Robert Hogan is the author of *The Experiments of Sean O'Casey, After the Irish Renaissance* and the six volume *History of the Modern Irish Drama.* His plays have been seen in New York, Los Angeles and Dublin.

James Douglas is the dramatist and short story writer who created *The Riordans.* His plays have appeared in Dublin at the Gate, the Olympia, and the Peacock, as well as on the BBC and RTE.

MURDER AT THE ABBEY THEATRE

A Comic Historical Novel

Murder at the Abbey Theatre

A COMIC HISTORICAL NOVEL

by

Robert Hogan and James Douglas

MOYTURA PRESS

DUBLIN

This book was typeset by
Gilbert Gough Typesetting for
Moytura Press, 4 Arran Quay, Dublin 7.

A catalogue number for this book
is available from the British library.

ISBN 1 871305 16 0

Printed in Ireland by
Colour Books Ltd

Some sixty years or so after the following events, an Abbey Theatre official knelt on one knee and reverently kissed the ring on the graciously outstretched hand.

Being beckoned to rise, he struggled to his feet and held out a handsome folio volume, bound in white leather.

"Eh, Your Holiness," he said, "it is an honour and rare pleasure to present to your Holiness one of our most prized national treasures, J.M. Synge's *Playboy of the Western World.*"

Cast of Characters

DIRECTORS OF THE ABBEY THEATRE:
W.B. YEATS, poet and playwright, early forties.
LADY AUGUSTA GREGORY, folklorist and playwright, middle fifties.
J.M. SYNGE, playwright, middle thirties.

MEMBERS OF THE ABBEY COMPANY:
WILLIAM G. FAY, chief producer and comic actor, middle thirties.
FRANK J. FAY, his older brother, chief verse speaker, middle thirties.
SARA ALLGOOD, leading actress, middle twenties.
MAIRE O'NEILL (Molly Allgood), Sara's younger sister, leading actress, early twenties.
ARTHUR SINCLAIR (Francis Quinton MacDonnell), leading character actor, middle twenties.
J.M. KERRIGAN, character actor, in his twenties.
J.A. O'ROURKE, character actor, in his twenties.
AMBROSE POWER, character actor, in his thirties.
BRIGIT O'DEMPSEY, wife of W.G. Fay, ingenue, early twenties.
MAY CRAIG, ingenue, nearly twenty.
ALICE O'SULLIVAN, ingenue, nearly twenty.
AUGUSTUS (GUSSIE) GAFFNEY, lighting technician, small parts player, early twenties.
LESLIE CHENEVIX PUREFOY, English character actor, middle thirties.

ABBEY THEATRE STAFF:
W.A. HENDERSON, Secretary, early thirties.
SEAGHAN BARLOW, stage carpenter and scene painter, in his thirties.
NELLIE BUSHELL, front of the house, about thirty.
MRS. SYBIL MULCASTER, cleaner, about forty.
B. IDEN PAYNE, prospective English producer, about thirty.

PROMINENT MEMBERS OF THE AUDIENCE:

OLIVER ST. JOHN GOGARTY, poet, physician and wit, in his late twenties.

JOSEPH HOLLOWAY, diarist and gossip, in his middle forties.

W.J. LAWRENCE, Belfast born journalist (and, subsequently, eminent theatre scholar), about forty-five.

GEORGE W. RUSSELL (AE), poet, painter, visionary and journalist, about forty.

SUSAN L. MITCHELL, his secretary, wit and poet, about forty.

PADRAIC COLUM, poet and playwright, in his mid-twenties.

ALICE L. MILLIGAN, Omagh born poet and playwright, in her early forties.

THOMASINA McFITZ, amateur tragedienne, about forty.

CHRISTINA McFITZ, her younger sister, housekeeper and poet, about forty.

GEORGE ROBERTS, publisher of Maunsel and Company, middle thirties.

MAIRE NIC SHIUBHLAIGH (Mary Walker), actress, middle twenties.

FRANK WALKER, her brother, amateur actor, middle twenties.

D.J. O'DONOGHUE, editor and librarian, middle forties.

"JACQUES", Dublin theatrical journalist.

JOHN BUTLER YEATS, father of W.B., painter and philosopher, late sixties.

PEARSE BEASLEY (Piaras Beaslai), patriot and Irish language enthusiast, middle twenties.

A PUGNACIOUS YOUNG MAN, in a smart topcoat.

Also PATRIOTS, POLICEMEN, REPORTERS, TRINITY COLLEGE STUDENTS and many others.

DUBLINERS:

ARTHUR GRIFFITH, editor of *The United Irishman*, middle thirties.

D.P. MORAN, editor of *The Leader*, middle thirties.

"PAT" (P.D. KENNY), journalist of *The Irish Times*, about forty.

GEORGE MOORE, eminent novelist, memoirist and wit, middle fifties.

EDWARD MARTYN, his cousin, amateur playwright and producer, late forties.

FRANCIS SHEEHY-SKEFFINGTON, socialist, pacifist and feminist, about thirty.

A LONG-NOSED, RED-EYED COMMON LABOURER, in cap and trenchcoat.

SEBASTIAN MELMOTH, a wraith.

SAMUEL BECKETT, a baby.

Also BERNARD SHAW, LEOPOLD BLOOM, BESSIE BURGESS, QUEENIE GILHOOLEY (McCLATCHIE that was), GYPO NOLAN, SKIN-THE-GOAT and many other Dubliners fictional, mythical and true.

A CAT.

Friday, January 25, 1907

Stately, plump Oliver Gogarty strode briskly along Eden Quay, the winter wind snarling after him and nipping the nape of his neck. He turned into Marlborough Street, and a few more brisk steps brought him to the entrance of the Abbey Theatre. Thankfully, he plunged under the portico, through the door and into the vestibule.

The box office was not open.

From the walls, several J.B. Yeats portraits of litterateurs and thespians impassively ignored him. Replying in kind, he stepped to the fireplace and regarded the ashes of last night's fire.

"Joking Jesus, it's as cold in here as it is outside."

He looked thoughtfully into the middle distance.

"As cold in here as a whore's heart? No. Obvious, too obvious."

Rejecting this offering of the muse, he raised his head and intoned, "Hello, hello! Anybody here a-tall, a-tall?"

One of the swinging doors to the auditorium opened, and a stout and red-faced woman appeared lugging a bucket of dirty water and a mop.

"Arrah, whisht," she muttered.

He was taken aback. "Eh, do they, I wonder, pay you to talk like that?"

"Pay, is it? Pay!" And she chortled to herself.

"Is the box office not open?" He took three steps to the box office, intoning, "Introibo ad altare Melpomeni. . . . Eh, the box office? Is it not open?"

The ample, red-faced woman raised her eyes from a dark contemplation of her water bucket and balefully fixed them upon the cubicle of the box office. After a period of sombre reflection, she replied dully, "It is not."

"Well, my good sibyl, could you possibly tell me when it does open?"

"Whin Misther Henderson wants ta open it." She plunged her mop into her bucket with dismal fury, and sloshed a stream of filthy water in the direction of Oliver Gogarty's gleaming and bespatted boots.

I

Athletically, he moved three brisk steps to the left. "And when might that be?"

"Ah!" she replied darkly, "Ah!"

He ruminated. "Ah."

"Why don't ya book at Cramer's?"

"They are sold out," he said, "for Saturday night's performance."

"Och," she said dubiously, plunged her mop into the bucket and directed another gush of water in his direction.

Taken off guard, Oliver Gogarty contemplated his bespatted and now bespotted boots. "Eh. . . ," he said, poising the syllable delicately between a clearing of the throat and a question.

Not unlike her sister, he thought, at Delphi, she remained inscrutable. In fact, she scrubbed.

"There are — ah — rumours," persisted Oliver Gogarty. "Rumours, you know, about Saturday's play. Eh?"

She looked up from her labours with a melancholy grimace. "Ha!" she said. "And why wouldn't there be?"

"Why, indeed?" he agreed.

She straightened up and kneaded the small of her back. "The problem is, ya see, this lot here wouldn't recognize a play if it was a tramcar and run 'em down." She produced half a cigarette from some secret recess and placed it carefully in the left corner of her mouth.

Oliver Gogarty produced matches. "Allow me."

"T'anks." She inhaled deeply and emitted two billows from her capacious nostrils. "No," she continued, "the class of stuff that gets on here would only stagger you with its — eh?" She paused for a word.

"Aestheticism?" he suggested.

"Not a bit of it; none of 'em takes any exercise. No, what it is, is they're just hopelessly out of it."

"Eh. . . out of what?"

She fixed a pitying stare upon him. "Life."

Quelled by the philosophic weight of that monosyllable, Oliver Gogarty contented himself with an acquiescent nod.

"Dead outa touch. What I mean is, all them ould gods and warriors spoutin' out their bits of poethical blather up there on th' stage." She struck a pose: "When you was an acorn on th' tree-top, / Then was I an eagle-cock; / Now that you are a withered old block, / Still am I an eagle cock." She snorted with withering disdain. "Sure, stuff fit only for chiselurs. And didja ever see little Misther Frank Fay pretendin' he was Coocoolin and holdin' up his mighty arm to be admired. Sure, I seen better pictorials on a match stick."

Oliver Gogarty nodded in appreciation of the imagery.

"Not to mention," she continued, "them poor gormless thicks of peasants her Ladyship has runnin' about and yammerin' some strange lingo nobody would ever say without first they took a header offa Nelson's pillar. And that man Synge, he doesn't write in English a-tall."

She exhaled blue smoke. "I'm goin' ta tell ya what it really comes down to. The problem of the theyater."

"Do," said Oliver Gogarty.

"This come to me," she whispered with a knowledgeable wink, "as I was walkin' down Sackville Street."

"What? Wait a minute!" said Oliver Gogarty, fumbling for his thin gold pen and small, embossed leather notebook. "As you were what?"

"It come to me," she said, "that *none* of these hoors here can write."

"Eh?" said Oliver Gogarty, blinking. "None?"

"Not a bleedin' one," she said dolefully.

"Hmm," he commiserated. "Hinc illae lacrimae."

"Yeh!" she nodded. "Exactly."

She extracted the last smokable half inch of cigarette from the left corner of her mouth and tenderly dropped it into her mop bucket. "Now for real writin', you'd wanta go to the Queen's. Oh, time was I never missed a Saturday night at the second house in the Queen's. Sittin' on the wooden seats in the gods, oh there was the place to see the classic plays and the most refined artistes. I remember Charles Warner in *Drink*, who could ever forget him? A shattered wreck of humanity he was, foamin' at the mouth, tearin' himself to pieces in his frenzy. Oh, powerful! Or John Lawson, there was an artiste, gentile to the fingertips and a master of restrained realism. Ah God, if ya could've seen him in the great fight scene in *Humanity*, completely wreckin' and totally demolishin' a drawing-room, smashin' all the windas, bustin' the pier glasses, the ancestral statues, the ornaments and geegaws, and then him and the villain crashin' to their doom on the collapsin' staircase."

"Holding the mirror up to nature, as it were," said Oliver Gogarty.

"Yeh — before they smashed it to bits, of course."

The door to Marlborough Street swept open, and an Arctic blast enveloped the two conversationalists in its icy embrace. Framed in the doorway stood a man resembling an old umbrella forgotten at a picnic. One spoke extended aloft, and at its extreme end was a hand with an upraised index finger.

"Though leaves are many," he chanted, "the root is one; Through lying lisps when I was young / I flaunted my foliage to the sun, / That what I said be seemly sung. . . . Hmm."

The frigid wind ruffled his locks, and one lank strand of jet black hair frisked about his ivory brow.

"Yiz have left the door wide open, Misther Yeats," remarked the sibyl.

He regarded her blankly. "Though leaves are many, the root is one; / Through luscious lisps when I was little / I bared my branches to the sun / That what I sung be brief and brittle."

"Jaysus!" said the sibyl, "It's only perishin' in here," and went to close the door herself.

The poet blinked, then sonorously intoned, "Good evening, Miss Allgood."

"Merry Christmas, St. Patrick!" she said, slamming the door.

"Yes," he agreed, turning absently away. He paused at the bottom of the stairs, and looked up to the balcony. "Luscious lips?" he queried. "Lascivious lisps?" Puzzled, he shook his head and, arm swaying in time to some internal music, disappeared up the stairs.

"Evenin', bedad!" snapped the sibyl. "Miss Allgood, moryah!"

"Bedad?" wondered Oliver Gogarty to himself. "Moryah?"

She retrieved her mop and resumed her moody ablutions of the floor.

"Eh?" said Oliver Gogarty, staying warily out of range. "Would you be one of the Allgood sisters?"

"Ya called me Sibyl," his companion retorted truculently. "Ya were right. Stand clear there."

"Really? Sibyl?"

"Mrs. Sibyl Mulcaster. Now clear on outa this. I'm behind meself, as it is."

Oliver Gogarty retired to the bench below the stairs and sat, his boots tucked safely out of the way. He poised his pen above his notebook and pondered. "There was," he wrote, "an old woman named Sibyl."

The door to Marlborough Street again banged open, this time allowing in both frigid wind and heated conversation.

Two little men stood in the doorway. The thin one suspiciously scrutinized a handful of coins. The tubby one panted behind him and clasped stubby arms around a small barrel of porter.

"One and six," marvelled the thin one. "Two bob. Two and thruppence. God Almighty, that's two shillin's from James's Street! Oh, don't the Dublin jarveys have it soft!"

"I — am — go — ing," said the other, who prided himself on distinct enunciation, "to dur-ropp — this bar-relll!"

Whereupon he did drop it, upon his foot, and remarked with great clarity, "Ayy-wahh-oooh-gahh!"

His pen arrested in mid-inspiration, Oliver Gogarty looked up in pleasant surprise. Ayy-wahh-oooh-gahh! A rumbling, deep-throated gurgle distinctly akin to the noise of the horn on Mr. Ford's new motor car.

"Oooh-gahh! Oooh-gahh!" the tubby actor cried, hopping about on one foot.

Oliver Gogarty abandoned his effort to immortalize an Old Woman named Sibyl, and jotted down instead, "There was a fat actor named Fay."

"Wouldja ever shut up and let me think!" rasped the thin one. "I've got a lot on me mind today."

"Would wan of yiz ever shut the bleedin' door!" said Mrs. Mulcaster.

"Two bob that cute hoor charged me. And me with no receipt. Well, I'm gettin' it off Henderson, and you can be my witness, brother!"

"Oooh-gahh!" the tubby one intoned, and sat on the barrel and massaged his left foot.

"Ah, luvva God!" said Mrs. Mulcaster, going to the door and banging it shut.

"A good thing you're my brother, or else you'd be getting yourself a puck — in — the — jaw!" remarked the tubby one, with some feeling.

"Looka, just shift that barrel onto the stage, and see if you can't sort your second act lines out into some semblance of sense."

The tubby one drew himself up into five foot four inches of affronted dignity. "I — am — not — in the least sure — it is my kind of rrrole!"

"Wouldja ever just stuff it? Just leave off your everlasting carping and whinging and whining and moaning! Amn't I only up to my eyebrows in coping with the set, and the props, and the bleeding costumes, and trying to memorize my own part."

"It is not possible — to — memorize these lines. They are too —

long. There is no place to bur-reathe. Also, you and Synge keep cutting and changing."

"I can't stand it," shrieked the thin one. "I've a good notion to throw the whole thing up. None of the yahoos around here are any help. Oh, if I only had the least bit of incompetent co-operation — ." He broke off in mid-lamentation and regarded his suddenly sodden boots and trouser cuffs. "Mrs. Mulcaster! You have just mopped my feet!"

"Yer in me way," she observed.

"Jaysus," he shrieked and made for the auditorium. "Yahoos!" Then he turned and growled, "Frank, are you bringing that barrel of porter in, or do I have to do everything?"

The tubby one regarded his disappearing brother and then regarded the barrel. "Did," he asked it lugubriously, "Burrrbage have to put up with the likes of this? Did Keannn? Did Coqqquelin?" And leaving the barrel in front of the door, he trod processionally across the vestibule and also disappeared into the auditorium.

Oliver Gogarty smiled at what he had written, then looked across the room at the portrait of the tubby actor by John Butler Yeats, and murmured, "There once was an actor named Fay / Whose speech resembled a neigh."

The door from Marlborough Street banged open again, and a heavy, swarthy man entered hastily from the wind and the wet, and barked his left shin on the porter barrel.

"Ouch, damn!" he said.

"Ah, Synge," called Oliver Gogarty, jotting down a line, "let me regale you with a new composition:

> There was an old woman named Sibyl
> Whose mop and whose mouth still would dribble;
>   Her last name was Mulcaster,
>   But though she mopped faster,
> That stopped not a quip nor a quibble.

"Eh?" said Mrs. Mulcaster. "Say that again."

"I shall be pleased to present you with a copy," said Oliver Gogarty.

"I think you'd better," she said. "Misther Synge, wouldja ever mind shiftin' yerself, as I have to mop around the porter barrel."

Synge moved heavily into the room. "Hello, Gogarty. Anybody here?"

"The brothers Fay have just disappeared into the inner recesses of the national temple of dramatic art. I say, Synge, you look rather seedy. Should you be out of your bed?"

Synge shrugged.

"Are you seeing someone?" said Oliver Gogarty, with a frown.

"Ball."

"Oh, a good, sound man. Look here, I've been hanging about trying to get tickets for your first night to-morrow, but you people don't seem to believe in cossetting the public by opening your box office."

Synge nodded wearily. "I'll see about it for you. Two?"

"Two, yes. I have recently joined the ranks of domestic bliss."

Synge's dark eyes seemed to wince. "Right then, two. I'll have them held for you. Now if you'll ex — ."

Gogarty laid a hand on his sleeve. "How is the play going?"

Synge grunted non-committally.

"There are a number of rumours — ."

Synge grimaced. "You'll really have to excuse me now."

Gogarty patted Synge's sleeve. "Right. Well, good luck anyhow." He stepped to the door, murmuring, "There once was an actor named Fay / With his intonations agley," and disappeared into Marlborough Street, leaving the door ajar.

"Jaysus!" remarked Mrs. Mulcaster, banging it shut again. "And the yobbo never give me my poem neither."

Synge sat lumpily down on the bench beneath the stairs. After a moment, he said, "Do you want to mop here?"

"Not a bit of it," said Mrs. Mulcaster. "Sure, who'll notice a little muck under there?" She retrieved her bucket, and trailing her mop behind her went into the auditorium.

For a moment, Synge looked unseeingly at the portraits of Frank and Willie Fay across the room. Then tiredly he produced some sheets of paper from an inside pocket, and glowered at them. "That stays in," he said and made a mark in the margin.

"Don't you do that!" piped W. G. Fay from the auditorium door. "I need every one of those goddamn cuts."

"Fay, we are butchering it."

W.G. Fay strode over and snatched the papers out of his hand. "Sure, it's it or us, isn't it?"

"How are the actors?"

"Ah, worried and bothered. Of course, they're always worried and bothered, especially the brother. . . . But this time they're talking it round — the bloody blabbermouths — that we could have a dust-up. If one of them mentions it to Holloway, it'll be all over town."

"How's Mol — Miss O'Neill?"

"Oh, she's the only one as has her lines. The sister, La Allgood, as usual hasn't. And me, I wish to God I had the half of them."

The door from Marlborough Street blew open again, and a weedy youth darted in and fell over the porter barrel. "You hoor," he addressed it feelingly.

"Gussie," said W. G. Fay, "will you shift that damn porter barrel onto the stage."

"I will, I will," said the youth, and picked himself up and trotted up the stairs.

"Then where the hell are you going?"

"I gotta check the lights on the balcony. There was some problem yesterday."

"Pain ever forever," remarked Synge.

A pale, thin face with a hatchet nose and a worn tweed cap pulled down over red-rimmed eyes looked in the open door from Marlborough Street. "That would be Shelley," he remarked and disappeared, closing the door behind him.

"I'll be inside," said W.G. Fay. "The others should be dribbling in shortly, so send them right onstage. I don't want them hanging round the Greenroom, brewing up pots of tea and hatching out treacheries." He hastened off to the auditorium with angry, little steps.

Synge leaned his head back against the wall and closed his eyes. Was this really worth it? Was it, after all? When what would come out would be a sham and a shadow, if not an outright travesty? His arms and his legs suddenly felt like lumps of lead. Yet Molly would be fine. And Sally, even though she would make a hames of the lines. And Sinclair would be too broad of course, but — .

"Lascivious laps," chanted a voice on the stairs.

Half-smiling, half-frowning, Synge rose and posted himself at the bottom. "Aren't you supposed to be in England?"

"Scotland. I am delivering a lecture for which I shall receive the useful emolument of two guineas. Always insist on guineas."

"Will you be back for the show?" Synge interposed swiftly.

"Show?"

"My show."

W.B. Yeats blinked. "*Riders to the Saints?*"

"*The Playboy of the Western World.*"

"Of course. Aeschylean, oh your most Aeschylean."

"Thanks," said Synge dryly. "Will you be back for it?"

"Oh surely, later in the week. On Thursday. Thursday definitely. Or Friday."

"I rather hoped you would be here earlier."

"Lady Gregory is coming up today. Did you see my gloves?"

"You're wearing them."

The poet peered suspiciously at his hands. "Lissome limbs," he murmured.

"I'm having a lot of pressure from Fay and Lady Gregory," said Synge patiently, "to make cuts. The actors are getting the wind up also, so I've made a few to keep everybody happy. However, my own inclination is to — ."

"Be bold!" said the poet, clapping him on the shoulder. "Be bold!" He strode to the door onto Marlborough Street. There a thought struck him.

He turned, lifted a long, tapering finger and whispered, "But not too bold."

As he went out, he bumped into a thin, rough-looking figure slouching beneath the portico.

"Pain ever forever," said the fellow.

"Browning," sniffed Yeats.

"Hunh!" said the fellow, tugging his old tweed cap contemptuously down over his red-rimmed eyes and mooching off.

Surly peasantry, thought Yeats, leaning into the wind and making his way to the quays.

"Good morning," said a chunky black-clad figure approaching him.

"Lascivious lips," acknowledged Yeats.

Filthy-minded as usual, reflected Mr. Joseph Holloway and proceeded into the Abbey Theatre. And even shut the door behind him.

No one was there.

He proceeded into the auditorium. He stood at the back where it was dim, a comfortable, well-fed, middle-aged man, unbuttoning his bulky overcoat but not removing the bowler hat which sat implacably untilted just on the centre of his head. With his second-best hand-kerchief, he wiped his baggy eyes of moisture. Dublin on a windy winter day was a place to watch one's eyes. Nothing, praise God, had blown into them, but one couldn't be too careful. About everything.

Rehearsal, he noticed dourly, was as usual late; and the auditorium was also as usual as cold as a —. Hmm. He sucked the ends of his straggly greying moustache reflectively, but no muse came to aid him. No muse ever had, and no muse ever would. He sniffed, instinctively distrusting the muses, one and all, who were, if truth be told, but heathen divinities.

He consulted his pocket watch. Rehearsal, he had been informed, was called for half-ten, and here it was well gone eleven. The Abbey people were distinctly unreliable. He buttoned himself back into his bulky overcoat, sat down and prepared to wait.

At seven past eleven, Gussie Gaffney ambled onstage, carrying a glass.

"Ah!" murmured Joseph Holloway, "we are starting at last."

Gussie came downstage, bent over a porter barrel, twisted the tap and filled his glass. "Ah!" he said, quaffing a big swig and then going off stage left.

"Ah, Jesus, Mary and Joseph!" muttered Joseph Holloway, reflecting, and not for the first time, on the unreliability, incompetence, tendency to sin and sheer shiftlessness of everyone even remotely connected with the Abbey Theatre. Except himself. Its renovating architect.

Fortunately he had a record of all their bungles and blasphemies. All sagely and safely jotted down. Two thousand words per day, day in, day out, and every three months taken to the binders to be encased in sturdy blue bindings. All some day, many years hence, to be presented to some reputable public body such as the Royal Irish Academy or the National Library. Oh, a grateful posterity would thank him. A weedy academic — necessarily American as the local lot didn't read — would pore over the millions of words, marvelling, ruining his eyesight, getting piles.

Heavens, where were the actors? Did they think he had all day?

He in fact did. Every day, and he was just beginning to wonder if he might not stroll over to Eason's and flip through the new magazines. But then the auditorium doors opened, and a Northern voice whispered, "That you, Joe?"

"Ah, Lawrence, sit down."

"Er, is anybody about?"

"Just us. The real lovers of the drama."

Glancing warily about, a raw-boned, red-haired man slipped silently into the next seat. "Yeets," he said, "would relish an opportunity like this."

"An opportunity like what?" said Joseph Holloway.

"An opportunity to say in his lah-de-dah voice, 'do you have permission to be here?' Oh, he'd love that, he would, the swine!"

There was a small silence, punctuated only by W.J. Lawrence remorselessly grinding his molars.

"Yeats has gone to Scotland," said Joseph Holloway.

"At a moment like this! With a dangerous new play in rehearsal!"

"Gone to Scotland," Joseph Holloway repeated. "That's all I know about it. Yet."

"Typical," said Lawrence. "Crept off like a cringing cur, leaving Synge and Lady Gregory to face the music." He took out a ratty-looking notepad, and jotted something down. "Might be worth a par in *The Freeman*." Then a thought hit him and he passed over a folded piece of paper. "Ran across this the other day. Thought you might like it for your collection."

"Ah!" said Joseph Holloway. About the drama, he was something of a pack rat, and his house in Northumberland Road was full to bursting with old theatre posters and programmes, even old ticket stubs, in fact every possible kind of theatrical memorabilia. Dusting was becoming quite a problem, but he had basically solved it by not dusting.

He unfolded the paper and read in his friend's neat, meticulous hand:

BY HIS MAJESTY'S COMPANY OF COMEDIANS
KILKENNY THEATRE ROYAL
(Positively the last night, because
the Company go tomorrow to Waterford)
ON SATURDAY, MAY 14th, 1793
will be performed, by desire and command
of several respectable people in this learned Metropolis
for the benefit of Mr Kearns the Manager
The Tragedy of
HAMLET THE PRINCE OF DENMARK

Originally written and composed by the celebrated Dan Hayes of Limerick, and inserted in Shakespear's works.

"My word!" marvelled Joseph Holloway. He quickly skimmed on down the page:

> The parts of the King and Queen, by directions of Father O'Callaghan, will be omitted, as too immoral for any stage.

"That point," he murmured, "has often occurred to me."

"Read it later," said W.J. Lawrence impatiently.

"Yes, yes," said Joseph Holloway, reading on:

> Tickets to be had of Mr Kearns, at the sign of the Goat's Beard, in Castle Street. The value of the tickets, as usual, will be taken out (if required) in candles, bacon, soap, butter, cheese, potatoes, etc.; as Mr Kearns wishes, in every particular, to accommodate the public.
> N.B. No smoking allowed. No person whatsoever will be admitted into the boxes without shoes or stockings.

"Ah," said Joseph Holloway, reluctantly tucking the paper away in his inside pocket, "They knew what theatre was in those days."

"Yes, yes," said W.J. Lawrence eagerly, "but what's new on the Rialto?"

"That's, of course, *Merchant of Venice*, Act One, Scene —."

"What's the word about this play!"

"Oh, they're very worried," said Joseph Holloway with a complacent smile. "Synge is having to change most of the original lines."

Lawrence nodded. "I've heard the language is something abominable."

"Disgraceful."

"It had to come to this with a creature like Yeets at the helm."

"A great poet," temporized Holloway, "but Pagan. Yes, Pagan."

"Hsst," said Lawrence, "someone's coming!" He slid down in his seat.

An uncommonly pretty young woman, wearing a large floppy hat, barged through the auditorium doors and halfway down the aisle.

"Miss O'Neill," whispered Joseph Holloway. "I'll ask her when the rehearsal starts."

"No!" whispered W.J. Lawrence, laying a restraining hand on his friend's arm. "I wouldn't like to be spotted. It ud get back to Yeets. He has his spies everywhere."

Halfway down the aisle, Molly O'Neill rested her scallop-shaped hold-all on the edge of a seat and let her eyes grow accustomed to the darkness.

Hah! she thought, nobody here, and me running the length of Lower Abbey Street, afraid I'd be late. She flopped down an aisle seat and rummaged through the debris in her hold-all for a cigarette. "Damn!" Finally she found one single crushed fag at the very bottom, and lit it.

Behind her, the swing doors opened again, letting the light in from the vestibule, and a female western voice rang out. "Dere is no smoking allowed in de auditorium, Miss O'Neill!"

Flustered, Molly jumped to her feet. "I'm sorry, your Ladyship. I forgot — oh, it's *you*! Very funny!"

A male chortle greeted her, the swing doors closed, and footsteps retreated.

"That couldn't have been Lady Gregory," whispered Lawrence.

"The new English actor, Purefoy," explained Joseph Holloway. "He's a mimic."

"Is it not monstrous," murmured Lawrence, "that this player here, but in a fiction. . . could force his soul so to his own conceit?"

"*Hamlet*," said Joseph Holloway. "Act Two, Scene Two, lines . . . eh?"

"Lines 517 to 519," said W.J. Lawrence.

Synge slipped through the swing doors and stood there for a moment, focusing his eyes to the darkness. Halfway down the theatre, the tip of a cigarette grew red and faintly outlined the floppy brim of a large hat. With a dour smile, he swung down the aisle. "Molly, you know you're not supposed to — Molly!"

"Oh, feck off!"

"What?"

"Look," she said, turning, "you're not fooling me twice in the same day — oh, Johnny! I thought you were that slimy Limey again."

"Purefoy?"

"He was just here doing Lady G."

"Umm," said Synge. "Let me in."

She drew back her legs, and he slid through and sat down beside her.

W.J. Lawrence tightened his fingers on Joseph Holloway's forearm.

"Just look at that!" he hissed.

Halfway down the theatre, the two dark shadows had merged into one.

"Disgusting," clucked Joseph Holloway.

"Revolting!" whispered W.J. Lawrence.

Joseph Holloway leaned over and murmured in his friend's ear. "And they think nobody knows about their carry-on. Well, the whole company knows."

"Reprehensible," said W.J. Lawrence.

"Very nasty," said Joseph Holloway.

"Ouch!" cried Synge.

"She's struck him!" whispered W.J. Lawrence, bending eagerly forward.

"What is it?" said Molly.

"That damn bird — or bunch of cherries — whatever is on your hat this time, has poked me in the eye."

"I just bought this hat in Clery's. I take it you don't like it."

"Well," he said, "it is a bit — extravagant."

"Thank you very much!"

"Shh!" he said. "Keep your voice down!"

"It is my voice," she said, but more softly. "And I'll do what I damn-well like with it."

"And do put out that cigarette. If somebody should come in and see us — ."

"You'd hate that, wouldn't you?" she said, taking a deep, defiant drag.

"It's a rule. And we can't have one rule for the rest of the company and another for you."

"That's just a problem you'll have to work out, Mr. Director." And she tapped her ash airily off onto the floor.

He sighed. "Oh, Molly, why do you go on like this?"

"I'm sick of how you ignore me in front of the rest of them."

"It's only till after the play is over, I promise. Then I'll tell them all — Yeats, the old lady, the actors, everybody."

"Your mother?"

"I — I — ." He relapsed into glum silence.

W.J. Lawrence snickered softly and bent over to Joseph Holloway's hairy ear. "We that are true lovers run into strange capers."

"*As You Like It.*"

"Act Two, Scene Four."

"Line — eh — 51?"

"Line 53," corrected W.J. Lawrence.

Synge took a scrap of newspaper from his inside pocket and unfolded it. "I was looking through the small ads. I've checked a couple of flats in Rathmines that might do for us."

"Have you been out to see them?"

"Er, ah, not yet. The play, you know — ."

She took the paper and lit a match to see better.

"But as soon as I get a minute free," he began.

She crumpled the paper up disgustedly and flipped it away.

"The date on the paper," she said flatly, "is two weeks old."

Again the silence dropped between them.

"Hee-hee," chuckled W.J. Lawrence.

Finally she said in an exaggerated stage voice, "Who, or what, do you have to kill before you come into your own?"

"That's a line from his *Playboy*," Joseph Holloway explained. "They were rehearsing it yesterday."

Halfway down the theatre, too low for them to hear almost, Synge murmured, "Each man kills the thing he loves."

"What's that?" she asked huffily. "More line changes?"

"No, that's Oscar Wilde."

"They're talking about Oscar Wilde now," said W.J. Lawrence, cocking his ear.

"Filthy," said Joseph Holloway.

"Nauseating," said W.J. Lawrence. Then his fingers tightened on Joseph Holloway's sleeve. "Good God, look!"

Onstage, a middle-aged figure in a bulky overcoat lumbered in from stage left. A bowler hat sat implacably just on the centre of his head, and beneath it dribbled a straggly, greying moustache.

"It's you, Joe!" said W.J. Lawrence, wide-eyed.

"Were you looking for something, Mr. Holloway?" Synge called out.

The bulky, dark-clad figure held a glass to the top of the porter barrel and filled it to the brim.

"Why's that old cod hanging about again?" muttered Molly. "And look at him, and he supposed to be teetotal."

15

"Can I do something for you, Mr. Holloway?" called Synge.

The figure straightened up, peeled off his moustache and swept off his bowler hat. "No thanks, old fruit," he chortled, and bounded off the stage.

"The slimy Limey again," said Molly. "He thinks he's so clever! Every time you turn around, he's taking somebody off."

"Good, though," said Synge. "He had Holloway's plodding walk down pat."

"My what!" said Joseph Holloway.

Synge stood up. "Let's see who's backstage. Maybe we can get this rehearsal started." Suddenly he grasped the back of the seat for support.

"Johnny!" She clutched his arm. "Are you all right?"

"Fine."

"You're not fine!"

"I'll be fine."

She bit her lip. "I'm sorry," she said, "about just now."

"You changeling," he smiled. "My own changeling."

She took his arm. "My old tramp."

"Thoroughly repugnant," said Joseph Holloway.

"Transformed into a strumpet's fool," clucked W.J. Lawrence.

"*Antony and Cleopatra*. Act One."

"Scene One."

"Line 11," Joseph Holloway interposed hastily.

"Line 12 actually."

Synge and Molly made their way, hand in hand, down the aisle.

"Don't worry about to-morrow, love. It'll go well. I know it will."

Synge paused at the little steps going up to the stage door. "The old lady wants more cuts yet. Otherwise, she says, there could be trouble."

"Oh, feck her, she wouldn't know a good line if she saw one. Sure, who can speak her old Kiltartan blather? It twists your tongue in knots. Not that your dialogue is all that easy!"

"Come on," he smiled, leading her up the steps.

"Wait!" She drew him back and kissed him lightly on the lips. "For luck."

"Things rank and gross in nature," snarled W.J. Lawrence, watching them disappear backstage.

"*Hamlet*, Act One, Scene Two," said Joseph Holloway. "Yet the poor fellow, he's not well."

"Line 136. Who's not well?"

"Poor Synge."

"He's well enough," spat Lawrence, "to produce his filthy play."

"Still," said Joseph Holloway, "he is an artist, no matter how morbid or perverse."

"Ill is he?" said Lawrence. "What's wrong with him?"

"Internal."

"It'll be external after to-morrow night!"

Suddenly the auditorium lights came on.

"Oh dear," said Lawrence, rising and scuttling through the swing doors.

W.G. Fay came on from stage left. "Act One!" he called. "From the beginning! Is everybody here? Finally!" His eyes scanned the auditorium and discerned one black bowler hat in the last line of seats.

"Holloway, I see you!"

"Eh," said Joseph Holloway, "I just popped in."

"Well, now you can just pop out."

Joseph Holloway arose in shambling dignity. "I have important business to transact with Mr. Henderson," he announced and made his portentous way out to the vestibule.

"I know your important business, you old busybody," muttered Willie Fay grimly.

Then he turned to the wings and bawled at the top of his lungs, "Beginners! Places!"

Friday, January 25: II

"Beginners!" Willie Fay roared.

Molly came out of the women's dressing-room, her costume hastily thrown on, but still wearing her Clery's hat.

Hmph, she thought, half the cast isn't here yet. Time for a quick cuppa.

She went into the Greenroom and found her sister Sally already pouring herself a cup. Each took a long, cool look at the other.

"Mnghh!" snorted Sally finally.

Molly's jaw set, and she turned away and surveyed her hat in the mirror.

Sally poured the milk into her cup, stirred it as though she were silently intoning "Boil and Bubble," and sat down in the middle of the couch. "So *that* was where you went — Clery's!"

"That *was* where."

She had, thought Sally, the amateur's knack of stressing the wrong word. Oh, a good thing for her sister she had a pretty face. Not that that would last forever.

Aloud she said, "And you *bought* it." She made "bought" sound like dire sacrilege.

"No, they gave it to me free because everybody thought I looked so gorgeous in it." Molly extracted two long hat pins, took the hat off and regarded it fondly. Then she tried it on again at a new angle.

"How much did it cost?"

"It's my money."

"It's Clery's money now."

Molly tossed her head impudently and re-adjusted her hat to a gravity-defying angle.

"Do you. . . want tea?" Sally finally tendered.

As well as tea, that pause meant the implicit offer of an olive branch. Clever, Molly marvelled, the wealth of meaning her sister could get into a pause. I must practice how she said that.

But out loud she said, "Isn't tea terrible for the complexion?"

Sally shrugged. "Suit yourself."

Amazing, she thought, sipping her own cup angrily and regarding her sister's backside, how she can eat anything and never put on an ounce.

Out loud she said, "Why are you smirking at yourself?"

"Somebody must love me," Molly smiled without turning around.

Gussie Gaffney poked his head in at the door. "Sure, and why wouldn't I? Aren't you only smashing?"

With mock ferocity, Molly snatched up from the table a prominently displayed volume entitled *The Poetical Works of W.B. Yeats, Volume I, Lyrical Poems*, and whirled around as if to hurl it. "Clear off outa this, Mr. Gussie Gaffney, if you know what's good for you!"

"Oh, I know what's good for me," he smirked.

She hurled the book at his head, but he plucked it out of the air, and grinned back at her, "Here now, here now, don't be makin' so fast and loose with the Holy Rot."

"Out! Out!"

He strolled in and replaced the book on the table. "Just thought I'd mention Willie Fay is yellin' for everybody onstage."

"Is he just yelling," asked Sally comfortably, "or does he mean it?"

"Ah, finish yer tea," said Gussie. "You've a good ten minutes before he busts a blood vessel." He settled down on the couch beside Sally. "Anything left in the pot?"

"Nothing for you!" said Molly. "Didn't you hear me say Out!"

He heaved a sigh and got back up. "Oi must aroise an' go now," he said, batting his eyes romantically at her and disappearing out the door.

"Eejit!" said Molly, not able to keep back a smile.

"*Which* he is it who loves you?" Sally asked after a minute.

'Oh, there must be hordes of them, hordes." Then she added seriously, "Johnny is the important one. Sure, I wouldn't give Mr Augustus Gaffney the time of day."

"Johnny," remarked Sally, with a heavy undertone of disapproval. "How could you tell?"

Molly poured herself a cup of tea, and then took her time spooning three loads of sugar into it. She wished she hadn't smoked her last fag. You could always cover an awkward moment with the business of lighting one. Instead, she sat composedly down in the big, ragged armchair and smoothed out her skirt.

Sally was cute at getting to people. Even onstage. But sure, she was always onstage.

"I've nothing against the man," Sally added lightly, and then came the significant pause. "He's the soul of propriety."

Good shot, thought Molly, wincing.

She pushed the bowl over, "Did you get sugar? Or are you still trying to diet?"

Sally's poker face still did not react, but her right hand gave a small, convulsive twitch.

Like to slap my face, wouldn't you, sister, Molly thought gleefully.

But Sally was working the pause again. "He is strange," she finally murmured.

"Do you think?" And then she worked the pause herself, and even amplified it a bit by licking a fingertip with her tongue and dabbing at her left eyebrow. "Perhaps you mean he comes from a different background?"

"From us."

Molly decided to ignore that. "Aren't you," she said inconsequentially, "letting the Widow Quin get a little, eh, large?"

Sally did not rise to the bait. "His strangeness," she mused. "He isn't our class or our creed."

"Oh, he's given up both of those."

Sally's eyes narrowed. "Has he now? . . . For *your* sake?"

Ah-hah, thought Molly, she laid it on rather heavily there.

Well, sister, the days are passed when you could send me blubbering to my room.

"For his own sake, I should think," said Molly with a nicely modulated casualness.

Sally stood up, strode across the room and then rounded on her, hands on hips — the same gesture she had rather overworked as Mrs. Fallon in *Spreading the News*. What was it with Sally? Dislike of Johnny? Vice versa? No, Sally had never really been attracted to him. Probably just jealousy that Johnny wrote Pegeen Mike for me and she had to play the Widow Quin. Great God, could Sally, with her bosom and backside, ever really hope to play Pegeen Mike?

"Ah, but still," Sally was saying softly, "he won't be seen with you; he won't acknowledge you."

So there it was, straight out. Molly sipped her tea, playing for time. Where had she heard Sally read a line like that? Yes, in their bedroom once, reciting Lady Macbeth. Good casting.

"Tea wet?" boomed a voice from the door. Without looking around, both sisters recognized the unconvincing joviality of Mr. Arthur Sinclair.

Molly swirled the teapot around. "All gone, Mac. We'll have to make some more, or is Willie getting too impatient?"

"Oh, he's good for five minutes more of fuming. Pay no attention to him." Arthur Sinclair lounged against the door post and stroked his tubby belly with absent-minded adoration.

"You know," he said, "I think I'm really making something quite nice out of Michael James now."

"Do you really, Mac?" said Sally with just the right touch of faint incredulity.

"Yes," he nodded humourlessly. "A pity that Synge left him out of the second act. Hurts the play, I'd say. Think I should speak to him about it?"

"Yes," said Sally. "I definitely would."

"And no time like the present," Molly added. "He's onstage with Willie Fay."

"Hmm," said Arthur Sinclair, "you could be right." He smoothed down his plastered red hair, and with lightly affirmative pats to his belly, withdrew with an air of purpose.

"Remember," Molly giggled, "when he was chatting us up and bent over and split his pants?"

But Sally was implacable. "*He* won't be seen with you," she repeated. "*He* won't acknowledge you."

And by "he," she didn't mean Arthur Sinclair.

"He?" murmured Leslie Chenevix Purefoy, pausing outside the Greenroom door. He who? What morsel of information was this? The more one found out about one's talentless colleagues, the better. Who knew what might prove useful?

Onstage he could hear Willie Fay roaring out some instruction. Uncouth sounds these Irish made. Ugh. Oh, this whole Dublin expedition was proving to be a catastrophic error. Yeats he had hardly seen. His one interview with that old frump Gregory had been most unfortunate, she being ridiculously unimpressed by his ability to manage an Irish accent. Her own constant substitution of d's for t's made her sound as if she had a potato in her mouth.

And the sombre Synge was so caught up with the problems of his idiotic play that he hadn't a word for anybody.

And that little martinet Willie Fay! Oh, Leslie Chenevix Purefoy still bristled at the memory of their last interview: "Och, Purefooey, this is not th' Covent Bloody Garden or th' Drury Bleedin' Lane. We don't go in for your 'forsooths' and your 'gadzooks' here. I mane this is not th' battle o' Dunsinane Hill we're rehearsin', is it? Tell ya what I'll do. Ya can play wan o' the 'Other Peasants.' A non-spakin' role."

Oh, hopeless amateurism! Oh, feckless egotism! Oh, what comprehensive ignorance of the great classic roles. But mention Richard III, Sir Giles Overreach or Claude Melnotte, and they would but blink their little pig-like Hibernian eyes, and mutter something about somebody called Conn the Shockruin.

"Outa me way, outa me way," squeaked a small, nasal voice, and Leslie Chenevix Purefoy suddenly found himself roughly bumped in the small of the back.

That surly dwarf, the stage carpenter Barlow, glared sourly up at him from under beetling brows, and trundled past with a ladder. "Warned ya! I warned ya!"

Oh, an impossible place. Leslie Chenevix Purefoy pushed his way angrily through the side door into the laneway, his features twisted into the moue of disgust so effectively developed for his brief (one matinee) but memorable appearance as Malvolio at the Theatre Royal, Cheltenham. Yes, an error of judgement to ally himself, even as a stop-gap between engagements, with these bogtrotters. Oh, it had seemed sensible at the time to accept the offer, and thus ingratiate himself with the dotty Miss Horniman, their English sponsor. Despite her insistence on casting his horoscope before hiring him, she was English. Also, she had money, and her plans to set up a repertory company in Manchester offered piquant possibilities. Yes, Manchester had its sooty charms, and no English company could be as gormless and uncouth as these barbaric Paddies. No, not even those amateurs at ghastly Aberdeen; and he shivered again at the recollection of four soggy weeks playing Banquo, Guildenstern and Sir Charles Pomander in that rain-sodden Athens.

But Aberdeen he could almost remember with nostalgia when he thought of the dismal incompetence he was now thrown amongst. The self-important Fays, that strutting tub Sinclair, the loutish O'Rourke and the gratingly cheerful Kerrigan. They had no more sense of the stage than a donkey would of ballet. They couldn't talk, they couldn't walk, they didn't know how to get on or get off. When someone else was speaking, they just stood there, hands flopped at their sides, eyes vacant, mouth gaping open, and spittle usually dribbling out of it.

The wind sweeping through the laneway made Leslie Chenevix Purefoy decide to find a cosier secluded haven to lick his many grievous wounds. He went out to Marlborough Street and came back in the front door. No one in the vestibule. Good.

Perhaps the balcony would be a secure retreat for binding up the ravelled sleeve of care. Quickly he mounted the stairs.

"Immmpossible!" F.J. Fay declaimed, folding his short arms over his pigeon chest. "I must — I repeat, must! — be seen Fullll Face!"

W.G. Fay executed an exasperated caper. "Dummy! Eejit! Upstage with ya!"

"Neverrr!" declaimed Frank J. Fay the implacable.

The only professional thing about those two clowns, Leslie Chenevix Purefoy decided, was that their whining voices carried to the back of the balcony. Carried with an ear-lacerating clarity, most unconducive to rumination or sleep.

Purefoy retreated to the hallway and noticed that the door to the little office was open. He peeped in. Empty. Ah, bliss.

Quietly he closed the door behind him, pulled out the comfortable-looking chair behind the desk, and sat. Ah!

Irish stout, he reflected presently, was an intriguing drink, although hardly on a par with Newcastle Brown Ale, and definitely not to be drunk with such carefree abandon as he had displayed last night at the premises of Mr. Davy Byrne in Duke Street.

He settled back in his chair and allowed his sleepy gaze to rove about the room. He should really not chance a nap. Rehearsals might actually commence in twenty minutes.

A breeze from the ill-fitting window caressed the nape of his neck, ruffled his prominent ears and fluttered a scrap of paper on the desk. Incuriously, he picked it up. Erse? No, just a strange, crabbed hand. Words could be made out. "Lascivious lips." His interest aroused, Purefoy studied the paper more seriously. Hmm, no, the promise of "Lascivious lips" did not seem to be fulfilled. But what was it?

Ah, of course, the short line lengths were the tip-off. Notes for a poem. And necessarily by the posing poetaster Yeats.

Furrowing his brow, Leslie Chenevix Purefoy studied the paper.

Then he put another blank piece of paper beside it. He took up a pencil, and, darting his glance back and forth between the two, essayed a copy.

Not too difficult really.

Thoughtfully, he folded both papers and put them in an inner pocket. Who knows what might prove useful? Perhaps he might forge a sharp note of reproof to the irritating Willie Fay. "Dear Fay, Your blunders to-night were more absurd than usual. Perhaps you had best return to your previous more congenial occupation at the abattoir. Yours truly, W.B. Yeats."

Perhaps better, though, to find some victim who would be unable to trace the interesting missive back to him. Hmm. What about those two extraordinary spinsters he was speaking to in the vestibule the other night? What was their name? McFitz. Yes, that might be a droll possibility. Or perhaps a stern communication to some of the more bovine members of the company. Such as that young lout, Gaffney. . . .

Gussie Gaffney passed the lavatory on his way from the Greenroom to the stage. Inside, somebody was making unsuccessful attempts to get the ancient and eccentric toilet to flush. Kerrigan had christened the toilet "Sally," as it would only work when it had a mind to.

"Ay!" bawled Gussie, putting his head up to the lavatory door. "Will ya ever get off Sally and come out here!"

He chuckled to himself and waited to see whoever, blushing, would emerge. "Gaffney," he had once heard W.B. Yeats intoning to Lady Gregory in a voice that carried all over the theatre, "Gaffney is the quintessential vulgar oaf, but he is the only person around here who can get the delicate lighting effects poetic drama requires."

Yah, reflected Gussie, silly old cod. And not for the first time he regaled himself with the memory of struggling with gels for an hour one afternoon while the poet kept repeating with infinite world-weariness, "That's not it, Gaffney. No, that's not it at all." And then, finally:

W.B. YEATS: That's it! Precisely the effect. Exactly what I envisaged!

GUSSIE: But Misther Yeats, th' fuckin' gel is on fire!"

Hee-hee-hee.

Gussie turned his attention again to the lavatory door. "Ay! Will ya stop yankin' and pullin' at Sally, and get out here!"

The toilet flushed, the door opened, and J.M. Synge emerged with a black frown and a pile of scripts.

"Eh. . . ah. . . ," said Gussie lamely.

Ah well, to hell with him anyway. Whatever could a dotey bit of goods like Molly ever see in gloomy old Synge? Molly was a girl who liked a few laughs and a good time, not having her nose forever pushed into some book.

And just what blabbermouth had told Synge the other day that Molly had been seen walking on Gussie's arm? Oh, Synge had heard that right enough. You could see it how he looked at you lately, bloody murder in his eyes. Sinclair maybe could have spilled the beans. Mac smiled a lot, but he sometimes had a mean streak. . . .

Mr. Arthur Sinclair (*né* Francis Quinton MacDonnell) always wore tight trousers. They nicely set off his powerful buttocks, his sinewy thighs and his meaty calves. "Too many actors," he was wont to pontificate, "are a disgrace when playing Shakespeare, Boucicault and other classic authors. They can't fill their parts because their parts can't fill their costumes."

"There's a fella," his colleague J.M. Kerrigan had remarked, "who could put the ham in Hamlet."

"Yeh," J.A. O'Rourke had agreed, "not to mention the brute in Brutus."

Now, however, as Mr. Arthur Sinclair made his way to the stage, the tightness of his trousers was occasioning more than a little discomfort in the vicinity of both crotch and bum. Momentarily he debated whether to re-adjust his braces, but, true artist that he was, decided against such crass self-indulgence.

"Excuse me, Mac."

Arthur Sinclair turned to see J.M. Synge balancing a pile of scripts in his arms.

"Ah," said Arthur Sinclair, "I've been looking all over for you. I crave a word."

"Now? Well, make it a quick one. We're late enough as it is."

"I have been thinking about my part."

"Glad to hear it. You were pretty fuzzy on your third act lines yesterday."

Mr. Arthur Sinclair closed his eyes in silent suffering.

"It is not my lines I have been thinking about."

"Apparently not," sighed Synge.

"It is the overall role," Arthur Sinclair whispered, bending conspiratorially forward. "The conception, ya might say."

What, Synge wondered, is that scent he uses? He must lash it on by the gallon.

"You'll agree that I have brought something to this part." He patted his rotund belly approvingly. "Fleshed it out, like."

"That," said Synge, "is true."

"So it seems a shame I'm not seen more of. It occurs to me that a few more appearances by Michael James Flaherty, as played by yours truly, could not but enhance the flatter portions of the entertainment. For instance, I am not used at all in the second act, and — how shall I put it? . . . "

"Put it quickly."

"The second act does sag. Now if we stuck in a nice soliloquy — ."

"A soliloquy?"

"Right. Suppose Michael James comes back from the wake."

"What on earth for?"

"What for? Why, so he can say his soliloquy. Sure, it's no good having him saying it off in the wings."

"I mean what would be his motivation?"

"Eh?"

"His reason for coming back?"

"Ah!" said Arthur Sinclair with an expansive smile. "Why, to check on Pegeen Mike."

"Mac, Michael James doesn't give a damn what happens to Pegeen Mike. All he's interested in is getting blind drunk at the wake."

"Ah well now, have you entirely plumbed his character? I put it to you, *why* does Michael James want to get blind drunk?" Arthur Sinclair donned the brooding expression that had been so admired in his portrayal of James II in Lady Gregory's powerful, if insufficiently appreciated, historical drama entitled *Kincora*. "Do you follow me?"

"If you would march onto the stage, I would be prepared to."

"Suppose now, that he was in love with the Widow Quin."

"Good God."

"Ah, startles you, doesn't it? Opens up whole new perspectives like! Now we could develop all this in his soliloquy. Or possibly two soliloquies might be better."

"If we ran them together, we could call it a dialogue."

"Eh?"

"Mac, we open to-morrow night."

"I'm a quick study. And then, you see, what I am suggesting would set matters up for the big confrontation scene between Michael James and the Widow Quin, although it would probably be better to put that in the third act. Right at the curtain."

"Well, I'm afraid there would be too many problems."

"Ah," said Arthur Sinclair with a knowing wink, "I see exactly what you mean. Poor Sally is not, like yours truly, quick at getting her lines. God knows, I've had to cover for her often enough during performance."

Synge tried to ooze his way around Arthur Sinclair's stalwart belly.

"You could write the scene so as to throw most of the lines to me. In fact, Sally really wouldn't need much more than a 'Yerra' or a 'bedad,' maybe only just a couple nods of the head. She does that well."

Synge raised himself onto his tiptoes and bellowed over Arthur Sinclair's large and fragrant shoulder, "Fay! Here are the scripts you wanted!"

Willie Fay darted to them, dragged Synge onstage and snatched the top script. "What kept ya?"

Synge decided not to answer that, and got down to the business at hand. "I've turned down the pages where I've written in changes. The very last changes."

Fay's finger darted to a speech at the bottom of a page. "You didn't do anything to this!"

"No, I definitely didn't. And I definitely won't!"

Upstage, J.A. O'Rourke jabbed J.M. Kerrigan knowingly in the ribs.

Willie Fay, who never missed a thing, caught that and tugged Synge by the arm. "Come over here. Let's talk about this for a minute."

"We can't keep on chopping and changing," said Synge, reluctantly following.

"And," said Willie Fay, "we can't — ."

A babble of voices interrupted them from stage left. Willie Fay cast an irritated glance in that direction and saw the two new girls, May and Alice, come in closely followed by the slimy Limey.

"Hold it down over there!" Willie Fay boomed. "We're about to start!" He turned back to Synge and jabbed viciously at the script. "Just look at this line here!"

"Fay," said Synge, "we open to-morrow night. The actors can't —."

"Purefoy!" yelled Willie Fay, without turning his head, "Get away from that porter barrel!"

Leslie Chenevix Purefoy came downstage centre and dramatically raised both hands above his head. "Why, oh why, did I ever come to this dreadful country?"

"Maybe," murmured Kerrigan absently, "it's that you can get bigger parts over here, Purefoy."

"Hee-hee-hee," snickered O'Rourke, an appreciator of broad irony.

"I assumed," said Purefoy, turning to them frostily, "that I would be acting major roles in verse dramas. Not be reduced to a mere walk-on. Not be apparelled in the rags of an unspeaking and unspeakable peasant."

"Purefoy!" roared Willie Fay, without lifting his eyes from the script, "Belt up!"

"Do you think," said O'Rourke to Kerrigan, "we could maybe sneak out to the laneway for a quick fag?"

And, like the experienced thespians they were, they did.

As they passed the Greenroom door followed by Purefoy hoping to cadge a cigarette, Molly was saying hotly, "I left home because I wouldn't put up with the way you kept on about him. And I'm not going to put up with it here!"

Purefoy halted to listen.

"Your head's turned by who he is," snapped Sally.

"Are you jealous of him and me? Is that what ails you?"

"Jealous! May God forgive you! I'm telling you, he's ashamed of you."

"He's not! He. . . gives me books and — ."

"Books! You! My God, that's like spittin' on the Sahara. Why won't he even introduce you to his people?"

Purefoy peeked around the door as Molly gave a defiant little shrug. "It might interest you to know, sister dear, that we're going public after this play gets on. We're telling every dog and divil. We're getting a flat. We're getting married. We. . . might even ask you to be bridesmaid."

After a long minute, Sally said quietly, "Moll."

"What?"

"Don't. . . ." A really long pause. "Do anything stupid."

Hmm, reflected Purefoy, interesting.

Saturday, January 26

Joseph Holloway, bowler hat set squarely on his head in dogged defiance of the icy gusts of Marlborough Street, thankfully entered the vestibule of the Abbey Theatre. Although some twenty minutes before the curtain, the room was already bustling with people and bubbling with noise.

"It was a great night at the Abbey Theatre," he mentally indited on the blank page of his brain, "and all artistic and literary Dublin was there."

At that instant, the door from the street swung sharply open, and Joseph Holloway was slammed between the shoulder blades and sent lurching forward into the small figure of Padraic Colum, poet and dramatist, who was just raising a cup of very hot tea to his lips.

"Oh!" exclaimed the poet, as the tea gushed down his shirt front. "Oh — my!"

"Sorry, sorry," remarked Joseph Holloway, simultaneously proferring his somewhat second-best handkerchief and peering over his shoulder to discern who or what had pushed him.

There, majestically framed in the doorway, was the prominent amateur tragedienne, Thomasina McFitz. It was unmistakably she — the lofty narrow brow, the noble waggling jowls, the commanding height, formidable girth and bohemian attire. At six foot four inches, she towered head, shoulders and sometimes even bosom over all there. The simple peacock feather rising from her green turban increased her height, while the billowing scarves swirling downwards and outwards enhanced her breadth.

Joseph Holloway had little leisure to admire the bangles that clanked about her wrist, or the encrustations of rings on her fingers, or the flowing gown of deep purple, or the leather sandals from which her massive toes emerged like bunches of unwashed carrots.

For at that juncture Mrs. Sibyl Mulcaster appeared in stained apron and filthy house slippers and shoved the consequential bulk brusquely out of the way. "Luvva God!" Mrs. Mulcaster expostulated, "Do yez not know the price o' coals?" And with some vehemence she banged the door shut.

"Ooh! Ooh!" came a piping cry from the other side of the door which promptly opened again, allowing the poetess Christina McFitz, a shorter, paler, and very much bonier version of her sister, to scamper in. From her turban trembled one bedraggled feather. Her gown was dusty grey. She wore no rings.

Thomasina waded into the throng, scattering bruised art lovers in every direction, and, as always, Christina tripped along in her wake.

"You have spilled my tea, I think," remarked Padraic Colum.

"Let's have another cup," said Joseph Holloway, and they moved over to the tea counter where Mrs. Mulcaster was again doing the honours.

"Do you think anything will happen to-night?" whispered Padraic Colum as they waited optimistically to catch her eye. Joseph Holloway swept his professional diarist's gaze about the vestibule, ticking off the luminaries present: Dr. Gogarty, George Moore, the Reddin brothers, Miss Sarah Purser, Maire Nic Shiubhlaigh. "Eh," he replied sagely, "you'd have to wonder."

"I've heard rumours," said Colum, "that the play is not — not quite — you know. . . ."

Joseph Holloway shrugged. "All true. But what can you expect from the theatre's pagan directorate? We must hope that Lady Gregory has exerted some restraining influence." But the eager glint in his moist eyes belied the sepulchral tone of his voice. . . .

Augusta Gregory closed the office door behind her, and smiled at the buzz of conversation from the vestibule below. She peeped over the top of the stairs and took a quick count of the people already there. Ah, to-night at least she would not have to go out the side door and come in the front door several times to make passersby think that an audience was collecting.

She brushed a strand of iron grey hair back in place, and frowned as she noticed Miss Walker and her brother talking to George Roberts by the fireplace. Nationalists they called themselves, and doubtless were, for they insisted on spelling their names as Maire Nic Shiubhlaigh and Prionsias MacShiubhlaigh on programmes. Malcontents and breakaways was what they really were. Nationalism didn't come into it. No, it was spite and envy and simply wanting more money. Well, Frank Walker was not worth any more than ten shillings. Roberts was a useful secretary, true enough, and it was good to have him still publishing some of the plays, but he was no great loss as an actor. No, Miss Walker was the loss. Such a beautiful girl, and almost as good as Sally in certain roles. Well, what could not be cured must be endured.

Obviously the Walkers were hoping for the worst to-night. They had never liked Synge's work. Ridiculous, for Mary Walker had one of her best parts in his little Wicklow play. Oh, they were all so young and so easily influenced by that fanatic Arthur Griffith and by that foolish woman — of course, she dare not describe Miss Gonne like that to Willie.

Vexing that he was not here, to-night of all nights. He could be such a tower of strength — whenever he was around. Curious, people thought him impractical. His manner, of course. Aloof, austere. Shyness really. Shyness and strength, what a queer mixture. It had been the strength in Willie that had estranged good-hearted, pompous AE. AE could have spoken sense to Miss Walker, all of those young people so looked up to AE.

Just as she thought that, she saw AE's burly figure shoulder through the door, his pipe jutting out from his tangle of beard.

Quickly she descended the stairs. "Oh, Mr. Russell, good evening."

AE looked around as if he had misplaced something. And yet in his way he was as able as Willie.

"Mr. Russell, how nice you've come."

"Eh? Ah, Lady Gregory." He shoved his hands into his pockets, then took them out again, then shoved them in.

What on earth was the matter with the man?

"You've a good house, despite the weather," he said finally.

"Yes, yes, I was terrified it would snow."

"Yes," he said. "Yes." Then embarrassed, he scrutinized his pipe, put it in his pocket, and then moved it to his other pocket. "Well," he said. "Well!" And he turned away.

Feuds, she thought. Dear, dear.

Suddenly he was back for a second at her side. "Good luck," he smiled beardily, and tapped her on the arm. "The best of good luck!"

Across the room, his secretary Susan L. Mitchell had seen him come in. She smiled protectively and adjusted her pince nez. What had he called her in the office today? "My dear twilight auraed naiad." Now why couldn't a man who could say something like that to you three or four times a day be young and thin and handsome and unmarried?

But AE could only be big and unbrushed and talkative. And seeing visions and fairies. And painting the visions and fairies like a talentless Blake. And dealing with the co-operative creameries. And editing a magazine. And having At Homes on Sundays where his wife served hot scones and weak tea to budding poets. (AE's canaries, Yeats called them.) Ah, why couldn't he be young, slim and romantic? And why couldn't she be in her twenties, not her forties? And wasp-waisted. And not near-sighted! And not half deaf!

But then he wouldn't be AE, and she wouldn't. . . have a sense of humour.

She cast her eye around the filling room and lit upon that prime inspiration for her sense of humour, Mr. George Moore. She ran over in her mind the lines she had written about him:

> If you like a stir, or want a stage, or would admired be,
> Prepare with care a naughty past, and then repent like me.
> My past, alas! was blameless but this the world won't see.

She envied Sarah Purser for the line, "Some men kiss and tell; George Moore tells and does not kiss."

A smile playing about her lips, and her good humour thoroughly restored, she closed her eyes and began fashioning a new stanza:

> The leaves of George's note-book shall be pruned by George's knife;
> "I'll renounce my *Esther Waters*, I'll divorce my *Mummer's Wife*. . . ."

George Moore, Oliver Gogarty was thinking, resembled an ambulatory pear. Yeats asserted that he was "a man carved out of a turnip." An arresting remark, but not a thorough-going metaphor. Now, if a pear, a rather over-ripe, moist, squishy pear; but, if a turnip — .

George Moore turned from an astonished contemplation of the milling crowd. "I find it incredible."

"What is that, Moore?" inquired Oliver Gogarty.

"That!" he cried, gesturing toward the gathering audience and accidentally flipping a raw-boned bystander on the nose.

"What's this? What's this?" Belfastianly expostulated the red-haired man, clapping a hand to his affronted nose.

George Moore surveyed him imperturbably.

"I said," repeated the red-haired man hotly, "just what do you think this is?" He pointed dramatically to his nose.

"It is amazing," mused George Moore, peering at the nose with myopic interest. "Rostand would adore it."

Oliver Gogarty firmly steered George Moore off into the crowd.

"I must come to the Abbey Theatre more often," said George Moore. "One bumps into the most extraordinary — *things*."

At that moment he collided with Miss Thomasina McFitz's capacious bust. He stepped back and regarded the impediment with perplexity. "Bumps . . . extraordinary."

"I beg your pardon!" she boomed in tragic affront.

"Granted," he allowed graciously.

"Over here," said Oliver Gogarty, tugging him away.

Moore patted his drooping, sandy moustache. "It all has to do with Yeats. He attracts a certain eccentric type."

"Isn't that your cousin Edward Martyn trying to attract your attention?"

"Dear Edward," said George Moore, watching his cousin burrow swiftly into the crowd, "has never succeeded in attracting my attention. Now, Gogarty, you were speaking of Yeats."

"No, I wasn't."

"Yeats knows nothing whatsoever of business, not to mention the theatre. Not, in fact, to mention life. The fellow is absolutely impractical. Lady Gregory once admitted that common multiplication is quite beyond his mental powers."

"He seems to have multiplied the audience," said Oliver Gogarty, raising his voice above the din.

"Fluke, pure fluke. Did I ever tell you about the time when we were rehearsing dear Edward's *The Heather Field* and Yeats' *Countess Cathleen*?"

"Eh, once or twice, yes."

"It will amuse you. He and that alarming Florence Farr were attempting to conduct the rehearsal. She, you may remember, was given to trailing around in a flowing Greek robe, or possibly bed sheet. Now, that bed sheet — ."

"What?" said Oliver Gogarty who was having trouble hearing above all the noise.

"That bed sheet!" shouted George Moore. "Remind me to tell you about the bed sheet — strictly in confidence of course!"

"Eh, I believe that's an old story."

"A good anecdote requires, like wine, a certain aging, Gogarty. I have sometimes pondered the feasibility of pulling off a three-volume anecdote."

"I don't think there's time before the curtain."

"Yes, and you were speaking about Yeats. Well, Yeats and La Farr would give these lectures-cum-readings. Yeats would favour their audience, composed mainly of middle-aged women of a certain financial standing, with his theories on the art of verse speaking. Then Miss Farr would provide examples, accompanying herself with twangs on that strange, lyre-like instrument, urm, what did they call it?"

"A psaltery."

"They should have called it," said George Moore, "an assault and battery."

The tall thin man with Synge flipped away his cigarette as they entered from Marlborough Street. His hair was brushed straight back from a high forehead, and he looked around the vestibule appraisingly. "Nice crowd. Is this usual?"

"Yes, for a first night," Synge said. "It tapers off after that."

"Eh! Mr. Synge! Eh! Mr. Synge!" cried a bearded, rabbitty man stationed unobtrusively just inside the door. "Nobody told me you were in the theatre."

"We seem to be filling up nicely," said Synge.

"Yes," said the rabbitty man with a nervous twitch of his nose. "But it's very crowded. Crowded. And they're restless. Definitely restless. I suppose everything will be all right."

"Perhaps," said Synge, "you might let them into the auditorium now."

"If you say so. If you say so. Do you think?"

"Yes. And Henderson — ."

Mr. Henderson gave a little, alarmed hop.

Synge turned to his tall companion. "Payne, this is W.A. Henderson, our secretary. Henderson, Mr. Payne who may be working with us."

34

"How do you do?" said B. Iden Payne, cordially extending his hand.

"Eh? Eh?" said Henderson flustered, and then hopped off into the crowd.

"What," asked Payne wonderingly, "does he do around the theatre?"

"Stands at the door and greets people. I am told that his geniality has built up our audiences."

"Really?" said Payne, wondering if he had heard aright.

"He also takes care of the accounts. But don't worry, he won't give you any trouble."

Payne looked quizzical. "Trouble?"

"Look," said Synge, "I really should go backstage. I'll talk to you later."

Payne nodded equably. Trouble . . .?

Twitching his nose, W. A. Henderson stood by the auditorium doors, troubled. Deeply troubled. Had Mr. Synge said to let the people in? For certainty's sake, orders should be said and then repeated. And then repeated.

"Ah, Henderson," said Joseph Holloway, appearing by his side. "Good crowd to-night. Congratulations. Where would the theatre be without you?"

"Er, yes," said Henderson miserably. "But it's pleasanter later in the week. Oh, much pleasanter. Fewer people to bother with. Lots fewer."

"Who came in with Synge?"

"With Synge? With Synge? Oh, Pine or something. He's going to be doing something here — or perhaps I didn't understand correctly. Dear, dear, if people would only keep their observations to themselves, things would all be simpler. Yes, to themselves. Simpler."

Joseph Holloway sucked the soggy left strands of his moustache. "Working here, you say?"

"I said nothing!"

Joseph Holloway was inured to the difficulties of extracting information from his friend. He proceeded with patience. "Is he Irish?"

"No," said Henderson, "I wouldn't know."

"Is he English?"

"Dear, dear, Mr. Synge remarked something about opening the doors just now. Now, did he mean now? Yes, English."

"English," said Joseph Holloway. "First they import that absurd Miss Darragh, and then the low mimic Purefoy, and now this one. Aghh!"

The "Aghh!" was occasioned by Miss Thomasina McFitz stepping on one of Joseph Holloway's multitudinous corns.

"Or did he," W.A. Henderson agonised, "mean open the doors later?"

"I don't know!" As usual Frank Fay was fussed about his make-up. "Nnno. I don't. . . know! Kerrigan, what do you think?"

"Terrific," said J.M. Kerrigan, picking up a newspaper.

"Eh?" said J.A. O'Rourke, "is that the late edition? See if it says who won the wrestling match at the Empire Palace."

"I put a couple of bob on Allen," said Gussie Gaffney.

"Allen!" O'Rourke scoffed, "couldn't wrestle his way out of a wet paper bag. Pat Connally is your only man."

Jem Casey, itinerant scene shifter, poked his head in the dressing-room door. "A pint o' plain is your only man," he observed with feeling.

"Maybe," said Frank Fay, "a little more shadow! Under the eyes! To show the suffering!"

"Connally has nothing to worry about," said O'Rourke.

"No good, lads," said Kerrigan. "This is an old paper. Ah! Here's something, though, — a review of our uncultured colleagues at the Queen's."

"Codswallop," sniffed Leslie Chenevix Purefoy, who had finished his make-up five minutes before but was still hogging a mirror.

"Maybe not," said Kerrigan. "Listen to this description. '*A Fight for Millions*, the powerful American drama.'"

"Codswallop!"

"Un-hand that mir-ror, Purefoy!" said Frank Fay.

"'See,'" continued Kerrigan, "'The Miraculous Escape in the Submarine Boat — Undoubtedly the Greatest Mechanical Effect ever presented.'"

"Now I wonder," Gussie Gaffney marvelled, "what that would be."

"Let us consult the review," said Kerrigan. "Ah yes — 'Mr. Ferris's company give a strong version of this stirring story which in its elucidation involves scenes at a country house on the Hudson, the pawnshop of a Jew, the Central Railway Station in New York City, the privacy of Sing Sing Prison, and even the bowels of a submarine boat, by means of which a wonderful escape is accomplished.'"

"Begod," said O'Rourke, "I wouldn't mind having one of them

submarine yokes anchored in the Liffey for our escape after this business to-night."

"'The part,'" continued Kerrigan, "'of Pearl Rivers, a true-hearted girl is played with fine dramatic force by Miss Alwynne Ernon.'"

"Alwynne Ernon!" exclaimed Purefoy. "Why, I played with her six years ago in Bury St. Edmund's, and she was no chicken then."

"Know where I'd like to be to-night?" said Gussie. "At the Rotunda. The Animated Pictures. Now, I'd say they'd give an audience something to remember."

"Remember?" said Kerrigan, digging O'Rourke in the ribs and gesturing to the concentrating figure of Mr. Arthur Sinclair who was pouring over his script in the corner. "Ah, little last minute freshener-upper on the old lines, Mac?"

"Ah, belt up!"

"Whisht!" said Gussie. "I think *Riders to the Sea* is over." He opened the dressing-room door and cocked his head to listen.

A wave of applause rolled in.

"At least they liked that," Frank Fay muttered gloomily.

Burly Ambrose Power, who was not on until the second act, came in wearing his street clothes. "Good house out there, lads."

"Hmmph!" said Frank Fay, profoundly unconvinced.

"Ah," said Kerrigan brightly, "Listen to this."

"Oh, shut up," said Arthur Sinclair feelingly.

"It says here Fred Karno's Company is at the Empire Palace tonight in *Mumming Birds*, supported by the Macarte Sisters in their amusing, graceful and unique performance, a serpentine dance in mid-air."

"Yeh?" said Gussie, "Now however would they manage that?"

"They didn't manage that at all well," pontificated Thomasina McFitz. "Especially old Maurya's last speeches. The performance of the play must depend upon how it is acted."

"Don't all plays?" said Susan Mitchell dryly.

"Or interpreted, wouldn't you say, sister?" interjected Christina McFitz, her prominent eyes bulging. "Upon how it is acted or inter-preted?"

Thomasina directed her most Medusa-like glare upon her sister.

"Ooh," said Christina abashed. "Sorry, sorry, sorry."

"And in this case," continued Thomasina, "the abject failure of Miss

Allgood in the central role of old Maurya let the play down very badly."

"Oh yes, tragically," said Christina.

"Not tragically," said Thomasina haughtily. "The play *is* a tragedy."

"Ooh. Sorry."

"Sara Allgood?" said Susan Mitchell. "Why, old Maurya is probably her finest role."

"Possibly," sniffed Thomasina through her cavernous nostrils, "but she does not gnaw the part to the marrow."

"The quintessential marrow," nodded Christina. "Eh, wouldn't you say, sister?"

Thomasina stroked the hairy mole on her chin. "Possibly," she conceded.

Christina bobbed her head enthusiastically at Susan Mitchell. "Thomasina has minutely analysed the part."

"Ah," said Susan Mitchell, who didn't hear her clearly but felt that some polite comment was required.

"In fact, Thomasina has sent Lady Gregory a detailed critique of how it should be played, and generously offered to demonstrate the more technical points."

Penned into the corner where the tea counter jutted out from the wall, Susan Mitchell did not know which was worse, the water vapour from the hissing urn that was fogging her pince nez, or the vocal vapour from the sisters McFitz that was fogging her mind.

"But this theatre," scowled Thomasina, "is obviously not interested in expertise."

"No, it is not," agreed Christina. "That is exactly so."

"Or in mere professionalism."

"Oh, that goes without saying," said Christina. "Otherwise they would not refuse to answer dear Thomasina's — ."

"Christina, *I* am speaking."

"Sorry, sorry, sorry."

"I was saying that — ."

"But," said Christina, unable to contain her enthusiasm, "for the theatre to ignore Thomasina's proven merit — ."

"Well," said Thomasina, mollified, "perhaps you are right. But as I was saying — ."

"Anyone who has seen dear Thomasina's Cassandra could never forget it."

38

"True," said Susan Mitchell. She suppressed a shudder.

"Or her brilliant Ajax!"

"Ajax?" marvelled Susan Mitchell.

"A private reading given for the pupils at Alex," Christina explained. "Several of the younger girls had to be taken out in hysterics."

"I can imagine," said Susan Mitchell. "Tell me, Miss McFitz, have you ever considered trying Tamburlaine?"

"No," said Thomasina. "I have, however, a few thoughts about Othello which should interest you."

"I think I heard the gong," said Susan Mitchell desperately. "*The Playboy* must be going to start." And peering through the water vapour on her pince nez, she fled.

She very nearly collided, however, with Mrs. Mulcaster who, with a bucket of coal dangling dangerously at the end of a hefty arm, was breasting the ingoing tide

"Outa me way, will yous! Stupid people! Sure, the cows coming down the North Circular Road have more sense."

"Oww!" cried Padraic Colum as the bucket banged into his shin and left a black smudge on his trousers.

Sally sat before the mirror and blended out the age lines in her make-up. "*Riders* went well, I thought," she said.

"Umm," said Molly, picking up the newspaper Kerrigan had dropped in the wings.

Sally looked around for someone to snarl at. Brigit O'Dempsey was combing her hair as usual.

"Miss O'Dempsey," said Sally in her iciest tones, "you flubbed the cue for my entrance again."

Brigit O'Dempsey smiled vacantly at her and fluffed up her hair. "Sure, and I didn't. I wonder where are those girls with the tea?"

"In fact, you mangled it. My entrance is when you say, 'Maybe when the tide turns, she'll be going down to see would he be floating from the east.'"

"Well, that's what I said."

"What you said, my lady, was, 'He'll maybe be floating down from the east when the tide turns.'"

"Well, that's shorter."

Fists clenched, Sally erupted from her chair.

"Tea!" called Alice O'Sullivan from the door.

Now why, thought Molly, couldn't she have been a minute later?

Alice O'Sullivan carried in the tray, and May Craig followed with the pot.

"What kept you?" growled Sally. "We've hardly got time now to have a sup in peace."

"We were peeping through the curtain," said May Craig. "Isn't it exciting!"

"Pour the tea," said Sally gruffly.

The two girls passed a look.

And Sally, her jawline hardening, thought that O'Sullivan had winked. The cheek of her! Nothing but cheap good looks to recommend her!

"I thought," said Alice O'Sullivan, pouring the tea, "you were really thrilling to-night, Miss Allgood."

"Oh," said Sally, nonplussed.

"So did I, Miss Allgood," said May Craig.

"Well. . . thank you, girls. Yes, it did go nicely to-night." She stole a triumphant look at Molly who remained obstinately immersed in the news of the world. As if Molly cared anything about the news of the world. Or about anything except silly hats and how she looked.

"Do call me Sally, girls."

"Did you model old Maurya on anybody in particular?" asked Alice O'Sullivan. "She seems so real."

"Well," said Sally graciously. "there was this old aunt of mine who had some peculiar mannerisms. For instance — ."

"Ostrich feathers!" cried Molly.

"What?" snarled Sally, whirling in a fury.

"'Boas, &c. Beautifully Cleaned, Dressed and Curled French Style. Prescott's Dye Works. Dublin, Cork, Limerick.' Hmm, how would I'd look in a boa?"

"Curtain in three minutes," barked little Barlow from the door. "Beginners onstage."

"Oh cripes!" said Molly, leaping up. "May, finish this fag for me."

"I don't hardly smoke, Molly."

"Give it a try. You're a long time dead." She glanced in the mirror, and twirled around.

"Janey, you haven't a bit of nerves, Molly!" said Alice O'Sullivan.

But a lot of neck, thought Sally.

Molly laughed and made for the door. "Wish me luck, girls!"

"Good luck, Molly!" they chorused.

What an odd play, thought Ben Iden Payne, making for the vestibule at the end of the act. He'd read Synge's earlier ones and liked them, but this one was hard to fathom.

He saw the rabbitty little man attempting to fasten back the swing doors.

"Ah, Mr. Henderson," said Payne, "very arresting stuff indeed, didn't you think?"

W.A. Henderson looked surprised. "Oh, I never watch the first acts. No, dear no, never. Haven't time."

"Oh?" said Payne, moving aside as the audience spilled out. Henderson was shrinking against the wall.

"The audience," Payne mused, "seems a little restive."

"Dear! Oh! Dear!" said Henderson, oozing off.

Payne pursued him. "Have you been working at the theatre long?"

"Long?" The nose above the beard twitched in alarm.

"Eh, for some time?"

"Eh, yes. Yes. Some time."

"You look after the front of the house and greet the people as they come in?"

"Oh, in a manner of speaking."

"A manner of speaking?"

"Well, I avoid saying very much. One can lock oneself in the box office."

"Er, yes!" said Payne. "Interesting work?"

"Interesting?"

"Er, yes — of interest?"

"I am very conscientious," squirmed Henderson.

"I am certain you are." And feeling that he had chewed all the gristle off this conversational bone, Payne turned to listen to what the audience was saying.

"One thing I like about it here," said Henderson behind him, "is that it allows me time to pursue my real work."

Payne turned back. "Your real work?"

W.A. Henderson quickly looked around and then leaned forward confidentially. "My research."

"Ah, and would that be connected with the drama?"

"Only the literary drama." W.A. Henderson cast another alarmed glance about and then lowered his voice. "I hope to prove that Shakespeare loved his father more than his mother."

"Oh! How do you hope to prove that? Not too much is known about Shakespeare's life."

Henderson gave a guarded wink. "By the plays themselves!"

"Ah. . . how by the plays?"

"Well, this is rather ingenious, and what I say must be held in strictest confidence. Thieves, you know."

"Yes. Yes, of course."

"What I do is to *count* the times that Shakespeare used the word 'father' and the word 'mother' in the plays. So far I have gone through eleven plays with surprising results."

"Eh, I daresay. Do you use the Variorum?"

"The very what?" asked Henderson, blinking his pink eyes rapidly.

"Eh, excuse me," said Payne. "I had better get back to my seat."

As he walked down the aisle, he began to have some second thoughts about this job. . . .

Frank Walker seized Padraic Colum's arm, thereby spilling half a cup of sugary tea on the poet's trousers. "Thanks be to God," he said fervently, "we're not mixed up with this crowd anymore!"

Colum instantly forgot his dripping trousers. "You don't mean you've cancelled my play!"

"Ah no, we'll still rent the bloody theatre from them. Here, here's a few flyers for you." He thrust some papers into Colum's hand. "Pass them around."

"The THEATRE OF IRELAND," Colum scanned, "at the Abbey Theatre, February 11 and 12. First production of Padraic Colum's THE FIDDLER'S HOUSE, to be preceded by Alice L. Milligan's —."

"Look here, Frank," said Colum, "I can't pass out advertisements for my own play." But Walker was gone. Oh dear, how embarrassing. Colum stuffed the papers into his pocket and looked guiltily around. His trousers were very damp. Oh, wouldn't the curtain ever go up? . . .

Lady Gregory met Synge on the stairs.

"It seems to be going all right," she said.

He shrugged.

"Are you sitting up here?"

He nodded.

"Are the voices coming across clearly?"

"So far. But that mumbler Power doesn't come on until this act."

He looked so miserable that she wanted to make some gesture of encouragement, but somehow one didn't do that with Synge. So she nodded and said, "I'll see you after," and went back down the stairs. . . .

As Joseph Holloway returned to his usual seat at the end of the second row, someone plucked his sleeve.

"Ah, Lawrence." He bent down conspiratorially. "What do you think?"

His friend glared. "The insufferable George Moore had the audacity to tweak — tweak! — my nose!"

"Eh?"

"Never mind. Read that." Lawrence shoved a notebook at him. "A direct quote. 'Wasn't I a foolish fellow not to kill my father in the years gone by.' Would you ever believe it?"

"We'll have much to discuss later," promised Joseph Holloway and continued on his way. Lawrence's nose? . . .

Arthur Sinclair, who was not in the second act, stood in the darkened wings and secretly undid the top button of his trousers. It was impossible to go over your lines when your loins — . But where was he? Pegeen's cue was. . . ? Was what?

Frank Fay peered around him at the stage, his face full of worry. "The brother's doing well, isn't he?"

"Umm," said Arthur Sinclair infusing into it a satisfactorily ambiguous note.

Someone coughed out front. Then someone else. Then someone else again.

Fay gnawed his lower lip. "That audience. . . ."

"We've not got them," Arthur Sinclair admitted. "We'll just have to hold on until my entrance in the third act."

"What an outrage!" exclaimed Frank Walker to his sister Mary during the next interval. "I'm surprised the audience has stuck it so far. By God, if we weren't renting the bloody theatre from them, I'd have boohed my head off."

A frown creased Mary's pretty face.

"And didja ever see such make-up?" her brother snarled.

Padraic Colum shook his head glumly. "Power especially. That bloodied bandage about his head certainly killed the atmosphere of high comedy."

"Power did look a fright," Mary Walker admitted.

"What a collection of thugs and blackguards," her brother snorted. "Just wait till *The Fiddler's House*. We'll show them what Irish life is really like. Oh, there's Roberts. Well, Seoirse, now you can see why we split off from this outfit."

George Roberts regarded him coldly. "You forget, Walker, I'm publishing the play."

"Yer jokin'!"

"And I am proud to publish it," Roberts said curtly, and walked away.

"Luvva God," said Frank Walker. "Didja hear that? Well, that fellow knows as much about the theatre as — ."

"He's a very good — that is, a conscientious publisher," said Colum, who had just given a copy of *The Fiddler's House* to Roberts that afternoon.

"How could any good nationalist," Frank Walker fumed, "publish a piece of filth like this? It defames the country!"

"Perhaps if it were played differently," his sister remarked unhappily.

"Well, I only hope somebody makes a protest," said her brother. "This stuff just turns your stomach. Come on, we'd better get back inside."

"Come on, I tell you," cried Sara Allgood from the stage in her thrilling stage voice, "and I'll find you finer sweethearts at each waning moon."

"It's Pegeen I'm seeking only," said Willie Fay mournfully, "and what'd I care if you brought me a drift of Mayo girls, standing in their shifts itself, maybe, from this place to the Eastern World?"

And then all hell broke loose. . . .

Saturday, January 26: II

The hisses and hoots and applause were subsiding, but the excited babble of the crowd was still intense as Joseph Holloway, rudely pushed and jostled, made his way from the auditorium to the vestibule. "Oof!" he cried, spinning off-balance into someone's steadying arms.

"All right, Joe?"

"Oh, O'Donoghue! Thanks. Dreadful crush."

"Dreadful night all round," replied D. J. O'Donoghue, the librarian. "Do you know MacNamara?"

"Joe and I are brother architects," said MacNamara.

"Well," said O'Donoghue, pushing his glasses up to the bridge of his thin nose, "I'm delighted that I didn't take my wife to this dirt."

"Aye," agreed MacNamara, "I was never so sickened in my life. Big difference from Boyle's *Mineral Workers*. Does no one supervise the plays?"

"Synge," Joseph Holloway pontificated, "is the evil genius of the Abbey, and Yeats is his able lieutenant. Lady Gregory, though she backs them up when they transgress good taste and cast decency to the winds, does keep clean in her plays, and William Boyle, as you say, is ever and always wholesome."

"Did you hear," said D. J. O'Donoghue, "the cry from the pit — 'This is not Irish life!' Oh, he put his finger right on it."

"That was Arthur Clery said that," said MacNamara. "He's covering it for *The Leader*. Moran, the editor, sent him because he feared to take his wife too."

"Well," said O'Donoghue, "after to-night the playgoers of Dublin will know exactly what to expect from J. M. Synge!"

"Yes," said Joseph Holloway, "the outpouring of a morbid, unhealthy mind, ever seeking on the dunghill of life for the nastiness that lies concealed there perhaps, but never suspected by the clean of mind. There is more to gaze on in a country scene than the manure heap!"

"Oh, you're absolutely right there, Joe," said MacNamara.

"Joe's always right in his facts," said O'Donoghue.

"Did you hear," said Joseph Holloway, basking, "that George Moore attacked poor Lawrence? Quite savagely."

"Really!" said MacNamara.

"Smashed him in the face."

"I just saw Lawrence," said O'Donoghue. "He looked all right."

"Oh, I had it from Lawrence himself," said Joseph Holloway. "It was a vicious coward's blow, utterly unprovoked."

"Well, as I said, Joe, you're always right in your facts," said O'Donoghue, with the sincere admiration of one rabid autodidact for another, but also with the scepticism of the true scholar.

"Yes," said Mary Walker, passing with a haunting smile, "Mr. Holloway is the finger we players keep upon the pulse of the Dublin public."

"Hem-hem," said Joseph Holloway, with a deprecatory smirk.

"Lovely actress," mused O'Donoghue.

"Whenever," reflected MacNamara, "there's a William Boyle play on here, the people come in droves."

Oliver Gogarty appeared amongst them. "Like sheep?" he inquired innocently.

"Bah!" snapped Joseph Holloway.

"Precisely," smiled Gogarty. "Anyone seen the author?"

"He was up in the balcony," said O'Donoghue.

"Skulking up in the balcony," Joseph Holloway amended.

"Ah, the reprobate," observed Gogarty pleasantly, and made his way off.

"Oh, that's the right boyo," snickered MacNamara.

"Someday he'll get his comedownance," said Joseph Holloway, "and richly deserved. Well, I'm going to find some fresh air."

He nodded to his friends, scowled piously, and tried to make his way to the door. The vestibule was still a churning mass of shouting people. More like a Tivoli audience on a drunken Saturday night, than a temple of uplifting, Christian Art.

"Here, Mr. Holloway." Frank Walker thrust a piece of paper into his hand, and Joseph Holloway nodded briefly and shoved onward. An earnest nationalist, Walker, but a terrible actor.

Joseph Holloway bumped into a diaphanous wall, which proved to be the massive back of Thomasina McFitz.

"It is not Art!" that lady was proclaiming.

46

Joseph Holloway's idea of Hell would have been an eternity at a play performed by Frank Walker and Thomasina McFitz. He was not entirely bereft of taste and judgement.

"Art," she declaimed, "is the basic and, indeed, the fundamental question."

"You are so right, darling," piped up Christina McFitz, also barring Joseph Holloway's way.

"I am," said Thomasina judiciously.

Joseph Holloway resigned himself to immobility. Then he recollected the slip of paper Walker had given him. A notice for Padraic Colum's *The Fiddler's House*, to be preceded by Alice L. Milligan's *The Last Feast of the Fianna*. Well, Colum was ever wholesome. As for Miss Milligan, hmm, an earnest Northern lady, and perhaps he could sit through her thing again. If he saw Walker, however, he might remark humorously that he hoped the Theatre of Ireland would provide a little more food on the table than had the Irish Literary Theatre in the original production. That was more a famine than a feast, as he had wittily jotted down in his journal on that patrotic, if somewhat lugubrious occasion.

"Ugh!" he gasped, as Christina McFitz trod on a corn on his right foot.

"Artistry above all," intoned Thomasina McFitz, stamping, with elocutionary fervour, upon Joseph Holloway's left foot.

"DAMME!" shrieked Joseph Holloway, thoroughly astonishing himself and all of those in his immediate vicinity.

Her pince nez was still not spotless. Susan L. Mitchell stopped short. Heavens, what a fussy old maid I am becoming. Queer how eccentricity creeps up upon one. Of course, a pince nez itself was the ne plus ultra in spinsterishness. How difficult it was to remain normal.

Particularly when listening to George Moore of Ely Place who was still holding forth.

"My dear AE," he expostulated, "*je suis enchanté*. Synge, save for the odd blemish to which I shall call his attention, has escaped Yeats' baneful influence, and the upshot is a great Irish play."

AE's face wrinkled. "Great? Irish?"

"*Un chef d'oeuvre!* Almost medieval in tone. Almost Rabelaisian. Well, Rabelaisian in an Irishly puritanic sort of way. Nevertheless, still too earthy, too *sensuel* for the national sensibility."

Susan Mitchell smiled, recalling her recent quatrain:

> Ah, since my views on Saving Grace
> The Puritans found flighty,
> Behold me now in Ely Place
> The priest of Aphrodite.

She removed her pince nez and gave them a slight, satisfying polish.

"Ah!" cried George Moore, "there is dear Edward. Edward!"

Edward Martyn burrowed frantically into the crowd.

"*Tiens*, didn't see me," said George Moore. "I'll chase after him. He'll be wanting my opinion."

"Och!" W.J. Lawrence exclaimed irritably as Edward Martyn in full flight stumbled into him.

"A bit wobbly on your pins, eh?" remarked "Jacques," the drama critic of *The Irish Independent*. "Happens to the best of us. Take my arm."

Lawrence got the full benefit of a whiskey-flavoured breath. Ordinarily Lawrence avoided his colleague who was no proper reviewer of plays at all, but merely a cretin from the sports desk.

However, they were both shoved together against the wall by the last balcony patrons crowding down the stairway.

"Well!" said Lawrence, "a fine exhibition in our so-called national theatre!"

"Ah, liked it, did you?" said Jacques upon whom irony, in the latter stages of the evening, was usually lost.

"An insult to the nation!" cried Lawrence. "No right-thinking Irishman will set foot in this place again."

"Oh, lurid, very lurid," agreed Jacques with a slight belch. "All them bloody-damn swear words."

"And that unforgivable reference to an article of female attire!"

"Eh?" said Jacques with woozy interest. "I must have missed that. What reference?"

"A word," said Lawrence stiffly, "not even privately expressed in Irish society. Or in any civilised society in modern times. There is an exactly analogous case in Dekker's play of 1604. You know the one I mean."

"Eh, " said Jacques blearily, "for the moment the name escapes me."

"*The Honest* — you know."

"Juno?"

"*The Honest* W-H-O-R-E."

Jacques' fuddled brain puzzled for a moment over the spelling. "Oh! Hoor!"

W.J. Lawrence winced at his companion's crudity. "In modern times, whenever it is revived, it is invariably called *The Honest Wanton*, and to my memory Barry Sullivan was the very last actor with the temerity to use the offensive Elizabethan title."

"Ah," said Jacques. "Barry Mulligan, entirely desperate that fella. But what was Synge's dirty word?"

"I should not," said W.J. Lawrence with dignity, "care to sully my lips with — ."

"Ah Jaysus," said Jacques, proferring a half-full naggin from his pocket, "wash it off with that."

Disdainfully, W. J. Lawrence brushed aside the offending bottle, and lowered his voice. "If you must know, it was S-H-I —."

"Jaysus, was it!" cried Jacques, lurching excitedly for the door.

"F-T," Lawrence concluded.

Ugh, he thought, casting his eyes thankfully aloft at his colleague's departure, what a low fellow. But who was that at the top of the stairs? Oh, this was too fortuitous to be missed!

He fought past the last few people coming down.

"Mr. Synge!"

The burly figure turned wearily. "It's Lawrence, isn't it?"

"W.J. Lawrence! I protest against this abominable presentation. This calumny! This disgrace to the Irish nation and this affront to Irish womanhood! It is shameful, sir! There! I have said it straight out!"

For a moment Synge looked down the stairs at him. "So you have," he said evenly, and turned and went into the balcony.

Ha, thought Lawrence, fled like a whipped cur!

Mary Walker had lost her brother. Well, he could find his own way. She'd catch the tram at the pillar.

"Maire! Maire Nic Shiubhlaigh!"

Mary Walker turned and saw trim little Miss Milligan making purposefully towards her.

"Oh, Miss Milligan, how lovely. We hoped you'd come down for your play."

Alice Milligan pressed her arm warmly. "I wouldn't miss it, my dear. But do let's get out of this crush."

Presently they managed their way out into Marlborough Street.

"Brr," the lively little woman said, "it's colder here than in Belfast. How are rehearsals going?"

"Oh, pretty well. You mustn't expect anything elaborate."

"My dear, I'm used to the simplest of productions."

They paused at the corner of Lower Abbey Street.

"I'm going to the Pillar," said Mary Walker.

"And I must turn off here for Gardiner Street. My temperance hotel closes its doors at an early hour."

Yet despite the cutting wind, each was reluctant to leave.

"What did you think of it?" Mary Walker asked finally, gesturing back to the theatre.

Miss Milligan compressed her lips and shook her head. "I'm afraid it's just what Yeats wants. He knows the value of advertising."

"The play itself," Mary Walker said uncertainly, "has a strange, nasty streak in it. Yet parts were beautiful."

"It's not Irish. Not Irish in the least."

"I think if we had played it, we could have hidden the nastiness. If we'd played it more for comedy."

Miss Milligan shook her head. "No. No, your Theatre of Ireland must go its own way, my dear. And so must the Abbey."

Mary Walker turned her beautiful head away. Not often, but sometimes, now and then, she had doubts. Not exactly regrets that she had joined the breakaway movement. An Irish theatre had to have Irish ideals. But the Theatre of Ireland productions were so hole-in-corner. And the Abbey had such a lovely little theatre. And she would certainly never play in London again, never with the Theatre of Ireland. . . . Her "wan, disquieting beauty," that famous critic had written.

"Who is right?" she asked softly.

Miss Milligan drew her collar tightly around her throat. "Time will tell, my dear. Good night." And with quick, businesslike steps she marched off in the direction of Gardiner Street.

For a moment Mary Walker — Maire Nic Shiubhlaigh — looked after her. So dedicated she was. So many poems she had written. And so many truly Irish plays. And yet *The Last Feast* was really not. . . awfully good. . . was it?

Too late to change now, thought Maire Nic Shiubhlaigh, and faced into the wind sweeping down from Sackville Street. . . .

The first to change, Molly O'Neill burst out of the auditorium into the now nearly deserted vestibule. On the stairway, a plump, stately young man stepped aside for her.

"Beautiful performance to-night," he said.

She flashed Gogarty a dazzling smile and hurried on.

"Johnny?"

A figure slowly rose from a front balcony seat, shadowy in the now darkened auditorium.

"Johnny!" She hurried down to him. "What did you think? Oh, not about how those few fools reacted. What did you think about us?"

"I — I thought you all did excellently."

She kissed him. "Who's asking about Sally and Frank and Willie? What about me?"

He managed a smile. "You were marvellous. Pegeen herself."

"La!" She hugged him. "But I'm not only Pegeen, you know. Oh, no indeed, sir. I'm a changeling — Pegeen to-night, Molly now, Mrs. John Synge to-morrow!"

Out in the hallway the office door opened, and they heard Henderson say, "Yes, your Ladyship, I've written it down. Where is it? Eh? Yes, here! I'll tend to it first thing in the morning. First thing." And they heard him hurry down the stairs.

He moved gently away from her. "We shouldn't be seen like this."

"Why? Won't everyone know to-morrow? Now, what will I buy to celebrate? Do you think — seriously now, I'm not jokin' — ostrich feathers look too depraved? I mean, for a young married lady."

"Is someone in dere?" Lady Gregory stood framed in the doorway to the hall.

"Yes," replied Synge quickly. "Yes, we're here. Me and Miss O'Neill."

"Oh. I couldn't see at first." Lady Gregory stepped into the balcony. "Well," she said, surveying the darkened auditorium, "it has been a memorable night at least."

"Yes, the most memorable night ever!" said Molly. "Because after to-night everybody, everybody, everybody will know!"

"What Miss O'Neill means," Synge began, "is, ah — ."

"Dat our little theatre will be notorious, yes," said Lady Gregory wearily.

"Yes, yes," said Synge. "Of course."

"Is that all they will know?" said Molly oddly.

"Quite enough," said Lady Gregory.

Molly squeezed Synge's arm in the darkness. "Is that quite enough?"

"Perhaps," he said weakly, "it is enough for one night."

"Do you want to look over de receipts, Mr. Synge?"

"No, no. I wanted — eh, well, what I wanted. . . ." His voice trailed off.

"I'll be on my way," said Molly harshly and made for the door.

"Wait!" Synge called. "I'll see you to — ."

"No need!" She turned back briefly in the doorway. "No need at all. You must have a good deal of *other things* to discuss!"

They heard her clatter down the stairs, and presently the outside door banged shut.

Lady Gregory raised a hand to see if her iron grey hair had come loose. It had not. "I had better wire Yeats. Ask him to come back as soon as possible, don't you think?"

"Eh, what? Oh yes, of course."

"I'll do it on my way. It's been a long day." She paused in the doorway. "Are you coming?"

"In a minute."

She nodded understandingly. "I'm not capable of talking about anything now. We should meet to-morrow though. You could come to tea."

"Yes."

"Get a good night's sleep."

He heard her make her way heavily down the stairs.

There were just a few sounds in the theatre now. The work light was on, lighting the stage dimly, leaving most in shadow. Someone laughed, and the side door slammed. Willie Fay and Seaghan Barlow came onstage, and Willie shifted a table and muttered something to Barlow, who nodded and went brusquely out. Then Willie took a last look round and followed him.

Time for him to go too, but he sank back down, without the will or energy to move.

On her way to the General Post Office in Sackville Street, Lady Gregory saw Joseph Holloway waiting for his tram.

She stopped. "What was the cause of the disturbance?"

"Blackguardism."

A small furrow came between Lady Gregory's brows. "On which side?"

"The stage!" he snapped.

She sighed and went on. . . .

In the deserted vestibule, Mrs. Sibyl Mulcaster contemplated the stacks of dirty delph. "Och," she said philosophically, "another night."

Sunday, January 27

He had lain awake for most of the night, listening to the wind and looking over at the square of not-so-dark that was the window, waiting for it to lighten into blue-grey.

Now he awoke, hearing church bells — Protestant and Catholic, vying to make more noise. He reeked of sweat, and his body ached, even to the bones. His mouth tasted of metal. The light in the bedroom was the colour of lead.

He resisted the desire to rise from the pillow and examine his face in the dressing-room mirror. No, he would not be morbid, not today.

'Fluish again? Yes, he felt like it. Perhaps it was 'flu, and nothing more. Had he imagined it, or did Gogarty — the doctor, not the dilettante — look at him curiously in the vestibule the other day?

"I say, Synge, should you be out of bed?"

The enquiry had been kindly — and one did not always expect kindness from Gogarty.

A bright, bouncy man. Always well togged out, smiling and smelling of expensive toiletries. Nothing morbid there. Mirthful mind, foul mouth. But somebody who could really crack jokes. But perhaps Gogarty's jokes were his way of insulating his essential self, the part that never appeared, except at odd moments in his poems. Not in his bawdy limericks. But even the poems were guarded, the spirit of the Latin poets falling like a toga over the modern man.

Was I much different with my Irish peasants? Only it's no toga I wear, but a stiff frieze coat from sheep that will never crop the Elysian fields.

Came up to me last night, after the performance, Gogarty. Ran me to ground in the balcony. Offered his flask: "A dollop of this. You'll prance like your Playboy."

We watched the last of the audience leave the auditorium, and then talked about the play. Surprising that Gogarty was so interested. There had always been, or so it seemed, a latent antipathy between us. Lack of sympathy, at any rate.

But be fair. Last night, he wasn't his usual mocking self. Before I was fully aware of it, he had me talking about the play.

The less a writer says about his work, the better. Why don the tweed or the toga, if you mean to walk naked? But it was good, if startling, to have someone really understand. Not even Willie Fay had completely done that. And, as for Yeats . . . well, why do I always feel myself something of a Konstantin to his something of a Trigorin?

What had she said, tossing aside the book I'd given her: "Oh God, Johnny, another Russian! What's this one's name — Feckoff?"

And what did Gogarty say? "Am I wrong, Synge, in thinking the style of the performance was at variance with the text?"

Surprised, I nodded an acknowledgment.

And puzzled, he shook his head. "Why was that? You and Fay produced it. Surely you could have done it exactly as you wanted to."

"No, not quite."

"Pressure from her Lah-dee-dahship?"

"No, she was worried but supportive."

"Janey Mac," he said, "don't make me think. Causes migraines. I'd better have another sup of the antidote. After you."

I barely touched the flask to my lips. No head for it.

"Let's see," he said, pursing his lips, "if I can state it simply. It's. . . well, very anti-social, your play. Boy doesn't get girl. No marriage feast at the end. In fact, boy really says that from here on in there's not a girl in the West that's safe from him. And he pushes the tyrannic old da out in front of him, saying in effect that he, the playboy, is the head buck cat there now. Why, man, you've kicked the foundations out from under our bucolic society!"

"I thought I'd disguised that."

"In the writing, yes. All flamboyant, ripe, bigger than life. And in the characterization too. But that story about Philly hanging his dog, and it barking at the end of the rope for an hour. Grotesque, my boy, even for Mayo."

"Extravagant."

"Very. But why, pray tell, didn't you make the playing extravagant too? That would have taken the offence out."

"Well. . . for one thing, our actors have not got all that much experience. Oh, they can play peasants, and even manage Yeats' poetry after a fashion. But a new unrealistic style — I'm not sure Fay and I could even have told them what we wanted."

That sounded plausible enough. Even if it wasn't quite the truth. But Gogarty was a perceptive fellow.

He frowned. "Yes, but why go for what one of our home-grown critics — Clery down there — called 'a brutally realistic playing'? Surely that's totally at loggerheads with your script!"

"Look, I really am feeling tired."

Instantly, concern crimped his face. "Of course, you must be whacked. Well, it's quite a play. And quite a night you've given us, laddie." And then he patted my shoulder sympathetically and dashed up the balcony steps. At the top he stopped for a moment and called, "Look here, Synge, get home to your bed."

Who'd have suspected Gogarty of such kindness?

Tired still today. But not all that ill. There had been worse days. Oh, much worse. . . .

Why really did I shackle the play with such realistic acting, brutal, everybody loutish, even Pegeen finally a shrew. I'd veered away from that question.

And I did court disapproval by how I directed it. I rushed — yes, rushed toward condemnation, embracing it, demanding the boohs and the hisses. And why?

To be punished? To punish myself in public, *before* the public, for all the weakness of my wretched life? My weakness with mother, who is the living embodiment of every value that I spurn, of every judgement that I discount, of every impulse that I would stifle. Yet what keeps me by her — the blackmail of the umbilical? Or do I love her too much?

And punishment for my weakness about Molly? Do I love her too little?

Oh God, that miserable moment on the balcony after the play, she so young, so radiant, waiting for me to tell Lady Gregory about us — and I couldn't.

Write to her, later on. Perhaps arrange to meet her to-morrow.

No, I couldn't see her so soon after that sickening scene with Lady Gregory.

But write to her. Perhaps in a letter it can be said. Easy to be courageous on paper.

Say that I will tell Lady Gregory when we meet later today. Yes, that would fix everything. She'll be delighted about that.

And explain how last night I was so worried about the play. So sick. She'll understand.

The pen and paper were there, on the desk.

But. . . wait!

Perhaps. . . perhaps I need only say in the letter that I will tell Lady Gregory this afternoon if. . . .

If?

Yes. . . if the opportunity arises. Yes, that's better. That is really much better. And I will, of course, tell Lady Gregory.

Oh, John Synge, liar! liar! Write to her straight out. Explain in words so that she can't fail to understand. She was improving, of course. Yes, she had a great natural taste and when she'd read a little more — .

Oh, prig!

Anyway, it's quite impossible. I've steeled myself to do it a hundred times. But how do you expose yourself that much?

But what if you lose her? . . .

Just now I haven't the strength to put my feet on the floor.

AE, seer and visionary, sat upon his usual stone at the top of Three Rock Mountain. His eyes searched among the rocks and ranged over the trees and between the bushes, seeking sight of those strange and timid creatures that he had so often visited here. And even painted.

"Hmm," Willie Yeats had said, inspecting one such canvas closely, almost too closely, and practically touching it with the tip of his aristocratic nose. AE chuckled in reminiscence, for he had been mischievously torn between a desire to say nothing and a duty to remark that the paint was not quite dry.

Too late.

"Do they," Willie had said, his nose now adorned by a small smear of Cerulean Blue, "really look like that to you?"

"Exactly like that. Why wouldn't they?"

"Well, ah, they appear to be somewhat boneless."

"Of course, they are boneless. They are spirits."

Silly fellow sometimes, Willie.

AE chuckled and glanced around again for his pet sylph. No, nothing to be seen today but Padraic Colum, who was little enough on a human scale. He had forgotten that young Colum was along on this Sunday morning tramp. Well, not surprising. Gentle Colum, so circumspect, so self-effacing.

He absently stoked up his old briar. The sight of young Colum, who crouched shivering in the lee of the rock, set him in mind of that trouble over Mary Walker and the others. Yeats had written a letter about that in his most imperious vein. *Acknowledging my personal strength and capability, but charging that I gathered about me the weak and incapable.*

Sitting below there, Colum did look weak and incapable. "AE's canaries," Yeats had quipped. *Which meant canaries have but a small, piping song. Which meant also by implication that if I took them under my wing, I could hardly use it to soar myself. Good man with a metaphor, Willie.*

Tut, unworthy thoughts. He and I are too different to be rivals. But wasn't that what he had also implied? I, twittering in my cosy nest among my adoring chirpers; he, lifting his noble voice alone on his lofty crag.

What had Susan said? "You are a really amiable man, AE." Hmm, well, it was to be hoped so; otherwise it would be difficult not to get irked with Yeats.

"Will you protest, AE?" said Colum.

"Ah no," said AE. "One takes one's friends as one finds them."

"Eh, what?" said young Colum." I don't follow."

"Oh!" said AE, laughing at himself. "I've been wool-gathering."

Young Colum's unlined face broke into a tolerant smile. "I was asking, are you going to protest against Synge's play?"

"Ah!" AE struck a match, cupped it expertly against the wind, applied it to his pipe, and drew deeply.

"That fuss about the Theatre of Ireland crossed my mind just now," said AE, leaning back and puffing.

"Yes, yes," said Colum unhappily. "Dear, dear."

"It could have been a minor little tiff in the theatre among friends, but it caused a quarrel with Yeats."

Padraic Colum, who had a great aversion to quarrels, winced.

"To protest against Synge's play," AE mused, "would be to quarrel yet again. Perhaps profoundly."

Down the slope Padraic Colum noticed a bird soar from behind a bush, circle and fly off. "I should not," he said, "personally like to offend Mr. Yeats. I am in a difficult position."

He shifted his small left buttock exploratively, removed an offending stone, and threw it down the mountain. "Both the Abbey and the Theatre of Ireland are interested in my work."

AE, his hands latticed comfortably behind his head, sent out billows of blue smoke. No man, he told himself, hates with more enthusiasm than Willie Yeats. It is a considerable talent. Something that I would not — . "Nor," he added aloud, "would you Padraic."

"Would what?" asked Padraic Colum, baffled.

"Enthusiastically hate."

"I don't hate Synge." said Colum. "We are sometimes compared, you know."

"Synge?" brooded AE. "I cannot agree with Synge. He would deny art a didactic dimension. Art should be always philosophic, laying bare both good and evil. Selfish psychological preoccupations are never enough. And therein lies the worthlessness of Synge's play — written, not for the common people, but for the psychological necessities of the author."

Now young Padraic Colum had a difficulty: how to understand all that AE had said? It was not that Padraic Colum was stupid, for he was not, but the compartment in his brain labelled "Generalizations, Philosophic" was a rather small, cramped one and easy to miss, hidden away as it was behind the larger one of "Opinions, Public and Politic," and the vastly larger one called "MY ARTISTIC ENDEAVOURS."

"But," Padraic Colum remarked diffidently, "there are common people in the play."

"No, Padraic," AE corrected, "there are most uncommon people in the play. Moonstruck mountebanks."

Not a bad description, he reflected wryly, of himself.

A clang of churchbells rose up the rocks from the Glen of the Pigs, the Glen of the Thrushes and the Country of the Trout.

"Time to be moving on," said AE, rising and lumbering cheerfully down the mountain.

He was never glum for very long.

Padraic Colum rose more unhappily and carefully picked his way after AE. Nothing was really answered for him, was it? How to act? What line to take?

Leslie Chenevix Purefoy was immured in his small, cold, upper room of the boardinghouse on Fitzwilliam Street kept by Captain Rex O'Growney-Greenway and his small, forceful and desiccated wife, Attracta. And her small, forceful and desiccated terriers. He belched.

For hours his digestive processes had been assailed by a lunch of bill-sticker's paste (described by his hostess in her Sunday voice as "celery soup"). Nor did the greasy boiled bacon, snaggy swede turnips and soapy, soggy potatoes help.

He ascribed the state of his stomach not only to the vile quality of the food, but also to the table manners of his host, a red-faced pukka sahib who claimed to have seen service on the Khyber, "bringing the demned natives to heel."

The soldier presided at table, a garrulous presence, complete with waxed moustache and parade ground voice. He ceaselessly regaled the starving assemblage of assorted theatricals, commercial travellers and counter-hoppers with blood-curdling tales of the North-West frontier.

The captain's diminutive lady always sat at the far end of the table, seemingly enthralled by her husband's gory accounts of foul Indian treason and fair British justice. If, however, the slatternly servant girl absently ladled too much food onto any plate other than sahib's or memsahib's, the pale little woman would snap her snuff-stained fingers instantly. And her three nasty terriers would yap. Oh, they knew which side their bones were buttered on.

There was a murderous east wind outdoors, and so Purefoy had spent the time since lunch paring his toenails and corns over an outstretched page of *The Irish Times*. It was not an absorbing occupation.

Why, oh why, had he ever allowed himself to be persuaded to come to this sodden, windswept country? He had been lured to this malicious land on false pretenses. "You can," burbled the enthusiastic Miss Horniman, "essay all the great parts on our small stage! You will be an inspiration to our peasant actors."

Ah, but the reality was different. Forced last night to play a walk-on! No lines! Costumed in rags! Nor had he understood what the wretched play was about if, indeed, anything.

In truth, he, Leslie Chenevix Purefoy, was much too much the professional for these dismal amateurs — these sometime schoolteachers, quondam clerks and cashiered shop assistants. He was jealously regarded by them as Miss Horniman's pet and spy, and, as such, was virtually ostracised. Conversation in the Greenroom ceased when he entered. Not that he was unduly troubled by this, for the talk was of an astonishingly moronic nature. "Lady Gregory, don'tcha think, is a better artist than Hamlet."

Oh, and the legend of the friendly, hospitable Irish was a myth — every bit as much as Captain and Mrs. O'Growney-Greenway's advertisement in *The Irish Times*: "Very superior board residence; personal supervision; homely touches; excellent table; fully heated; terms moderate; trams pass frequently."

Well, Leslie Chenevix Purefoy, actor, would one day show them all! He was not quite sure, yet, as to how he would visit his vengeance upon them — but vengeance there would be! Again he belched.

He gathered up the newspaper, with its parings and slicings and rubbings, and padded to the grimy window. The bottom part of this window was stuck permanently in the half-opened position. He inserted the newspaper into the aperture, shook it free of all that it contained, and belched again.

Joseph Holloway, passing on the street below, felt his face smitten.

Snow? He raised his eyes to search the low and sullen sky. Or was it a sign from heaven?

Joseph Holloway, as he walked along the windy streets, had been engaged in an examination of his conscience, a favourite pastime.

Did he, after all, commit sin last night by his attendance at that play, which was simply the outpouring of a morbid, unhealthy mind ever seeking on the dunghill of life for the foulness concealed therein? A well-turned phrase, he noted with satisfaction.

But if he, Joseph Holloway, had sinned, then so too had Synge. Which was a consolation.

Synge had gone too far. What had happened last night on the stage of the Abbey Theatre was unforgivable. There were many present whose righteous anger would be hard to appease. Yes, oh indeed, yes!

Murder most foul had been committed for less.

Across Pembroke Road, Joseph Holloway espied the Fays — Willie, Willie's wife Brigit, and the brother Frank.

It was possible that, humiliated by their part in last night's squalid proceedings, they would attempt to scuttle off and avoid a piece of his mind.

In fact, they were hastening to the corner. Must not have seen him.

"Ah!" hailed Joseph Holloway, "all out for a bit of a stroll to cleanse the stench of last night?"

"Oh, was that you there, Joe?" said Frank. "Now don't be so hard on us."

"Hmmph!" said Willie Fay truculently.

"Oh," said Joseph Holloway, wiping the drop from the end of his nose, "I'm not hard on the cast, at all. I pitied you last night up there on that stage having to speak such gross and offensive lines."

Willie Fay scowled. "If you think," he said contemptuously, "what you heard was bad, Holloway, you should have seen what we cut."

Joseph Holloway's eyes gleamed moistly. "There'd be no chance, I suppose, of seeing the cuts?"

"None!" Willie Fay said. "That's theatre property."

"I was merely thinking," said Joseph Holloway, "it would make an interesting note for my journal — which could be very valuable one of these days." Joseph Holloway's words were accompanied by a rapid succession of muscular twitches about his left eye. In a more attractive individual, his action might have been construed as a wink.

Willie Fay gazed stonily into the middle distance.

"Did you notice, Mr. Holloway, that I missed a cue?" asked Brigit O'Dempsey.

"Missed your cue?" Joseph Holloway couldn't believe that so season-ed a trouper as Miss O'Dempsey would ever miss a cue. "Did you? You didn't! Ah, no!"

Ah balls, thought Willie Fay, watching his wife's lovely but vacant face light up happily. "Yes," she chirped. "Missed it Missed it! Ha-ha!"

"Hardly her fault, Joe," explained Frank Fay. "All the cuts. None of us knew where we were."

Frank Fay had spent many pleasant hours in Joseph Holloway's incredibly cluttered study in Northumberland Road, sipping tea and gossiping away about G.V. Brooke and other thespians of yesteryear. Not a bad old sod, Holloway. No need to be as brusque with him as Willie was.

"Well, madam," continued Joseph Holloway, trowelling it on heavily, "I noticed not a thing, being too taken with the charm of your acting."

"Oh, but would you listen to him!" simpered Brigit O'Dempsey.

"Hunh!" said her husband.

Ordinarily Joseph Holloway would then have launched into a lengthy eulogy of her acting. Actors seemed able to listen to that sort of thing for hours. Usually, though, he served up a few mild barbs at the end. But on this occasion, the lust for gossip was too pressing.

He turned to Willie. "You wouldn't ask himself, would you?"

"Ask who what?" said Willie Fay, knowing perfectly well who-what.

"Synge. If I could glance over the cuts."

"I'd rather you did that yourself. After all, it's his play."

Joseph Holloway did not quite succeed in keeping the huffiness from his voice. "Oh, it is indeed; indeed it is, his play. The play of the evil genius of the Abbey Theatre."

"Oh," said Frank Fay quickly, "there's some excuse for himmmm."

"Well," said Joseph Holloway, raising his bushy brows, "he's Protestant, of course."

"I meant," said Frank Fay, "that poor Synge has had little joy in his life."

"Joy!" said Brigit O'Dempsey. "And he might not find it where he's looking." There, that would serve that Molly O'Neill for saying I'm stupid.

"Oh? Where's he looking?" asked Joseph Holloway, the tip of his nose quivering.

"Well!" began Brigit O'Dempsey, lowering her voice.

"Biddy!" snapped Willie Fay.

"Oh!" she said. Her eyes resumed their usual pleasant vacancy, and she fluffed her hair. "Isn't it getting awful cold."

"To be standing here blathering," said Willie Fay.

"Yes," she giggled, "blathering." And cast a meek and adoring look at her husband.

Frank Fay, ruminating as usual, had missed all this, and began explaining, as much to himself as to the others: "No, no joy in his life — and until there is, we may expect some strange — plays."

"He could finish the Abbey," said Joseph Holloway, "if he's let."

"There's some people," said Willie Fay, fixing his eye firmly on Joseph Holloway, "as wouldn't mind that at all."

"Heavens!" said Brigit O'Dempsey. "Who on earth?"

"Let's be off home!" said her husband.

Frank Fay, however, was still ruminating. "Oh, your pal came round afterwards, last night, Joe."

"Pal?" asked Joseph Holloway a trifle coldly, as he regarded the concept of "pal" as the kind of vulgar notion that might be current in Ringsend.

Willie Fay snorted. "Lawrence, the Belfast beagle."

"Sure," said Brigit O'Dempsey vacantly, "that accent of his would set your teeth on edge."

"Now there," said Joseph Holloway stoutly, "is the one man who could cause the dramatist of the dungheap and his able lieutenant, Mr. William Butler Yeats, a terrible lot of trouble. He would put no joy in their lives, hee-hee-hee."

"If I were Lawrence," said Willie Fay, "I'd think twice about tackling Bill Butler Yeats." And taking his wife and his brother by the arms, he marched them away.

Having in the privacy of the well-ventilated room completed his toilet, Leslie Chenevix Purefoy was engaged in the throes of composition.

"Dear Sir," he wrote, "As an Irishwoman, I desire to enter a most emphatic protest against Mr. J.M. Synge's new comedy, *The Playboy of the Western World*.

"I am well acquainted with the conditions of life in the West, and not only does this play not truly represent these conditions, but it portrays the people of that part of Ireland as a coarse, besotted race, without one gleam of genuine humour or one sparkle of virtue."

He paused. A modest beginning in his campaign of vengeance, but it was only a beginning. He returned to his labours.

"We have now an Irish dramatist putting on the boards of a Dublin theatre a play representing Irish people actively sympathising with a parricide, while Irish girls fling themselves into his arms, and an Irish peasant woman, who has made herself a widow, proving herself to be a liar, an intriguer, and a coarse-spoken virago, whose honesty is purchasable at the price of a red cow. Could any Irish person accept this as a true picture of Irish life? Fancy such a play being produced in England!"

Edward Martyn glared in disgust at the plate on which reposed a scanty three tea buns. "I understood I was invited for a meal."

George Moore poured the tea. "Irish servants, dear Edward. I have been, alas, deserted again." The rattling of a cane along his area railings, a noise he found acutely abrasive, distracted George Moore, and he sloshed some tea into his cousin's saucer. Infuriating neighbours, they do that in childish protest against the patriotic green I have painted my front door. Oh, a race bereft of visual sense. "In fact," he added aloud, "a treacherous race. Low, begrudging, pathetic in their native malice."

"It is your own fault, Moore, that you cannot keep servants," said Edward Martyn pulling the plate of tea buns over and calculating which was the largest.

"Servants," sniffed George Moore. "I shall spare you the sordid details of their latest effrontery." He poured the sloshed tea from his cousin's saucer into his cup, and presented it with a flourish. "Milk and sugar are by your side — prepared, of necessity, by myself."

Edward Martyn cranked his head on its short, fat neck and surveyed the milk and sugar. "You should have taken me to the Kildare Street Club. In fact, it is probably not too late."

"Ah, but I wanted a tête-á-tête. Eh. . . Edward, that is the fourth sugar you have put in your tea."

Edward Martyn impassively shovelled another teaspoon in.

Dear Edward, George Moore mused, one must think of his good qualities.

He did so. It took two seconds.

"Let us talk of Synge now, Edward," he said firmly.

"There is no butter, George."

"Butter? We are about to discuss art."

"I like butter."

"That is not a major fault," George Moore conceded. "In time it can be corrected. But now, dear Edward, pay attention. I have seen Synge's play, and I declare that at long last Ireland has begotten a masterpiece. Eh," he amended, "a dramatic masterpiece."

"Butter," muttered Edward Martyn, gnawing his bun gloomily.

"Synge has managed — for the most part — to disassociate himself from the baleful influence of our quondam colleague Yeats, and the result has been — for the main part — masterly. Now you and I, Edward, should be able to isolate the few disfiguring Celtic Twilightisms that still sully his text. He will be much beholden to us, as will posterity."

"I don't like peasant plays," said Edward Martyn, embarking upon the second largest tea bun.

"I appreciate your biases, Edward," said George Moore, drawing the

plate hastily to him, "but in this island the peasant is the wellspring of all
— ."

"His *Well of the Saints*!" snorted Edward Martyn, his large face turning
faintly purple. "All this sneering at Catholic practices is utterly distasteful
to me. When I hear the Sacred Name — ."

"Eh, you mean the name of God, Edward, don't you?"

"I never like to mention it. The Sacred Name is sufficient."

"But, Edward, when you are speaking French, you say '*Mon Dieu!*'
at every other sentence. Surely what isn't wrong in one language can't
be wrong in another."

A pitying smile trickled across Edward Martyn's large, round face.
"*Mon cher* Moore, France is France, and blasphemy is blasphemy."

What a delicious character, reflected George Moore, dear Edward is
going to make in my memoirs.

"And further," his cousin continued, "the hooting and outraged
protests which commenced in the third act at the words 'If all the women
of Mayo were standing before me, and they in their — in their —'. "
Edward Martyn blushed and shrank from completing the sentence.

"Oh, I agree with you, Edward," said George Moore innocently,
"that shift evokes a picture of calico, but if you recall the delightful
underwear of Madame — ."

In spite of himself Edward Martyn giggled. "Now, George," he
deprecated. "None of your Parisian anecdotes." And then amused at his
own folly, he began to laugh wheezingly.

Sensing an advantage, George Moore quickly said, "As an artist,
Edward — " (a hypocritical phrase but forgivable, as most hypocritical
phrases, George Moore had long ago decided, were), "you know that
art has its own morality."

Edward Martyn fixed his small perplexed eyes on his friend.

Ah, thought George Moore, that got his attention.

"Are you going to eat that last bun, George?"

"Yes!" said George Moore, appropriating it hastily. "But to the
point, Edward. You have a duty to see the play again. I have proclaimed
it a masterpiece."

"Oh you, George," shrugged Edward Martyn.

"A masterpiece which you, in pure and total ignorance, condemn."

"Ignorance," said Edward Martyn, "is never pure and never total.
Besides, Synge's language is something abominable."

"Synge's language!" cried George Moore in real astonishment. "Edward, you know nothing of language. I am the connoisseur. Remember how I had to rewrite *The Tale of a Town* for you."

"Butchery."

"Edward, Synge's mastery of language is apparent in his very first lines. Pegeen Mike's letter to Mr. Michael Flaherty, general dealer, in Castlebar, for six yards of stuff for to make a yellow gown, a pair of boots with lengthy heels on them and brassy eyes, a hat suited for a wedding day, a fine-tooth comb — oh, what a picture of peasant life in a few lines. And at every subsequent sentence my admiration increased. At the end of Act One, I cried out, 'A masterpiece! A masterpiece!' — Edward, don't go to sleep!"

"Eh?" said Edward Martyn, blinking his little eyes and shaking his burly frame. "Heard every word. However, I am not going to agree with you. That," he added, chuckling, "would be bad for you."

"But the style, Edward!"

"It isn't English. I like the Irish language and the English language, but I don't like the mixture. I like — " and he paused, "the intellectual drama."

This assertion, repeated at drearily regular intervals, always reduced George Moore to stupefaction. It did so now. When he had sufficiently recovered to return to the attack, he perceived that his cousin had fallen asleep.

Lady Isabella Augusta Gregory was very much at home in her private sittingroom in the Nassau Hotel. She liked the heavy, upholstered furniture, embossed wallpaper and bobbin-fringed curtains.

"Perhaps," she said to the man in the window embrasure, "we should have the light on."

"If you like," he answered, staring at a tattered newspaper being blown along the street below. Now it was spread, breathless, against the railing of Trinity College.

"Come join me at the fire," said Lady Gregory.

"Yes," he said listlessly. The wind was now buffeting the paper across College Park.

He was brooding over last night's row, she thought. Or perhaps also on her coming unexpectedly upon him and Miss O'Neill in the balcony. Silly man, everyone in the theatre knew about him and Miss O'Neill.

Perhaps she should make a friendly inquiry about the girl. But it was all so difficult with Synge.

"Here comes one of our new Englishmen," he said dully.

"That new actor?"

"Purefoy? No, the other one. Payne."

"How is the actor turning out?" she enquired.

"Early to say. I believe he's quite a good mimic, but I don't think the other actors greatly care for him."

She sighed. "I know. They feel he's imposed from outside, different from them, better. Oh, how I wish — ." She broke off, for she had intended to say, "I wish Miss Horniman would mind her own business."

"Pardon?" he queried dully.

"I wish our little family could be more content. Sometimes it seems just one bickering after another. Why do we generate so much anger, so much hatred? Arthur Griffith who used to be our friend, Miss Gonne, de Walkers. . . ."

"Why, indeed?" he said sourly. "Well, yesterday night gave one good answer — my plays."

What could she say?

"Payne's coming in," he observed and turned and trudged across the carpet to sit opposite her at the fire. "Is he joining us?"

"He's booked in here for a few days. Yeats — and we, of course — will want to talk to him about his duties."

"You wired Yeats then?"

"Yes." She lifted the lid on a dish of buttered toast on the small table between them. "I adore buttered toast. Have some."

"I'm not really hungry."

"I'll pour you some tea."

"When will Yeats be here?"

"Tuesday."

"And what about tomorrow?"

"Well. . . I suppose we hope for de best. One should always hope for de best."

He made a faint wry grimace.

Her small, white teeth bit noiselessly into a piece of toast. "Do you like Payne?"

He pulled himself restlessly up. "Oh, I don't know him. But I don't like the idea."

"Yeats says he requires him."

"Umm."

"His plays, after all, are our *raison d'être*. My own little comedies are just stop-gaps, better I should hope than Boyle's, but just little pieces to keep de theatre open."

"They are, I think, much better than Boyle's, as you know."

She looked at him levelly. "I do not underrate them. However, Miss Horniman was right about one thing at least — Yeats. She gave us de theatre primarily for his plays. And she was quite right about Yeats' value. He is only beginning to find himself, to grow. He needs de theatre. And if it's imperilled by — ." She stopped abruptly.

"By my plays."

Involuntarily her cup rattled against her saucer. Carefully she put them down on the table.

"You have never quite liked *The Playboy*," he said, without accusation.

"It is very strong."

A clinker cracked on the fire.

"I was afraid," she admitted, "of its effects. We have all worked so hard for de theatre. To lose it now — ."

"There are various ways we could lose it. Not only through me."

"What do you mean?"

He took up his cup and sipped it. "Payne may be a fine producer, but he is not one of them. Oh, I know that Willie Fay can be abrasive, but still he is one of them. They're loyal to him in their way. In fact, I have some loyalty to Fay."

"But Fay is still to do all de peasant plays — yours, mine, Boyle's, Colum's. Payne is just to do Yeats' poetic dramas. Or if we should ever do Shakespeare. Or Molière perhaps."

"We're creating, in the minds of the actors at least, two classes of work — the kind they can do naturally, and the kind in which they must be tutored. Or even replaced by English actors."

"Ah," she smiled, trying to lighten the conversation. "Can you imagine Ambrose Power playing Coriolanus?"

He massaged the bridge of his nose. "Payne is going to be making a good deal more money than Fay."

"Miss Horniman insisted dat we pay properly for somebody good."

He sighed and remained moodily silent.

"And Yeats wants — ."

"Yes," he said. "He arrives Tuesday, eh? I wonder what he will do."

"I wonder," she murmured, "What our audience will do."

They sat in silence for a long minute.

"Despite *The Playboy*," she said finally, "Yeats will be de one dey hate. Not you."

"Hate?"

She shivered slightly. "Yes."

Grinning, Leslie Chenevix Purefoy signed his composition with a flourish:

> Yours truly,
> A WESTERN GIRL

In his flat at 10 Adelphi Terrace, London WC, Bernard Shaw was going through the Sunday papers with his customary dispatch. "Disturbance at the Abbey Theatre," he read, and his tufted eyebrows twitched with interest. Twenty seconds later, having thoroughly digested the story, he gazed out at the Thames.

"How extraordinarily nice," he reflected once again, "not to be in Ireland."

Monday, January 28

Thomasina McFitz, majestically arranged on the tattered chaise lounge with the wonky leg, waited impatiently. "Well!" she finally bellowed in her resounding baritone.

From the hallway, came a mouselike rustling. The door opened tentatively, and Christina slipped through, hastily stuffing a paper into her apron pocket.

"What is that?" demanded Thomasina.

"Bill from Arnott's."

"Throw it on the fire. Anything for me?"

"Eh, just this, darling." Christina held out an envelope which her sister snatched.

Yes, his hand! She slipped the envelope beneath her great buttock and glowered at her sister. "Tea!"

"Eh . . . ?"

"Is something perchance amiss with my enunciation?"

Having often accompanied her sister on gusty Sunday afternoons to Bullock Harbour for the purpose of practicing vowel sounds in defiance of the elements and to the alarm of the gulls, Christina was aware that elocution was one of the multitudinous strong points upon which Thomasina congratulated herself.

"Oh, no, no," she bleated. "Tea. Of course, tea." She progressed in frantic birdlike skips to the door.

"And biscuits!"

"Eh. . . you ate all the biscuits, darling."

"Then muffins! Scones! Toast!"

"Yes, yes, yes. Pardon. Sorry," said her sister, slipping out.

"Or meringues," rumbled Thomasina deeply in her goitrous throat.

But there were no meringues, nor had there been since her twenty-first birthday party when poor Papa had blown his brains out. And merely because silly Mama, whom Christina so unfortunately resembled, had decamped with the handyman. And the butler and the maids — there were a butler and maids then — had all scampered into the study, leaving the entire platter of meringues unguarded. A moment to treasure.

She retrieved her letter. The third since Friday! She shivered. So did the wonky leg of the chaise lounge.

"Adored one!" she read.

In the kitchen Christina scraped bits of blue-green mould off the bread. "Ooh-ooh-ooh!" she cooed, thinking of the missive secreted in her little apron pocket. She was able to resist no longer. She snatched out the letter, her third since Friday, with her thin, pale fingers.

"Adored one!" she read.

> ... until you triumphantly embody my Countess Cathleen, my Deirdre, my Cuchullain upon the stage of the Abbey Theatre,
> > I remain
> > > dear Artiste,
> > > > Your servant,
> > > > > Your faithful Admirer,
> > > > > > Pantingly,
> > > > > > > W.B. (Liam) Yeats

"Oh, ye gods!" ejaculated Thomasina classically and collapsed athletically upon the chaise lounge. "Oh, meringues!"

The traitorous wonky leg collapsed also.

> ... until the dulcet euphonies of your delicate phancies find their full expression upon the stage of our national theatre,
> > I remain,
> > > Beloved Artiste,
> > > > Your servant,
> > > > > Your faithful Admirer,
> > > > > > Palpitatingly,
> > > > > > > W.B. Yeats (Guillaume)

> P.S. I don't think your sister is right for the heroine. She has, *au fond*, an animal crudity and would speak your lines as if she were spitting dung on a sapphire.
> > In fond frankness,
> > > G.

"Quite right!" said Christina and spread the mould back on the bread.

"Allow me!" said Leslie Chenevix Purefoy, opening the stage door so that Gussie Gaffney could carry his bicycle out into the lane.

Purefoy wasn't such a bad old skin — for an Englishman, thought Gussie.

A lot of the company didn't like him, but Gussie enjoyed his fund of theatrical stories and his mimicry of Irving and Barebum Tree. Sure, if they were half as good as Purefoy's take-offs of Yeats and Frank Fay, they must be dead-on.

Gussie set his bike down at the corner of the laneway and Marlborough Street and, getting astride it, resumed their intriguing conversation.

"And you really think that, do you, Mr. Purefoy? — I'm wasting me talent here?"

"Nothing surer, my dear boy. You are blushing unseen." And his hand came to rest paternally on Gussie's shoulder.

"Eh? What?" said Gussie uncomfortably.

"London," said Purefoy stroking his shoulder, "beckons! Shaftesbury Avenue was paved for your feet."

"That's a street in London, is it?"

"A street containing prominent theatres." Purefoy bent confidentially closer. "Unlike," he whispered, "the temple of Thespis at my back."

"Eh, the temple of what?"

"This doss-house of the drama that we labor in!" explained Purefoy. "The paucity of talent among our co-workers precludes their crossing even the malodorous waters of the Liffey. Not to mention the Irish Sea."

"Ah, you're dead right there," agreed Gussie. "Sure, you couldn't hardly see a one of them acting at the Gaiety or the Royal. Sure, not even at the Queen's."

"Precisely. Whereas you, my dear Augustus, have a potential of truly enormous proportions. I perceive all — and I do mean all — of the great roles as falling within the penumbra of your personality. You could play them all!" The corners of his mouth twitched faintly, and he added, "As they have never been played before."

"Yeh," said Gussie enthusiastically. "The great parts — Shaun the Post, Myles na gCopaleen!"

"Lear, Hamlet, Thisbe," agreed Purefoy.

"Be the hokey!" murmured Gussie. "Oh, by the way, that half-crown the other day — ."

"What about it?" snapped Purefoy.

"No hurry on it. Whenever you have it, will be more than time enough."

Oliver Gogarty had come to the offices of *Sinn Fein* to deliver another of his contributions in the series "Ugly England." He now sat with his bespatted feet up on the editor's desk, his hat tilted in the general direction of Ugly England, his topcoat unbuttoned and falling to the floor, smoking a cigarette.

"And Juiceless Jimmy said that, did he?" Oliver Gogarty murmured. "Well, isn't he the bitter boyo!"

Arthur Griffith looked up from Gogarty's manuscript. "I wanted you to hear it from me rather than from some publichouse gossip. Dublin being Dublin, some gobshite would be bound to blab it just to get a rise out of you."

"Who told you?"

"Somebody who was talking to the brother."

"Ah, the punctilious young Stanislaus. That hoor never liked me. In fact, if you can imagine it, he always blamed me for introducing Juiceless Jimmy to the delights of dubious doxies." Oliver cackled. "Oh, dear delapidated Jaysus! Like introducing a fish to water. Harkee:

> There wance was a poet named Joyce
> Who wished to be wan of the boys,
> And begged his pal Noll
> To find him some doll,
> Not unnecessarily choice."

"Stannie," Griffith resumed, "sent the brother the piece you wrote on your honeymoon."

"And our continental litterateur replied, 'Mrs. Gogarty mustn't have been very entertaining.' Yes, 'tis his fashion. I can hear his sniff and see his smile — rather like an anus in agony. Oh, very Irish."

Griffith took his chauvinism seriously. "How so?"

"Well, doesn't what emerges from the bard's lips, my pen and your press have something Celtically in common?"

"Such as?"

"Bullshit. From a registered Irish bull."

Imperturbably, Arthur Griffith turned away in his chair, took off his pince nez and polished them. If one liked Gogarty, and he did, one had to be imperturbable.

Oliver Gogarty leaned forward with an earnestness that he exhibited to few people. "I think, Arthur, that Barnacle Jim should have his bottom scraped, and I'd be charmed to do it without an anaesthetic, but to the more important matter — what I write and what you print is a bit insulting to the intelligence. 'Ugly England,' say I. 'Burn everything English, except her coal,' say you."

Arthur Griffith replaced his pince nez. "Whether we entirely believe it ourselves is beside the point. We're trying to resuscitate the notion of nationhood."

"And how do we resuscitate / The notion of a nation state?" remarked Oliver Gogarty metrically.

"By tactics," Arthur Griffith snapped. "And while you're looking for a rhyme for 'tactics,' let me point out that's why this business at the Abbey is so serious." He scratched his jaw. "An extravagance, Synge called it?"

"So he said. Ha, what a pair of national bards. Juiceless Jimmy and Joyless Johnny. Poor Synge, trying to write an extravaganza. I admire him, but he's as hilarious as a multiple fracture."

Griffith pounced upon that. "They say he's not a well man."

"Oh, far from it. Sick in mind and body."

"In mind?"

Oliver Gogarty shot his friend a quick look. "I see what you're after — diseased play by diseased playwright. Not nice, Arthur."

"You're a medical man," Griffith persisted. "In your opinion, is he sick in mind?"

"Well. . . not exactly sick, no."

"Disturbed?"

Oliver Gogarty shrugged. "Who's not disturbed?"

"Do you think that this play of his could fairly be called the expression of a disturbed mind?"

"Are you interested in being fair, Arthur?"

"I am interested," said Griffith quietly, "in winning."

"That row a couple of years ago over Synge's *Shadow of the Glen*," said Gogarty. "You stirred up a lot of angry feeling against them. In my opinion, needlessly."

"I had great hopes for that theatre. I supported it. It could have been a voice in the national struggle. But if it attacks the national ideals — well, it can still be useful as a whipping boy in arousing public opinion."

"I also remember at the time your paper printed a sort of antidote to *The Shadow of the Glen*. A piece called — ?"

"Called *In a Real Wicklow Glen*."

"I never knew who wrote that. But I always suspected you."

"I should prefer," said Arthur Griffith, an almost invisible smile flickering at the corner of his mouth, "not to plead guilty."

"A sound preference, as Synge's was drama, and yours was only propaganda."

Arthur Griffith turned his chair fully toward Oliver Gogarty and placed his palms down on the desk. "Am I in the business of creating a literature or a nation?" He paused for a long moment. "Now tell me about Synge's play."

How different he and Griffith were, Oliver Gogarty reflected. And even more curiously, the qualities he admired in his friend were precisely the ones that he himself lacked — certainty, intensity, single-minded ruthlessness.

"It's perhaps a great play."

Griffith brushed away the comment with a gesture. "Tell me something I can use."

"It's anarchic," said Oliver Gogarty slowly, and then dourly saw his friend jot down the word. "That appeals to me, especially coming from somebody of his class and background."

"Your typical Anglophile," said his friend dryly, "is not frequently noted for anarchy."

"Synge is hardly an Anglophile," said Oliver Gogarty getting exasperated. "Your West-Briton is generally over-fed, smug and constipated. Synge is hardly representative of that class."

"Nor of ours," Griffith stated emphatically and blew Oliver Gogarty's cigarette ash off his desk.

"No, but he represents himself, and that's imperative for every artist. Your valued little contributor Padraic Colum, couldn't have written a Playboy in a hundred years, and the reason is he has only a commonplace little individuality to represent. All Colum can do is hold up a mirror."

"To nature," said Arthur Griffith. "The classic place, I believe."

Oliver Gogarty took out another cigarette from his gold case. "I must never forget," he said, "that you use words too. And quite well. But I wonder if they always have to be used as a weapon."

"The play?" Griffith persisted.

"You could say that the play is a violent and bizarre — ." He sourly watched Griffith jot the words down. " — indictment of peasant life in the West. Of peasant life at its most grimly unglamourized. It is all utterly realistic, and all utterly Brobdingnized."

"Exaggerated," murmured Griffith, adding the word to his notes. "The printer could never spell Brobding-whatever. Well, I've a thousand things to do. Shall I see you Saturday morning at the Forty Foot?"

"Wife and weather willing." Gogarty stood up and buttoned his overcoat. "You haven't even seen the man's play."

Arthur Griffith smiled in dismissal. "No time." And buried himself in his papers.

Oliver Gogarty went out into the wintry wind. He should really drop by the College of Surgeons. Instead he turned into the nearest pub and called, "A short hot one. No cloves."

He regarded the smoke-smudged wood of the ceiling and presently murmured to himself:

"Jimmy and Johnny were the boyos who got
Arthur and Oliver's communal goat,
Yet in every way
The quartet did display
Minds stubbornly not to be bought."

He took out his small gold pen and his leather notebook, and entered the latest gift of his sub-muse.

When his drink came, he drained half of it at a gulp. As it seared his throat, he added:

"Dogs in the night barking at naught."

Jacques, a prudent man who had no wish to be kept from his bed till all hours putting his copy together, sat in the stalls of the Abbey Theatre, scribbling the first paragraph of his piece. The curtains had just closed on *Riders to the Sea*.

"It would not be true to say," he wrote, "that the Abbey Theatre was packed to capacity last evening for the second public performance of Mr. John Millington Synge's controversial piece, *The Playboy of the Western World*. Only the pit was packed; the rest of the house showed many vacant seats.

"In the pit, a mostly young, mostly male audience, some armed with sticks and speaking Gaelic, had sat with respectful admiration through a fine performance of the curtain-raiser, *Riders to the Sea*, also by Mr. Synge. The impression gained by this reporter was that these denizens of the pit had seldom been to a play before. They were awed by Miss Allgood's moving portrayal of 'Maurya,' an old woman, whose sons are stolen by the deep, and were generous in their applause. However, from the buzz of conversation during the interval, it was plain that their presence was caused by what was to follow."

At this point, Jacques wondered if there were time to nip across the street. Newspaper reporting is thirsty work.

In the ladies' dressing-room, Sally Allgood was completing the changes to her costume. She looked around to see were they alone for a moment. The young girls were clustered in the corner giggling at some piece of malice that Brigit O'Dempsey was giving out with. "Moll," said Sally, lowering her voice, "don't tantalize them to-night. Now, sure you won't."

Molly regarded her mockingly. "What do you mean, tantalize them?"

"You know fine well what I mean. I'm talking about the way you threw yourself about on Saturday."

Molly shrugged and stubbed out her cigarette. "Some of us have something to throw about. Watch this." She threw her head up, tossed her shoulders back, and clapped her palm against a jutting hip. "Amn't I the fine, frisky woman in red flannel!"

"Peals of applause," said Sally wryly. "From the pit!"

In the men's dressing-room, Arthur Sinclair sat at the make-up table and for the umpteenth time read "H. S. D.'s" review in that evening's *Mail*.

"*The Playboy of the Western World* is a remarkable achievement, a comedy brilliantly written and brilliantly acted."

"Does he single out Michael James for particular notice?" said Purefoy sardonically.

"Hmmph!" said Arthur Sinclair, and turned back to the mirror in lordly dismissal. Envious, talentless, English sod, he thought, wetting his finger and re-arranging his left eyebrow into a rakish tuft.

Big Ambrose Power came in and went over to the clothes rack. "I wonder," he said, "does me bandage have enough blood on it."

"It may after to-night," said Willie Fay grimly.

"Ohhh," his brother groaned miserably.

Seaghan Barlow scowled in at the door. "Two minutes to curtain!"

Jacques did indeed have time to nip across the street, and with the expertise of the born journalist downed a double whiskey. That, on top of a pork chop with kidney for supper, rendered him somewhat drowsy, and soon after the start of *The Playboy* he dozed.

A violent hissing and a shower of saliva abruptly woke him. It was a vehemently gesticulating man in the row behind. The whole house, in fact, was in an uproar.

"Wha-wha-what's the matter?" he cried.

"See that little grimy bugger up there! Well, that lovely Irish maiden is running after him. It's disgusting. Booh! Booh! And he's going to spend the night with her on his bloody lone. Oh by God, the filth of it'd turn yer stomach. Booh! Booh!"

"God save Ireland, cried the hayroes," boomed a ragged chorus from the balcony.

"Let you stop a short while anyhow," cried Pegeen Mike. "Aren't you destroyed walking with your feet in bleeding blisters, and your whole skin needing washing like a Wicklow sheep."

"We won't have this!" raged a voice from the pit.

"God save Ireland, cried they all!" came from the balcony.

"Now, by the grace of God," yelled Jimmy Farrell, "herself will be safe this night, with a man killed his father holding danger from the door — ."

"It is not good enough for Dublin!"

"Sinn Fein abu!"

"Whether on the gallows high / Or on battlefield we die!" roared the balcony.

"Sure, you can't hear a thing from the stage," said Jacques.

The Playboy detached himself from his stool by the bar and came forward to the footlights. He held up his hands, and in a moment got a comparative calm.

"A nation wance again," quavered one off-key tenor from the balcony.

"Shh! Shh!"

"Now," said Willie Fay from the footlights, "as you are all tired, I suppose I may speak."

"Booh! Booh!"

"We won't have it!"

The reporter's pencil flew over his pad.

"There are people here," shouted Willie Fay, "who have paid to see the piece. Anyone who does not like the play can have his money returned!"

"Irishmen do not harbour murderers!"

"We respect Irish virtue!"

"Where's the author? Bring him out and we'll deal with him!"

"Sinn Fein for ever!"

"I will send for the police," roared Willie Fay, "and every man who kicks up a row will be removed."

"Send for them! We'll deal with them!"

"West Briton!"

"Shoneen!"

"Up Sinn Fein!"

With a snort of disgust, Willie Fay turned on his heel and motioned offstage. Immediately the curtains began to close, and a loud cheer broke out when they met.

Joseph Holloway and W.A. Henderson came out into Stephen's Green from the Large Hall where they had listened with pleasure and profit to the lecture "Pigmy Races and Fairy Tales," delivered by Dr. Bertram C.A. Windle, M.A., President of Queen's College, Cork, and presented under the auspices of the National Literary Society.

"Nice little crowd to-night," said Joseph Holloway, setting his bowler hat firmly and squarely on his head. "Wonder how they're doing at the Abbey."

W.A. Henderson shook his head gloomily. "I have to go down and count the evening's receipts now. I dread it."

"Hmm," said Joseph Holloway. "I daresay you're right. Well, I'll just walk along with you to see what's going on."

Joseph Holloway plodded, and W.A. Henderson hopped silently down Grafton Street.

"Well," said Joseph Holloway with measured solemnity, "after Saturday night's disgrace, you might expect the devil and all." He smiled complacently. "Yes, the devil and all."

His companion twitched his nose, and gave a lugubrious peep.

As they lumbered and hopped past Brown Thomas, Joseph Holloway contributed another philosophic reflection. "Oh, but hasn't Synge got a nasty mind."

"Indeed he has," said W.A. Henderson. "Just imagine the like of a man who would store up all those crude, coarse sayings from childhood, and then to put them into a play!" Both walked on, silently marvelling at the depravity of man.

As they passed around by Trinity, Joseph Holloway contemplated the underslung chin of the poet Goldsmith and then clucked, "Literature. . . . The influence of Hauptmann must be upon him. It's the only possible explanation."

From his exalted position above the urinal, the beefy figure of Tom Moore seemed to raise an admonitory finger.

They proceeded into Westmoreland Street.

"Joe," said W.A. Henderson, "I'm getting out."

"Out?" said Joseph Holloway. "We are out."

"Out of the Abbey," said his companion. "It's that or the boot."

"They'd never sack you, sure."

"Oh, would they not! Nothing surer."

"Blackguards," snorted Joseph Holloway. "And after all you have done to build up the attendance. No man more faithful. Eh — why weren't you there to-night?"

"Ah, Monday's always slack. Miss Bushell can manage."

They crossed O'Connell Bridge, and Henderson paused to look at the black, flowing river. "You see, the English manager starts with us soon."

"Ashe," said Joseph Holloway.

"True," mourned W.A. Henderson. "Dust and ashes — life!" His nose twitched tragically.

"No," said Joseph Holloway with mild irritation. "Ashe, his name.

Or is it Spruce?"

"No. Pine."

"Oh, Pine!" said Joseph Holloway.

"Ah, there's better than that," said W.A. Henderson spitefully. "His wife's name is Mona Limerick."

"I don't believe it!" chortled Joseph Holloway.

"Perhaps it's her stage name. She's an actress."

"Pity she didn't pick Mona Mullingar. Oh, they must think we're all eejits."

"There's talk of her for Yeats' *Deirdre*."

"An English actress? Never!" said Joseph Holloway stoutly, as they turned into Marlborough Street.

"Ah, that's the way things are going," said W.A. Henderson. "And your man is to get five pounds a week as against my thirty shillings."

"Disgraceful!" said Joseph Holloway.

Two policemen were in the vestibule as they went in, and there were many more in the doorway to the auditorium.

W.J. Lawrence stood by the fireplace, smirking with dour glee. "Ah, Joe! You're after missing it!"

"Dear!" said Joseph Holloway, his moist eyes sparkling. "I hope there was no trouble."

"Trouble! Peelers all over the place. The play stopped three or four times. D'ye hear that? It's still raging!" They listened to the uproar from the auditorium.

"Come on," said W.J. Lawrence. "Let's see this."

"Coming, Henderson?"

"Ah no, ah no!" said Henderson scuttling into the safety of the box office cubicle.

W.J. Lawrence barged through the clump of puzzled-looking policemen, and Joseph Holloway trotted nimbly in his wake.

The curtains were just drawing apart, and, as they found seats, Willie Fay came forward and held up his hand. Presently there was a bit of a lull.

"You who have hissed to-night," cried Willie Fay, "will go away saying that you have heard the play, but you haven't!"

"We heard it on Saturday!" howled a voice from the pit.

"Sinn Fein abu!"

"Ireland forever!"

"Bring out the author!"

"Kill him!"

Lawrence leaned over and whispered with relish, "Few love to hear the sins they love to act."

"Eh," said Joseph Holloway. "That must be *Antony and Cleopatra*. Act Four, Scene — ."

"*Pericles*," said his friend snappishly. "Act One, Scene One, line 92."

"Of course, you're right," said Joseph Holloway, "line 92."

Why do I bother with him at all, thought W.J. Lawrence. *Antony and Cleopatra*, indeed!

Error irritated W.J. Lawrence.

Much later, Sara Allgood stood on the corner of Marlborough Street and Eden Quay. The after-theatre crowd had dispersed, and few people were about. A scouring wind blew up the Liffey from off the bay. The clock at Brunswick Street Fire Station struck.

She was all at sixes and sevens to-night. It was that disgusting business with the Holy Water that had started her off.

There she was, onstage, having delivered — and very well too — that gorgeous speech all about the wind and the dark nights after Samhain. Immersed in the part, the whole house in the hollow of her hand, she had then asked "Nora" for the Holy Water to sprinkle "Bartley's" body.

Normally, the vessel contained just water. Oh, but not to-night. To-night, there had been something altogether different in the vessel, put there by some prankster to destroy her performance. She was too experienced an actress to lose the grip on herself. But oh, the smell — it had to be cat — when she dipped the bit of palm twig into the vessel had only been something disgusting.

Yes, there was a terrible lot of jack-acting and interfering with props going on in the theatre lately. She had her suspicions about who was doing it; she certainly had. Just who did Mr. Arthur Sinclair, Esquire, think he was, going on like that? Envy it was, pure venomous envy of her. Oh, he had a very fine opinion of himself, indeed, did Mr. Arthur Sinclair. Well, he would just — .

"Ah, Sally love, is that you?" came the unmistakable drawl of Arthur Sinclair behind her.

She whirled, ready to give him the full benefit of her exasperation

— but, no, it was the English fellow, Purefoy, showing off his stupid talent for mimicry again. Pure fool would be a better name, she thought, sourly regarding his jaunty stance, his mouldy astrakhan collar pulled up, his trilby rakishly tilted above his prominent ears.

"Waiting for a cab, perchance?" he drawled in his plummy voice. "Perhaps we could share it?"

The more she looked at him, the more her distaste grew. Oh, she'd seen enough of his type before with their coat thrown carelessly over their shoulders, with their little cane. Oh, yes, these provincial English actors, who come swanking over here as if they were F. R. Benson, looking down their long, runny noses at the mere Irish. Well, she'd played Isabella at William Poel's personal request and got rave reviews for it in *The Manchester Guardian*, and she was having nothing whatsoever to do with his lah-de-dah.

"No, I amn't waiting for a cab," she said in her stiffest manner.

"Miss Allgood," he said mournfully, "I receive the distinct impression that you have formed an aversion to me."

"If that means that I don't like you, you are absolutely right. I wouldn't let the likes of you in under my umbrella, not even if it were raining cats and dogs for forty days and forty nights." And she turned magnificently on her heel and stared out over the river.

The Tivoli turned its lights out.

"But how, Miss Allgood," he said, gliding around to the front of her, "have I offended? If so, I am deeply affected. Deeply distraught. Only tell me what the sin, whether of commission or emission, and I will mend my erring ways."

"I don't like you, that's all, and there's an end to it. Now kindly take yourself off. I'm waiting for somebody."

"Of the opposite sex, may I enquire?"

"No, you may not! Stop butting into other people's business."

"Very well, Sara."

Sara! The cheek of him!

He placed his hand on his heart, emitted a long sigh and sloped off into the night.

Shades of *East Lynne*!

Her fingers twitched with the desire to box his prominent ears.

It suddenly seemed very quiet. It was madness, of course, her being here, on this windy corner, waiting. Well, not so much madness; more curiosity. The letter had been waiting for her at the stage door. They'd all been mad for her to open it, there and then, to see what it was about. Molly especially.

Well, she hadn't given any of them the least satisfaction, and had waited till she was alone to open the embossed envelope. The stationery was that of the Shelbourne Hotel.

> Dear Miss Allgood,
>
> I am a fervent admirer of your extraordinary talent, as moved by the heart-felt intensity of your acting as by your incomparable grace and beauty.
>
> Now, in town for a few days and staying at this hotel before embarking for my plantation in the Antipodes, I should deem it a signal honour if you would allow me to give you supper, over which I might express in person the gratitude I so warmly feel for the pleasure that you have bestowed upon me. I realize that you must be the recipient of hundreds of such embarrassing requests, but I can only hope that you will cast a benevolent eye upon the plea of one who will have so few memories of home to cherish in the many lonely nights out there on the veldt.
>
> Yours respectfully,
> Gordon Fitzmaurice Tollemache
>
> P.S. My equipage will pass down the quays after the theatre to-night. Its coat of arms depicts one gull rampant in an azure field.
> G. F. T.

Her watch was stopped. She crossed the quay to look down at the clock on the Custom House.

Good Lord! Five to twelve!

Normally, she wouldn't bother her head about any stage-door Johnnie — not that you got many of those at the Abbey. But this was different.

She envisioned Gordon — as she had already come in her mind to call him — holding the chair out gracefully for her, his long artistic fingers barely touching her shoulders as he took her wrap, the waiter hovering discreetly in the background by the rich tapestries, the dying fire in the grate — .

His glossy black hair, a touch of distinguished grey at the temples, the flickering candlelight, and then after the champagne had been poured and the obsequious waiter had disappeared behind the ormolu vase. . . then Gordon would lift his glass and, with the deep but obscure pain in his eyes, murmur softly, "To you!"

"To us!"

He would push away his platter of oysters under glass, stride impulsively to the marble portieres, and cry in gargled anguish, "Ah, this one night!"

"Yes," she would reply huskily, sensing the deep need in him, and fluttering like a wounded bird to the muscular nest of his enfolding arms. "Our night!"

"And then . . . I will have my tender memories. . . and you will have your lonely art!"

It was inexpressibly sad. . . .

Leslie Chenevix Purefoy snuggled beneath the thin blankets in his select but windswept room in Fitwilliam Street. Still, he reflected with a smile, it must be colder standing around the quays at this time of night. He smiled.

From the foot of his bed a tethered cat meowed.

In the offices of the *Dublin Evening Mail*, the young reporter returned to his typewriter, consulted his notes, and typed six more lines. Then he pulled the sheet from the machine, put it with three others, selected a well-gnawed pencil and read what he had written.

"Mr. Synge, who had promised me half an hour after the play was over, was scarcely in a mood for being interviewed. He looked excited and restless, the perspiration standing out in great beads over his forehead and cheeks, and, besides, he seemed just then in extraordinary demand by sundry persons, who had all sorts of things to say to him. I practically had to collar him and drag him away with me to some quiet spot. But the quietest I could find was the narrow passage leading up to the stage from the entrance hall, and that was anything but quiet. We were continually jostled and interrupted, and the draughts, too, were blowing from all directions, but I was not going to grumble. I was conscious of the one thing only — that I had cornered my man, and must have it out with him. Neither was there any time to waste; so I began straight away.

"'Tell me, Mr. Synge, was your purpose in writing this play to represent Irish life as it is lived — in short, did you think yourself holding up the mirror to nature?'

"'No, no,' Mr. Synge answered, rather emphatically."

The reporter corrected a typo and continued to read:

"'What, then, was your object in this play?' I asked after a while.

"'Nothing,' Mr. Synge answered, with sustained emphasis, due probably to his excited condition, 'simply the idea appealed to me — it pleased myself, and I worked it up.

"'It does not matter a rap. I wrote the play because it pleased me, and it just happens that I know Irish life best, so I made my methods Irish.'

"'Then,' I interposed, 'the real truth is you had no idea of catering for the Irish National Theatre. The main idea of the play pleased your own artistic sense, and that you gave it an Irish setting is a mere accident, owing to your intimate knowledge of Irish life.'

"'Exactly so,' he answered.

"'But you know,' I suggested, 'the main idea of your play is not a pretty one. You take the worst form of murderer, a parricide, and set him up on a pedestal to be worshipped by the simple, honest people of the West. Is this probable?'

"'No,' replied Mr. Synge. 'It is not; and it does not matter. Was *Don Quixote* probable? and still it is art.'

"'What was it that at all suggested the main idea of the play?' I asked.

"''Tis a thing that really happened. I knew a young fellow in the Aran Islands who had killed his father. And the people befriended him and sent him off to America.'

"'But did the girls all make love to him because he had killed his father, and for that only, the sorry-looking, bedraggled, and altogether repellent figure though he was personally?'

"'No. Those girls did not, but mine do.'

"'Why do they? What is your idea in making them do it?'

"'It is to bring out the humour of the situation. It is a comedy, an extravaganza, made to amuse.'

"At this point the lights went out and we were left in complete darkness. For the matter of that, I shall always remain in the dark as to Mr. Synge's ideas on art.

"His excitement seemed to go on growing at the interval, to ruffle him still more. He went on talking to me at a rate which made me glad I was not taking him down in shorthand. I cannot believe there is a pencil on earth likely to have kept pace with him then. I was just able to catch him up at the end, to the effect that the speech used by his characters was the actual speech of the people, and that in art a spade must be called a spade."

"'But,'" the young reporter continued reading, "'the complaint is, Mr. Synge, that you call it a bloody shovel. Of course I am not speaking from personal experience, for I have not heard a word at all from the stage, though I could not possibly be nearer it. And that reminds me, Mr. Synge, what do you propose to do for the rest of the week, in face of what has taken place to-night?'

"'We shall go on with the play to the very end, in spite of all,' he answered, snapping his fingers, more excited than ever. 'I don't care a rap.'"

Much later, he found the latch-key. He let himself in, and softly closed the door so as not to awake his mother who was a light sleeper. He took off his boots and, carrying them in his hands, trudged up the interminable stairs to his room. He was too tired to take his clothes off. He slumped down on the bed and stared at the darkness. He closed his eyes, but he did not sleep.

Tuesday, January 29

Despite the greasy breakfast provided by Mrs. Attracta O'Growney-Greenway, Leslie Chenevix Purefoy sauntered cheerfully into Amiens Street Station. This might well prove a useful little excursion. He took the telegram out of his pocket. It was addressed to Lady Gregory, Abbey Theatre, Dublin, and read, "Arriving Amiens Street ten A.M. Yeats."

It wanted ten minutes of the hour. Good. Time to marshal one's thoughts. The poet, after all, was no Gussie Gaffney or Sally Allgood. He would require a certain finesse; and dashing down here from Abbey Street after discovering the unopened telegram propped up on the ledge of the ticket booth in the theatre vestibule had not afforded Purefoy time for proper reflection.

A little quick planning of the strategy was now in order, for the poet was distinctly a rum one. A challenge. Discerning from which gate the Great Man must emerge, Purefoy found a nearby bench. Pity there was no time to hatch something intricate. As a connoisseur of the drama as well as a thespian, Purefoy's taste inclined to the devious convolutions of comic, even farcical plotting. Now Ben Jonson, there was a man to spin a juicy and complicated plot. It was one of the bitter disappointments of Purefoy's professional career that he had once at the ghastly Theatre Royal, Aberdeen, been passed over for the part of Mosca in the master's consummate *Volpone*.

But to Yeats. What was initially needful was to ingratiate oneself with the pompous ninny. Which should be easy enough, he was so mountainously egotistic. Now, Leslie Chenevix Purefoy was not precisely lacking in a complacent self-appreciation himself, but the difference between him and Yeats was that Yeats had the freedom of parading his quirks and peccadilloes to a doting public. Thus far he, Leslie Chenevix Purefoy, had been obliged to dissemble, to be sickeningly amiable, even at times to be a bit of a lickspittle. Ah, but this would all change — and soon!

Meanwhile, Yeats. Perhaps something sexual could be arranged for

Yeats. Yes, something in the Wilde line. Oh, intriguing to contemplate, and just what the portentous poet richly deserved, bugger him. Leslie Chenevix Purefoy grimly remembered when the credulous Miss Horniman had first introduced him to the patronising poet, and the poet's glazed eyes had passed disinterestedly over him, and he had mumbled, "Chenevix, in a fix. . . Purefoy, hoorboy."

"He's always composing," Miss Horniman had gurgled adoringly.

Pleasanter, Leslie Chenevix Purefoy had reflected, to think of him decomposing.

"Oof!" he said, as a beefy woman plopped down on the bench and shoved him over with a brisk twitch of a mountainous thigh.

"I beg your pardon, madam!"

"Well, ya may, ya popinjay, hogging the entirety of this public facility. Well, Bessie Burgess is also a member of the populacity and well aware of her rights and concomitant privileges!"

Purefoy contemplated accidentally knocking her well-stuffed bag to the floor, but the train was pulling in. He solaced himself with the reflection that hers was a savage race, and took up a position near the gate.

The first passengers were alighting. Ah, there was the tall, black-suited figure of the poet. What on earth was the fool doing? He was going the wrong way, back up the platform! No, a conductor had turned him around and propelled him in the proper direction.

"Ah, Mr. Yeats!" called Leslie Chenevix Purefoy. "Here I am!"

The poet blinked vaguely and looked in every other direction.

"Right here, Mr. Yeats! This way!"

His abstraction having been momentarily penetrated, the poet padded in the proper direction and attempted to navigate, not without some little difficulty, the exit gate.

"Ah, Mr. Yeats," said Leslie Chenevix Purefoy, extracting the poet and taking his bag. "Welcome back. I have come to meet you."

"You?" said the poet blankly and without recognition.

"Yes! Leslie Chenevix Purefoy, late of the Theatre Royal, Cheltenham, and recently engaged by you and Miss Horniman to play leading roles in the poetic drama — a matter which we must discuss at our earliest mutual convenience."

"Purefoy, hoorboy," remembered Yeats.

This denigration, whether intended or not, Leslie Chenevix Purefoy mentally added to the extensive list of affronts to be dealt with at some later stage. For the nonce, he composed his face in an engaging smile, and prepared to suggest that he and the poet repair to the nearby railway buffet to refresh themselves, the expenses of said treat, although Leslie Chenevix Purefoy did not intend immediately to express himself on the matter, to be defrayed by the poet.

"Perhaps, sir, a glass or two of sherry after your tiring journey," said Leslie Chenevix Purefoy solicitously.

"Journey," mused Yeats sleepily as he brushed back a lank, raven lock. "Ferny, tourney."

"Yeats!" called an approaching voice, and Leslie Chenevix Purefoy saw Synge and Lady Gregory bustling toward them. Drat, how did they get wind of it?

"Ah," said Lady Gregory, "why didn't you send your wires earlier? We didn't know when you were coming or where you would arrive."

"Wires?" Leslie Chenevix Purefoy wondered.

"When Yeats is arriving, he always sends half a dozen wires to let us know," Synge explained.

"Oh, what a hustle and pother," said Lady Gregory. "I think we might have a cup of tea at de buffet."

"Ah!" said Yeats, his flashing eyes suddenly gleaming with intelligence. He abruptly stalked off, nostrils dramatically flaring.

"No, Willie!" cried Lady Gregory, bouncing after him with an alacrity surprising in one ordinarily so stately. She snatched his sleeve. "Dis way!"

"Ah!" said Yeats staring at her either profoundly or near-sightedly.

Ah, thought Purefoy, mentally smacking his lips at the thought of non-greasy refreshment, all is not lost.

"Mr. Purefoy," Lady Gregory called over her shoulder as she steered the poet toward the buffet. "You might leave Mr. Yeats' case in at de theatre. We'll be back shortly."

Flashing the brilliantly dissembling smile that was so effective in the role of Sir Francis Levison in Mrs. Woods' immortal claptrap *East Lynne*, Leslie Chenevix Purefoy prepared to lug the heavy suitcase off. Then a thought struck him, and he turned back to Synge who was moodily rolling a cigarette.

"Eh, why," he enquired, "does Mr. Yeats think half a dozen wires necessary to announce his arrival?"

"That's in case he forgets to send some of them," said Synge, licking his cigarette and ambling after his companions.

"Hmmph!" said Leslie Chenevix Purefoy, and lugged the poet's valise to the door and down the steps into Amiens Street. "Damned heavy," he remarked, as he trudged through the biting wind.

But then he brightened. If the office were empty, there might be a moment to glance through the poet's things. Possibly a few useful documents there amid the mouldering socks. Further examples of handwriting would come in handy. Perhaps even a holograph poem that could be sold at some later date, in the remote case that the poet's inflated reputation had not collapsed.

Intrigued by the thought, Leslie Chenevix Purefoy deposited the poet's valise in the middle of a pile of fresh horse dung, and smiled broadly. His was basically a buoyant nature.

Synge came back from the counter with tea for each of them and two cherry buns for the poet.

Yeats frowned. "Only two buns?"

"De situation," Lady Gregory was saying, "is extremely serious."

"Umm," said Yeats, taking wolfish bites.

"Last night was derrible. It was unbarallelled disorder."

The poet shook his head in comprehension and gnawed away.

"I don't know," she said slowly, "dat we can afford another such situation. Another such night." She looked at Synge, who shrugged and stubbed out his cigarette.

"Mr. Synge and I agreed to wait for your opinion. Willie, what should we do?"

"Do?" he said, his mouth full. "Fide!"

"What?" she said.

"Fight!" he cantilated.

In the middle of the afternoon, a gust of January wind roared through the unclosable window and blew the holograph revision of "The Lake Isle of Innisfree" to the floor. That revision, never subsequently published, read:

> I will arise and go now, and go to Innisfree,
> And a great mansion build there, of brick and mortar made;
> Nine great whores will I have there, and have them frequently.

The remainder was undecipherable. Perhaps it was all for the best.

Leslie Chenevix Purefoy retrieved the errant paper and put his inkpot on it to hold it down. Beside it he placed another but blank piece of paper. He dipped his pen in the inkpot and, biting his tongue, his eyes darted back and forth between both papers. Finally he painstakingly wrote, "Entrancing Vision!"

Yes, he thought, his eyes darting back and forth between each crabbed scrawl, perfect!

In the early evening, J.A. O'Rourke entered the shop on the corner of Marlborough and Abbey Streets. "Eh, gimme ten Afton, will ya?" he said and plunked threepence down on the counter. As he came out, he bumped into Kerrigan who was ambling along the dark street, trying to read a newspaper.

"Yer going to get yerself run over," he said.

"Eh?" said Kerrigan. "Just reading about last night's festivities."

"Hunh!" said O'Rourke, as they crossed the street. "Look and see what it says about the 3.15 at Gatwick, the Tantivy Steeplechase."

"Good God," said Kerrigan, "here we are in the middle of theatrical history in the making, and all you can think of is the gee-gees."

O'Rourke lit his cigarette. "Jujube with Donnelly up." Reflectively, he plucked a shred of tobacco from his lip. "Five year old. Eleven stone, five pound."

They turned into the laneway.

"His last time out — ," continued O'Rourke.

Kerrigan put a hand on his arm. "Hi, look at that now, would you."

He pointed to a file of policemen, waiting at the stage door. Then the door opened, and they marched inside.

Kerrigan whistled. "Now what do you think of that?"

"His last time out he won in a walk. Two and a half lengths, if I remember."

"Ah, dry up," said Kerrigan.

The din in the auditorium was swelling, and Gussie Gaffney took a peep out through the curtains. "Pit's well filled up," he said, and turned around to see Synge crossing the stage. "Eh, looks like a good house for a Tuesday."

Synge grunted and continued on.

"Old grump," muttered Gussie.

Lady Gregory and Yeats were in the wings.

"Willie's lost his watch again," she said. "How long till the curtain?"

Synge drew out his own watch. "Twelve or thirteen minutes. You can hardly move in the Greenroom, with all of the police."

"I pray dey won't be required," she said.

Yeats smiled beatifically and brushed back a dark lock of hair. "A necessary precaution. One of several."

"What do you mean?" frowned Synge. "One of several?"

Yeats serenely settled his flowing tie, and brushed at some fluff on his sleeve. "We've decided that I shall come out just after *Riders* and make a few remarks."

"To defuse things," said Lady Gregory.

"O," Yeats blinked. "Defuse, refuse."

Synge listened to the growing clamour from the auditorium. "One?" he asked uneasily. "What did you mean, one of the precautions?"

"I've arranged for a claque. Quite the traditional thing in the eighteenth century. They should be arriving about now."

Synge pushed past him and went out the door and down the three steps into the auditorium.

Miss Bushell, with a sheaf of programs in her arms, plucked at his sleeve. "Mr. Synge, this gentleman has been asking for you."

A young man appeared grinning behind her. "Mr. Yeats said we were to be admitted to the stalls."

"We?" said Synge.

The young man turned and indicated a knot of people nearby. "I've brought some supporters."

"All right, Miss Bushell," sighed Synge. "Let them in. There are certainly plenty of seats."

They bustled past and took their seats. Many wore long college scarves. Trinity boys.

"Good Lord, how many of them are there — twenty?"

"Twice that, sir," said Miss Bushell. "There's more out in the vestibule."

One of them wearing a smart-fitting overcoat turned and bellowed at the pit, "Any of you who don't like this play will have to answer to me!" He swayed and waved his fist. "I hereby throw down a challenge to you, any of you! Misbehave, and you'll answer to me!"

A hoot of laughter greeted him from the pit.

"Oh my God," murmured Synge.

"Come on, any of you, step right up and fall right down!"

"Ah, gowan home to yer mammy!" cried a voice from the pit.

"Sure, we'll wipe the floor with you," cried another.

"This," said the young man, swinging his arm aloft, "is a fist!" Then he lurched forward and would have fallen over the back of a seat had some hands not reached out and caught him.

"This is terrible," said Synge, and made his way back down the aisle.

"Look at him run for cover," said W. J. Lawrence, his thin lips curving in contempt.

The young man in the smart overcoat was on his feet again. "I am a little bit drunk," he shouted, "and don't know what I am saying."

In the wings, Leslie Chenevix Purefoy inserted a tundish into the depleted barrel of porter. Then he uncapped a small bottle, and upended it over the tundish. Its liquid contents made a satisfying gurgle.

Onstage, Sara Allgood's beautiful voice rose above the keening of the women. "Michael has a clean burial in the far north, by the grace of the Almighty God."

The keening fell off into a murmur and then silence.

"Bartley will have a fine coffin out of the white boards, and a deep grave surely. What more can we want than that?"

The theatre was utterly still now.

"No man at all can be living for ever, and we must be satisfied."

Slowly she bowed her head, and slowly the curtains closed.

From the auditorium came the sound of hearty clapping.

Molly gave her a spontaneous hug. "You really got them to-night, Sal!"

Surprised, Sally did not have time to reply, for W.B. Yeats strode on from the wings, a hand lifted in benediction. He made his way through the curtains, and the applause died.

"Bill Butler's going to make a speech," said Willie Fay, sitting up from his prone position on the table.

"Wouldn't you know?" said Brigit O'Dempsey, producing a cigarette from behind her ear. This was one of his wife's unprofessional habits which Willie Fay had thus far been unable to correct. "Sure, the audience

95

can't see it," Brigit had stoutly stated. "I've got lovely, fluffy hair."

"Hush, let's hear this," said Molly.

The actors crowded up behind the curtain, cocking their heads and listening.

"A difference of opinion," they heard, "has arisen between the management of this theatre and some of the audience as to the value of the play which we are now to produce. . . ."

"Difference of opinion!" said Brigit O'Dempsey. "Would you listen to that!"

"Shhh!" said her husband, digging her in the ribs.

". . . and as to our policy in producing it. If any of you wish to discuss the merits of the play or our rightness in producing it, I shall be delighted to discuss it with you, and do my best to answer your arguments. I will endeavour to get an audience, and to invite any who wish to speak to come on the stage and do so."

"I have one thing to say — !" a voice cried from the audience.

"Order! Order!" came shouts from other parts of the house.

In front of the curtain, Yeats raised his hand pontifically. "On Monday evening I shall be pleased to hear you. We have put this play before you to be heard and to be judged — ."

In the pit, D.J. O'Donoghue leaned over to W.J. Lawrence in the row in front of him, and whispered, "We have judged it!"

"And it's not going to be heard again," said Lawrence grimly.

"Every man," continued Yeats, "has a right to hear it and condemn it if he pleases — ."

"I should certainly hope so," muttered Joseph Holloway to nobody in particular.

"But no man has a right to interfere with another man hearing a play and judging for himself!"

"Hear, hear!" roared an Anglo-Irish voice from the stalls.

"The country that condescends either to bully or to permit itself to be bullied soon ceases to have any fine qualities, and I promise you that if there is any small section in this theatre that wish to deny the right of others to hear what they themselves don't want to hear — ."

"We will put them out!" cried the man in the stalls.

"We will play on, and our patience shall last longer than their patience." Having delivered himself of that dictum, Yeats with his haughtiest stare commanded a second of silence. Then he waved his

96

hand, as if in dismissal, turned on his heel and disappeared behind the curtain.

Applause mixed with groans followed him, and as he passed languidly into the wings the actors looked at each other uneasily.

"Come on, come on," snapped Willie Fay. "Let's get changed!"

As the curtains parted for Act One of *The Playboy*, J.M. Synge checked his watch again. It was three minutes past nine, and in the silence Molly's clear voice rang out: "Six yards of stuff for to make a yellow gown."

Just in front of him, fidgeting even more than usual, Frank Fay was waiting for his entrance. Synge patted him on the shoulder and whispered, "Good luck."

Startled, Fay jumped and shot back a frightened look. His mouth twitched nervously, but before he could reply Molly was saying, ". . . best compliments of the season. Margaret Flaherty." And Frank Fay jerked himself onstage.

"Where's himself?" he croaked, not at all in his usual mellifluous moo.

Poor Fay, reflected Synge, always a worrier, but now an excited bundle of nerves. Well, at least that wouldn't much hurt his first scene because his character, Shawn Keogh, was too.

Synge found himself with his ears cocked more to the audience than to what was being said onstage. Dead silence so far out there, but an ominous silence, not the warm, thick silence that meant you had the audience captivated. No, more like everyone out there was holding his breath.

Then Shawn Keogh said, ". . . when we're wedded in a short while you'll have no call to complain, for I've little will to be walking off to wakes or weddings in the darkness of the night." And he got a little ripple of laughter. Not bad for Frank who couldn't play comedy at all. That might just give him a little confidence and settle him down.

Then Molly pushed her next line to try to build on Frank's laugh. "You're making mighty certain, Shaneen, that I'll wed you now." Too big entirely, but it worked and got the larger laugh. Maybe everything would be all right.

She had courage, Molly. He wanted to hug her for throwing out that line so boldly. He must find the courage to speak to her.

Synge grimaced. Torturous, this waiting. He'd step out in the lane and roll a cigarette. Perhaps decide what he could say to her after the show. As he turned toward the door, he bumped into a tall dark figure in the gloom. Yeats.

"Perhaps it will be all right," Synge whispered.

"Instead of a Parnell, a Stephens, or a Butt," Yeats murmured, "we must obey the demands of a commonplace and ignorant people."

"What?"

"Who try to impose some crude shibboleth on their own and others' necks."

"What are you talking about?" Synge whispered.

"The mass," said Yeats, his eyes glazed over, "can only be converted by terror, threats and abuse."

Good God, it occurred to Synge, he's composing his next curtain speech. "Yeats, listen to me. You can't go out there and say that!"

"Sorry!" said Arthur Sinclair pushing past. "My entrance is coming up."

As O'Rourke and Kerrigan followed him, Synge tugged Yeats back out of the way.

"Yeats, the audience seems fairly receptive. We — ."

The poet came out of his trance, and raised a benedictory hand. "Receptive, deceptive," he smiled agreeably.

Hopeless, thought Synge, and ridiculous. He took himself a few steps off and leaned limply against the wall. And waited.

At first it was hardly even a noise, just a rustling that he could sense rather than actually hear. Then Kerrigan said, "What is there to hurt you, and you a fine, hardy girl would knock the head of any two men in the place?"

Then it was like a storm breaking. He couldn't hear the actors anymore, just the roar from the pit. He pushed forward to see onstage. They were bravely going through the motions in dumb show, but he couldn't catch a word. In fact, except for Molly tilting her chin a little defiantly higher and flashing her eyes a bit more fiercely, it was as if the players weren't even hearing that battering wall of sound. Good for them!

Oh, no! Frank Fay was bolting for the wings, blast him! Then Synge caught a couple of the words: ". . . scarlet-coated bishops of Rome!" Ah, it was Fay's normal exit line.

"Mother of God," said Frank Fay, tumbling into Synge's arms.

"That's something fearful out there."

Willie Fay strode off and pushed past them with a scowl. "Fearful!" he snorted. "Bah!"

"Don't inflame them, brother," Frank pleaded. "Don't inflame themmmm!"

"Wouldja ever shut up," snapped Willie Fay. "How the hell am I going to catch me cue!"

W.B. Yeats peered delightedly over their heads and tapped Synge on the shoulder. "I think we must go forth and assay the matter. Come, come, come!" And he pulled Synge toward the house door.

In the stalls, the pugnacious young man in the smart-fitting overcoat was leaping up and down.

"Look at that," said Joseph Holloway to no one in particular, as no one could have heard him.

"I am spoiling for a row," announced the pugnacious young man, unbuttoning his smart-fitting overcoat, so as to afford a more fluent facility for his flailing fists to assault the unoffending air.

"Let him have the row!" cried a dishevelled youth nearby with a grin.

W.J. Lawrence looked back over his shoulder. "Look!" he gestured toward the front of the house. "Here comes the reprobate Synge now!"

D.J. O'Donoghue saw Synge pushing his way between the rows of seats toward the pugnacious young man.

"Let the licentious Synge reap what he has sown!" chortled Lawrence.

"Licentious?" said D.J. O'Donoghue, remembering the quiet, courteous young fellow he had known in Paris. "Oh, that's rot, Lawrence!"

"Let slip the dogs of war!" howled W. J. Lawrence.

The pugnacious young man in the stalls smote whatever bleary wraith rose up to assault his befuddled eyes. In fact, he brought his right fist down upon the balding pate of the burly gentleman in the seat in front of him who was just at that moment attempting, in apparent alarm, to rise. That gentleman — Edward Martyn, Esq., of Tullira Castle, Co. Mayo, appreciator of Palestrina, follower of Ibsen, and devout Roman Catholic bachelor — exclaimed, "Jesus, Mary and Joseph!" and relapsed into his seat.

"Shite and onions," blearily agreed John Stanislaus Joyce who was sitting immediately to his left.

"I think," said the dapper Hugh Lane, bending toward the ear of his aunt, Lady Augusta Gregory, "that Yeats must bring in the police. A show of strength would quell these bog-trotters."

"Oh, dear," said Lady Gregory.

At this point the poet Yeats stalked into the licensed premises of Michael James Flaherty, raised his hand in the manner of the orator Grattan, and asked the audience to remain seated and to listen to the play of a man who, at any rate, was a most distinguished countryman of theirs. An observation variously greeted with applause, groans and hisses.

Oh my God, thought Synge, and, despairing of making his way to the pugnacious young man, fought a path to the aisle, hoping to get backstage and at least stifle Yeats.

"Mr. Synge deserves to be heard!" cried the poet. "If his play is bad, it will die without your help; and if it is good, your hindrances cannot impair it, but you can impair very greatly the reputation of this country for courtesy and intelligence!"

The poet then stalked offstage to a crescendo of cheers, groans, hisses and, ringing out from the balcony, the notes of a bugle.

"Woa!" cried the pugnacious young man to the departing bard. "Woa, you chap there!"

The middle-aged reporter of *The Freeman's Journal* observed the confusion surrounding the pugnacious young gentleman, and in his efficient shorthand jotted down: "His friends then gathered around the speaker and tried to pull him out of the hall. He resisted violently, and others supported him, with the result that chairs were overturned and the excitement was considerably increased. Finding it impossible to force him out of the hall, persuasion was next resorted to, with the result that in a short time the overcoat was seen to disappear through the stage door, amidst renewed uproar on the part of the occupants of the pit."

Out of breath, Synge dashed into the wings and snatched at Yeats' coat-tails. Too late, the bard had again entered the shebeen of Michael James Flaherty, and was remarking, pugilistically in tone and buglistically in volume, that, "We have persuaded one man who was, I regret to say, intoxicated, to leave the meeting. I appeal to all of you who are sober to listen!"

"We are all sober here!" retorted Frank Walker from the pit.

Lady Gregory made her way backstage, tugged at Synge's sleeve and gestured toward seven stolid constables who were emerging from the

Greenroom. "Shall we?"

A roar from the auditorium engulfed them.

"It's our theatre," she said grimly. "He who pays de piper calls de tune."

Miserably, Synge nodded his acquiescence.

When the seven stolid constables filed down the steps into the auditorium, a sudden silence descended.

"Perhaps it will be all right now," said Lady Gregory peeping out after them. "We don't want de theatre damaged."

A gentleman from the stalls mounted his seat and cried, "Just one word, as a member of the public!"

"Who are you?" demanded a voice from the pit.

"It doesn't matter who I am. I am a member of the public. The management are responsible to me for having brought me here."

"And to us also!" retorted the voice from the pit.

"They are responsible for giving me something," cried the gentleman, "and they are not allowed to do so. You also have made a contract, and want something for your money — to see this play. Have you seen the play?"

"Yes" bellowed a dozen voices from the pit and balcony.

"I say you have not, and you have no right to judge it until you have!"

Hugh Lane rose hotly from his seat and accosted a solid, stolid constable. "Arrest those two men!" he demanded, pointing to two gesticulating pittites.

"Eh, I dunno," said the constable.

"I will charge them," said Hugh Lane. "Arrest them. I demand their arrest!"

The old, pale, thin-chested reporter for *The Daily Express* recorded in his notebook the following information: "At this point Inspector Flynn entered, and on Mr. Lane's demand he had one of the men removed. When the curtain rang up for Act II, a large number of constables had been drafted into the building. A few minutes afterwards Mr. Lane demanded the removal of another man, who was accordingly hustled out by the police. There was not much noise until the point in the play where Pegeen asks Christy Mahon was he the man who killed his father. On his replying in the affirmative Pegeen exclaims, 'Then a thousand welcomes to you.' This drew forth a perfect Bedlam of yells, and various cries, such as 'That is not the West; I defy you to prove it.' 'Travesty,' etc. From this point a steady drumming of feet was sustained, through which the play could only just be followed. By direction of Mr. Yeats another man was removed. Mr. Yeats and the police were loudly boohed."

Sara Allgood made her second act exit followed by Brigit O'Dempsey, Alice O'Sullivan and May Craig. Instantly the three younger girls put their heads together and whispered excitedly.

"Whisht, whisht!" snapped Sally, "the audience'll hear you!"

"Oh, whisht yourself," said Brigit O'Dempsey. "They couldn't hardly hear us when we were onstage roaring our lungs out."

Synge peered glumly over their shoulders. Shawn Keogh was presenting Christy with a new coat and hat and breeches. "I'll give you the whole of them, and my blessing, and the blessing of Father O'Reilly itself. . . ."

A new wave of hissing and boohing broke out, and one familiar Northern voice could be heard roaring apocalyptically above the din, "The little travesty should be beaten off the stage."

"Oh dear," mourned Lady Gregory appearing by Synge's side.

"They didn't even hear the rest of the line," said Synge. "— 'if you'll quit from this and leave us in the peace we had. . . .' There's nothing to offend in that!" He stalked into the Greenroom, threw himself down in a chair and tried to roll a cigarette.

Big Ambrose Power looked in, his head swathed in old Mahon's bloody bandage. He shuffled his large feet.

"Must be close to time for my entrance," he said unhappily.

What does he want me to say to him, thought Synge, that it's not? That we've decided to cut Old Mahon to-night?

"Must be. Good luck."

Ambrose Power nodded miserably and disappeared.

At least, thought Synge, it won't matter to-night that he hasn't got all his lines off.

In the men's dressing-room, O'Rourke threw the newspaper away with a snort. "Bleedin' Jujube!" he spat out. "Bleedin', bloody Jujube!"

"God, Joe," said Kerrigan, "I believe you'd try to place a bet on the Day of Judgement."

Another muffled roar came back to them.

"It sounds like the Day of Judgement," said Arthur Sinclair.

Kerrigan consulted his watch. "No, it sounds like the second act curtain."

Frank Fay came in, wiping his streaming face and smudging his make-up.

"All going well?" Purefoy enquired innocently.

Willie Fay bustled in carrying the Playboy's new clothes. "Outa me way, for God's sake. I've got to make me change."

"Once more into the breeches again," remarked Kerrigan to the ceiling.

Molly Allgood swirled into the Greenroom and picked up the kettle. "Stone cold! Bloody marvellous!"

Synge stood up. "Molly — ."

She glared at him and stalked out.

Humbly he went over to the gas ring, produced a match and lit it.

In the crowded vestibule, Joseph Holloway stroked his waggling jowls. "That old man the police took out, I know him from somewhere."

"I've seen him once or twice at the National Literary Society," said D. J. O'Donoghue.

"Of course, of course!" said Holloway, his baggy eyes glinting. "That's young Colum's father!"

"Oh, a fine business!" exulted W. J. Lawrence. "A fine piece of work entirely!"

In the small orchestra pit, Arthur Darley conducted his three musicians in a medley of lugubrious Irish airs. Nobody listened.

Backstage, Leslie Chenevix Purefoy ambled over to the Props table and tapped little Seaghan Barlow on the shoulder. "We mustn't forget to bring on the barrel of stout for this act."

Seaghan Barlow gave him a glance of withering pity and stomped away.

"Ah, Augustus," said Leslie Chenevix Purefoy, "Mr. Synge asked me to make sure the barrel of stout gets on for this act. Would you give me a hand? Oh, my back!" Purefoy lurched, stumbled and staggered in a remarkably accurate recreation of Henry Irving's portrayal of the mad scene in *The Bells*.

"Eh, are you all right, Mr. Purefoy?" Gussie enquired.

"Oh," groaned Purefoy, "it's just my old back injury. I once had a terrible fall during the equestrian scene in *Salome*. But it's all right, I'll manage to go on. Ugh!"

"You better take it easy, Mr. Purefoy," said Gussie, patting him on the shoulder. "And don't worry about this old barrel of porter. I'll place it."

"Merci, Augustus," said Leslie Chenevix Purefoy, "you are more than kind."

During the third act, the middle-aged reporter from *The Freeman's Journal* jotted down these higgledy-piggledy impressions:

"During the third act the stamping of feet in the pit and occasional outbursts of indignation were pretty constant. Referring to the murder of Old Mahon by his son, the publican said, 'It is a hard story,' whereupon a member of the audience aptly remarked, 'It is a rotten story,' a remark which was loudly applauded.

"The revulsion of feeling on the part of the village people and 'Pegeen Mike' when they discovered that Christopher Mahon was not entitled to be regarded as a hero, as he had not succeeded in murdering his father, caused a further outburst of groans and hisses. The drunken, idiotic appearance of the publican returning from a wake was accompanied by expressions of well-merited reprobation."

Onstage Arthur Sinclair as Michael James Flaherty drew a drink from the barrel of porter on the bar and remarked, ". . . aren't you a louty schemer to go burying your poor father unbeknownst when you'd a right to throw him on the crupper of a Kerry mule and drive him westwards, like holy Joseph in the days gone by. . . ." And then Arthur Sinclair, as directed by Willie Fay, took a hefty swig from his glass.

"Gahhh!" he remarked, departing somewhat from the author's lines and spewing porter behind the bar. "What the bloody hell!"

"The revulsion of feeling. . . ," continued the reporter for *The Freeman's Journal*, who had a turn for the genteel literary phrase.

"Eh?" said his elderly, pale, thin-chested colleague of *The Daily Express*, tapping him on the shoulder, "What's up with Sinclair? He looks to be puking his guts out."

"He is a sensitive artiste," said Joseph Holloway two seats over.

Further aesthetic conversation along these lines was interrupted by a particularly virulent outburst of groans and hisses.

At twenty past ten, the young gentleman in the smart overcoat re-entered and announced that he stood firmly on his rights. He did not, however, stand firmly. He swayed considerably.

"Matters," continued the reporter from *The Freeman's Journal*, "continued in this way until the play concluded. From start to finish not half a dozen consecutive sentences had been heard by the audience."

As the curtains closed, Yeats' claque united in a boisterous rendition of "God Save the King."

"Oh dear," moaned Lady Gregory, "I do hope Willie didn't put dem up to dat."

In the wings, J.M. Synge waited miserably for Molly to come off. When she did, she froze him with a glare.

In the men's dressing-room, Arthur Sinclair was groaning and spitting into a bucket.

W.B. Yeats was not to be seen, for he was upstairs in the office attending to serious business.

"£12.10.1," he concluded. "Not bad for a Tuesday."

Wednesday, January 30

Joseph Holloway caught W.J. Lawrence's eye and motioned to an empty place beside him.

"These proceedings are a disgrace!" hissed Lawrence. "Have I missed anything?"

"Old Colum's case has just come up. That's him over there, the little white-haired man."

"Good Lord!"

"Shhh," said Holloway.

"Now constable," said the prosecutor, "tell us in your own words what you observed last night about the behaviour of the defendant on the premises of the Abbey Theatre?"

The constable produced a small notebook from his tunic, consulted it, and then said in measured deliberation, "Well, sir, I was on duty in the Abbey Theatre on Tuesday evening when the disturbance occurred. It commenced between ten and eleven o'clock at the performance of the play."

"You mean Mr. Synge's play, *The Playboy of the Western World?*"

"Yes, sir. When the disturbance commenced, I observed the defendant stamping his feet and heard him boohing and hissing."

"Did this cause disturbance and annoyance to the audience?"

"Yes, and some of them called 'Hush.' A number of others also caused disturbance."

"Did the defendant say anything?"

"Yes, when I put my hand on him, he said, 'Who are you, you —?' And used a particular word. He refused to stop creating noise."

The prosecutor nodded and sat down.

"All very cut and dried," whispered Lawrence, writing in his notepad.

"Here's Lidwell, old Colum's lawyer," whispered Holloway. "I know him."

"Constable, at the time in question was there great noise and confusion in the theatre?"

"Yes sir. There was great noise. We were called in to quell the disturbance. Some of the·audience wanted to hear the play and some did not."

"Did you hear any offensive word used on the stage?"

"I heard one offensive word."

"As offensive as anything said amongst the audience?"

A grin cut across the stolid constable's face.

"No further questions," said Mr. Lidwell.

"There are quite a lot of further questions in my mind," whispered Lawrence hotly.

"Shh, shh!" said Joseph Holloway. "I think they're going to call Yeats."

"Is he here?" said Lawrence, half-rising. "Where?"

The poet took his place in the box, brushed a wandering raven lock from off his noble brow and looked vaguely over the heads of the crowd.

"Humbug, thy name is Yeats," said Lawrence.

"Yes," the poet was saying melodiously, "I am managing director of the Abbey Theatre. I was there last night when a play called *The Playboy of the Western World* was performed. From the first rising of the curtain there was an obviously organised attempt to prevent the play being heard."

"Hah!" snorted W. J. Lawrence.

"That," continued Yeats, "was from a section of the pit. The stalls and balcony were anxious to hear the play. The noise consisted of shouting and booing and stamping of feet. I did not hear six consecutive lines of the play last night owing to the noise."

"Good!" said Lawrence.

"The section that caused the disturbance was not part of the regular audience. The conduct of the section was riotous and offensive, and disturbed and annoyed the audience."

"It was the play disturbed and annoyed the audience," said W.J. Lawrence.

Thomasina MacFitz tapped him on the shoulder. "Shh!" And her trained baritone caused many members of the assembly to look round in alarm.

Lawrence glared back over his shoulder. Silly old bag, and a rotten actress too. In his irritation he dropped his notebook and fumbled about on the floor for it. When he got himself settled again, Lidwell was cross-examining the poet.

"Did you read this play?"

"Yes, and passed it."

"Is it a caricature of the Irish people?"

Lawrence nudged Joseph Holloway. "Good point."

"It is," Yeats said smoothly, "no more a caricature of the people of Ireland than Macbeth is a caricature of the people of Scotland, or Falstaff a caricature of the gentlemen of England. The play is an example of the exaggeration of art."

"Is the play," persisted Lidwell, "typical of the Irish people?"

"No," Yeats said equably. "It is an exaggeration."

"Then you admit it is a caricature?"

"An exaggeration," Yeats corrected politely.

"I am satisfied," said the judge, "that the defendant was guilty of disorderly behaviour, and order him to pay a fine of 40s, with the alternative of one month's imprisonment, and to find sureties of £10 for his future good behaviour."

Padraic Colum slipped out of the building, his face burning. Oh, this was terrible. Of course, his father should not have hissed and boohed. And cursed. He himself would never have, never. But his father was his father.

And not for the first time the thought crossed his mind of how arresting a character his father would be for a play. Properly disguised, of course. There had been something of him in *The Fiddler's House*, but more might. . . .

Impatiently he pushed the thought away, and addressed himself to the problem of the moment.

A stand would have to be taken. He winced at that uncomfortable idea. But it would. His father would have to be defended. With dignity. In a letter perhaps. Yes, a letter to the press. A restrained letter that had in it nothing of the brawling tumult to be seen in the theatre.

But would the theatre itself have to be criticized?

Oh dear.

Oh dear, indeed!

Perhaps it could be a private letter. No, he pushed that temptation away too. It would have to be a public statement. It would be difficult to maintain a balance, a judicious equipoise. So as to defend, not offend. Yes.

And as always the problem of manoeuvering words happily absorbed him.

Sir, he might begin, The organised attempt to prevent a hearing for *The Playboy of* — .

"Pat."

On the other hand, it seems to this correspondent that the management of the Abbey Theatre — .

"Pat."

On the same hand — .

"Pat!" His father thumped him roughly on the shoulder. "Let's go. I paid the bloody fine."

"I saw," W.B. Yeats said firmly, "the defendant at the performance last night in the Abbey Theatre. There was an organized disturbance by a section of the pit to prevent the play being heard. I saw the defendant arrested, and saw him before the arrest rise up and yell at the top of his voice."

"Who is the defendant?" Lawrence scribbled on his notepad and passed it to Joseph Holloway who immediately began to sketch a profile of the young man in the dock. Joseph Holloway was much given to making sketches of the many actors, lecturers, singers and various interesting people he encountered in the busy round of his day. These sketches were invariably in profile, as Joseph Holloway had difficulty with a three-quarters or full-face view. This did not dissuade him from frequently presenting his sitters with a copy of his efforts. At best these individuals were puzzled, but a few concluded that a portrait was intended. Often, that conclusion resulted in a certain coolness between subject and artist.

"Joe! Who is the defendant?"

"Beasley. A prominent Gael from London."

Yeats had turned to the judge. "He addressed some words to me in Irish."

"Were they complimentary or the reverse?"

W.B. Yeats mournfully shook his head. "I am sorry to say I understand no Irish."

"Well," chuckled the judge, "I know some Irish, and I know that one can say very scathing things in Irish."

The court dutifully tittered.

"Now, Mr. Beasley," said the judge, "what have you to say?"

The young man met the judge's eyes. "If your worship had been present last night you would have heard nothing unedifying from me. I am no member of any organised gang who went to the theatre for the purpose of objecting."

"Hear, hear!" muttered Lawrence.

"I cannot hear!" Thomasina MacFitz spat wetly into his left ear.

"I went with two friends and did not know the other objectors, but my blood boiled at the attempt to coerce public opinion. The men in the stalls were standing up and shaking their sticks at us. Mr. Yeats stood over me and said he would give in charge the next man who boohed."

"Just so!" said W.B. Yeats firmly.

"Just then a particularly objectionable expression was used on the stage, and I, in common with a number of others, boohed. Mr. Yeats then pointed me out to the constable, and I was taken in charge."

"Yes, quite," said W.B. Yeats.

"No threats or penalties," said young Beasley, "will deter me from objecting to what I consider an outrage on the Irish people."

"Hear, hear!" muttered W.J. Lawrence.

"Noisy man!" spat Christina MacFitz into his right ear.

"Before this," said Pearse Beasley, "I had been an admirer of the Abbey Theatre and a regular supporter of it."

"Yes," mused the judge out loud, "this is a different case from the last."

"I have made my protest, and I consider that every true Irishman would act in the same way."

The judge cleared his throat, and bent forward. "You are entitled to indulge in legitimate criticism and also in a reasonable form of disapproval, but you are not entitled to be guilty of such behaviour as would be offensive to other persons in the play and prevent their performance. I understand you are an enthusiast in Celtic matters, and I do not want to be too severe on you if you will give an undertaking that you will not take any part in these disturbances again."

"I would be satisfied with such an understanding," said W. B. Yeats.

"No," said Pearse Beasley, "I will make no appeal to Mr. Yeats. I wish him to push the matter to the utmost extremity. You will then have the spectacle of a man brought into the Police Court for making a protest against an outrage on Irish nationality."

The judge was frowning. "A protest which the law does not permit. Surely you can make a protest without breaking the law."

Pearse Beasley shook his head. "Mr. Yeats pointed me out to the police and is responsible for this prosecution."

"I must fine you 40s," said the judge, "or in default, a month's imprisonment, and I will take your own sureties for good behaviour."

"Come, sister!" said Thomasina MacFitz, rising in disgust and perhaps inadvertently knocking W. J. Lawrence sharply on the back of the head.

"Is it over?" said Christina.

The young reporter found them just sitting down to lunch at the Metropole. He approached the table, hat in had, and said, "Pardon me, gentlemen. I am from the press, and I wonder if I might have just a few words with you about Mr. Synge's *Playboy*."

Synge sighed and looked away. Perhaps he could excuse himself and slip off for a moment to the G.P.O. to send a wire to Molly. He could say. . . .

W.B. Yeats looked over the top of his menu. "Mr. Synge's play is a masterpiece, but we are dealing here with a much more important question than the merits of a play. We are dealing with the freedom of the theatre. And also lunch."

The young reporter wrote on his pad. "Yes, sir, but the play — "

W.B. Yeats put down his menu and sternly folded his arms. "The play has been attacked on grounds which have nothing whatever to do with art."

"Yes, sir, but many people feel that the play defames the Irish peasant."

"Art," said Yeats, his nostrils curling in marvellous disdain, "as a certain French writer has said, is 'exaggeration a propos'."

"Eh, what French writer would that have — ?"

Yeats frowned him down. "Have our critics read *Bartholomew Fair* by Ben Jonson?"

"Eh," said the young reporter. "Is that S-O-N or S-T-O-N?"

Yeats leaned over to Synge. "Did he say something?"

"He wants to know how to spell Jonson."

"One E," said Yeats.

A waiter appeared. "Are you ready to order, gentlemen?"

"I'll just have coffee," said Synge.

"He'll have what I'm having," said Yeats. "I'm having a mixed grill. All great literature deals with exaggerated types, and all tragedy and tragi-comedy deal with types of sin and folly."

"And you, sir?" repeated the waiter to the young reporter.

"A dramatist," boomed Yeats, getting into his stride, "is not an historian!"

"Eh, coffee," said the young reporter meekly.

"Tea all round," said Yeats. He turned to the young reporter, waving a tutorial finger. "If the critics were right about the play, that would not make their conduct less than outrageous. A serious issue has been rising in Ireland for some time. When I was a lad, Irishmen obeyed a few leaders, but during the last ten years a change has taken place." He paused and waited for the furiously scribbling reporter to catch up with him.

Synge rolled a cigarette.

"For leaders we have now societies, clubs and leagues. Organised opinion of sections and coteries have been put in place of these leaders, one or two of whom were men of genius. Instead of a Parnell, a Stephens, or a Butt, we must obey the demands of commonplace and ignorant people, who try to take on an appearance of strength by imposing some crude shibboleth on their own and others' necks."

"Eh?" said the young reporter, flustered.

"Shibboleth has two b's," murmured Synge, noting his problem.

"Yes, but where?"

"They do not persuade," intoned Yeats, "for that is difficult. They do not expound, for that needs knowledge."

Well turned, thought Synge, wondering if it were true.

"The mass," said Yeats, pushing back his chair and rising to address the room, "only understand conversion by terror, threats and abuse!"

"Here's our tea," said Synge.

"Ah!" Yeats resumed his chair. "Pass the sugar."

"Do you think," said the young reporter, "the opposition last night represented this school of criticism?"

"Yes," said Yeats. "The protestors who came down last night, not to judge the play, but to prevent other people from doing so, merely carried out a method which is becoming general in our national affairs. They have been so long in mental servitude that they cannot understand life if their head is not in some bag."

"Em," said the young reporter cautiously, "are you going on with the play?"

Yeats looked at him astonished. "Of course, we are going on with the play. We will go on until the play has been heard, and heard sufficiently to be judged on its merits. We had only announced its production for one week. We have now decided to play all next week as well, if the opposition continue. With the exception of one night when I shall lecture on the freedom of the theatre, and invite our opponents to speak on its slavery to the mob if they have a mind to."

"You will extend the run then?"

"We shall go on thus," said Yeats, throwing his head back magnificently, "as long as there is one man who has wanted to hear the play and has been prevented by noise. Anyone who writes that he has not been able to hear shall be sent a free ticket."

Synge looked up, bemused. "Wouldn't that mean giving free tickets to the opposition?"

"Can't be helped," said Yeats airily. "If our critics wish to make liars of themselves, it is not our affair."

"Two mixed grills," said the waiter.

"That one's mine," said Yeats.

"Eh, Mr. Synge," said the young reporter, "the word which caused the uproar on Saturday night — ."

"An everyday word in the West of Ireland," said Synge wearily. "It was used without objection in Douglas Hyde's *Songs of Connaught* in the Irish."

"Do you agree with Mr. Yeats' theory that art is an exaggeration?"

"Yes, he does," said Yeats lavishly buttering his toast.

"The play," said Synge, "I have called an extravaganza, but — ."

"Synge, pardon me!" said Yeats and bent intently across the table.

The young reporter, pencil poised, also bent avidly over.

"Do you want that second rasher?"

Yeats strode off down Lower Abbey Street to the theatre.

Odd, thought Synge, how lecturing, as he did to that reporter, fires him up. In a few minutes of course he would be back in his trance, staring unseeing at the world, his hand raised to conduct the mute music of his mind.

Perhaps he should have walked Yeats to the theatre, just to see that he didn't halt in the middle of Lower Abbey Street to unravel a line as he unknowingly snarled up traffic.

How unlike Yeats was from his energetic father. And, as if on cue, old John Butler Yeats, his beard buffeted by the wind, plunged out of Eason's doorway and made across Sackville Street.

Yes, old J.B.'s energy and his talk never let up.

Tiredly, Synge turned toward the Post Office. The wire was a simple problem in words.

Simply write, "I love you. I want to see you. Your old Tramp."

He reached the colonnade of the G.P.O. and steadied himself against the first pillar.

Strange that it was possible to want two opposites simultaneously.

To want to smash that howling mob and force the play down their throats. To rub their noses in it.

To want to throw Molly down on the mountainside and fall upon her.

And to want the opposite. To want peace and quiet, darkness, silence, his room.

His knees buckled under him, and he quickly caught himself.

The wire would wait. The theatre would still be there to-morrow. And the world. And Molly.

Blindly he staggered off for the Dalkey tram.

Much later that evening, W.B. Yeats brushed back his wandering raven tress and settled down at the office desk. He opened the metal box and contemplated the satisfying sheaf of bills and the small mountain of loose coins. He did not bother to count the money himself, for Lady Gregory said that Henderson was scrupulously accurate. And besides his own computations never came out the same way twice.

W.B. Yeats was attracted to arcane mysteries, but somehow arithmetic had none of theosophy's fascination. Madame Blavatsky had, of course, lectured him on the powers of certain mystic numbers, and even Annie Horniman found numbers indispensable in casting horoscopes, but to him columns of naked figures proved more conducive to headaches than to revelations.

Nevertheless, he patted the money happily, and turned to Henderson's tally for the evening:

Wednesday, January 30, 1907
Box Office Receipts, for a total of 421 paid admissions —
£24. 13s. 6d.
Free List — 33.

33! He frowned.

In his airy room in Fitzwilliam Street, Leslie Chenevix Purefoy was smiling.

Thursday, January 31

Yeats had spent a profitless day of smoky images and unsatisfactory rhymes, to wit:

> That if the dancer stayed his hungry foot
> It seemed the sun and moon were all the fruit. . . .

In the boot, perhaps? Were never caught? Were all for naught? Or perhaps, thirsty boot? Would that make sense? Vague sense?

Overcome with the fatigue of it all, he threw himself down on the divan. Really, the atmosphere in that sitting room which he shared with Lady Gregory in the Nassau Hotel was not conducive to poetry. He touched his throbbing temple.

And it was then that he heard the voice.

"O, poet, great poet," it intoned.

"I shall really have to stop talking to myself," said the poet to himself. "Despite the interest of the conversation."

"Poet!"

Save for himself, the room was empty. He sat up, mildly disconcerted. "Who whereupon speaks whereat?"

Silence.

"I charge you," he bellowed. "Come forth! Be a man!"

"A little late for that," wailed the voice.

"Oh. You are fleshless, then? Bloodless?"

"Also, alas, boneless."

Hmm, pondered the poet, difficult to ask him to have a seat.

He cleared his throat. "Can it be that I have been privileged with an emanation? Or is this, merely, a subjective, a cognitive intensification of my own personal spiritual aura? Which I am assured by MacGregor Mathers is extremely strong."

"Be apprised," said the voice, "that this is Aeschylus."

Ah!

"All hail, Aeschylus! I have long admired some bits of your work. We probably have more than a little in common."

"Such as what?"

"Oh, the implacable austerity. The monumental grandeur."

The Voice emitted a series of irritating, high-pitched snickers.

"Are you sure you are Aeschylus?" said the bard, with more than a touch of asperity.

"Oh, quite sure," chuckled the Voice.

"Well, then," said the poet, "tell me if you are in touch with Sophocles."

"It is impossible for spirits to be in touch."

"I spoke idiomatically."

"That is a fault of you regional poets."

Yeats was tempted to retort with some heat, but he merely remarked, "I have a particular reason for wishing to speak with him. I am contemplating a translation of his *Oedipus the King*."

"That has come to his attention, and he is somewhat irate."

"Irate?"

"More than a little incensed."

"About what, might I ask?"

"About your gall, impertinence and effrontery, you might say."

The poet drew himself up stiffly. "I would not say that at all. In fact, you can tell Sophocles to kiss my arse!" Whereupon, sweeping back the raven lock from his brow, he left the room, banging the door behind him.

In the corner of the room, the door of the dumb waiter slowly opened, and Leslie Chenevix Purefoy extracted himself from his cramped quarters with a grin.

Sally peered into the mirror, mechanically smoothing out old Maurya's age lines. She must pull herself together, concentrate. She had just walked through the part to-night, and the Widow Quin was still to come.

It was the clippings distracting her. One in the morning's post, one in the afternoon's, and one actually taped to the dressing-room mirror when she came in this evening. Thank God, she had come in early and been the first one here.

They had all been neatly cut from something. Not a newspaper certainly. What? *Thom's Directory*?

They were all burned into her mind:

DUBLIN BY LAMPLIGHT, BALLS-BRIDGE
Superioress — Mrs. M. G. Keating

"That they may recover themselves out of the snare of the devil, who are taken captive by him at his will".
2 Tim., ii.26

This valuable Institution is supported by voluntary contributions and by the inmates' own exertions. It has an excellent laundry attached, furnished with all modern appliances.

That had been in the morning's post, and it was merely puzzling. But then in the afternoon's "ST. MARY MAGDALEN'S ASYLUM, DONNYBROOK" which "provides in every respect for 100 penitants, who contribute to their support by washing and needlework." And now to-night, taped to the mirror — oh, if that had been seen!

MAGDALEN ASYLUM, 8, Leeson-Street, Lower
Founded by Lady Arabella Denny,
1765
Patroness, Lady Ardilaun

This Institution, the oldest Magdalen Asylum in Ireland, is intended only for young women who have for the first time fallen into vice.

"Why, Sally," cried Brigit O'Dempsey, "whatever have you done to your make-up? You've smudged it all up."

"I was trying something new," Sally snapped, and reached quickly for the cold cream.

"Oh?" said Brigit O'Dempsey strangely, and then stretched for Sally's purse. "Mind if I borrow a fag?"

"Yes! I do!"

"Sorry!" said Brigit O'Dempsey, and retreated to the far side of the room to whisper something to May Craig.

Seaghan Barlow looked sullenly in. "Miss O'Neill! Five minutes!"

"Right!" said Molly. As she passed, she bent down to her sister and whispered, "That Brigit O'Dempsey makes far too free."

118

She patted Sally's shoulder and went out to the wings. She could hear the hum as the audience moved back to their seats.

"How's about a drink after the show?" said a voice behind her.

"Oh, Gussie," she said, "Are all the props in place? Last night there was no bar rag behind — ."

"Not to worry your pretty head," he said, giving her a tickle in the ribs.

"Clear off!" she said, the softness of her voice belying the flounce of her head.

Well, why not? It wouldn't hurt Johnny to be a bit jealous. He hadn't even thought her performance important enough to show up to-night.

Serve him right!

Idly she picked up a newspaper from the prompter's chair, and an advertisement caught her eye.

J.H. WEBB & Co.
Iron and Brass Bedsteads
200 to Select From

Double Size Bedstead, Brass Rails, Rings and Spindles (as per illustration), 25/-
With 3-ply Wire Mattress, Pure Hair Mattress, Feather Bolster and Pillows, Complete for £4 8s. 6d.
All Brass Bedsteads — £5

Hmm, she thought, tearing it out and stuffing it into her apron, I must show that to Johnny. If I decide to speak to him again. If he speaks to me. . . . Abruptly she dropped the paper back onto the chair and went onstage to check her props.

Arthur Sinclair came into the wings and watched the sensuous sway of her hips as she sauntered onstage. A nice bit of goods Molly, much trimmer than Sally. Trouble was, she held her nose so high in the air now that she and Synge were doing a line. Well, who needed her? When he went into management one of these days, she'd sing a different tune. "Oh, please, Mac," she'd whine, unbuttoning her blouse down to her navel. "Couldn't you find me a small part, a walk-on?"

An ad in the newspaper caught his wandering eye. Hmm, he thought, and picked it up.

Ask Your Grocer for a Sample Bottle of
"Kandee"
(The New Irish Sauce)
Appetizing — Delicious — Digestive

Hmm, well, he'd had no problem with digestion after some bollocks had laced the Guinness with paraffin oil. My God, he'd forgotten to ask Fay if he'd replaced it with the real stuff. He went onstage to check his props.

Och, clucked Gussie, look at Mac spraying my newspaper all over the floor.

"Ah, dear boy," said Purefoy, appearing behind him. "This bag has just been handed in at the door for Miss Allgood. Could you see that she gets it?"

"Oh, sure, Mr. Purefoy. Hunh," he prodded the cloth bag, "wonder what this is?"

"Doubtless from an admirer. Now, Augustus, you remember my coaching for to-night?"

"Ah I was wondering, Mr. Purefoy, do you think I should really chance it? I mean — ."

"Tush, you must call the callous world's attention to your true abilities."

"Eh, yeh, but. . . ."

Purefoy patted him caressingly on the shoulder. "Only think of your name in the morning papers, dear boy! Now I do believe the curtain's about to go up. You'd better get that bag to Miss Allgood."

Great, reflected Gussie, hurrying off on his errand, to have some real professional coaching for a change. Willie Fay wouldn't have the time to do anything but grouch at you, and tell you to go out and make the tea.

He knocked at the women's dressing room. "Sally, here's something been handed in for you."

"Gussie Gaffney!" snapped Brigit O'Dempsey. "You're not to knock and stick your fat head in! You're to knock and wait until you're asked to enter. I mean, you might otherwise see something you're not supposed to." She cackled at the blushing Gussie and turned back into the room with the bag. "This is for you, Sally."

"Me?" said Sally. "What's in it?"

"Lah-de-dah!" said Brigit O'Dempsey, untying the draw string and emptying the contents on the table. "Oh! Oh, wouldja look at this!"

The girls clustered around.

"Men's socks!" said May Craig.

"And underwear!" marvelled Alice O'Sullivan.

"Men's dirty underwear!" gurgled Brigit O'Dempsey in delight.

Sally jerked convulsively and sent powder furiously flying all down her blouse.

Friday, February 1

W.J. Lawrence stalked out of the *Independent* offices fuming. Only a guinea, and the piece was twice as long as usual. And represented a good four days' work in the National Library. "Heblon" would get that for one of his vapid "Pieces in Blue" that wouldn't cost him an hour's work.

He had another headache coming on. Lack of sleep. Perhaps a cup of tea and a bun would drive it away for the moment. He turned into the nearest cafe on Sackville Street, found the place empty, selected a corner table and scowled at the three empty cups, the sloshed tea on the greasy surface, the crumbs. It was never like this in Belfast.

A waitress sauntered past carrying an empty tray, humming to herself. "Miss!"

Gone! And that would never happen in Belfast either.

Oh, his head! He took off his cap, placed it on the chair beside him and kneaded his brow. Tiredness, that was his trouble. Still, nice to sit down and stretch out. Close his eyes for a minute, and maybe the headache would go away. . . .

"Mind if I join you?" someone said, and sat down before Lawrence could reply. Cheek!

"Miss," said the mild voice opposite.

"Yes, sir," said the waitress, hastening over. "Just let me clean this off for you. Now, sir, may I take your order?"

"Coffee, I think. Very black. Ah, wait, have you taken this gentleman's order?"

"Oh," said the waitress, regarding W.J. Lawrence without enthusiasm. "Did you want anything?"

W.J. Lawrence exploded. "Tea! And a rock bun!"

His companion took off his curled-brim hat, flicked off a speck and put it down on top of Lawrence's cap. "Daunting name, rock bun. Of course, it seems to promise so little that it can hardly disappoint greatly."

W.J. Lawrence scowled at the pale, fat, pasty, amiable face opposite him. "I like rock buns!" he said.

"Ah," said the other mellifluously, "always or just during Lent?"

W.J. Lawrence's scowl deepened into a glower as he regarded this gaudy popinjay, overdressed in checked tweeds, with a fat and blubbery mouth.

"Always!" W.J. Lawrence announced, and took out the *Independent* which he had abstracted from the office as his just due as a contributor. No matter how insufficiently valued.

"Always." His companion was amused.

This impertinence would not do. W.J. Lawrence snapped the paper down on the table. "I said, with perfect clarity and total sincerity, 'always!'" Hah, that should put him in his place! Unblinkingly, he continued to glare until the vulgar creature would look down abashed. Or, even better, shamefacedly remove his obnoxious presence to another table.

He found himself, however, favoured with a disarming smile.

W.J. Lawrence was not a man to be disarmed so easily. Particularly when the smiler had a mouthful of discoloured teeth.

"A little sincerity," remarked his tablemate easily, "is a dangerous thing — and a great deal of it is absolutely fatal."

Intolerable! W.J. Lawrence looked around for another table.

"Yes," murmured his companion, covering his teeth with a pudgy, beringed hand. "A man cannot be too careful in the choice of his enemies."

W.J. Lawrence, although taken aback at how correctly his mind had been read, retorted, "Unfortunately in a public place one does not always have a reasonable choice."

"Reason," came the equable reply, "is but choosing." The large flabby fellow smiled pleasantly and languidly removed a second glove. That pudgy hand was also much-beringed.

Lawrence grimaced in distaste.

"But perhaps," his companion drawled, "you are not interested in art."

"I am extremely interested in art."

The shrug was nonchalant. "All art is quite useless."

Lawrence frowned. Had he misjudged this fop?

"It is only shallow people who do not judge by appearances," the fellow smiled, once again seeming to read his thought.

"Eh?"

The other produced a gold cigarette case, and extracted a black cigarette. "Mind if I smoke? A man should always have an occupation. What, one wonders, is yours?"

"I am a drama critic, an historian and a journalist."

"Yes, weren't you at the Abbey Theatre the other night? Was it in your treble or tribal capacity?"

"I reviewed the wretched piece for *The Stage*."

"Wretched? Hmm."

W.J. Lawrence narrowed his eyes in anger. "It was both unintelligible and immoral!" And, noting that his rock bun had arrived, he emphasized his moral fervour by taking a savage bite.

His companion raised his coffee cup, sniffed dubiously and replaced it on the table. "I fancy, that if a work of art was immediately recognised by the public through their medium, the public Press, as intelligible and moral — I fancy the artist must question seriously whether the work was second-rate or of no artistic value whatsoever."

"That play," snapped Lawrence, "is morbid!"

"Morbid," pondered his companion who then blew three smoke rings. "Now 'morbid' is a word that the public do not often use. Its meaning is so simple that they are afraid of using it."

"Afraid!"

"Also, it is a ridiculous word to apply to a work of art."

Lawrence slammed his tea cup back into its saucer.

The other seemed not to have heard. "The public are all morbid because the public can never find expression for anything. The artist is never morbid."

"J.M. Synge," W.J. Lawrence snarled, "is a notoriously morbid artist!"

"Ah, but the true artist notoriously, and incomparably, expresses everything. To call an artist morbid because he deals with morbidity as his subject-matter is as silly as if one called Shakespeare mad because he wrote *King Lear*."

"You'd compare the glorious Shakespeare to the exotic, unhealthy Synge! Bah!"

And thumping the table, W.J. Lawrence inadvertently hit the corner of his plate, an action which occasioned his rock bun to describe a graceful parabola through the air and then to descend with a dramatic splash into his full cup of tea.

His companion continued imperturbably. "Within the last few years two other adjectives have been added to the limited vocabulary of art-abuse at the disposal of the public press. One is the word 'unhealthy'; the other is the word 'exotic.' The latter merely expresses the rage of the momentary mushroom against the immortal and exquisite orchid."

"Mushroom! Are you implying that I am a — !"

"Now the word, 'unhealthy' is interesting. So interesting that those who use it do not know what it means."

"I — I — I — !" spluttered W. J. Lawrence.

"Ah, you have a nautical background also. Well, I am pleased that you agree."

"I do not ag— !"

"But what is a healthy or an unhealthy work of art? All terms that one rationally applies to a work of art have reference to either its style or its subject, or to both together. From the point of view of style, a healthy work of art is one whose style recognizes the beauty of the material it employs, be that material one of words or of bronze, of colour or of ivory, and uses that beauty as a factor in producing the aesthetic effect."

"Bah!"

"From the point of view of subject," his companion continued equably, "a healthy work of art is one the choice of whose subject is conditioned by the temperament of the artist. In fine, a healthy work of art has both perfection and personality. Of course, form and substance cannot be separated in a work of art; they are always one. But for purposes of analysis, and setting the wholeness of aesthetic impression aside for a moment, we can intellectually so separate them."

"Grrmm," growled W.J. Lawrence, feeling a curious lassitude envelope his limbs. If not, he should surely have smashed his fist into that pale, pasty, bloated, revoltingly amiable face.

"An unhealthy work of art, on the other hand, is a work whose style is obvious, old-fashioned and common, and whose subject is deliberately chosen, not because the artist has any pleasure in it, but because he thinks that the public will pay him for it. In fact, the popular novel or play that the public call healthy is always a thoroughly unhealthy production; and what the public call an unhealthy novel or play is always a beautiful and healthy work of art."

His companion placed his black cigarette precisely in the centre of his mouth and inhaled. Then he blew a fat, enlarging and perfect smoke ring. Slowly it floated across and encircled W. J. Lawrence's angrily dilating nostrils. Somehow Lawrence was unable to raise his hands to wave it away. And somehow it did not dissipate. It clung there quite ludicrously.

His companion continued. "I do not complain that the public and the Press misuse these words. But how, with their lack of comprehension of Art, could they possibly use them in the proper sense?"

Languidly he dropped his black cigarette into his untasted cup of coffee.

"The misuse, of course, comes from the natural inability of a community corrupted by authority to understand or appreciate individualism."

He retrieved his fawn-coloured gloves and lazily pulled them on.

"In a word, it comes from that monstrous and ignorant thing called Public Opinion, which, bad and well-meaning as it is when it tries to control action, is infamous and of evil meaning when it tries to control Thought or Art. Well, I trust this has been illuminating."

He rose and placed his hat carefully on his head. Then as an afterthought gave it a slight rakish tilt. "We must discuss these matters again." And he turned and lounged lazily to the door.

Lawrence gathered himself with an effort. "Who are you?"

"Melmoth," came the distant reply.

Lawrence blinked several times, conscious that the waitress was shaking him. "This isn't a doss house," she was saying. "You can't sleep here!"

"I merely closed my eyes," he retorted stiffly, and raised his cup to his lips.

"Aghh!" he exclaimed and spat out the soggy remains of a rock bun.

Thomasina McFitz was growling in the privacy of her boudoir, clad only in her tentlike peignoir.

"Wahr!!! Wahrrr!!!" she growled, thereby causing the crack in the ceiling to extend itself another three inches and a bit of plaster to fall.

Again she smoothed out the crumpled letter, and again she read it:

Entrancing Vision!
It is with inexpressible lugubriousness that I take up my quill

to pen this last, most melancholy farewell. Blasted all my hopes and riven all my plans for our future bliss connubial. However, your ever solicitous sister has made me face, albeit with bitter reluctance, the fact that I must not obstruct your future triumphal progress in the thespianic art. Your sister is right — you belong to the world not to one mere man, no matter how doting he be! "L'Art," remarked Horace, "c'est tout!" And I, who perhaps in my small way, am also an artist shall not stand in your inexorable way.

Farewell Forever from
The Lorn and Lonesome,
The Bereft and Bereaved,
W.B. (Liam) Yeats

P.S. I append a poesy upon the heretofore referred to topic:

ALAS, THE LOSS
Roses are still red,
Nasturtiums chartreuse,
The macaws still chirp,
And Quack! goes the goose!

But my love is fled;
Alas, I let her a-loose,
My love sweeter than syr'p,
My Lost Amoreuse!

Thomasina McFitz crushed the letter in her powerful fist and roared such vast, all-encompassing, reverberating bellows that the last remaining bit of Waterford, a vinegar cruet, cracked in twain.

"OH, YOU UNNATURAL HAG!" she remarked, referring to her absent sister, "I WILL HAVE SUCH REVENGES ON YOU THAT ALL THE WORLD SHALL — I WILL DO SUCH THINGS — WHAT THEY ARE, YET I KNOW NOT; BUT THEY SHALL BE THE TERRORS OF THE EARTH!!!"

Half a street away, Joseph Holloway paused. "*Lear*," he murmured.

"Act Two," said W. J. Lawrence.

"Scene Four," said Joseph Holloway.

"Lines 277 to 281," said W.J. Lawrence. "But slightly misquoted."

Once again Joseph Holloway marvelled at his friend's erudition.

Christina McFitz was weeping in the privacy of the library amidst the rising damp and the musty odour of the few moistly mouldering books that had not been previously sold to Greene's of Clare street.

"krik-krik-krik," she wept, in unobtrusive lower case.

Again she smoothed out the tear-blubbered missive, and again she read it:

> Ineffable Saint!
>
> It is with inexpressible lugubriousness that I take up my quill to indite this last, most melancholy farewell. Blasted all my hopes and riven all my plans for our future union spirituelle. However, your ever-solicitous sister has made me face, albeit with painful reluctance, the fact that I must not obstruct your future spiritual development as a Poor Clare among the benighted natives of far-off Pago-Pago. Your sister is right — you belong to the Lord, not to one mere mortal man, no matter how adoringly reverent he may be! "La Vie Religeuse," remarked St. Paul, "est la moment le plus superbe dans l'existence d'une femme." And I, who perhaps in my miniscule way, am also a devotee of the higher life ("It is better not to yearn" — cf. also St. Paul) shall not stand in your way.
>
> Farewell until a brighter Day
> Hath Dawneth,
> The Chaste and Chastened,
> But Bruised and Battered,
> W.B. Yeats (Guillaume)
>
> P.S. I append a poeme upon the heretofore adverted to topic:
>
> A LASS THE LESS
> Violets are still blue
> And pansies viridian,
> I stumble through
> My lorn life quotidien!
>
> She labours anew
> In climes Antipodidian,
> But my love is through
> Below my Meridian!

Christina McFitz unbuttoned her blouse and placed the sacred letter against her cold bosom. She said nothing, but her pale lips compressed in thin determination.

The Greenroom was chock-a-block with people, the occasion being the introduction to the company the new English manager-elect. An aura of festivity permeated the room, save for that small corner in which W.G. Fay glowered as his wife, the fluffy-haired Brigit, consolingly patted his hand.

Now, with the inevitable ten minute oration by W.B. Yeats concluded, and with two or three diffident words spoken by B. Iden Payne himself, there was to be performed one of the theatre's rituals. Her Ladyship had brought the barmbrack from Coole Park, and a great quantity of strong tea had been brewed.

The cake, covered with a large napkin, was set upon a salver in the centre of the table, surrounded by many heavy white cups and saucers of an institutional nature.

"Jaysus," whispered Arthur Sinclair to Ambrose Power, effecting unobtrusively some momentary relief from the constriction of his stylish but tight trousers, "what a bloody waste of valuable drinking time."

"Shush!" said Ambrose Power. "The old lady'll hear you."

"What a splendid idea," B. Iden Payne was heard to say.

"Thank you," said W.B. Yeats. "Which one of mine?"

"This celebration. Do you do it often?"

Lady Gregory was pleased. "Fairly often. No matter what our droubles or dravails at de theatre may be, if we can all meet and take tea and cake, well, I feel dat we shall always overcome dat which besets us."

"Oh, quite," said B. Iden Payne. "Jolly good idea!"

"Simplicity, of course, is all," said W.B. Yeats, absently picking up a tea cup.

"Pardon?" said Payne.

"Particularly in rehearsal. Now I once had the idea of contriving a number of barrels mounted on wheels, and providing myself with a large forked stick to prod the barrels about with. What do you think of that?"

"Barrels?" said Payne.

"Or boxes," said Yeats, sipping from his tea cup. "Perfectly immaterial — and so is this tea."

"I don't quite follow," said B. Iden Payne. "Why would you want barrels or boxes?"

"Mr. Yeats," said Lady Gregory, with a perfectly straight face, "had de idea of putting de actors in de barrels."

"Oh!" said B. Iden Payne. Then feeling that something more was required, added nervously, "Well, ha-ha, do you think the actors should hide their light under a barrel?"

"Perhaps," pondered W.B. Yeats, "the problem is that there is no sugar in my cup."

"Nor," said Lady Gregory, "is dere any tea."

"Oh?" said W.B. Yeats. "I suppose, Payne, you are aware of the theories about acting formulated by my friend, Gordon Craig?" He set his cup and saucer down on top of the barmbrack.

Lady Gregory retrieved them and looked about. Yes, young Miss O'Sullivan and young Miss Craig were there, giant teapots at the ready. "Pour Mr. Yeats some tea, my dears. He takes three spoons of sugar. Oh, Miss O'Neill, where is Sally?"

"Right here," said Molly. And where was Johnny, she wondered unhappily. Perhaps he was ill, or — oh, she should write or wire. No, damned if she would!

Her sister, Lady Gregory's usual handmaiden on these occasions, brushed past her roughly.

"The cake slice, Sally, if you please," said Lady Gregory.

As the company fell silent, Leslie Chenevix Purefoy, keeping well out on the periphery, stood up on his toes.

"May I be of some assistance?" enquired B. Iden Payne.

"Ah, perhaps!" said W.B. Yeats, who was never one to miss the symbolism of an event. "You might enfold Lady Gregory's small hands with your own capable ones and aid her to wield the blade. And I shall place my hands atop both."

"Sort of a hand samwich," came the poet's own inimitable voice from the periphery of the crowd.

Lady Gregory's eyes glinted dangerously, and she resolved to query Sally later about the identity of the mimic. However, she quickly said, "What an excellent idea. Step right up to de cake, Mr. Payne. Dis will be your initiation into de theatre."

As she positioned the cake-slice over the barmbrack, and Mr. Payne awkwardly put his hand on hers, and W.B. Yeats solemnly lifted off the napkin, Leslie Chenevix Purefoy with difficulty suppressed a giggle.

For as the trio sliced into the cake, it collapsed of a sudden into a vile mess of foul-smelling matter which all Irish writers with the deplorable exception of the scatological former Dean of St. Patrick's consider too indelicate to name.

In the aghast silence, the foul odour pervaded the room.

"In stinks like cat," said Ambrose Power.

Leslie Chenevix Purefoy slipped, silent and smiling, out the door. Well worth all the time and trouble and now he could get rid of that one-eared cat that he had tethered to the leg of his bed.

In an upper room in Fitzwilliam Street the cat, a battle-scarred veteran of Dublin's back alleys, finally gnawed through the confining twine, and streaked through the permanently open window.

Saturday, February 2

It had taken a long time for Joseph Holloway to arrange a meeting with his confessor, Father Quince. Letters had been written by Joseph Holloway, notes had been dropped in at the presbytery, appointments made, and appointments broken by the cleric. One would wonder, wondered Joseph Holloway, plodding past the Royal Irish Academy of Music, if the clergy nowadays has its former enthusiastic interest in sin.

Well, Joseph Holloway certainly had. Particularly in the sins of other people.

As he padded flatfootedly along to the Church of St. Andrew, a theological thought struck him. He stopped short. Wouldn't it be a good idea to be a surrogate sinner? Not, he crossed himself piously, a bona fide sinner, but a humble confessant of the sins of others?

In a sense, of course, he was. Did he not daily write down in 2,000 words in his journal a detailed account of the evil deeds of his fellow citizens? Posterity would thank him, yes, but was that enough? If he confessed the sins of others, surely Heaven would thank him too. A surrogate confession.

He walked up the steps of the church, pushed his way through the doors into the comforting gloom, and knelt in a pew in a side chapel to contemplate his recent sin, namely his attendance at a certain notorious play in the Abbey Theatre.

The church was largely empty and quiet except for the occasional mutter of prayer and the tinkle of small coins being dropped into the candle boxes by the shrines. Incense clung to the stale, cold air. Polished nailheads glinted from the bare floor.

Dublin has always had its share of strange characters, and now a seedy, saturnine individual entered the pew without genuflecting, scowled at the altar and sat beside Joseph Holloway.

"I am the Prince of Darkness," he announced through toothless gums.

"We have not met," said Joseph Holloway primly.

"You think not?"

"Oh no, I should have remembered, as you look extraordinarily like Sir Henry Irving in his classic role of Mathias in *The Bells*."

"Oh, go to hell," said his companion, moving off. Then he quickly returned and fervently remarked, "No, don't!"

"Or like Joseph O'Mara as Mephistopheles in *Faust*."

"My God, my God," remarked his companion hastily disappearing, "why hast thou forsaken me?"

The door from the sacristy opened and closed with an echoing bang. It was Father Quince in his soutane, but wearing a woolen muffler around his throat rather than a stole.

Well, allowed Joseph Holloway, with Christian charity, perhaps it has been blessed.

A rotund man with bald head, florid face and pitted carrotty nose, Father Quince saw Joseph Holloway, sucked in a copious quantity of the stale, cold air, and released a monumental sigh flavoured with the aroma of peppermint and whiskey.

Joseph Holloway padded to the end of the pew where he made a half-genuflection and headed for Father Quince's confession box.

"Well, Joe," Father Quince said resignedly, "I suppose we may as well make a start with it."

Joseph Holloway, head hung low, opened the confessor's compartment to allow his reverence to enter in. Father Quince was carrying a Foxford rug and a thermos flask.

Joseph Holloway's puzzlement communicated itself to Father Quince. "I suffer," said that holy man with rasping dignity, "from poor circulation in my nether extremities. Hence, the rug. And, in the flask, there is a little weak tea."

They entered their respective compartments.

"Oh, my God!" Joseph Holloway heard his confessor moan quietly on the other side of the lattice.

"He is praying," thought Joseph Holloway. He waited for what he considered a discreet interval. Then he pressed his loins reverently against the wall of the compartment, and cleared his throat.

The slide shot back.

"Well, Joe," said Father Quince, belching delicately. "Let her rip."

"Bless me, Father," began Joseph Holloway, "for we have sinned."

"You and who else?" said Father Quince with interest.

"The world," said Joseph Holloway.

133

Father Quince uncapped his thermos flask.

Thomasina McFitz gingerly shifted her expansive bulk on the chaise lounge with the wonky leg and mangled a piece of Turkish Delight between her yellow fangs.

It was half two in the afternoon, but the drapes were already drawn, and the threadbare room was seen at its best in the wan light of the austere Protestant fire in the grate.

She heard Christina close the front door, and presently the little birdlike steps tripped down the hall toward her. She had had the whole thing out with her sister the previous evening. A little abasement was good for Christina, but ultimately Thomasina had condescended to forgive her. In any event, it was blindingly obvious that Christina had not attempted to come between her and Liam. No, Christina was entirely too simple. Still, Thomasina frowned, something was peculiar. Was Liam himself at the bottom of it? O treachery!

"Oh? Oh? Oh?" came several humble chirps from the door.

"Entrez!" Thomasina thundered. It would not do to allow Christina any imperious over-confidence.

"Oh, Thomasina darling, oh, oh!"

"Close the door, Christina!" Thomasina commanded. "Have you forgotten my larynx!"

"Sorry, sorry, sorry, darling!" Christina bleated and noiselessly closed the door behind her.

"Sometimes you are extremly heartless, sister."

"Oh, oh!" said Christina, a small tear scraping down her thin cheek.

"And!" Thomasina intoned, thumping the back of the chaise lounge, "you have not replenished my incense!"

The wonky leg shivered, as did her sister.

"Oh, oh, oh, sorry, sorry, sorry!" said Christina. "I was just about to, darling, when the postman rang." She held up a large manila envelope.

"Bills," remarked Thomasina. "Well, I hope there are a lot of them. Roll them up tightly and put them on the fire; it is getting cold."

"It is not bills this time, sister darling."

"Not bills!" said Thomasina hotly. "Incredible how unbusinesslike Dublin merchants are! Well, roll up some more of those manuscripts that Sir Samuel Ferguson sent to dear Papa."

"Thomasina, the Abbey Theatre has returned my play."

"Returned your play," rumbled Thomasina in her magnificent baritone. "What effrontery!" Her eyes bulged alarmingly.

"My *Doom of Dervorgilla*," wailed Christina, "written expressly for you."

"He will pay," thundered Thomasina.

"It is a cabal to keep you down," moaned Christina. "Perhaps we should go back to Mullingar."

"Was there a letter? Did he dare to sign it?"

"Eh, who?"

"Liam — I mean Yeats, the poetaster."

"Eh, yes, he did."

"Get," growled Thomasina, "the keys to Papa's chemical laboratory."

"Good-bye," said Susan L. Mitchell, going out the door, "and mind you don't forget to lock up."

"Of course. . . . Eh, what did you say?"

Susan L. Mitchell rolled her eyes drolly and went off.

AE regarded the closed door and then took out his key and locked himself in. I really shouldn't do this, he reflected. I do have a reputation for benevolence and gravity. Then irrepressibly he grinned.

He sat down and picked up his pen. His hand raced over the paper, and this is what it wrote:

BRITTANIA RULE-THE-WAVE
A COMEDY
(In One Act and in Prose)

CHIEF POET OF IRELAND: What is that sound of boohing that I hear?

CHIEF ACTOR OF IRELAND [*Going to the window and looking out*]: I see nothing.

CHIEF POET OF IRELAND: I must have been dreaming. We have had nothing but boohing for the past week, and it has got on my nerves. I hear a hissing sound in my ears all the time. I think if we hired a policeman by the day to stand here, it would give a sense of security.

CHIEF ACTOR OF IRELAND: It's very expensive. I could borrow the uniform from the Castle and put one of the company in it. Would that do?

CHIEF POET OF IRELAND: There it is again!

CHIEF ACTOR OF IRELAND: It's nearer now.

CHIEF POET OF IRELAND: Send some one out to see what it is. They may be coming to attack the theatre. Ring up the police at the Exchange.

CHIEF ACTOR OF IRELAND: I'd better look out first. No, there's nobody! There's only a stout old lady. She couldn't make all that noise. By the holy, she's coming here. She's knocking at the door. I never saw anybody like her before. Wanting to be charwoman, maybe.

[Old Lady, very stout, enters. She has got a brilliant shawl round her shoulders of red and blue striped and crossed. She wears an antique bonnet of Grecian helmet shape, with horse hair on the crest, and she carries a three-pronged fork.]

CHIEF POET OF IRELAND: What do you want? Where do you come from?

OLD LADY: Oh, I'm very sick. I came a long way. I crossed the Channel this morning. Oh, I'm very sick.

CHIEF POET OF IRELAND: Who is she, do you think?

CHIEF ACTOR OF IRELAND: I don't know. Maybe she's a comedy character wanting an engagement.

CHIEF POET OF IRELAND: Do you want an engagement here?

OLD LADY: Oh, I have had a hard time of it. They have hissed me through the streets. I have had a very hard time of it.

CHIEF POET OF IRELAND: And what did they hiss you for, ma'am? Was it the play or the acting?

OLD LADY: Oh, it was my beautiful play. There were miles and miles of soldiers in my play, and miles of policemen, but it never got a fair hearing.

CHIEF ACTOR OF IRELAND: Would you like a job here, ma'am?

OLD LADY: Yes, I would like to come here. I would like to put a lion and unicorn over the door. I would like to make it into a Royal house.

CHIEF POET OF IRELAND: A Royal house! What a splendid idea. Tell me more.

OLD LADY: I have many Royal houses in my own country. There were many songs made about me. Many men were knighted for love of me. There was an Alfred of the Austins and a Rudyard of the Kiplings and an Albert of the Quills. There were many hundreds of them.

136

They will all be forgotten to-morrow, but to-morrow there will be hundreds more, and they will all sing songs for my sake. They were knighted for love of me; some of them were knighted yesterday and some will be knighted to-morrow.

CHIEF POET OF IRELAND [*Eagerly*]: Is it in Ireland they will be knighted to-morrow?

CHIEF ACTOR OF IRELAND: Don't listen to her. We have wasted time long enough. I don't think she would be any use to us here. They don't like her style in the theatre.

CHIEF POET OF IRELAND: Oh, I want to listen to her. Tell me about the songs that were made about you.

OLD LADY: I heard one this morning as I came over. Listen.

[*Chants*]: They will be respectable for ever,
    There shall be money in their pockets for ever,
    They shall go to the Castle for ever,
    The police shall protect them for ever.

CHIEF POET OF IRELAND: Who will the police protect?

OLD LADY: Those who enter my service. Those who were pale-cheeked, they will be red-cheeked. Those who were thin, they will have fat paunches. Those who walked before, or went in trams, will drive in carriages. Those who took off their hats will have hats taken off to them. Those who had no balance in the bank will have big balances in the bank. They will all be well paid.

CHIEF POET OF IRELAND: What is your name, ma'am?

OLD LADY: There are some that call me Seaghan Buidhe, and there are some that call me Brittania that Rules the Waves.

CHIEF POET OF IRELAND: I think I have heard that name in a song.

OLD LADY [*Going to the door*]: I must be going now. I must be going to the Levee. All the titled doctors in Dublin are gathering to greet me. All the heads of departments. They are the Upper classes to-day, and they will be the Upper classes to-morrow. They will have no need to work. They will have no need to work. [Goes out chanting]:
    They will be respectable for ever,
    The police will protect them for ever.

CHIEF POET OF IRELAND [*Going after her*]: Wait a minute. I will go with you, ma'am.

CHIEF ACTOR OF IRELAND: Where are you going? You forget about the rehearsal here. You are forgetting you are building up a Theatre for the Nation.

CHIEF POET OF IRELAND [*In a dream*]: What nation are you talking about? What nationality are you going to build up? Oh, I forgot!

[*Scene Shifter rushes in.*]

SCENE SHIFTER: There's a yacht in the harbour. King Edward has landed in Kingstown. The police are all going down to see the King.

[*Chief Poet of Ireland goes to the door.*]

CHIEF ACTOR OF IRELAND [*Detaining him*]: You are not going with the police. You are not going to meet the King.

VOICE [*Heard chanting down the stairs*]:

> They will be respectable for ever,
>
> The police will protect them for ever.

[*Chief Poet of Ireland breaks away. Chief Actor of Ireland and Scene Shifter look at each other.*]

CHIEF ACTOR OF IRELAND: Here's a holy sell. Did you see a fat old lady going down the stairs?

SCENE SHIFTER: Faith, I did. She was the very spit of the image on the new penny. And there was a mangy old lion from the Zoo walking by her side.

CURTAIN

AE put down his pen and read what he had written. Oh, I must tear this up. I must not publish this. He sighed. Very difficult being a sage and a saint.

No, I could not publish it. Under my own name. Or in my magazine. But, he laughed, I might slip it to Griffith.

Arthur Griffith heard his printer let himself out. They were all gone now. Time for some serious work.

He rolled a piece of paper into his typewriter, reflected briefly, very briefly, and then wrote:

THE FABLE OF THE FIDDLER
By 'Shanganagh'

There was once a Fiddler who opened a Booth in a Fair, and Over the Booth he wrote: "The Only Genuine Irish Fiddler. The Only Genuine Irish Music. Beware of Foreign Imitations. Come! Come!! Come!!!"

The Irish Public was at the Fair. He Read the Writing, and said: "I am glad I can at Last Hear Genuine Irish Music. I shall Beware of Foreign Imitations. I shall Go in Here."

And the Irish Public asked the Fiddler, "How much?" And the Fiddler answered — "Sixpence — same as the Foreign Imitators." And the Irish Public paid his Sixpence and Walked Inside.

And the Fiddler took his Fiddle and drew his Bow up and down the Strings, and instead of emitting Music the Fiddle snarled and barked and shrieked until the Irish Public's ears could stand it no longer, and he said: "But that isn't Genuine Irish Music." And the Fiddler replied: "You are an Ignoramus. You don't know anything about Ireland."

The Irish Public was astonished, but he was a mild man, having been Educated in the Belief that he was Full of Sin, and he said gently:

"But Surely it is not Music at all?"

"You Wretched Lout," replied the Fiddler. "What do you know about Music? How dare you presume to Criticise an Artist?" And he drew his Bow, and made the Fiddle screech till the Irish Public felt his nerves going, and said:

"But, please, won't you play me 'The Coulin,' or 'The Fair Hills of Ireland,' or — ."

But the Fiddler with a Great Roar stood up and cried, "You Impudent, Ignorant, Illiterate, Interrupting Imbecile, do you not know it is the Fiddler who Calls the Tune?"

"I really didn't know," said the Irish Public apologetically. "I thought when you asked me to come here instead of going elsewhere, and when I paid you my money that — ."

"Shut up," interrupted the Fiddler in a disgusted voice. "What does a Fellow like you know about Art?"

And the Fiddler rasped at his Fiddle until the Nerves of the Irish Public gave way altogether, and he gasped —

"Well, then, won't you please stop Playing?"

This exasperated the Fiddler, who called for the Police; and when the Police came in, he pointed to the Irish Public, and said: "Keep your eye on that Scoundrel. He is an Organised Interrupter." And the Police Smiled in Joy and drew his Baton and held it over the head of the Irish Public, and the Fiddler rasped worse than before, so that the Irish Public's Nerves wholly gave way and his Teeth Chattered.

"You heard him," said the Fiddler to the Police, "deliberately Interrupt."

"But," protested the Irish Public feebly, "I can't help it. Your frightful rasping sets my Teeth on Edge" — and his Teeth Chattered again at the recollection, and the Police broke in his Skull with the Baton and Kicked him along the Road into a Police-Cell, and next morning brought him before the Law, who said:

"He is a Guilty-looking Scoundrel. What is the Charge?"

"I heard his Teeth Chatter when the Fiddler rasped the Fiddle," said the Police.

"I distinctly heard him Moan," said the Fiddler.

"Forty Shillings or a Month," said the Law, "and 'God Save the King.'"

"Hip, Hip, Hurrah for Freedom," said the Fiddler.

Moral — This is Ireland.

Arthur Griffith pulled the paper from the typewriter and read what he had written. His face was totally without expression. Arthur Griffith's face was usually without expression. That perhaps gave people the impression that he did not feel. It was a quite erroneous impression.

In Ely Place, George Moore delicately slit the envelope. Type-written. But signed by, ah-hah, Synge! His hand found the sherry decanter and poured a generous dollop. Yes, this might be rather pleasant. The most prominent disciple about to be detached from Yeats' retinue. He giggled, took an appreciative sip, and allowed himself the luxury of prophesying the contents. Something along these lines, no doubt:

> Cher Maître,
>
> I am bedazzled by your brilliant explication of the multi-tudinous faults of *The Playboy*. Folly to have let myself be influenced by the driveller Yeats. Now, thanks to you, the scales have fallen from my eyes.
>
> All of your criticisms are eminently just, utterly accurate and inimitably acute. May I submit the play for a comprehensive rewriting by the practised hand of *le maître plus grand de la prose dans tout le monde?*
>
> > Hopefully and abjectly,
> > J.M. Synge

Smiling in anticipation, George Moore unfolded the letter and read:

> Dear Moore,
>   Thanks for offering to rewrite *The Playboy*, but I rather fancy it as it is.
>   Yours,
>   J.M. Synge

The incredibly tasteless ingratitude!

In shocked indignation, George Moore crumpled the letter and thrust it from him, thereby toppling his glass of sherry which sloshed over his well-polished table and dripped unheeded onto the well-worn but expensive Turkish rug.

Synge must be made to cringe — but, stay, was there not a defter hand than his in this? Was there not the sneering venom of a certain vastly over-rated bardlet?

George Moore drummed his pudgy fingers thoughtfully upon his wine-besplattered table.

It was twenty five minutes past four in the Church of Saint Andrew, Westland Row, when Mrs. Queenie Gilhooley (MacClatchie that was — oh, why did she ever change it? Duped, yes, duped!) thankfully allowed her birdlike legs a respite from the burden of conveying her tanklike body. She made a semi-genuflection, and semi-knelt in her favourite pew, neatly balancing her massive buttocks on the seat behind her. She lifted the netting on her bonnet and with satisfaction contemplated the crucifix on the High Altar.

Yes, the figure did bear a remarkable resemblance to her lord and mister, Thaddeus Gilhooley, devil. Her eyes played gratifyingly over the crown of the thorns, the nails in the palms and insteps, the dribbling wound in the side.

She mumbled the principal words of the Hail Mary, and shoved her haunches all the way back in the seat. Should she slip off her shoes and get comfortable? Why not?

Thus cosily disposed, she continued her religious meditations which ran to such matters as to where sharp nails might be purchased, were the opportunity for their use ever to present itself, as someday it surely must.

Oh, but wasn't Thaddeus the surly go-boy to swagger home every night, his little belly bloated with beer and his little brain bulging with badness! Her mammy had been right — "Marry that pup, and it's sorrow you'll sup!" Which was what she had only that morning repeated to her neighbour in the first floor back, Mrs. Boyle, who God knows had her own cross to bear with that bowsie the captain and his cadging crony Daly.

Yes, nails, and she could borrow a hammer from Mr. Good, if he wasn't fluthered. One sudden, sharp nail into the temple. Or a spike, positioned nicely in the centre of his scaly, unwashed bald spot, and then WHAM! and SPLAT!!!

She had once in the course of confession mentioned this holy work to Father Quince who savagely snarled some nonsense about wifely duties. "No more snivelling now," he said. "Grin and bear it!"

That was perfectly fine as far as his reverence — God bless him, God blast him — was concerned. But he didn't have to lie under a slobbering bowsey and think of the Five Sorrowful Mysteries.

What a lovely cleaver the butcher in Dorset Street had. Slish, it went through the rosy beef; crunch, through the white bones.

Speaking of Father Quince, what were those sounds coming from his confession box?

". . . and that," she heard, "saving your holy presence, is the way that I see the whole sordid episode, and it was the mention of shifts that did it."

There followed a provocative silence.

"Can you," the same voice asked, "can you absolve me?"

Another, longer silence. Jesus, Mary and Joseph, marvelled Mrs. Gilhooley, what's going on in there?

"Father Quince, Father Quince?" The voice was now distraught. "Have I shocked you too much?"

"Wha — ? Wha — ?" boomed Father Quince. "I'll have three rashers, Biddy."

"Father Quince!" implored the penitent.

"Oh! Oh!" said Father Quince. "Ah, yourself, Joe! Of course! Good man! Now, where were we, a-tall, a-tall?"

"I have just finished explaining my predicament," said Joseph Holloway.

"Well, hem," said Father Quince. "We deal with grevious matters here, Joe. Grevious."

"I am truly distressed that your ears should be sullied, father."

"Ah, that's all right, Joe," said Father Quince. "And you're all finished now, are you? There's nothing more you need to say? No, no, of course, there isn't! Well, say three Hail Marys."

"Just three?"

"Ah, say four."

Christ Almighty, three Hail Marys! Well, thought Queenie Gilhooley, that beats all! And me never getting less than the Stations of the Cross!

Joseph Holloway emerged from the confession box and consulted his watch. Exactly two hours and two minutes, he noted proudly, a personal record!

Mrs. Queenie Gilhooley was again engrossed too deeply in religious meditation to see Joseph Holloway leave the church. Didn't Mr. Good also have a lovely saw among his tools? Yis, and rusty too. Rust, she had read in the medical column of the "Weekly Indo," when it enters the bloodstream could corrode the entire musculiar-vasculiar-peculiar system.

The office of *The Leader* was at last deserted save for the presence of its editor, D.P. Moran. And the presence of the office cat, a scarred veteran of Dublin's innumerable filthy laneways.

The cat was not as young as she used to be. No, in cat terms, she was incredibly ancient.

She had even lost most of one ear in some forgotten catastrophe or cataclysm.

Nor had she the benefit of a name, except the generic one of "damn cat!"

The cat in ancient Egypt was held in immense, almost deific esteem, but no one in this benighted Northern clime had ever paid her the least honour. Or attention, except, of course, when she had toppled a bin over, and they had bunged a rock at her. And except for that curious bloke who tied her up in his room.

Well, it takes all kinds, and that made for an interesting life, although rigorous. Now rigour, while excellent in the formation of character, finally exacts its toll. And the cat had begun to yearn for small comforts. The saucer of warm milk. The cosy fireside. And that was why she had impulsively dashed through the momentarily open door of *The Leader* office.

Presently she was noticed. "Hey, Boss, dere's a cat in here."

"Cat?"

"Will I be after putting it out?"

"Emh, leave it. Maybe it will get rid of the rats."

Newspaper offices are traditionally infested with rats, but *The Leader* had not been doing all that financially well lately, and many rats had decamped for pastures new.

As far as the cat was concerned, that was to the good. Dublin rats were large and vicious, and the cat preferred to give them a wide berth. A small mouse now and then was amusing, but even they seemed to run faster than they used to.

By and large, the cat was finding life at *The Leader* pleasant enough. Occasionally, the copy boy, an irascible urchin named Leo, would provide a saucer of milk. And there was some heat to be had from the small fire in the grate.

Really the only drawback was the humans — burly men who shouted and cursed. Quite the worst was the editor; he tended to hiss with grisly relish while sitting at his desk and tapping a machine with his fingers.

He was doing that now. Then he stopped, extracted a paper from the machine and regarded it. As he did, he emitted an even more unpleasant sound, a sort of sibilant snicker.

The cat undulated silently out of the door, made its way to the press room and found a cosy heap of oily rags to curl up in. Anything for a quiet life.

D.P. Moran, sounding like an excited tea kettle, read what he had just written:

> . . . And yet Mr. Synge was all the while writing without any particular motive; he was merely writing to please himself and to make people laugh. . . .

"Ssss, ssss, ssss," he hissed appreciatively.

> A county or a country cannot, unfortunately, take a criminal libel action against a "comedian" who intended to make its people laugh! If we worked up a sketch composed of such ingredients

as a murderer, a fool, a forger, a harlot, a drunkard, an adulterer, a Freemason, an Orangeman, and such like choice specimens of West Britons, and if, to heighten the humour of the sketch, to make the matter an extravaganza, we called all the male blackguards after Mr. Yeats, Mr. Synge, and their friends, and all the female bad characters after the female relatives and friends of these gentlemen, would they object? What would they say if we told them that in objecting to the names we gave our extravaganza that was meant to make them laugh, that they were outraging literary freedom and the "freedom of judgement," that for our part we might have called the low women any other names, and that they were not really intended to represent Mr. Yeats' women relatives and friends, and that for the rest we did not "care a rap" whether they felt pained or not? We suspect that under the circumstances we would hear very little from Mr. Yeats about his friends and his relatives' "mental servitude," but would rather be the recipients of a writ for criminal libel.

. . . Dimly, for she was almost off to sleep, the cat heard another noise, puzzling and curious. She went to investigate. She poked her head into the editor's office. The sound was coming from him. He was peering at a piece of paper and purring. The cat faintly shuddered. Time for the roads again.

After the matinee, Leslie Chenevix Purefoy and Augustus Gaffney were met with a strange sight when they entered the dim interior of Mister Tommy Lennon's public-house on Lower Abbey Street. The patrons stood motionless in a large semi-circle about the bar, mouths open and eyes fixed on Frank J. Fay, who lay sprawled in the sawdust, his head resting heavily on the bar-rail. Standing over him with small, balled fists was the heavily breathing figure of his brother, the prominent comedian William G. Fay.

This arresting tableau was dissolved by the arrival of Murty, the big-bellied Cork barman. He carried a bucket of water, and called past the bent-shank pipe clenched between his teeth, "Gangway! Mind yerselves before yiz gets drenched!" Then, standing well back, he struck a delicate balance with the bucket, intoned the words, "I baptise thee in the name of the Father and of the Son and of Charles Stewart Parnell," and sloshed the water full into Frank's face.

In the dripping interval that followed, Bantam Lyons, well-known turf philosopher, hazarded the opinion that, "If he's not battered to death, he's probably drownded."

Just at that moment, however, the supine Frank emitted a sigh which was distinctly audible even to those on the outer fringe of the circle. He was always noted for clarity of enunciation.

Groggily he shook his head. "Whattt hittt me?"

"I hit you," glowered Willie, extending his hand. "Now get up out of that."

"You dastarrd!"

"Yeh," said Murty, going back behind the bar, "he's gameball! Business as usual, gents. Belly up!"

Frank J. struggled to his feet, brushing aside Willie G's proferred hand. "I'll get you for your coward's blow, brother. You're going to be woeful sorry, you incontinent bull's pizzle!"

"Oh yeh! We'll see about that, sonny boy!" said Willie G., suddenly very angry again also.

"Perrr-dition and dammm-nation!" said Frank J., stumbling to the door and bumping into the inoffensive mass of Leslie Chenevix Purefoy on the way. "Out of me light, you big-eared Pommy bastard!" And he tottered out onto Abbey Street.

Leslie Chenevix Purefoy struck a pose adapted from Herbert Beerbohm Tree in the sinister role of Svengali. "What," he asked Willie J. Fay, "was that all about?"

"Ah, feck off, you!" suggested Fay, retrieving his hat from the sawdust and truculently following his brother into the street.

"A strange country," Purefoy noted, turning to the jakes. "I shall shed a tear for its inhabitants."

"Ah," called Gussie after him, "You wouldn't want to be minding ayther Frank nor Willie, Mr. Purefoy."

"Indeed?" queried Purefoy, arresting his progress.

"Ah, no," said Gussie. "It was probably all over some disagreement."

"Augustus," said Purefoy in all sincerity, "you astonish me."

"Yeh," said Gussie, and then noted the prepossessing form of his colleague Mr. Arthur Sinclair, who was sitting at a nearby table and opening his *Evening Mail* to scrutinize the early racing returns. "What was that about with Frank and Willie, Mac?"

146

Arthur Sinclair took a swig from his ball of malt and sloshed it about in his big fat mouth before making a reply. "Ah, a bit of a cafuffle about Pierre Corneille. I wasn't giving it me full attention." He returned to his perusal of the budget of equine intelligence, murmuring, "Drummer Boy let me down at Newmarket."

"Do you," said Purefoy, "mean to intimate that what we have just witnessed was the result of a discussion on poetry? I can't believe it."

"Oh," said Gussie, nodding sagely, "we have our traditions, the bards and all, ya know. The hedge schools."

"True," said Arthur Sinclair abstractly, "we're a volatile race."

"Now more than ever," said Purefoy, taking himself off, "must I shed that tear. Augustus, will you do the honours?"

Gussie dutifully approached the bar, but had difficulty claiming the attention of the industrious Murty, who lent his ear to the loudest shout. So embarrassed by his ineffectuality did Gussie become that Arthur Sinclair took pity on him. "What's your call?"

"A pint apiece for meself and Mr. Purefoy," replied Gussie.

"You're standing for that cadger, are ya?"

"Hunh?" said Gussie innocently.

"Ay, Murty," Arthur Sinclair bellowed, "Murty, oul' son! Whenever yer ready."

Murty danced to attendance. "What'll it be, Mr. Sinclair, sir?"

"Two pints with a good head. Eh, might as well make it three."

"Sartinly, Mr. Sinclair! Sartinly!"

Gussie marvelled and pulled out a chair. "Jay, I've got to hand it t'ya, Mac. More style nor the Lord of Lucan."

Arthur Sinclair shifted his beefy legs in their constricting trousers. "Nothing to it. All you need is a magnetic personality. But listen to me, Gussie. If I was you, I'd watch that Hoorfoy."

Puzzlement creased Gussie's face. "Mr. Purefoy?"

"One bad bit of goods. And also there's some very peculiar things going on around the theatre ever since he showed up."

At that moment, Purefoy returned, reflecting as he sank gracefully into a chair, "One would require Wellington boots in that unspeakable place."

"There's some," said Arthur Sinclair, "as just require boots." And with that enigmatic utterance, he drained his tumbler, collected his paper, and retired to the bar to conclude his researches.

"Most peculiar fellow," said Purefoy.

"Eh. . . ," said Gussie, scratching his head in perplexity.

"Ah!" said Purefoy, noting the approach of their pints.

As W.J. Lawrence made his way angrily into Great Brunswick Street, his attention was arrested by the lighted windows of Charles W. Harrison and Sons, sculptors and monumental masons. He halted abruptly. Ah, the tombstones on display had been changed for the first time since before Christmas!

As usual, the contemplation of well-designed and executed grave-markers provided its pleasures. Fancy was the fungus of the intellect; nevertheless, W.J. Lawrence did relish the picking out of tombstones for those of his acquaintance who deserved them. A rather large number.

A monument for Yeats, now, had an unfailing fascination. Perhaps something symbolic. The Romans were given to adorning their churches with statues of the Virgin, crushing the head of a serpent. Perhaps something along the lines of the poetic muse, tastefully adorned in a clinging Grecian gown, crushing a foot as massive as that of Thomasina McFitz onto the head of the serpent Yeats. His eyes popping, his cheeks hideously bulging, his mouth slobbering.

And some appropriate inscription would be needed. Perhaps:

BENEATH THIS STONE MISERABLY ROTS
THE MOULDERING BONES OF
W.B. YEATS
WHOSE DARK SPIRIT GROANS
IN UNSPEAKABLE TORMENTS!

"Despicable termites?" queried a voice behind his thin right shoulder.

He turned to observe Joseph Holloway regarding him curiously.

Not for the first time did W.J. Lawrence squelch a private regret that he and Joseph Holloway were bosom friends. The architect afforded piquant possibilities for graveyard inscriptions.

"A strange observation," said Joseph Holloway, fractionally adjusting his bowler hat so that it sat precisely upon the middle of his fat head. "Are you in good form, Lawrence?"

"Of course, I am!" snarled W.J. Lawrence, waving a balled fist dangerously.

A large, passing policeman, usually on duty at the bottom of Grafton

Street, roused himself from pleasant thoughts of Mary Makebelieve, and stared suspiciously at W.J. Lawrence. "Here now, here now!" he said sternly. "Don't be accosting that inoffensive man!"

"What?" said W.J. Lawrence, in outraged dignity.

Young Gypo Nolan, his knobby forehead contorted by the unaccustomed activity of thought, paused, hoping for free entertainment. Maybe a nice dust-up that he could wade into. His hammy hands clenched and unclenched in an inchoate desire to smash somebody, anybody.

"It's nothing, constable, nothing at all," said Joseph Holloway, securing his friend by the arm and hurrying him off down the street.

"Hmm," said the policeman, "you see some quare ones."

"Ughh," said young Gypo Nolan disconsolately.

"Well, I've just come from confession," said Joseph Holloway.

"Oh?" said W.J. Lawrence coldly. "Is that so?"

Joseph Holloway allowed a satisfied smile to appear beneath his drooping moustache. "I feel as if a great weight has been lifted from me."

"Here lies Joseph Holloway," thought his friend, "an ignorant Southern bigot."

Across the street, Padraic Pearse, schoolmaster and Gaelic Leaguer, paused briefly to survey his natal home, and thus did not note Joseph Holloway's wave.

"Yes," said Joseph Holloway smugly, "I've just been shriven. And I lit a penny candle at the shrine of Saint Francis of Assissi on your behalf."

Two strong hands, with iron fingers, could be placed just above his friend's wing collar, W.J. Lawrence reflected. Then they could slowly press and squeeze and. . . .

"Going into town are you?" asked Joseph Holloway. "I suppose you'll look into the Abbey. Things I believe have calmed down since early in the week."

"Yes, Yeats' uniformed thugs have squelched any hope of honest protest. But things will be different on Monday."

"Ah," said Joseph Holloway, sucking the right end of his drooping moustache. "The debate."

"I'll see you there."

"Ah, well, eh," said Joseph Holloway uncomfortably. "Do you think it is liable to be heated?"

"Red hot!" snapped W.J. Lawrence with relish.

"Ah, well, ah, on Monday night it is my custom to attend the meetings of the National Literary Society."

"What!" said W.J. Lawrence in astonishment. "And miss Yeats' discomfiture! His humiliation!" And he ground his teeth in delight. "Oh, it will be memorable."

"Evening," said a citizen emerging from D'Olier Street and touching the brim of his hat deferentially.

"Good evening," said Joseph Holloway.

"Who's that?" said W.J. Lawrence. "I see him all over the city."

"Oh, that's, ah. . . I can never remember his name. Blazes Boylan calls him the celebrated Hebernian. Witty, eh? Hebernian!"

W.J. Lawrence contemplated the joys of strangulation.

In the dark laneway behind the theatre, Leslie Chenevix Purefoy efficiently went through the pockets of his spiflicated companion. Eightpence. Only a miserable eightpence.

Lady Gregory's unmistakable lisp approached from the corner.

Quickly he entered the stage door, making sure to leave it ajar so that the light would catch the supine Gussie very nicely.

Sunday, February 3

The room seemed crowded by the presence of his mother and the doctor, both looking down upon him in the bed. His mother had letters for him in her hand. Letters to-day? Why had she not given them to him yesterday? But yesterday was something of a blur.

"'Flu?" his mother questioned. "You're sure it's just 'flu?"

He wished she would not detain the doctor. There might be a letter from Molly.

Still, he managed a smile. "Isn't 'flu enough, mother?"

Anxious to be away, the doctor fiddled with his stethoscope. "A few days' rest should see him right, Mrs. Synge."

"Well, that is a relief," she said. "One never knows what he'll pick up from those people."

He smiled for the doctor's benefit. "Mother's afraid I might have caught Catholicism."

"Or been poisoned!" his mother said.

"Poisoned?" said the doctor with a nervous little laugh.

"They'd poison us all!" said Mrs. Synge.

"Umm," said the doctor.

"Well, come along," she said peremptorily, deciding that the doctor was as much a fool as his father, the old doctor, had been. "I will see you to the door."

As she led the way down the stairs, she decided to unburden herself a bit. "I begged him not to go out on Friday. But, of course, he wouldn't listen to me. I think really you should tell him to be more cautious. He went to Bray, of all places!"

He shook his head, bemused as he listened to their voices fade away. Bray, of all places. He should have chosen malaria-infested Calcutta.

Eagerly he took up the letters.

No, none from her.

Oh, why doesn't she write? Even just a line!

He glanced through a letter from little Colum. Courteous but firm. Colum did not like *The Playboy*, and had written to tell him so. No one was remaining neutral. If gentle little Colum could be almost brusque, some hothead like that Lawrence fellow must be foaming at the mouth.

Augusta Gregory gave the steaming contents of the tumbler a vigorous stir and, tapping the spoon against the rim of the glass, said, "Here, drink this!"

W.B. Yeats was standing, his back to her, in the window embrasure of the hotel sitting room. Slowly he raised his right hand above his head and murmured, "As the congregation genuflects before the altar, so must the audience immolate itself before the drama!" He shook his raised hand emphatically.

Strolling along Nassau Street, Joseph Holloway was not unnaturally surprised, but waved back. Stiffly.

Lady Gregory wondered how best to engage Willie's attention. She never liked to intrude on these moments, but his throat was sore. She would try her usual ploy — approach closely and wait till he accidentally struck her with one of his gestures. With a caution born of experience, she took off her glasses, and insinuated herself between the poet and the window.

"The stage, we must always remember, is an altar! The dramatist, we must always remember, is its high priest!" And he vigorously slapped Lady Gregory in the face.

"Jaysus! Wouldja look at that!" cried Frank Walker, pausing in the middle of Nassau Street. "He's after batin' her."

"For your throat," said Lady Gregory, smiling through a tear and profferring the steaming glass.

"Smells lethal," he demurred, retreating backwards into the room.

"Lemon juice, honey, sugar, hot water and cloves. It will be good for your poor throat."

"Ah," said the placated poet, accepting the glass and sipping. "My goodness, my throat feels better already." And he put the drained glass down on the table that had elephant tusks for legs.

"To-morrow night will be arduous for you," she said. "And dangerous for us."

"Arduous for me? Dangerous for me? Nonsense, I am quite looking forward to it. We may defeat the mob once and for all, and see the beginnings of a party of the intellect in the arts and in the nation."

Lady Gregory considered making a caustic comment about the

inclusion of Miss Gonne in such a party. Instead she said, "Our enemies are many. Even some who were our friends — ."

"A theatre," he interrupted, "must be a temple, a cathedral of art. If a few shamrocks should fall off the facade in the scuffle — ."

"Well, it's not merely the Gaels," hesitated Lady Gregory. "There's something else at work. Some spirit of mischief around the theatre lately."

But W.B. Yeats had again drifted back to the window embrasure. "An audience," he intoned, raising his right hand in an unconscious imitation of Grattan, "must be taught, must if necessary be whipped!"

Leaning against the wall of Trinity College to remove a pebble from his shoe, W. J. Lawrence glowered at the poet's salutation. "Wait till to-morrow night, you hypocritical southern swine," he snarled.

"Eek" cried Christina McFitz, who was passing by on an errand for dear Thomasina. "Eek!" And she scampered on.

> Dear Synge,
>
> I am grieved that you spurned my well-intentioned offer of assistance with *The Playboy*. I had thought that some few bits might be salvaged. On reflection, however, I was probably optimistic.
>
> > Yours,
> > George Moore.

Synge tossed the letter onto the floor, and selected another.

The handwriting was unfamiliar. He'd received some odd letters over the past week. Much less restrained than George Moore's. Some odious ones too, full of threat and venom.

> Dear Mr. John Synge,
>
> I was surprised that Molly was still a virgin. With your sensitivity to words, you'll notice I use the past tense.
>
> What a responsive little creature she can be — given, that is, something big to respond to.
>
> Who am I?
>
> Well, that scarcely matters. You'll know me easily enough from the satiated smile on my face.
>
> > Yours (or should I say hers?),
> > A REAL MAN

A lump came to his throat.

Padraic Colum, shivering under the portico of the Seaman's Mission, came down the steps to stand in front of them.

"Ah, Mr. Colum," said Lady Gregory. "How nice to see you."

W.B. Yeats stared about with myopic hauteur. "To see who?"

"Padraic Colum," the little poet said with a rare edge to his voice.

"Oh," said Yeats sadly.

"May we expect you at de debate to-morrow?" Lady Gregory said with a warm smile.

"No," said Padraic Colum. "I have a rehearsal."

"What on earth of?" W.B. Yeats inquired vaguely of a passing seagull.

"I have been waiting to see you, Lady Gregory," Padraic Colum said.

She put up her umbrella and held it over Yeats. "Come into de theatre out of the wet."

He shook his head. "I wanted to thank you for your offer to pay my father's fine. We have paid it."

"Oh!" she cried in concern. "But forty shillings. It's so much." She paused in embarrassment. "It was all a derrible mistake."

"Isn't it raining?" asked Yeats.

Padraic Colum gave him a long, hard look. Then he turned up his coat collar and walked stiffly off.

She followed him with her eyes. "Oh, dear me. Dere was almost hatred in his look."

"Really?" said Yeats. "Perhaps we should take another glance at that last script of his."

Was he dreaming? Or daydreaming? Or remembering?

They came out of the teashop, the only one open on the front to-day, and drifted back to the railings. The waves were rolling in now, and low, dark clouds heavy with rain scudded across the sky. She saw the big wave coming and tugged at his sleeve.

"Come back, Johnny. We'll be drenched."

His fingers tightened stubbornly around the railing, and he shook his head. For a moment she looked like scampering away, but then she placed one hand over his and stood beside him.

The wave struck the seawall, shuddering it so that they were unsure of their footing. They stood an instant, rigid, frozen against the shock. Great white masses of spumy water spun high into the air, blotting out the grey light, to fall suddenly in a heavy cascade upon them both.

He laughed unexpectedly, being suddenly thrilled, feeling a wild exhilaration out of what seemed to be a sudden, strange understanding of the sea.

He turned to her, beads of water glistening in his moustache, and touched her hat. "Your pigeon is soaked."

She smiled up at him. "It's a wren," she said.

He leaned heavily on the railings and gazed out at the whitecaps with their broken crests spuming in the wind. "I'm glad that you came."

She leaned her head onto his shoulder. As always, he glanced around to see if they were observed.

She sighed. "There's no one else out walking to-day."

Disturbed by her tone, he looked down at her.

"Come on, my old tramp," she said. "Let's walk along the shore."

"Your pigeon will get his feathers wet."

"Everything has to take its chances. Mind your step coming down."

He drew back. "It'll be harder going on the stones."

"When hasn't it been?" she said, and walked away.

"Come back!"

He peered after her. But there was no one there now. No one at all. Abruptly he sat up in the bed, sweat pouring down his face.

At her desk in the corner, Susan L. Mitchell was scribbling on her pad:

> There once was a poet called Colum
> Whose manner was meek, mild and solemn,
> But when incensed by Yeats
> His loves turned to hates,
> And he wanted to pummel and maul 'im.

Hmm? Should it rather be, "But when incensed by Willie / His reaction was silly"?

"Will we see you at Garville Avenue to-night, Padraic?" she heard AE ask.

"I hardly think hatred," Padraic Colum mused outloud. "I should be sorry if it were hatred."

"Hatred?" said AE, puzzled. "Well now, we do not live in an ideal world, of course." From out of the corner of his eye he caught the little sylph sitting on top of the bookcase. She blew him a kiss. "Entirely ideal," he amended. "And if you want to make your way in it, you must be prepared to give as good as you get. Is the tea drawn, Susan?"

Susan L. Mitchell got up to look. "Yes." And then she added a propos of something on her mind, "Of course, W. B. isn't above the odd bit of a pose, you know."

"Give as much as you get," Colum repeated. He turned to Susan Mitchell. "But he wasn't posing. His eyes were. . . alight."

"A light," said AE, patting his pockets. "You wouldn't have a match, would you?"

"I don't smoke," said Padraic Colum.

Or fume either, thought Susan L. Mitchell.

There was a French language magazine lying open on AE's desk, and from it he tore a spill for his pipe.

"Oh, really, AE," said Susan Mitchell. "That was Synge's review of your poems."

AE shrugged. "Echoing his master's voice, he doesn't think my poetry has much merit."

"Sugar?" said Susan Mitchell, turning back to Colum. "One teaspoon? Two? Three?"

"Hmm?" said Padraic Colum, gazing blankly at her spooning sugar into his cup. Then he started and said, "I think I'll chance a bit of lemon. As an experiment."

She took the cup and put it on AE's desk. "Here, AE, your tea."

"Emm," said AE, inserting the reflections of J. M. Synge between the coals. When it caught, the sylph mischievously fluttered down and blew it out. "Now stop that," whispered AE.

"What," pondered Padraic Colum, leafing unseeingly through a much underlined copy of *Esoteric Buddhism*, "would a sour taste be like? — Eh, give me lots of lemon."

She did, and then she retrieved the slightly charred considerations of J.M. Synge from AE's paw and lit them.

The sylph retired to the bookcase and huffily sat down on a copy of *Isis Unveiled*.

"Careful," cautioned Susan Mitchell, "you don't burn your beard. Puff now, puff."

"Yes!" exclaimed Padraic Colum. "Sometimes you do have to puff yourself." He raised his cup and sipped. "Very bracing! Will you go to the debate to-morrow, AE?"

"Emm, yes," said AE from a cloud of smoke. "But I'll sit in the balcony."

"Where the enemies of the theatre sit?" asked Padraic Colum.

"No," said AE, "It's the estranged who sit in the balcony. The enemies sit in the pit."

"The pit!" cried Padraic Colum. He slammed down his teacup, strode to the door, and his brisk footsteps clicked off down the hall.

"Emm," AE presently rumbled, "just what was all that young Padraic was saying?"

"He may finally," said Susan Mitchell, "be starting to smoulder."

Monday, February 4: I

Leslie Chenevix Purefoy had made the pleasant discovery that visitors to the Guinness Brewery were treated to free samples. His visits to that enterprising establishment had become so frequent, however, that he thought it wise to vary his costume. In his present cassock and Roman collar, temporarily borrowed from the Abbey Wardrobe, he had just consumed six pints.

Now, at ease with the world, he ambled down Thomas Street in the pale sunlight. He must purchase the ingredients for a late lunch on his way back to the theatre. The three shillings he had "borrowed" from Frank Fay should see him with a fillet of beefsteak, a crusty loaf, a dollop of salty butter, a pungent trio of Spanish onions and a thrupenny bottle of the excellent Kandee sauce, a brother of which he had recently extracted from the overcoat pocket of Mr. Arthur Sinclair.

Because of the evening's debate, or whatever it was supposed to be — the mind boggled at the combative Celts engaging in anything so coherent as a polite exchange of points of view — he should have the Greenroom to himself, and would be able at leisure and in comfort to prepare his repast.

Infinitely preferable to sitting at the Captain's table, being spittle-spotted in company with the various meek clerks and seedy counter-hoppers. Not to mention the Captain's mummified lady and her levee of terrible terriers.

The lady Attracta's cross-eyed stare made one uncertain of where exactly one should be, but someplace else seemed always preferable. No, today he would have to make no manful attempt to eat her "shepherd's pie," Monday's inevitable luncheon abomination. In his last week's monastic portion, he had actually come upon two feathers. "I must spur my dull revenge," he remarked out loud.

The deserted Greenroom would give him opportunity to compose his thoughts for his evening's entertainment. And he was not thinking of the aesthetic debate advertised by the theatre's directors (sold out, incidentally, but at half price).

There would be much confusion to-night. What better time for his master coup? A stroke more deadly than all that had gone before! "The worst is death," quoth Richard II, "and death will have his day."

Death.

Slightly awe-stricken at the thought which had come so easily to mind, he resolutely put the matter away from him. For the moment. Until his head had cleared.

There was a nice bit of heat in the pale February sun. Pleasant, and Dublin, he was finding, was not entirely unpleasant either. Filthy, of course. Squalid. Provincial and pretentious. But not unlovely.

Food was definitely required. Bread before beauty.

His muddled brain did not instantly respond to the call of reason, for the thought of beauty brought irresistibly to mind the warming vision of the younger Miss Allgood. Yes, more should be attempted there. The letter to Synge was but the opening wedge.

The door to Arthur Griffith's office banged open, and a great draught blew a blizzard of paper all about the room.

Frantically, he beat down the swirling sheets of paper. The door banged shut.

"Arthur, what the hell is this I hear?" Gogarty stood in the centre of the office, looking very angry indeed.

"Well?" Gogarty demanded.

Griffith retrieved a paper from under his desk. The new effusion from Miss Twigg. He sighed.

"Oliver, look at my papers — the morning's work."

"I'm interested in to-night's work."

"I don't know anything about to-night. Oh, look at my office."

"It will not do, Arthur!"

"I haven't the foggiest notion what you're talking about." Griffith sat down and sorted out those papers within reach. He put Miss Twigg on the bottom.

"Arthur!" Gogarty bent close. "It won't do!"

Griffith regarded him calmly, "I didn't arrange it."

"But you can stop it!"

Griffith shruged. "I haven't got that much authority."

"Yeats has offered a fair and free discussion. Anybody can speak up. Every point of view can be heard."

"Above the hissing and boohing?"

"I've heard of stink bombs. And violence."

"In that case, Oliver, I should steer clear of the place."

"For God's sake, man! Yeats is right. A free discussion of the issues. Isn't that what a democratic society is all about?"

"Ideally. Oh, I don't hold your friend Synge all that responsible, but Yeats knew what to expect. Inside that foppish exterior, our poet has a finely calculating mind. He wants a row. I have no patience with the man. He's egotistic, he's perverse, and he's totally irresponsible. A national drama, indeed! A national drama must mould opinion against England and prepare for the day of —. Hmm, I'm making a speech."

"Go to the theatre to-night and make it. That's what a free country is about."

"There's freedom and there's freedom."

"By hell, no! Freedom is absolute. You don't reserve it for your own view."

Griffith arose and went around the room picking up his papers.

"Listen, my friend," said Gogarty. "What kind of a state will there be when, and if, you come to power? Will you impose a censorship of books and plays you don't like?"

"A case might be made for that."

"I shouldn't like to live here then."

Griffith replaced the last of his papers tidily on his desk. "I should miss you."

"Arthur, stop this thing to-night."

Griffith slowly shook his head. "I cannot do that. Yeats must be taught a lesson."

Leslie Chenevix Purefoy, a little gaseous after his satisfying lunch, undid the button of his waistband through a hole in his overcoat pocket. Standing in the vestibule of the theatre, he congratulated himself. They were going to debate, were they? Well, he would give them something to debate about.

But now there was the minor problem of diversion for the dreary hours till it was time to put the master plan into effect. Surely there was some company which, with the price of a drink, he could edify with a few circumspect accounts of his past exploits? Alas, he had but a mere tuppence left after the lunch. Perhaps providence would present him with a sheep to be shorn.

At just that moment, Gussie Gaffney entered from Marlborough Street.

"Ah!" cried Purefoy.

"Eh, Mr. Purefoy," said Gussie, uneasily wondering just what his colleague had to do with dumping him in the laneway. Oh, Lady Gregory gave him down the banks about that.

"Augustus!" Purefoy beamed. "I was so worried about you. Where did you disappear to on Saturday evening? I thought you looked a bit under the weather."

"Eh, no. . . just sleepy."

"Good, good! I looked all over for you."

"Eh," said Gussie, changing the subject, "didja get in touch with Mr. Synge all right?"

"I? Synge?" Purefoy blinked twice in an accomplished simulation of peasant bafflement, copied from Gussie's ordinary stage expression.

Gussie blinked twice also.

"Well," Purefoy continued, "such minds as ours — yours, dear boy, and mine — do sometimes fail to take cognisance of the minute and mundane. *N'est-ce pas?*"

"Ah, yer dead right there, Mr. Purefoy. Bang on."

Purefoy stroked Gussie's young, broad shoulder with his long, tapering fingers. "By the by, my sincere congratulations on the light and shade of your peasant portrayal during the last exciting week. I am delighted by how you followed my advice."

"Well, I only done me best. But I amn't too sure Willie Fay liked it all that much. He said if he caught me spitting on the stage again, I would have to scrub it down."

"Fay!" sniffed Purefoy, tossing his head. "A pipsqueak of minor talent and a popinjay of major jealousy, Augustus. Now I know for certain that Lady Gregory has her eye on you."

"Ah, she does, begod," said Gussie uncomfortably.

"And as a reward for your being an apt pupil, I shall allow you to stand me a pint."

"Eh, I dunno, Mr. Purefoy. I'm kinda off the drink."

"Perhaps," said Leslie Chenevix Purefoy, taking him firmly by the arm and steering him to the door, "even two pints!"

"Well!" said Sally Allgood, standing just inside the door of the smoky Greenroom, her arms straight down by her sides from the weight of the shopping bags. "Cast an eye on that!"

"Disgusting!" agreed Molly, standing behind her, similarly laden.

After a sisterly couple of hours going about the shops, the sisters were really parched for a cup of tea.

"Who's done this?" barked Sally in disbelief at the state of the Greenroom.

"Some pig, by the looks of it," said Molly. "Jacobs! The arse is burning out of the pan!" Molly dashed to the glowing stove and snatched up the prop frying pan and clattered it down on the fender.

The table was littered with onion peels and pieces of bread; there were bloodied wrapping papers and an upset sugar bowl; and milk and tea were slopped everywhere. There was a used mug and a plate with bits of yellow fat congealed in a sea of grease.

"Yes, some pig!" said Molly, freeing a lump of trodden bread from the spike of her heel.

"Sinclair!" accused Sally, holding up an empty bottle of Kandee sauce. "He swims in the stuff."

"No worse than that cologne," said Molly.

"Maybe we should clean up," said Sally.

"Are you daft?" Molly banged on the window with the heel of her hand and got it open.

"But there'll be all sorts of toff-tiffy people in here to-night. And, anyway, I'd never enjoy a sup of tea amid this dirt."

Her coat off, her blouse sleeves rolled back, but her bonnet still secure upon her head, Sally set about putting the room to rights.

Molly smiled. Wasn't it just like Sally, all this maternal fussing? Would she herself feel like that when she and Johnny — ? Cross that bridge when you come to it. The first problem was to get him to the bloody bridge. She touched the crumpled telegram in her overcoat pocket. Well, why hadn't he said he had been sick? Oh, he never looked after himself. But he could have wired. Yes, he could have. And she would be a little distant with him at first. No, she wouldn't. Yes, she would.

"You can close that window now," Sally said, "it's only perishing in here."

Molly lit a cigarette and watched her sister swabbing off the table.

Then she fished in her scallop-shaped holdall for that letter. She hesitated and then said, "I don't think I showed you this."

Sally looked. "Oh! Somebody's sending them to you too."

"You've had one?"

Disturbed, Sally nodded. "Three. And the other night didn't Gussie Gaffney give me that pillowcase all stuffed with filthy, smelly clothes. Men's clothes."

"You think it's Gussie who's been playing the bold prankster around here?"

"Gussie?" said Sally, beginning to sweep the floor. "He's too innocent."

"Whoever it is," said Molly grimly, "better watch out. If I find who's doing it, his wife's wedding present will be in an awful lot of danger!"

"Maybe it's not a he."

Molly thought. "Well, it's not Brigit. She's still in awe of her lord and master, Mr. Willie Fay, to have anything else on what passes for her mind. . . . One of the young ones maybe. I saw that May Craig making up to J — to Synge last week. A gawky snip like that!"

Sally flung the broom into the corner. "Why does he always have to be dragged into it? We got along grand all day without a mention of him! And all the trouble last week — that was his fault, but where was he? He left us to face it."

"He's going to be here to-night."

"Well, isn't that grand!" Sally dumped the dishes in the sink and ran some water.

"It's not easy for Johnny and me right now," said Molly, determinedly blinking back tears. "You might at least try to understand. The row about the play, our own troubles, and now this filthy letter —." She caught her breath. Suppose Johnny had got a letter too.

"Oh, I understand perfectly!" said Sally. "He thinks he's too good for you."

"He doesn't! He's been sick. He's had the 'flu."

"I won't see you throw yourself away on the likes of him!" cried Sally. "I won't, I say! I will not! I tell you plainly I'll do anything to stop it!"

W.J. Lawrence passed the portico of Lady Morgan's house and crossed over, head bowed against the wind sweeping down Kildare

Street. As he turned in at the National Library, he noticed the well-swathed George Moore ambling in his direction.

Another of the literary heathens, he sniffed, and made for the sanctuary of the library. The cold, columned vestibule was scarcely warmer than the outside. Lyster, the Quaker librarian, came out of his office, rubbing mittened hands together, and disappeared downstairs to the jakes.

W.J. Lawrence consulted the clock on the wall. A good two hours he could put in before a quick bite and then the theatre. With relish, he rehearsed his opening remarks as he climbed the stairs, past the windows of the mad-looking Michaelangelo and the wall-eyed Leonardo. Despite a distinctly similar expression, W.J. Lawrence did not give them the time of day, but made his way up to the great reading room. As he passed through the turnstile and surveyed the scholars hunched over their desks, a change came over W.J. Lawrence's own expression. A calmness came into his eyes. His features seemed almost to soften.

Happily he went to the counter and made out his docket.

Mr. George Moore, despite the savage wind, paused to regard the stone monkeys playing billiards on the side of the Kildare Street Club. An apt advertisement for membership. But hold — was there not a resemblance to Yeats in the monkey on the left? A low cunning. Extraordinary he had never noticed it before. Had the afternoon not been so frigid, George Moore could have found a good deal of charm in several moments of contemplation.

As it was, he hastened inside, doffed his hat, his muffler, his gloves and his coat with the astrakhan collar, and made his way to the library. Ah, there he was, curled up as usual in his usual chair by the fire, mouth as usual open and emitting rhythmic honks, a copy of *The Irish Times* fluttering on his chest.

"Edward! Wake up!"

"Not asleep. Resting my eyes."

"Edward, wake up instantly. I require your attention."

Reluctantly, Edward Martyn's eyes opened. "Oh, it's you, George. Kindly go away."

"No. I want to talk to you."

"I am busy."

"Bah!" said George Moore, drawing up a chair. "We are going to the theatre to-night."

"What's on?"

"Nothing is on. To-night is — ."

"Just like you, George. Nothing is on. You get more and more absurd."

George Moore resisted an impulse to kick his friend in the shin. "Yeats is having his debate to-night."

"Oh heavens, Moore, we've both heard Yeats. Much too often, in my opinion." And Edward Martyn closed his eyes to rest them some more.

"Edward, this is an irresistible opportunity to show that charlatan up. You shall rise and — Edward, you shall rise!" This time George Moore did not resist the impulse to kick his cousin in the shin.

"Ouch! Whatever are you doing, Moore! I shall summon the porter."

George Moore extracted several typewritten sheets from his inside pocket. "Here, Edward, are some trenchant remarks that I have jotted down for you."

"I don't want them."

"In this paper, I expose in devastating detail how Yeats, by egotism, perversity and lamentable incompetence destroyed the Irish Literary Theatre!"

"I think," said Edward Martyn, "it is time for tea. George, do you see the — ?"

"When you read this paper to-night, it will crush him. His reputation will be in flitters. His name anathema to true sons of the Gael."

"You read it."

"Edward, dear Edward! Is this the thanks I get for my time and effort? Is this — ?"

"Hello there! May I order tea. For one!"

"I am not taking no for an answer, Edward. And you know how determined I can be. Mr. Martyn will have tea for two!"

The long disused attic laboratory of Oscar Cornelius McFitz, B.A., P.L.G. (deceased) was stale and musty at the best of times. Now it was permeated by strange smells and suffocating fumes. A cloud of green vapour bubbled from a retort, and Christina McFitz huddled by the door, waving her dainty hanky to ward off the noisome odours.

"Oh, oh, oh," she whimpered. "I wish you wouldn't do that, sister. You remember all the trouble dear father had with his explosions."

"Boil and bubble," gloated her absorbed sister, lighting the bunsen burner. "Boil and bubble!"

There was a letter on the mat inside the door. Mechanically Oliver Gogarty tore it open and read:

> Dear Noll,
>   I cannot stop busybodies and bigots and madmen, but there will be no organized disturbance to-night. We might meet at the Bailey for lunch to-morrow.
>   Art O Griofa

A smile broke over Oliver Gogarty's face. "A Roland for an Oliver," he murmured, pulling on his overcoat.

In the office of the Abbey Theatre, W.B. Yeats stood some distance from a pocket mirror that was propped against an unopened package addressed to the theatre in the tidy handwriting of Mr. G. Bernard Shaw and doubtless containing several more dramatic works by that prolix worthy. They must, reflected W.B. Yeats, be acknowledged one of these days. Perhaps even opened.

W.B. Yeats dismissed such mundanities from his mind. There was no time to lose. Soon he must go down onto the stage and chastise the unruly mob. But still it would not come right. Most vexing. It had to seem natural, unarranged, without artifice, with an undulant flow. As with the best poetry, so too with his lock of raven hair.

Could one describe AE's poetry as uncombed?

Augusta Gregory entered the office and saw his predicament. "Tut, let me do dat."

"Umm," he said, bending toward her. "Such a bother, vanity. My one fault, perhaps."

"Now how could it be a fault?" she said primly, as she primped and poked. "Dere. But be careful how you move your head."

"That's difficult. My first significant gesture is to be an intractable toss of the head. Something plain yet arrogant, to set the tone. Eh, have copies of my impromptu remarks been delivered to the newspapers?"

"Henderson's gone with dem."

"Good. One fears misquotation from those cretins, the journalists. Eh, did you know that even in prose one can get the effect of a caesura?"

"Hail, Caesar," she thought of saying, but turned away to disguise her smile. "By de semi-colon?" she said instead.

Inspecting himself in the mirror, he replied with a mild hauteur, "I was speaking of vowels, not bowels."

"I think," she sighed, "it is more probably howls we shall be concerned with to-night. Ones of execration."

"Ah yes," he said, rubbing his hands gleefully. "I shrink from the encounter."

She poked into her bag. "I've had a wire from Payne."

"Pain ever forever — where did I hear that lately?"

"B. Iden Payne," she explained. "He's back for de moment touring with his company in de south. He wishes us luck."

"Luck," said Yeats, "will have very little to do with it." He pocketed the mirror, opened the office door a crack and listened to the raucous invective from the vestibule and auditorium.

"In Swift's time," he mused, "we had the stocks, the gallows. . . disembowelment. . . ."

"De crowd seems in an ugly mood," she said unhappily. "Don't excite dem."

He turned, surprised. "When," he protested, "have I ever been anything but diplomatic?"

From where he sat in the Greenroom, Leslie Chenevix Purefoy could hear the audience pouring in for the debate. Here, the long table was already set with the heavy cups and saucers. But he would not be taking tea. Indeed, no!

Sally Allgood entered briskly, followed by Mrs. Mulcaster limping after her and burdened with two massive kettles. "Put them down there," she said.

Mrs. Mulcaster thumped the tea kettles down. "There! I hope that's to yer sub-Ladyship's satisfaction. Now I have me own duties to attend to in the vestibule." And Mrs. Mulcaster limped righteously off.

"That woman!" Sally snorted, casting her eye around for another target for her wrath.

"Purefoy, shift yourself!"

"Perhaps I might be of some slight service, dear lady?" inquired Purefoy at his most humble.

"Hmmpp!" she grunted and commenced re-arranging plates, cups and saucers more to her satisfaction.

"Dear lady," he said courteously rising, "it pains me to see you so active whilst I am so idle. How may I assist?"

"By taking yourself out of here!"

"Dear lady, dear lady, if I have unwittingly offended, I apologise abjectly." He had once done a highly admired Uriah Heep at Bromley.

"Oh, all right," she said truculently. "Spread this butter on that bread."

"Dear lady, you have filled my heart with joy! I quiver with gratitude."

"Don't spread it on too thick."

"Eh?"

"The butter," she said wryly.

"Certainly not, certainly not!" he said, reassured. He hung up his topcoat and felt its pocket as he did so. Yes, his package was safe.

His head throbbing, he turned into the laneway. At the stagedoor he stopped and put his hand out against the wall for support. His legs weakened under him.

"Misther Synge," came a voice behind him. "Misther Synge, are ya all right?"

"Wha — ? Oh, it's you, Gaffney. Would you open the door?"

"Jay, Misther Synge, should you be out?"

"Just open the door."

Gussie opened the door, and Synge allowed him to take his arm and help him in.

"Will I find Lady Gregory for you, or — or — Miss Allgood?"

With an effort, Synge shook his head and smiled. "No, no. But — thank you, Gaffney."

Gussie looked at him uncertainly.

From the stage came the vigorous, resonant voice of W.B. Yeats.

It had started.

Monday, February 4: II

"I would never like," cried W.B. Yeats, sweeping back the raven lock from his ivory brow, "to set plays before a theatrical audience that was not free to approve or disapprove."

WIDESPREAD GROANS AND A GRUFF CRY FROM THE PIT OF "WHAT ABOUT THE POLICE?"

"Disapprove even very loudly, for there is no dramatist that does not desire a live audience," added the poet with a jovial smile that had cost him some practice. Stupid facial expression really.

LAUGHTER, CHEERS AND HISSES.

"But!" [A SOLEMNLY IMPRESSIVE FIVE SECOND PAUSE.] "We had to face something quite different from reasonable expression of dissent."

"OH!"

"On Tuesday, and on Monday nights, it was not possible to hear six consecutive lines of the play!"

"QUITE RIGHT!"

"This deafening outcry was not raised by the whole theatre!" [STERN PAUSE.] "But almost entirely by a section of the pit."

"NO! NO!"

"It was an attempt to prevent the play from being heard and judged!"

CHEERS AND CRIES OF "QUITE RIGHT!"

Doctor Sigerson completed his introductory remarks to polite applause from the middle-aged ladies, weedy enthusiasts and eccentric old gentlemen who comprised the usual attendance at the National Literary Society's Monday evenings.

But what on earth had he said, pondered Joseph Holloway. And who was the speaker who now so unctuously arose, polished his spectacles and approached the podium clutching a formidable sheaf of notes? Who was he? And what was he on about? Faeries? No, that was last week. Dolmens? Ogham writing?

So difficult to concentrate, knowing the scenes that were even now being played out at the Abbey. Historic scenes that required an intelligent, unbiased, devoutly Catholic reporter. Oh, what a brilliant entry it would have made in his journal! It probably would have been no occasion of sin to attend a mere debate.

However, reflected Joseph Holloway, I have my schedule, and it is laid exactly down for every minute of every busy day. A schedule was, after all, a schedule, and Monday night was for the National Literary Society. This admirable civic and Christian body had early in its distinguished career invited him, Joseph Holloway, to lecture upon a subject of his choice. He had hit upon the attractive topic of "Elocution, Its History and Beneficial Effects for Mankind, with Illustrations from the Classic Works of Edgar A. Poe, Thomas Moore and William McGonagall, Poet and Tragedian." Despite the richness of the material, he had never been invited again. A deplorable oversight doubtless. But hard to know, some people are such fools.

There was nothing to prevent him from hurrying down to the Abbey after this lecture, whatever it was about — beehive huts? standing stones? — was over. Yes, he might even catch the last of the debate, or at least get a glimpse of Yeats being huddled off the stage by his chagrined Anglo-Irish toadies. Perhaps even pelted by the Christian members of the audience!

What a sheaf of notes in the speaker's hands. Ah well, he, Joseph Holloway, would pay close attention and offer it up for the lost h-rl-ts of the eighteenth century stage.

Hmm, wasn't that little Miss Milligan in the second row?

It was.

"Mr. O'Donoghue has said in to-day's *Freeman* — "

Oh blast, thought D. J. O'Donoghue, writhing. Why did I send that in? Stephen Gwynn's letter was perfectly adequate.

" — that the forty dissentients were doing their duty — "

CHEERS.

" — because there is no Government Censor in Ireland — "

CHEERS.

"The public," roared W.B. Yeats magnificently, "is the Censor when there is no other!"

DEAFENING CHEERS FROM THE PIT. CRIES OF "DEAD RIGHT!" AND "BANG ON!"

"But were these forty alone the public and the Censor?"

GROANS.

"What right had they to prevent the far greater number who wished to hear from hearing?"

HISSES AND GROANS.

"We called to our aid — "

CRIES OF "THE POLICE!"

" — the means which every community possesses to limit the activities of small minorities who set their interests against those of the community. Yes, the police!"

GREAT GROANING.

Her tea had gone cold, and the fire was going out, but still she did not move. Perhaps she should have gone with Frank to-night, but no, no, she couldn't have faced it.

Mary Walker was not a coward, or at least she didn't think so. But when you are not sure, how can you. . . ?

Again she picked up this morning's *Freeman* and looked at Miss Milligan's letter:

> . . . let me say that I have never missed a performance at the Abbey Theatre when it was within my power to attend, even by undertaking a long journey from Belfast, or some country place, for the purpose. And though given to frequenting the cheap seats in other theatres, and travelling third-class on railways, I always made it a rule to take stall tickets at the Abbey for myself and some friends to accompany. I have bought all their playbooks and publications, and. . . .

Mary Walker's glance strayed to the bookcase on the wall. They were all there, the *Samhains* with Yeats' brave remarks, and Dr. Hyde's and Lady Gregory's plays, and old Mr. Yeats' fine drawings of Willie Fay, of Frank Fay as Cuchulain, of Mr. Synge and Padraic and Sally and Mac. Not Mr. Yeats' lovely one of her. Oh, she would have liked that, to have been in *Samhain* with the others.

And they were all there too, the pretty paper covered Irish Theatre Series that George Roberts had brought out. All ten volumes, just as fresh and crisp as when they'd come from the printer. She turned them over, one by one. *The Well of the Saints* with Willie as Martin Doul and

Vera Esposito (very bad) as Mary, and George Roberts as Timmy the Smith, and Sally as Molly Byrne, and her in the tiny part of Bride, and her brother Frank as Mat Simon. *Kincora* with her in a really good part as Gormleith, and her brother as Sitric, and Seumas O'Sullivan as a really terrible Maelmora, King of Leinster. Little Padraic's *The Land* with Willie so good as Murtagh Cosgar. . . and her brother not so good as his son Matt. Yet they had all tried, done as best they could. And sometimes they were good. When she'd replaced Miss Gonne as Kathleen Ni Houlihan, Yeats had complimented her. But, oh, how could you not read those thrilling lines and feel almost as if Ireland were speaking through you?

And yet Miss Milligan had said. . . . She picked up the paper again:

> . . . there is no doubt that both Mr. Yeats and the Messrs. Fay brought with them to the Abbey Theatre enterprise a considerable heritage of opposition and enmity. . . .

Oh, Mr. Yeats did put people off all right, and so did Willie Fay in his different way, but all they all ever really wanted was just to put on the plays. How often she had run through the rain up Camden Street to their little hall behind the pork butcher's, saving the tram fare, without tea, tired from the day's work, but just bursting not to be late!

Her eye lit again on Miss Milligan's letter:

> . . . It has cost me a certain amount of self-repression and self-restraint not to have been in the thick of this opposition. . . . Mr. Yeats would then be in his element, debating on the freedom of the Theatre as against the freedom of the Press, and as even of more importance the freedom of Ireland. . . .

Impulsively Mary Walker swept up all of the books in her arms and took three quick steps to the fire.

But no, no, she couldn't throw them in! She just couldn't!

"The struggle of last week has long been a necessity," Yeats cried.
CHEERS.
"Various paragraphs in newspapers, describing Irish attacks on theatres, have made many, mostly by young men, come to think that

the silencing of a stage at their own pleasure might win them a little fame
— "

HISSES.

" — and, perhaps, serve their country. The last I heard of was in
Liverpool — "

A SMALL CLUSTER OF HISSES FROM THE MIDDLE BALCONY.

" — and there a stage was rushed, and a priest who set a play upon
it came before that audience and apologised."

"YOU SHOULD HAVE DONE THE SAME!" AN ERUPTION OF
CHEERS.

"We have not such pliant bones! We did not learn in the house that
bred us a so suppliant knee!"

GROANS AND HISSES AND STAMPING OF FEET.

P.D. "Pat" Kenny, pamphleteer and journalist for *The Irish Times*,
arose and pounded his gavel on the table. "Please! Please! Ladies and
Gentlemen! Fair play! I appeal to you to give the speaker a fair hearing,
just as you expect a fair hearing yourselves!"

"Let me conclude!" roared W. B. Yeats above the din.

"SOONER THE BETTER!" LAUGHTER.

"Manhood!" cried W. B. Yeats. [WITH ARMS ALOFT, A MAGNIFI-
CENT FIVE SECOND PAUSE.] "Manhood is all!"

LAUGHTER, CHEERS, CLAPPING, GROANS AND ASSORTED NOISE.

"Ooh, ooh, ooh," trilled Christina McFitz.

Her sister seized Christina's little right finger and twisted it straight
back. "Shut up!" she growled.

George Moore clung to his hat brim and cursed roundly. The wind
off the Liffey was Siberian, and had given his pasty face, at least what was
visible beneath its enveloping muffler, an uncharacteristically rosy blush.

"You idiot, Edward! Why didn't you let me call a cab?"

Edward Martyn continued his imperturbable progress across
O'Connell Bridge. "I like a nice walk after dinner."

"This is not a nice walk!"

"It will settle my digestion."

"We are late!"

Infuriatingly, Edward Martyn came to a complete halt.

"What are you doing? We can't stop here, man. We shall be blown into the river."

"Boots, boots, boots," rumbled Edward Martyn.

"This is hardly the time, Edward, to indulge a bizarre taste for Kipling."

"My boots, George. Take a look at my boots like a good fellow."

"I don't give a damn about your boots, and I am not a good fellow," raged George Moore.

"I have a feeling that one of my boots has come unlaced."

"If your feet are like mine, they can't have any feeling. They are entirely frozen." And he jerked his companion roughly by the arm.

"One can take a nasty spill by stepping on an unlaced bootstring, Moore."

"Then tie it, you fool. Tie it!"

"My old back injury precludes my bending down. One should never stray too far from one's valet."

George Moore departed from his own usually lofty standards of conversation, and remarked, "Oh, shut up!"

"I think, Moore, that you are behaving very badly. In the circumstances, it would be the part of a friend to offer to lace my boot."

"LACE YOUR BOOT!"

"If you please."

George Moore considered the options, such as remaining on the polar bridge for a lengthy period. Consequently, shivering with cold, he went down on one knee. As his abdomen rendered that position ineffectual, he reluctantly went down on both knees. The pavement proved to be wet.

Mon Dieu, he thought, what if some admirer should chance along? What if some enemy? Such as that venomous Mitchell woman with her tasteless doggerel particularly on the subject of himself.

As quickly as possible he located his friend's right bootlace. It was snugly tied, and so was its brother.

"Edward!" he roared, rising, "your boots were not untied!"

Just then a strenuous buffet of wind swept his hat out over the stone railing of the bridge, and it was shortly to be seen bobbing along the black waters of the Liffey.

"My hat," he said grimly, "has blown into the river!"

Edward Martyn patted his own warm deerstalker whose flaps were securely knotted with a small ribbon beneath his chin.

"You really should be more careful, Moore," he remarked complacently.

Bristling with outrage, W. J. Lawrence rose to the accompaniment of loud cheers.

"I speak as an Irishman and an Irish playboy!"

LAUGHTER AND APPLAUSE.

"I am not a member of any League or Society in Ireland!"

APPLAUSE.

"In some of his recent writings, Mr. Yeats has said that praise, except it came from an equal, was an insult. I am not going to praise Mr. Yeats to-night. [AN EFFECTIVE THREE SECOND PAUSE.] I come to bury Caesar, not to praise him!"

APPRECIATIVE LAUGHTER AND ENTHUSIASTIC CHEERS.

"I was present four nights last week, and I was present on the first occasion. Mr. Yeats was not. I am therefore in a position to speak in regard to the reception the play got on the first night. I have twenty-five years' experience as a playgoer, and I have never seen a more thoroughly intellectual, representative audience. There was no predisposition to damn the play. It got a fair and honest hearing."

VOICE FROM THE STALLS: "IT DIDN'T ON MONDAY!"

VOICE FROM THE PIT: "THROW HIM OUT!"

"At the end," cried W. J. Lawrence, "the protest was made on the indecent verbiage, blasphemy and Billingsgate that was indulged in."

CHEERS.

VOICE FROM THE STALLS: "NONSENSE!"

"There was not a single call for author," said W.J. Lawrence emphatically. "That indicated the condemnation of the play!"

MANY VOICES: "HEAR, HEAR!"

In the men's dressing room, Mr. Arthur Sinclair rattled his newspaper. "Didja read this!" he cried to the room at large.

"Yeh," said O'Rourke in disgust, "Syd's Baby in the 2.30 at Cheltenham."

"Boyle's letter! He's withdrawing his plays!"

"That so?" said Kerrigan, looking up with interest. "What's he say?"

"Just this," said Arthur Sinclair. "'I regret to be obliged to withdraw my three plays — *The Building Fund* and *The Eloquent Dempsy* and *The*

Mineral Workers — from the repertoire of the National Theatre Company as a protest against the action of attempting to force at the head of a riot, a play on the Dublin public, against their protests of its being a gross misinterpretation of the character of the Western Peasantry.' Well, that's done it! Without Boyle, the theatre might just as well close its doors."

"Umm," mused Kerrigan philosophically, "What would the public do without your Eloquent Dempsy, Mac?"

Arthur Sinclair cast a quick, suspicious glance at him.

"The quare thing is," rumbled big Ambrose Power from the corner, "that Boyle hasn't read nor seen *The Playboy*."

"G'wan, Amby," Kerrigan said, "How wouldja know that?"

"Mister Holloway told me the other day."

"Well," said Kerrigan, "Boyle was always a bit of a so-and- so."

"Boyle is a loss," gloomed Frank Fay. "Yeats has a lotttt — to answer for — there."

Mr. F. Sheehy-Skeffington, the well-known idealist, vegetarian and supporter of women's rights, arose, adjusted his one-piece Jaeger suit, and cried out in his fluting treble, "I have divided this subject into three parts!"

"Omnia ballia," reflected Oliver Gogarty, "divisa est in partes tres. Seems somehow unnatural."

"The play, the disturbance, and the methods employed to quell the disturbance." [HERE F. SHEEHY-SKEFFINGTON PAUSED FOR A POR-TENTOUS TWO SECONDS.] "The play was in my opinion bad, the organised disturbance was worse — "

UPROAR.

" — and the methods employed to quell the disturbance were worst of all."

CHEERS.

"Mr. Yeats has alienated from the National Theatre the great mass of Dublin playgoers and deprived himself of their support. Even if the opposition to the introduction of the police was entirely fantastic, Mr. Yeats, as a director of the theatre, should have known better than to bring them in and alienate the public. This introduction of the police was the worst feature of the whole business."

Behind the curtain, Lady Gregory nodded in agreement. "I am afraid dat he is only too right dere."

Synge, sick at heart, nodded too. "But had we a choice?"

" — and that has led," F. Sheehy-Skeffington continued, "to such extravagant conduct as that of the Western Board of Guardians which, without having seen or heard the play, has condemned it by resolution."

LOUD LAUGHTER.

Lady Gregory tapped her foot impatiently. "I fear too dat dis debate will only make matters worse. It will only make people more angry."

And how, Synge wondered silently, could we have stopped the debate? Tied Yeats up perhaps?

"My opinion," a new speaker was saying, "is anti-Yeats!"

CHEERS AND BOOHING.

"Who is dat?"

Synge peeked out through the curtain. "Cruise O'Brien, the journalist."

"The quiet audiences toward the end of the week have been quoted," continued Cruise O'Brien, "as justifying the play. My contention is that the first audience was the best test."

CHEERS.

"The supporters of the theatre were fully represented on the first night. These were people who had come to the theatre since its inception, and supported it loyally all through. There were no rival mobs of boohers on the one hand, or of a claque on the other. The first-night audience came to discriminate and to judge. And having judged and found the play wanting, it should then have been withdrawn at once. In face of the enormous disturbance which took place on the next night, it then most certainly should have been taken off the stage to prevent the theatre being turned from a place of art into a bear garden."

"Dis will only hurt our audiences for de future," Lady Gregory mourned.

"Well. . . perhaps not," Synge said.

"Yes, yes, and just when we have so much fine new work about to come out."

True, he reflected wryly and silently. Your *Jackdaw*, your *Rising of the Moon*, your *Poorhouse*, and your friend Blunt's *Fand*.

"I think," he said aloud, "I'll see if the tea's wet yet. Would you like a cup?"

"And such good new work it is too," she said bitterly. "Oh, sometimes I think I could kill Willie!"

Huddled in her seat, Christina McFitz blubbered to herself. Her hand fluttered to the poem she would slip into his pocket:

IN MEMORIAM: GUILLAUME
What boots the broil and strife,
The storms that wracked us,
When once upon my desert life
You bloomed, my cactus!

But Guillaume had to perish. Thomasina was as always right. Yet he was so beautiful. . . .

His teeth clattering, George Moore looked up at the portico of the Abbey Theatre. "At last!"

Edward Martyn solidly planted himself and regarded the entrance. "Do we want to go in?"

"Yes!" said George Moore. "It's going to rain!" He entered the comforting warmth of the vestibule and made at once for the glowing fire.

"Here now, here now!" came a stern voice from behind the tea counter. "Jist what do ya think yer after doin'?"

"G-g-going to the theatre," George Moore managed to reply through his clattering teeth.

"Not to-night yer not! The debate has already started, and I have strict orders not to let its progress be discomposed!"

"Madam, don't be ridiculous!" said George Moore, making his way to the auditorium door.

The woman limped athletically from behind the counter and took up a position in front of the auditorium door. "Buzz off!"

"I demand admittance!" shrilled George Moore. "I demand it as an artist! I demand it as a member of the Gaelic League! I demand it as —!"

"Do yez have a ticket?"

"Ticket?"

"Yiz look loike wan o' them trouble-makers to me," she said shrewdly.

A roar of hoots and jeers erupted from the auditorium.

"An' we've more than our share of them to-night. So just take yerself on outa this. Quick step, march!" And she pushed him to the door.

"Madam, stop this at once! I will expose you to the newspapers. I will write to *The Irish Times!*"

"Never read it."

"You are interfering with my freedom of speech!"

"G'wan, and you bawling at the top of yer lungs. Now, off with yez, and don't come back till yer sober."

George Moore found himself ejected onto the footpath. "You will rue this!" he shrieked.

"Aww, go soak yer head," she said and slammed the door.

"Some difficulty, Moore?" Edward Martyn enquired from the shelter of the portico.

"Did you hear that harridan just tell me to go and soak my head?"

"Ah yes," said Edward Martyn sticking his hand out tentatively. "It is starting to rain."

And so it was. Heavily.

A STORM OF GROANS AND HISSES.

Mr. P.D. "Pat" Kenny again arose from the chair and pounded the table hotly with his gavel. "Order! Order! Order! The Chair recognises that gentleman!"

Pearse Beasley arose and slowly surveyed the audience. "I find it," he said dryly, "very hard to understand Mr. Yeats's view to-night, but I found it easy last week when Mr. Yeats charged me in the Police Courts."

GROANS AND CRIES OF "POLICE!"

"Order! Order, please!" exhorted P. D. "Pat" Kenny, thumping his gavel.

Pearse Beasley turned an ironic eye upon the chair. "We have as chairman," he said with exaggerated politeness, "a gentleman who has already expressed his views in the congenial atmosphere of *The Irish Times.*"

"HE OUGHT TO BE VERY IMPARTIAL." LAUGHTER.

"Mr. Yeats," resumed Pearse Beasley, "said he came as an artist."

LAUGHTER.

"De young poltroon!" exclaimed Lady Gregory, "to say dat!" And she turned on her heel in disgust and bumped into the avidly listening Alice O'Sullivan and May Craig. "Girls! Girls! Don't listen to such nonsense. Go into de Greenroom and help Sally!" And clucking briskly, she shooed them out before her.

"He came," said Pearse Beasley, "posing as an artist. Well, I hope

Irishmen will never forget his pose in the Police Court!"

Susan L. Mitchell took a sip of hot cocoa, pulled up the duvet and
settled back cosily on the propped-up pillows. She smiled, took her pad
and pencil, and reached for the copy of the *Freeman* containing the
sentence she had circled.

"This play, in which one of the characters makes use of a word that
no refined woman would mention, even to herself."

She gazed at that, and presently began to write:

> Oh no, we never mention it, its name is never heard —
> New Ireland sets its face against the once familiar word.
> They take me to the Gaelic League where men wear kilts,
>   and yet
> The simple word of childhood's days I'm bidden to forget!

She paused to consider her rhymes — ease, please, breeze, trees; drift,
sift, gift, lift. Then she wrote another stanza:

> They tell me no one says it now, but yet to give me ease —
> If I must speak they bid me use a word that rhymes with "sneeze."
> But oh! their cold permission my spirits cannot lift —
> I only want the dear old word, the one that ends in "ift."

With trepidation, W. B. Yeats saw his father rise to speak. Oh bother,
he thought, here is where the debate becomes a soliloquy.

"I have not read the play," said old J. B. Yeats, stroking his long,
white beard. "I have seen it twice but have not heard it."

"DIDN'T MISS A THING!"

"I know Mr. Synge," J.B. Yeats continued imperturbably. "I know
that he has an affection for these people he has described in *Riders to the
Sea*."

LOUD LAUGHTER AND CATCALLS.

"His affection for them is based on a real knowledge."

"NO, NO!" ALSO CRIES AND GROANS.

"He has lived amongst them, and is their friend!"

CRIES, GROANS AND CONSIDERABLE DISORDER.

J.B. Yeats stared unabashed around the house and then raised his hand high above his head. "I know," he roared above the crowd, "that this is the Island of Saints!"

APPLAUSE.

And then he threw his head back, and his old eyes mischievously glinted, and his white beard floated out like a banner. "Plaster Saints!" he cackled.

Placid amid the ensuing din, W. B. Yeats smiled proudly.

As Brigit disappeared into the Greenroom, Willie Fay turned away and stalked up and down. The noise from the front of the house had grown deafening. No point in listening to it. Just blather. Oh, Bill Butler was an egotistic fool. It wasn't a theatre he wanted; oh, no, it was a podium. Anywhere he could make a speech. Well, damn him, a stage was a stage, and only a stage. A place to put a play on, and all of this debate nonsense just interfered with the work. God, it would turn your stomach.

"Eh, Willie."

"What?" he rasped.

Seaghan Barlow glared up at him from under beetling brows. "This sketch you give me for *The Jackdaw* — I can't build it. It won't work. In fact, it's stupid."

At another time W. G. Fay might have directed a few blasts of invective at the small, opinionated stage carpenter.

To-night he turned and said thankfully, "Let's have a look, Seaghan."

As the young Gael rumbled on, Thomasina bent over to give a sharp twist to the little finger of her sister's right hand. "You understand?" she whispered.

"Y-y-yes, sister," whimpered Christina, ineffectually trying to disengage her finger.

"You have the maid's cap?"

"Right here."

"Right where? No, don't show it to me, fool! We might be seen. You have the apron?"

"Beneath my coat."

"Good. And then?"

"When the crowd disappears, I am to creep backstage and help serve tea."

"You have the phial?"

"No! What for? To saw through the bars when I am captured?"

"You are not going to be captured, stupid. You will not even be noticed. Nobody ever notices you."

"Oh, of course, yes. But where will you be?"

"Waiting for you in the vestibule."

"But won't you be noticed? I mean, people do notice you."

Was there a tinge of cattiness in her sister's tone? Thomasina put that distraction aside to be dealt with later. Vigorously, if necessary. Aloud she said, "I will hide inside the box-office cubicle. As soon as you're done, come out."

"You mean after I have helped with the washing up?"

Thomasina sharply twisted her sister's finger. "No. Immediately. Just as soon as you have done what you're supposed to do. Come out into the vestibule and knock three times on the box-office door."

"Three times, yes," said Christina. "And then what do we do?"

"We go home! Heavens, what a muddlehead you are!"

"George Moore will not be so easily thwarted," said George Moore, as the rain poured down on his bared head and dribbled coldly down inside his collar. "Oh, why didn't I bring an umbrella?"

"Ah!" said Edward Martyn, reaching beneath his ulster and drawing one forth. "Just the thing." He unfurled it above his head. "Very good thinking, indeed."

"Bring that over here, Edward. I am soaking."

"I don't think so, George. It's not a large brolly. There is really only room for one."

George Moore growled, pulled up his coat collar and went on down the laneway. "Come here," he said, "and light a match."

"When did you take up smoking, George?"

"I do not want to smoke, idiot. I want to see!"

"It occurs to me," said Edward Martyn, trundling after him, "that there is little to see in this laneway. It is too dark, and it would probably not be a very interesting vista at the brightest of times."

"Damn!" said George Moore. "I have stepped in a puddle. "Bring me the matches."

"Oh, very well," said Edward Martyn, proferring a solitary match.

"And the box, fool! How do you expect me to strike it?"

"Ah, want to strike it, do you?" He held up the box for George Moore to strike the match.

It flared, and instantly went out.

"Give me another."

"Why didn't you cup your hands around that one?"

"Just give me another."

"I don't know, Moore. I only have sixteen left. Why can't you buy your own matches?"

"Edward!"

"Oh, very well. But this time bend over like this." Edward Martyn inclined in his companion's direction.

"OOF!"

"Now what is it? Do stop jumping up and down, Moore."

"You have poked me in the eye with your damned brolly!"

"Quite unintentional. You should look where you are going. Here is another match. And absolutely the last one."

"Thank you, my childhood friend!"

"That's all right. Just don't forget to cup your hands." Edward Martyn observed his friend closely. "Cup them, George. You were always clumsy, you know, even as a boy."

With some self-restraint, George Moore lit the match. This time it did not go out.

"Ah!" he said. "As I suspected! A door! See, Edward!"

"Yes, always been there. The side door to the theatre."

"Why didn't you tell me?"

"I didn't know you were interested. I mean, it's not the door of Cologne Cathedral, is it?"

"Oh! The damn thing is locked! Those buggers have locked it from the inside!"

"I'm going home now, Moore. Have a nice hot toddy and put my feet up."

"You are not going home! You are seeing this thing through with me."

"What thing?"

"A window! A window!"

"Well, there is very little to see in this wretched laneway, even if we had a window. Really, I think you get more and more eccentric."

Thundering down the stairs, and then shoving D.J. O'Donoghue and Arthur Clery to one side, and thrusting Frank Walker and George Roberts to the other, Thomasina McFitz made her way through the otherwise empty vestibule to the box-office door. Unobtrusively, she opened it and — it was quite a tight fit — inserted her bulk inside.

"Owwtch!" cried a small, rabbitty voice.

Thomasina looked down at the small, contorted face. With great presence of mind, she clapped her paw over the mouth.

"Beware!" she commanded.

"Mmmpff," W.A. Henderson replied.

Monday, February 4: III

Molly clattered through the laneway on her high heels and tried to protect her new boa from the rain. "Damn, damn," she mumbled, fumbling for her key to the side door. How could she be so late? She gave herself plenty of time, so she had, but she wanted to look just right to-night. Hmm, perhaps she should have left off the boa till a less trying time.

And if she was late — where was that key? — it really was his fault. Didn't she have to practise just what to say before the mirror? First, she would be distant. Reserved. But not for too long. Just long enough to make him good and sorry. Then gradually she would relent, and — .

Ugh, ugh, the lock always stuck. Why couldn't that sour old Barlow ever fix anything?

Ah! She thumped the door open, but caught her brolly going through and completely turned it inside out.

"Do stop that banging!" came a harsh voice. "And close that door!"

"Oh, wouldja ever give over!" she cried, wrestling with her brolly. "This is destroyed entirely. Just shut up!"

"All right," came the voice she knew.

She turned just in time to see the bleak look on his face as he walked away.

The brolly fell unheeded into the laneway.

The rain had now turned to sleet, and it stung George Moore's chubby cheeks into an almost cherubic red. His expression, however, was far from cherubic. Indeed, it possessed a disturbing intensity, and the eyes had an unblinking glare to them.

"Unlatched! Come here, Edward."

"Oh drat, Moore, you are most unreasonable. I could put up with weather like this for something intelligent like fishing."

George Moore did not think that fishing was intelligent, but he allowed the remark to pass.

"Come here at once, Edward. It is time for you to make your contribution."

"You are not getting any more matches."

"The window, Edward."

"Oh, back on that hobby horse, are you?"

"The window," George Moore explained patiently, "is too high for me to reach. Consequently, it will be necessary for you to bend over and allow me to climb up on your back."

"That does not strike me as in the least necessary," said Edward Martyn. "In fact, I can think of three insuperable obstacles to it. Imprimis, your boots are muddy."

"Edward!"

"Secundus, it is bad for me to bend with my chronic back trouble."

"Edward!!"

"Tertius, I don't care to. It is undignified."

"All right, but you can cup your hands and — ."

"No more matches, George."

"Just cup your hands, idiot, and give me a boost up."

"I don't think so."

"Edward!"

"Oh, very well, very well. Take off your boots."

"My boots!"

"Yes, your boots."

"Do you want me to get my feet soaked?"

"Better your feet than my new kidskin gloves, George. You can tie your laces together and hang your boots around your neck."

Squelching some reflections of his own about necks and hanging, George Moore tore off his boots. "Oh, my God! My feet are freezing!"

"Yes," said Edward Martyn sagely, "I should be very surprised if you didn't come down with quite a nasty cold."

"Ah-ah-ah-choo!" sneezed George Moore.

"Pneumonia even."

"Just cup your hands."

"Like this?"

"Not like that, booby! Lace your fingers together. Brilliant!"

"Nothing to it."

"All right now, Edward. I am now going to put my foot in them, and then my knee on your shoulder."

"You didn't mention anything about your knee on my shoulder."

Growling, George Moore heaved and hoisted his pearlike body up more or less according to plan.

"Oof! This is very uncomfortable, Moore."

"Shut up, Edward. Our next task is to lift this window."

"It is not my task. I take no interest in the matter."

"Ugh, it's stuck. Oh, merde, this is a problem."

"You had better solve it quickly because I am going to drop you."

"Edward, you are not going to drop me! I am going to get this wretched window open, and then, when I give the word, you are going to heave me through."

"What is the word?"

"The word is 'heave'."

"Heave. Very well, but you had better say it shortly, or I am going to drop you."

"Ugh!" said George Moore, struggling with the window. "Ugh!"

"Moore?"

"What?" gasped George Moore.

"What did you say was the word?"

"I said it was 'heave!' Heave, you lunatic, heave!"

With a tinkling of shattered glass, George Moore disappeared through the window.

"I certainly," panted Edward Martyn, "wouldn't care to do that again. Moore, don't think you can count on me to do that again. I am quite puffed."

There was no answer.

"Moore? Moore? Moore, I am not going to stand around here all night. This is quite ridiculous. . . . Ha, what have we here? I say, Moore, you've forgotten your boots. Hmm. Well, perhaps he doesn't want them."

Musing yet again on his friend's increasing queerness, Edward Martyn shook his head, dropped the boots back into their puddle, and placidly made for home.

Thomasina removed her hand from her companion's mouth.

"What are you doing here?" she demanded. "Don't lie, or it will go hard for you."

"Ah-ah-ah," he whimpered. "I think my foot is bleeding."

Again she clapped her hand over his blubbering mouth and ground her foot into his boot.

"I will crush your miserable toes," she whispered. "I will grind them into a bloody, mangled pulp. Do you understand?"

"Urk!" he replied emphatically.

"Very well." She took her hand from his mouth and grasped instead his short, grey beard. "But I warn you if you attempt to raise an alarm, I will probably break your jaw. The choice is entirely yours."

"P-p-please don't do that!"

"Who are you, and what are you doing here? If you make me ask you a third time, you will regret it."

"I am Mr. W.A. Henderson, and I am counting up the box-office receipts."

"I want my money back," she said promptly.

"Madam, I would gladly give you your money back. And everybody else's! But I cannot reach it. I can hardly move. I am not sure that I can breathe."

"It is not necessary that you breathe."

"You are crushing me!"

She thrust herself vigorously against him. "Stop that insipid whining, or I will break your ribs."

"Aaaahh!"

> O cruel Gaelic Leaguers! cruel Sinn Feiners all!
> Have you no little sisters, who once when very small,
> Before they knew what sinfulness could lurk in one
>   wee word —
> Have you not from their artless lips its simple accents heard?

Susan L. Mitchell re-read the verse and smiled at her old teddy at the foot of the bed. She had had that bear long before President Roosevelt's election, and they had been christened Ted. Dear Ted, the confidant of so many secrets. Oh, stop, stop that maundering. Consider your rhymes.

She did. Bays, drays, lays, praise. And then she wrote the last stanza:

> Then by those early memories, hearken to one who prays
> The right to mention once again the word of other days,

Without police protection once more her voice to lift —
The right to tell (even to herself) that still she wears — a shift!

Again she smiled. And then the smile slowly died.
The right to tell (even to herself) that still she wears — a shift!
But who cared if she did or not?

Mr. D. Sheehan arose from the stalls. "I come," he announced, "to defend the play. I do so as a peasant who knows peasants, and also as a medical student!"

LOUD LAUGHTER AND GROANS.

P.D. "Pat" Kenny tapped his gavel and grinned. "Listen to a peasant on peasants!"

LOUD LAUGHTER.

Oh, God, moaned W.B. Yeats, shifting uncomfortably. He should have had Lady Gregory bring along a pillow.

"I claim my right to speak as a medical student. Mr. Synge has drawn a type of character that, as a student of science, I have paid strong attention to. I refer to the sexual melancholic."

Backstage John Synge winced.

"In any country town in Ireland you will get types of men like Christy Mahon."

VOICE FROM THE PIT: "NOT SO!"

"I refer you to the lunacy reports of Ireland!"

DISORDER AND STAMPING OF FEET.

"I refer you to Dr. Connolly Norman's lectures at the Richmond Lunatic Asylum!"

VOICE FROM THE BALCONY: "I REFER YOU TO THE MINUTES OF THIS MEETING!"

Medical students, sniffed Oliver Gogarty, were less sententious in my day.

Shifting his buttocks in the uncomfortable stalls seat, he scratched his nose with his small gold pen, re-opened his leather notebook, and jotted down his third effort of the noisy and unruly evening:

There once was a house called the Abbey,
Less sumptuous than it was shabby,
Which catered to Art,

And no other part,
Unless posteriorly flabby.

"The chair," said P. D. "Pat" Kenny, "recognises the young man in the smart overcoat."

The young man, Oliver Gogarty observed, had some difficulty in remaining perpendicular.

"I say," said an intense-looking person next to Oliver Gogarty, "I'm from *The Daily Express*, and I've just broken my pencil. Borrow yours? Thanks awfully!"

And snatching the pen, the intense-looking person, glanced hastily from auditorium to page and scribbled the following:

> . . . a young gentleman in an advanced stage of inebriety, who, while apparently anxious to say a few words, seemed to have lost the power of speech. A key to his condition was found when, after being gently removed from the stalls, he made a second attempt to mount to the stage, and a large bottle fell from his pocket and crashed to the floor. With this incident his oratorical ambition disappeared.

"Snappy copy that," he said.

"My pen!" said Oliver Gogarty. "I have better uses for it."

"Madam, I implore you, madam!"

"What now?" snapped Thomasina McFitz.

"I cannot b-breathe!"

"I am getting impatient with your incessant complaining."

"If you could extract your bo-bo-bo — ."

"Don't cry. It's unwomanly."

"Your bosom!"

"You filthy little beast!"

"Your chest I mean, your chest! If you could only extract it from my m — ."

"Bah!" growled Thomasina, who was by nature contemptuous of human frailty, and therefore thrust herself even more forcefully against him.

"Mrrmmf!" he exclaimed in a strangulated fashion.

Her own sensation, Thomasina realized, was novel and interesting. She thrust herself, with even increased vigour at him.

"Madam, I am a family man!"

"You little beast," she cried, crushing him in rhythmic bounces against the wall. "Are you trying to inflame me!"

Christina slid out of her coat and hid it away beneath her seat. Then she affixed the maid's cap in her thin hair, smoothed down her frilly apron, and made her unobtrusive way out of the balcony.

But suddenly the voice, that voice, from the stage transfixed her.

"The author," it cried, "of *Kathleen Ni Houlihan* appeals to you!"

She stood transfixed amid the cheers and cries.

"Oh, Guillaume, Guillaume," she wept, "I will never forget you!" And clutching the phial she hurried down the stairs.

"We were offered," intoned W.B. Yeats, sweeping his raven tress imperiously back, "the support from the garrison if we took *Kathleen Ni Houlihan* from our list of plays. And we refused!"

ENTHUSIASTIC CHEERS FROM ALL PARTS OF THE HOUSE.

"And now the author of that play refuses to give up the work of a man of genius!"

In the wings, John Synge looked distractedly around. Where is she?

In Rathgar, AE was immersed in the Upanishads.

"George!" his wife called. "Aren't you coming to bed?"

"Shortly, dear, shortly." Hmm, his pipe had gone out. He rummaged in his baggy pocket for a match. Must be getting old when he forgot even to keep his pipe lit.

Wasn't there something else he had forgot to-night? Hmm, must not have been too important.

Disengaging himself from the congratulations and handshakes of P. D. "Pat" Kenny, Hugh Lane and Oliver Gogarty, W.B. Yeats hurried through the nearly empty auditorium.

A remarkable night! "The author of *Kathleen Ni Houlihan* appeals to you!" Brilliant that. The memory of the spontaneous applause warmed him.

Perhaps he should not have said "appeals." No, "demands" would have been much better. Ah well, memorable enough. Triumphant really. Yes, a lesson had been taught.

The insufferable Lawrence and the unspeakable Holloway were conferring in the back row. With his most practised vagueness, he looked straight through them.

Emerging into the deserted vestibule, he noticed curiously that the box-office was trembling. Another manifestation of the impertinent Aeschylus?

The box-office tipped precariously to the left, and then swayed marvellously to the right.

Was it Dante, perhaps? Virgil?

The box-office shuddered and then toppled to the floor with a crash of rending wood.

From the dust and debris, a figure in flowing robes magnificently arose.

"Homer!" exclaimed W. B. Yeats. "Hail, colleague!"

"Rape!" boomed Thomasina McFitz.

Monday, February 4: IV

It was too noisy, too bright, too cold, too wet. She slunk unobtrusively, surreptitiously along the cold quay wall.

"Rowerr!"

"All right, get her, boy! Get her, Garryowen!" a Citizen encouraged gruffly.

She sensed the swirl. The mad rush at her back. Panic-stricken, she leapt upon the quay wall.

"ROWERRR!" It was huge and almost upon her, fangs bared, and instantaneously, without thought, she sprang across the footpath into the terrifying tangle of clopping hooves and rumbling wheels.

When she emerged on the other side and silently blended into the shadows, her eighth life lay expiring on the roadway behind her.

Lady Gregory closed the office door, thus muffling the still resonant bleats of Miss McFitz. Under Sally's motherly influence, the blasts of the first five minutes had now considerably abated. Well, thank heavens, the audience had practically all left. Oh, utterly the last straw should the story get about. She could see the headlines. "Abbey Official's Savage Attack upon Lady." Or even worse, "Further Depravities at the Abbey."

Oh dear, something would have to be done somehow to placate the hysterical woman. But what? Lady Gregory paused by the door to the balcony to consider. Money was out of the question, for the theatre had none. And Lady Gregory winced at the idea of approaching Miss Horniman again.

The house was still lit, and Willie was there on the forestage. Pacing back and forth and flailing his arms about. Heavens, he must be re-enacting his last speech of the evening. Oh, she must get down there and stop him before someone saw him.

As she turned to go, Yeats' unmistakable voice trumpeted out not from the stage, but just below her. "Turn off the stage lights, Barlow! Lights cost money!"

What? Were her eyes betraying her? She stepped out onto the balcony, and saw Yeats hurrying down the aisle.

"Out! Out with them, man!"

"Put out the light, and then put out the light!" declaimed a plummy voice from the forestage, and the black-suited figure turned toward the footlights.

Why that was not Yeats onstage at all. It was the new English actor. How could her eyes play such tricks upon her? The Englishman did not really look like Willie. It was just that for a moment his walk, the way he tossed his head back — .

She hastened out into the little hall.

Synge was coming heavily up the stairs.

"How is Mr. Henderson?" she asked.

He joined her. "Holloway and that Lawrence fellow are with him. He's calming down."

"Oh dear, Mr. Holloway is de worst gossip in de city. And dat Mr. Lawrence hates us."

A sepulchral moan came from behind the office door.

"Good God!" he said. "What's that?"

"Dat's Miss McFitz, de — de victim."

"Victim?" he marvelled. "She might be a victim of an earthquake, but I hardly see how an ordinary male — ."

"Particularly Mr. Henderson," she smiled.

"He's stopped weeping. I think the best thing is to get him out of here. As quickly as possible."

"Yes, yes. Do you have any idea where he lives?"

"Holloway said something about Howth. Perhaps if you went down and talked to them — at your most tactful."

She sighed. "Me?"

"I'm afraid so. Lawrence looks about to erupt if I'm in the vicinity. Perhaps you could get them to see him home, or at least put him in a cab."

"A cab? Oh dear, I don't know if I have enough money."

"I salvaged £9 or so from the shambles of the box office."

"But we should have had over £16."

"Mrs. Mulcaster," he said dryly, "was assisting me."

"Very well," she said, taking the money from him and making a mental note about Mrs. Mulcaster.

She turned to the stairs, putting on a mask of concern. Oh, what a hypocrite one must be. I really don't give a — a damn! Yes that was what dear John Quinn would have said. A damn!

"Oh, Mr. Henderson!" she exclaimed aloud. "Dis is derrible, derrible! You poor man!"

Mr. Arthur Sinclair sat glowering in the men's dressing-room. It was not the first time that Kerrigan had made a defamatory remark about his acting. "The public won't take kindly to being deprived of your 'Eloquent Dempsy,' Mac." Oh, a right nasty, built-in slur there.

And Kerrigan was cute enough to hoodwink such asses as Holloway and Lawrence into thinking they had seen real acting. But the man was just a magpie, picking up bits of his better's technique. Oh, he could sing a bit, although what music-hall had to do with the legitimate drama Arthur Sinclair could not fathom. Mere playing to the gods.

And of course, Kerrigan had nothing of Arthur Sinclair's own consummate ability to milk a laugh. Oh, there was no way that Kerrigan could fill out a big, crowd-pleasing role like Dempsy. God, the fellow was barely taller than the Fays. And getting fat.

Here, Arthur Sinclair thoughtfully patted his own stomach. No, not the same thing at all; he had the height to carry it.

Well, there was no way that Kerrigan could hurt him by any true and honest artistic standard. It was only those sneaky little bits of business he inserted — particularly at moments when he, Arthur Sinclair, was delivering some vital and important speech. Then Kerrigan, the rat, would be pulling his earlobe, scratching his nose, fiddling with a button, ugh!

This was what he would have to watch out for when they started rehearsing *The Rising of the Moon*. If he had to play his big scene sitting back-to-back with Kerrigan on that damned barrel, oh there was no telling what nose-scratching treachery the swine would be up to. And the little rat had a song.

"Hey, Mac," called J.M. Kerrigan's cheerful voice from the door. "All on your lone-i-o? Favour us with some of your eloquence in the Greenroom."

Arthur Sinclair swivelled his large, florid head angrily around.

"O, then tell me, Sean O'Farrell," sang Kerrigan owlishly, "where the meetin' is to be!"

And then the little rat winked and disappeared.

That tore it! Arthur Sinclair strode to his overcoat.

He extracted a murky-looking bottle and secreted it in his rear trousers pocket. There might be an unsightly bulge there, disrupting the flowing contour of his right buttock. But Arthur Sinclair was an artiste and undaunted by necessary sartorial sacrifices.

"It was dreadful," blubbered W. A. Henderson, as he was led gently out the door.

"You should offer it up," said Joseph Holloway consolingly.

"You should sue the theatre!" snarled W. J. Lawrence.

Lady Gregory pretended not to hear that.

"There are worse stories," Joseph Holloway added as they came out onto Marlborough Street. "On the African missions, for instance. Nuns, saintly Christian brothers — who in this world is safe?"

From the open doorway, Lady Gregory watched them totter off to the corner. A group of men clustered across the street stopped chatting and took it all in too.

George Roberts detached himself from them. "Is everything all right, ma'am?"

"Fine," she said. "A little mishap."

Frank Walker muttered something to Seumas O'Sullivan, who pulled his moustache and looked bland. Like his poetry.

She glimpsed Padraic Colum amongst them.

"Mr. Colum," she called, "would you step inside? I'd like a word."

Slowly he approached, and she took him by the arm, steered him into the vestibule and closed the door. "Too brisk to talk out dere."

He regarded the toes of his boots.

This was going to be difficult, but she should make the effort.

"How did you think it went to-night?" she asked.

He looked up sharply, his mild blue eyes flashing. "It was a bad night for the theatre. A black night."

She favoured him with her pleasantest smile. "And dat is why de theatre needs its old friends around it."

His face set stubbornly.

"Come back with me to de Greenroom, and have a cup of tea with de actors."

He was about to refuse, when the street door swept open.

"Oh my!" cried AE, his beard blowing wildly in the wind from the street. "Over, is it? How stupid of me. I rushed right in from Rathgar as soon as I remembered."

"Shut de door, Mr. Russell," said Lady Gregory, "before we're swept away. Come backstage. Mr. Colum and I were about to have a cup of tea."

"Ah, tea!" said AE, brightening. "Hello, Padraic."

"Eh, no!" protested Padraic Colum as AE's beefy hand closed about his thin arm and impelled him forward.

W.J. Lawrence and Joseph Holloway watched the cab rattle off down Sackville Street.

"Who would have thought," said W. J. Lawrence, "that the rot could have so quickly penetrated so deeply?"

"Eh?" said Joseph Holloway, perking up his hairy ears in interest. "What rot?"

"Into poor Henderson."

"Poor Henderson?"

"Who," repeated W.J. Lawrence dolefully, "would have thought it?"

"Have thought it?"

Holloway had lately developed an irritating habit of repeating the last words of a remark. Doubtless, W.J. Lawrence surmised, a consequence of having no original thoughts in his own hollow head. A leech he was, an intellectual leech.

"Have thought it?" Joseph Holloway repeated.

"I mean," said W. J. Lawrence with barely suppressed irritation, "who would have thought that the decadent ambience of that den would have driven him to this?"

"To what?"

W.J. Lawrence wanted to scream. And did.

"RAPE!"

Father Patrick Dineen passing by, hands as usual clasped behind his back, paused and raised his pale, scholarly face to the heavens. "Rape?" he remarked. "Considered substantively and poetically, that would be 'Fuadach.' But considered substantively and juridically, 'Eigniu.' But should the word properly be included in a dictionary at all?" In some perplexity, he passed on.

W.J. Lawrence noticed this. He also noticed that the tall policeman, usually stationed during the day at the bottom of Grafton Street, was eyeing him dubiously. "Let's go," he said, catching Joseph Holloway's arm and marching him away, "or we shall miss our last tram."

"Eh, ah, er," said Joseph Holloway. "I think I shall walk home. You run on ahead, or you'll miss it."

"Walk? On a night like this?"

"Er, walk, yes. I have a bit of a headache." And Joseph Holloway involuntarily crossed himself.

How can it be possible, wondered W.J. Lawrence, to have an ache in a void?

"All right," he said. "I'll possibly drop by Northumberland Road to-morrow." And he stepped off to catch the Number 6, 7 or 8. Then a thought struck him. Holloway had crossed himself, and Holloway only did that when passing a church or when telling one of his frequent but palpable lies.

Miserable hypocrite!

Then a second thought struck him. As he had been assisting the depraved Henderson out of the theatre, Lady Gregory had seemed to murmur something to Holloway.

Or at least she inclined her head definitely in his direction. Why?

A: It was a gesture of respect.

Eliminate possibility A.

B: To kiss him.

W.J. Lawrence suddenly erupted into raucous laughter.

"Ouch," he said.

Eliminate possibility B.

That, ergo, left — possibility C. Lady Gregory had whispered something to Joseph Holloway. What?

W.J. Lawrence stepped into a darkened doorway and peeped back down the street. Yes, there he was, bulky in his overcoat, his hard hat set implacably on the centre of his fat head, flitting across Sackville Street. Unusual for Holloway to flit. Practically impossible. Oh, something was in the wind, and, like the wind from the state of Denmark that something definitely stank (*Hamlet*, I, iv, 90).

W.J. Lawrence quickly followed, keeping well behind. The burly little figure presently turned into Abbey Street. Oh, the wretched hypocrite was returning to the theatre!

Yes, now he turned into Marlborough Street. And now, with a furtive look, he darted through the portico. The filthy, conniving little sneak! And after all he, W.J. Lawrence, had done for him!

As W.J. Lawrence stood outside the portico and looked at the closed door, a frigid blast swept up from the river. And he had probably missed the last tram. Drat.

In fact, damme!

There was a certain archaic literary flavour about "damme" that somehow mitigated its bisyllabic vulgarity.

With a sudden resolve, W.J. Lawrence dashed up the steps into the portico. Quickly he opened the door, just an inch. Then an inch more.

He did not notice the small, shadowy figure at his heels.

Someone had piled the splintered pieces of the box office in the corner. How symbolic that was, Joseph Holloway reflected, the box office literally exploded, laid low and destroyed. Savouring the poetic justice of it all, and sucking on the lefthand strands of his straggly moustache, Joseph Holloway made his placid way into the darkened auditorium.

Yet he felt a bit sad. He had spent many happy and not always sinful hours here. And Miss Horniman had chosen him as the renovating architect. Oh dear, he lamented, what would Dublin do without its Abbey? What would he do?

A wave of laughter came from the Greenroom. He compressed his lips. What unspeakable vileness were they up to now?

Happily, he hastened to see.

The rain had turned to sleet, and the dishevelled cat seized the opportunity to slip through the door just on the man's heels. The vicissitudes of a bohemian life had years before turned her into an opportunist.

The room was warm but too bright, and the man, feeling her slither by his ankles, aimed an angry kick at her. Expecting such a predictable human response, the cat deftly evaded the heavy boot, and in four lithe leaps disappeared into the darkened auditorium. She then slithered under a row of seats and huddled in a motionless ball.

He did not follow.

Still she did not move, for Life had taught the cat much. Silence, exile and cunning. Such qualities had served her well in a precarious life. She had survived much, lived hard, lived long. Lived, in fact, very long. Lived through at least eight normal cat lives.

In the crowded Greenroom, J.M. Kerrigan was jostled into W.G. Fay. "Say, Willie," he surprised himself by saying, "have you decided on the casting of *The Rising of the Moon* yet?"

W.G. Fay frowned. "It's you and O'Rourke for the polismen."

"Oh? I thought I read the Ballad Singer pretty well the other morning," said Kerrigan.

"Yes, pretty well."

J.M. Kerrigan found himself growing unaccustomedly irked. "Only pretty well?"

"Her Ladyship doesn't want to take any chances with it," said W.G. Fay.

"That means you'll be playing it."

"That's right."

J.M. Kerrigan gave him a long, expressionless stare. "Good luck with the song," he said flatly, and turned away.

Begrudging bastard! thought Willie Fay.

J.M. Synge thought of slipping silently away.

"Hello," she said.

He flipped the boa contemptuously with his finger. "Wherever did you acquire that vulgarity?"

For a second nothing happened. Then Molly O'Neill's eyes hardened, and she turned on her heel.

Oh fool, Synge raged, miserable fool!

Gussie was feeling peckish, but he didn't like to step up to Lady Gregory who was carving fat slices from the barmbrack. No, after the other night in the laneway, he didn't fancy doing that at all.

"Gussie, I'm going home."

"Eh? Oh, right, Seaghan."

"Shift them chairs and the table off the stage, and see the lights are all out when they finally decide to go home," said Seaghan Barlow, surveying the crowded room sourly. "God, I hope they're planning to clean up in here."

"Oh, not to worry, Seaghan."

"You'd worry if all the dirty work fell on you."

"Right, Seaghan, right," said Gussie humbly.

He watched the little stage carpenter stamp angrily to the door. Sure, why was Seaghan always so grumpy, Gussie wondered. In fact, why was everybody so out of sorts lately? Weren't they, after all, all doing what they really liked to do? Putting on plays and all. Gussie really enjoyed running the lights, and helping out backstage, and doing the odd walk-on part. Sometimes even a part with a couple of lines. Well, as the nice Mr. Purefoy said, it was only a matter of time till he got the really big parts — Cuchulain and Dempsy and Martin Doul.

Ah, maybe he was just codding himself. Maybe he should just chuck the whole business and look around for something else. Seaghan was so grouchy, and Willie Fay was a holy terror. And there was no money in it, God knows. Sure, after he'd paid the Mammy, he hardly had enough left over for a pint and a packet of fags.

He went through the wings and out onto the stage. The work lights were on, and Michael James' shebeen was half dismantled. It looked eerie-like, it did, in the half darkness. Gussie never really felt easy about being alone on the stage after the theatre emptied. But everyone was laughing off in the Greenroom. Still, the place had been the city morgue at one time, and according to Mrs. Mulcaster there was the ghost. . . ah, what a lot of rubbish.

He poked his way through the front curtains. Seaghan had put the houselights out, and the auditorium was quiet, not a sound. The balcony door was open, and some weak light spilled in. Well, shift them chairs, and then grab a cup of tea when Lady Gregory wasn't looking. Molly would get him one. Or Alice O'Sullivan — a cute little piece that.

A seat somewhere in the auditorium suddenly bumped up. Alarmed, Gussie peered out at the darkened house.

"Who's that?"

Nothing.

"Who's there?"

Nothing.

But there was something. A quick, black sort of movement, a swirl of motion in the balcony.

And then he heard — another bump.

Jaysus! He clawed his way back through the curtains, across the stage, through the wings, back to the comforting light and noise of the Greenroom.

Mother of God, Mrs. Mulcaster's copious collection of corns and bunions were only an agony. "Here, you!" she cried hotly to the small, snivelling figure huddled against the wall. "Who are you?"

"Irk," whimpered Christina.

"Hanh!" snorted Mrs. Mulcaster, regarding with ill-disguised repulsion the snowy-white little maid's apron. "Some posh rig-out yer wearin! Didja forget to leave it behind at the Papal Nuncio's? Ya hear me talkin' to ya?"

"Yes, yes, yes. You're loud and forceful."

"What?"

"Thank you," said Christina piteously.

"Humph!" said Mrs. Mulcaster suspiciously. "Well, serve these around! And look smart about it!"

Christina accepted a trayful of steaming mugs of tea. The tray was very heavy.

"Get to it!" snapped Mrs. Mulcaster.

"Tea?" she whispered. "Tea anyone?" She took two birdlike steps away. Where could she go? Where could she hide? Where could she get rid of these horrible, heavy cups of tea?

She poured one into a flower pot.

Sally threaded her way through the crowd. "She's gone to sleep."

"Extraordinary," said Lady Gregory. "Perhaps I should send Dr. Gogarty up to look at her."

"Let her sleep," said Sally. "I'll snatch a cup of tea and go up and sit with her."

"Have your tea in peace. I'll look in on her presently. Later we'll send her off in a cab. But, eh. . . ?"

Sally turned back.

"Did she," asked Lady Gregory softly, "say anything?"

Sally arched a well-practised eyebrow. "About Henderson? He'd need to be Finn MacCoul to have his way with that one."

Lady Gregory smiled. Her first real smile of the night.

"Eh," said J.M. Kerrigan, moodily holding out his cup, "I'll chance a sup more of that."

May Craig swirled the contents of the teapot about and frowned. "I think this is about gone."

"Give it to me," said Arthur Sinclair quickly, "I'll make us a fresh sup."

Taking the pot and turning away from his surprised colleagues, Arthur Sinclair patted the bulge in his back right trousers pocket.

Frank Fay had fallen into the clutches of old Mr. Yeats. The painter had inserted a bony finger into the buttonhole of Fay's lapel and was drowning him in the stream of monologue that gushed out of his long, white beard.

Synge took the opportunity to inch away and to let his eyes sweep over the room. Yes, there she was, chattering with Brigit O'Dempsey and Miss Bushell. The peal of her laugh swept out above the clamour of the room. Oh sullen fool, he raged, do you want to lose her? Go to her.

"Ah, Synge, are you flying from the wisdom of the sages?" said Oliver Gogarty.

"Old Mr. Yeats? Well, I suppose he is wise."

"And witty. To judge from his contribution to to-night's farrago."

"Oh," said Synge, trying to keep his eyes on her, "he's more trenchant than witty."

"Well, you'd know. You've been painted by him. What do you think of him as a painter?"

Synge stifled his impatience. "He's a garrulous painter. He spends more time talking than painting."

"Here," said Gogarty, "give me that." He emptied Synge's cup into a nearby potted plant. "From what bog do you people import your tea?"

"Eh?" said Synge abstractedly.

Oliver Gogarty turned to the wall, deftly produced a pocket flask and poured Synge's teacup half-full. "Just," he said benignly, "what the doctor ordered."

Synge sipped. "You're right."

"Invariably. Now all I have to do is convince the world." He tapped the rim of Synge's cup, and said seriously. "I want you to finish that and go home."

Was that her, over there behind O'Rourke?

"You were asking something," Synge said, "about old Yeats' painting?"

"Yes. How good is he?"

"His little black and white sketches are fine. Those he just tosses off in a few minutes. But if you're giving commissions, I'd put my money on Jack."

"The brother?"

"He's good. Eh, look here, Gogarty, could you finish this for me?"

"Well, all right, but — ."

Synge abruptly nodded his thanks and fled.

Strange fellow, Oliver Gogarty pondered. Was he offended because I didn't talk about the play or the debate? No, just shyness, no doubt. With a grimace of distaste, Gogarty remembered how once he and Juiceless Jimmy had pissed on Synge's doorstep. What was their limerical eloquence on that occasion? Berated, micturated?

"Ah, Gogarty!" said Yeats, tapping him on the shoulder, "I want you to hear this. It's quite new."

Slim chance of W.B. ever forgetting one of his.

First! The horrible Mrs. Mulcaster had demanded where all the cups and mugs had gone. Well, she would not find them, Christina reflected smugly, for they were well hidden, behind the piano and under the couch.

And second!

Second, He had spoken to her.

"Did you misplace my cup of tea? Do fetch me another."

The words trembled in her memory.

Her brave little heart was full of conflicting emotions, just as her pale little hands were too full of cup and saucer and phial.

She set the cup and saucer carefully on the window sill. That left only the phial to be dealt with. Ugh, ugh, the top was stuck. So like Thomasina. She didn't know her own strength. Christina remembered all those fruitless struggles with the lids of jam jars jammed into irre-movability by her sister's massive strength and moral fervour.

"What seems to be the matter, little lady?" said a plummy voice. "Perhaps I can be of assistance?"

"Eh, well, it's this top. I can't seem to get it off."

The man plucked the phial from her fingers and observed its green contents with interest.

"Eh, it's medicinal," she explained. "Mr. Yeats requires it in his tea."

"Really?" he said, uncorking the phial and sniffing. His eyebrows rose in the direction of both large and outstanding ears. Then he smiled winningly, and with a courteous bow returned the phial.

"Th-thank you," she said and scuttled away.

"My pleasure entirely," murmured Leslie Chenevix Purefoy.

Tea and tobacco perfectly complemented each other, and AE satisfyingly exhaled a halo of smoke and finished off his third cup. Curious-tasting tea, but not unpleasant.

"Padraic, when you next approach the teapot, would you refill my cup? I have been there several times already, and don't want to appear piggish."

"I — I don't really want any more tea, AE. I'm not sure it agrees with me."

AE saw beads of perspiration popping out on the little poet's broad forehead. "No, you don't look so well. Stuffy in here."

"I'm grand, grand," said Padraic Colum. "Give me your cup."

He moved queasily off into the crowd. This was very embarrassing, and he should never have allowed himself to be dragged into it. He was in an utterly false position. Oh, not that he was an enemy of the theatre; indeed, he preferred not to be an enemy of anybody. But he could hardly be called a friend either. No, not after that business with his father. And certainly not after the letter he had sent to Synge. Not that he repudiated his stand in that letter in the least. His firm stand! But if he should bump into Synge — .

And just at that moment he did.

"Oh, hello, Colum. You here?" said Synge disinterestedly, and passed on.

Oh, this was terrible. And he felt awful. He must leave. Must get out into the air.

But two implacable figures barred his way.

"I won't hide the fact, Mr. Yeats," said Willie Fay hotly. "I'm very unhappy about it."

"No need to feel unhappy, Fay," said the poet, "not at all."

"Mr. Yeats? Mr. Yeats," whispered a small voice near Padraic Colum's ear. "Your tea."

"You will," said Yeats, "have complete control over our peasant work. The work which, possibly, we are most noted for." He looked up thoughtfully. "Possibly."

"Oh dear, oh dear," whispered the small voice near Padraic Colum's ear. "It's getting cold."

Padraic Colum twisted his head around to see a small, pale woman plaintively proffering a cup and saucer.

"There's Synge's fine work. Lady Gregory's. And that other fellow, eh, that little fellow, eh, Cousins, was it?"

"Not Cousins," said Willie Fay. "We dumped Cousins three years ago."

Padraic Colum felt a gentle nudge in the ribs. "Please," said the small voice, "could you ever hand him this?" And she shoved the cup and saucer into Padraic Colum's unwilling hands.

He looked at it. How curiously green it was.

"Dumped?" said W.B. Yeats. "Then who am I talking about?"

"You must mean Colum," said Willie Fay impatiently.

"Oh, Colum. Upright young fellow. Easy to forget. What did James Whatsisname call him? Ah, Patrick What-do-you-Colum. Ha! They're all alike."

It was done in an instant. Padraic Colum felt for the little tin of pills in his pocket, flipped it open with his finger nail, and dropped them all — every last one — into the cup. With a peremptory tap on the poet's arm, he cried, "Your tea!" Then he thrust it into the outstretched hand and plunged toward the doorway.

Oh, dear God, he moaned, as he clawed his way out of the Greenroom, he was going to be very sick.

He heard a gush of water, and a door opened, and large Ambrose Power emerged swaying from the toilet cubicle. "What a night," he said huskily.

Padraic Colum had to agree.

Joseph Holloway, clutching his fifth cup of tea, made his unsteady way out of the Greenroom. He did not feel well at all.

He tottered to the small toilet cubicle, but it was locked on the inside,

206

and he heard someone working the recalcitrant chain and vehemently swearing.

Oh dear, was he going to be sick? Blindly he blundered on and found himself onstage. His head was throbbing queerly, and the chatter and laughter from the Greenroom were a distant irritation. He groped through the front curtains and sunk down on one of the chairs left on the forestage.

Oh. Oh dear, that was better. It was mercifully quiet here. And dim, almost pitch dark. No one could surely see him, and so he undid his waistcoat buttons. Ah!

Perhaps also the top two buttons on his trousers? No, better not.

"Ah, my dear Holloway," came the well-known, resonant voice behind him.

Yeats?

The arrogant poet was actually deigning to speak to him?

Squinting in the gloom, Joseph Holloway saw a dark figure brush back a tress of hair.

"I have been hoping that we two might have a quiet moment. I have so much on my mind, and there are so few real devotees of the theatre to whom I can turn for sound, Christian advice."

"Well ah, well ah!" said Joseph Holloway, considerably flustered. "Anything I can do, any small service I can — !"

"You are entirely too modest."

"Perhaps, perhaps," said Joseph Holloway, to whom that thought was not exactly novel.

"One must not," said the noble voice, "be born to blush obscene."

"*Antony and Cleopatra*," said Joseph Holloway tentatively.

"But I see your cup is empty. Pray, have this fresh one, and as soon as I fetch another for myself, we shall have a nice titty-tat." A black sleeve reached over Joseph Holloway's shoulder and exchanged teacups. Then as quickly steps receded behind the stage curtains.

Well, thought Joseph Holloway, isn't that something! Yeats, for all of his aloofness and rampant egotism, was a true poet. Quite as true as Ethna Carberry, and as perceptive and subtle, so naturally he would sense a sympathetic spirit. Ha, wouldn't Lawrence be only livid with envy!

Before he could sip his fresh cup of tea, his stomach heaved alarmingly, and he quickly put the cup down.

A nice titty-tat. Fine poetic phrase that. Whatever could it mean?

Not Irish, of course, for Yeats had no Irish. Latin? Greek? He sounded it out. "Titty-tat?"

As if in answer he distinctly heard a small meow.

Yes, there, stage left, curled up in the lighting trough, a cat. Joseph Holloway was not ordinarily fond of cats or, indeed, dogs, cows, horses, gazelles or any animals large or small. In the ordinary course of events, animals galloped, leaped, climbed, waddled, slithered or swam their way, and Joseph Holloway plodded his.

But to-night was somehow different, and a benign numbness began to steal over Joseph Holloway. With an unpractised yet benevolent smile beneath his straggly moustache, he slopped some of his tea into the saucer and placed it on the floor. "Puss, puss, puss," he called kindly.

Those words struck an almost buried but still responsive chord in the old cat's normally suspicious mind.

"Meow!" she murmured, and almost like a kitten scampered trustingly to him.

It was a mistake.

J.A. O'Rourke barely made it to the men's dressing-room. After he had heaved into the wash basin, and then heaved again, he looked up weakly. "Joe, give us a fag."

J.M. Kerrigan sympathetically supplied one and lit it.

"It's that bloody Gort cake, Joe," said J.A. O'Rourke. "Begod, she can sack me before I touch a crumb of it again."

The rain and sleet had stopped, but it was bitterly cold out in the laneway. Alice O'Sullivan leaned her forehead against the wall, and made dry, awful, retching noises.

"What's she been drinking?" asked Molly.

"Just a glass of sherry before the debate. That's all, Miss O'Neill, honest it is," May Craig protested.

Molly found a cigarette and tried to light it in the wind. "Damn," she said. "Stay with her, May. I'll get her coat and be back in a sec."

People were beginning to emerge from the Greenroom as she hurried back inside. To tell the truth, she didn't really want the fag, for she didn't feel all that good herself.

"Molly!"

His fingers closed and tightened on her shoulders.

"I'm busy now!" she said harshly.

"Don't. Please don't. I know I was wrong."

She turned to him angrily. "Oh, you know now, do you?"

He winced, stepped back, and said almost too low to hear, "Yes, I know now."

"Well, now's a bloody rotten time. The O'Sullivan girl is sick as a dog out in the laneway. God, it's as cold in here as outside. Somebody's left that little window at the back open."

"Just a second to set things straight."

"It takes more than just a second, John Synge!"

He pulled her roughly to him. "I'll give it all the time you want. All the time in the world."

Despite herself, she lifted her face to his.

"Oh Christ!" he cried desperately. "Someone's coming!"

Lady Gregory felt deeply weary as she emerged from the Greenroom. She paused and leaned back against the wall. There was a terrible draught from somewhere.

Behind her, she could hear Sally giving out to Mrs. Mulcaster about where so many teacups had disappeared to. Then Kerrigan's light laugh and Power's throaty rumble came from the men's dressing-room. And Brigit O'Dempsey's brainless giggle came from the women's. Well, at least the actors weren't downcast.

She was. Profoundly.

Oh, it would be good to get back to the hotel and a nice cup of tea. What with the fuss and the bother, she hadn't got one at all. Oh, a most wearing day, and was there really much point to it? Hadn't they merely stirred up matters even worse? Made people even angrier? Well, no point in thinking any more about it to-night.

She stirred herself and went out the little door and down the three steps into the auditorium. The light spilling in from the vestibule silhouetted Yeats making some excited point to Dr. Gogarty.

A pity that Boyle — but, of course, he was always difficult — had withdrawn his plays. *Dempsy* would have been just the simple crowd-pleasing comedy to draw people back into the theatre next week. But at least the first readings of her new piece, *The Rising of the Moon*, were going well. Too bad she could not cast Kerrigan as the Ballad Singer, for he could sing so much better than Fay. But one couldn't ruffle Fay any more than he already was. Oh, there were so many people that one couldn't ruffle!

She paused halfway up the aisle for a last glance round the house. Seaghan hadn't removed the table and two chairs from the stage. Oh, what did it really matter?

She turned away to join Yeats in the vestibule, but something stopped her. Something not quite right.

She peered back through the gloom. Was one of the chairs onstage somehow bulkier than the other?

She retraced her steps back down the aisle. Yes, someone was there, sitting at the table.

"Mr. Synge," she called, "is dat you?"

No, it was a figure in an overcoat, his head bent down on his chest, and a bowler hat set squarely on his head.

"Mr. Holloway?"

Oh heavens, the silly man had gone to sleep. Sighing, she went back up the steps, through the little door and out onto the stage. Fumbling her way through the drawn curtains, she came out onto the little forestage.

"Mr. Holloway, wake up. We're all going home." She touched him gently on the shoulder. "Mr. Holloway."

Joseph Holloway slowly slipped sideways in his chair. His hard hat tumbled onto the floor. Beneath his ragged moustache, his mouth lay open.

Tuesday, February 5

Oliver Gogarty straightened up and stood staring down at the still form of Joseph Holloway. "Well, he's rather dead."

Synge pulled out his watch. It had just gone twelve.

"Dead?" mused W.B. Yeats. "How extraordinary."

"Speaking professionally," said Oliver Gogarty, "I would say it's normal enough."

"Oh dear!" said Lady Gregory, and then bit her lip to avoid adding, "Why did he have to do it here?"

Synge sensed Molly standing just behind him. He turned to her, and took her hand. Damn whoever saw them!

"I suppose we should notify somebody," Lady Gregory murmured unhappily. "De police? Eh, Dr. Gogarty, de police?"

But Oliver Gogarty was bending over the table and peering intently into the cup on it. "Queer looking tea," he observed. "Lady Gregory?"

Not relinquishing Molly's hand, Synge drew her with him and looked over their shoulders. The cup was about half full, with a milky green colour.

Gogarty sniffed it and frowned. "I don't like this."

"Ugh," Yeats agreed. "Cold tea."

Molly suddenly pressed Synge's hand. "Johnny, the saucer on the floor."

Nobody seemed to notice her calling him "Johnny," for everybody was staring at the saucer. It was on the floor, near the left front leg of the table, its bottom also tinged a milky green.

"Chaucer," murmured W.B. Yeats thoughtfully.

"Why would he set it on de floor?" asked Lady Gregory.

Oliver Gogarty swept his eyes along the forestage. "Synge," he said quietly. "Look over here."

Reluctantly relinquishing Molly's hand, Synge followed him over to the proscenium arch stage right.

"See there," said Gogarty, pointing to the lighting trough.

"What is it?"

"I'd say it's a dead cat," said Gogarty, squatting down and poking it with a forefinger. "Stiffening."

"My God," said Synge, certain implications suddenly striking him.

Gogarty rose. "I think," he said softly, "we should keep everyone from leaving the theatre."

"I've rounded up everybody who's not left already," said Synge, coming back through the wings. "They're all in the Greenroom."

Gogarty produced his pen and notebook. "Who've we got?"

"Most of the actors. The Fays, Sinclair, Kerrigan, O'Rourke, Power, Purefoy, Gaffney, Sally Allgood, Molly — er, Miss O'Neill I mean — Brigit O'Dempsey. Who else? The young girls have gone. Miss O'Sullivan was ill, and Miss Craig saw her home. Mrs. Mulcaster, the charwoman, is still here, but Miss Bushell has already left. AE's here, and Colum. Yeats is up in the office, probably totting up the receipts, and Lady Gregory must be with him. That's the lot, I think."

"Yes. . . ." Oliver Gogarty ran his pen down the list. "Quite a lot of us."

"It's poison, isn't it?"

"Certainly looks like it. Just what kind I don't know. It would have to be analysed."

Synge looked from Joseph Holloway to the cat.

"Yes," nodded Gogarty, "Holloway came out here to have his tea, sat down, saw the cat and put some down in the saucer for it. Seems clear enough, don't you think?"

"I think," said Synge, looking back to the sprawled figure of Joseph Holloway, "it would be a good thing to cover him with something."

Gogarty rubbed his chin abstractedly. "Yes, I daresay. I would like to know what this stuff is, though. It's got rather a pungent smell to it. Wouldn't you say?"

Ignoring Joseph Holloway as best he could, Synge bent over the cup. After a moment, he straightened up frowning. "Yes. And a rather familiar smell."

Gogarty nodded. "I can't put my finger on what it is, though." He paused and then added, "Of course, the real question is how did it get in the cup?"

"Some ghastly accident," said Synge unhappily. "But I suppose we had better notify the police."

212

"It seems like a person would notice whatever is in there," said Gogarty. "The colour is not only weird for tea, but you'd notice the odour."

"The police will have to sort it out."

"Perhaps," Gogarty puzzled, "it was something Holloway was dosing himself with."

"Joe Holloway," came a voice from the auditorium, "didn't put it in."

Startled, they both turned and peered into the darkness.

"He didn't put anything in it!"

Gogarty tapped Synge on the arm and pointed. "Up there."

Synge made out a dark figure standing in the front row of the balcony. "Who's that?" he called.

"Ring the police!" the figure cried. "What are you waiting for?"

"Who's there?" called Synge.

For a second the figure didn't answer. Then he cried harshly. "Lawrence! W.J. Lawrence!"

"What are you doing up there, Mr. Lawrence?"

Again there was a second's silence.

"That's not important. What is important is that I saw who gave poor Joe the tea. It was that dastard Yeets!"

"You stay right where you are," called Oliver Gogarty. "We're coming up." He gestured to Synge to follow him into the wings.

"Listen," he said softly, "get someone from the Greenroom to stay with the body, and then come on up yourself. Eh, whatever is that fellow Lawrence still doing in the theatre?"

"Who knows?" said Synge. "Better get on up to him."

Gogarty nodded and clattered off toward the auditorium.

Synge's head was throbbing. He rubbed the heels of his palms over his forehead. And an hour ago he'd thought things couldn't get any worse! Well, this was no time to dawdle. But as he turned quickly to the Greenroom, a clicking sound caught his ear.

There was a dim figure by the stage door.

"Who's that?"

"Leslie Chenevix Purefoy, Mr. Synge," came a plummy voice. "I was just stepping out into the laneway for a breath of air."

"I'm afraid no one can leave the theatre for the present, Purefoy. Come with me."

Synge waited until the Englishman came up to him. "Into the Greenroom, please."

Inside, people were standing uneasily in hushed groups of two or three. As Synge entered behind Purefoy, all eyes turned to him.

"Look here," said Arthur Sinclair importantly, "just what is going on? It's after twelve, and we've all missed our trams already."

"Oh, shut up, Mac," snapped Willie Fay, "a walk home for once won't hurt you."

"Be good for your figure, Mac," J. M. Kerrigan suggested innocently.

"Well, I'm not about to walk all the way home," cried Mrs. Mulcaster. "Not with me poor suffering feet!"

"All right, all right," said Willie Fay. "Just everybody keep quiet, and hear what Mr. Synge has to say."

"The fact is," Synge said, "there's been an unfortunate accident, and we'll all have to remain in the theatre for the moment."

Instant hubbub greeted this announcement.

"What kind of an accident?"

"Who to?"

"Stay in the bloody theatre!"

"Does he know what the time is?"

He saw her standing by her sister. She smiled faintly and gave him a little nod of encouragement.

He held up his hand for quiet. "I know you're all tired and want to go home."

"We do!" shrilled Brigit O'Dempsey. "I feel rotten enough as it is."

"Bridie!" rasped Willie Fay. "Everybody!"

Again there was silence.

"Has anyone been hurt?" AE rumbled mildly through a fog of pipe smoke.

"Yes," Synge admitted. "It's Mr. Holloway. He seems to have had a — a heart attack possibly."

There was a buzz of muffled exclamations.

He held up his hand again. "We'll all have to be patient for just a few moments. Dr. Gogarty is with him."

"Is he dead, the ould bugger?" queried Mrs. Mulcaster in fascination.

"Mrs. Mulcaster!" Sally growled.

"I'll tell you everything I can," said Synge, "just as soon as I know more. In the meantime, I would like you all to stay in here, just where you are. We will be as quick as possible."

They muttered unhappily.

"Eh, Fay." Synge gestured toward the door; and, as he turned to go, he caught Molly's eye and nodded reassuringly.

Willie Fay joined him outside.

"The situation is this," said Synge quietly. "Holloway is onstage, and he's dead. I want you to stay with him — or no, it's better you stay in the Greenroom and keep order. But put Gaffney with him or somebody you can trust."

Fay nodded in quick understanding. "Kerrigan."

"Good. And — you might cover him up with something."

Fay nodded brusquely and turned back into the Greenroom. "All right, all right, everybody. This won't take too long. Kerrigan, I want you. And Sally, organise a cup of tea for everybody?"

"No!" cried Synge, bursting back in. "No tea!"

In the dim light of the upstairs hallway, Oliver Gogarty, with his most suave bedside manner, patted W. J. Lawrence on his thin, trembling shoulder. "Yes, yes," he said, "that must have been most startling."

"It was the perfidious Yeets!" Lawrence snarled.

"Quite. Now let's just see if I've got all this straight," said Oliver Gogarty soothingly. "You were in the balcony searching for your lost wallet?"

"Yes!" snapped Lawrence. "Do you doubt me?"

"No, of course not. But then what happened?"

"I heard someone come onstage and sit down. I looked up and saw it was Joe. Poor old Joe."

"What was he doing there?"

"Doing there! How should I know? He sat down."

"Just so. And then what?"

"I want to make my statement to the police. Where are the police?"

"They're on the way," lied Oliver Gogarty soothingly. "And then what happened?"

"Well, I was just about to call out to him that — that I had found my wallet, when Yeets came out through the curtains."

"I see. And they talked?"

"Of course, they talked."

"Did you hear what they said?"

"How could I hear what they said?"

"Well, I've never sat in the balcony, but I assumed the acoustics of the theatre — ."

"They — they murmured."

"Ah, naturally," said Oliver Gogarty. "And then what?"

"And then Yeets gave him the cup of tea and left."

"You're absolutely sure it was Yeats? I mean, it's dark down there."

W.J. Lawrence snorted. "How could anyone mistake him!"

Oliver Gogarty could not answer that.

Synge was coming up the stairs.

"No," said Gogarty. "Don't you go with him. Next to Yeats, you seem to be Lawrence's favourite *bête noir*."

"Well," said Synge, "Frank Fay is a friend of his. He could look after him."

"Is there any place private we could put the two of them?"

Synge rubbed his throbbing forehead. "Eh, let me see — the men's dressing-room."

"All right. I think it's important we keep Lawrence away from the others."

Synge nodded and hurried back down the stairs.

"And Synge!" Oliver Gogarty followed him a few steps down. "Before we do anything else then, it's important we talk. Yeats, Lady Gregory, us. Very important, I think."

Padraic Colum had found a chair in the corner of the room. He was feeling a bit better now. That horrible session in the lavatory had got rid of most of whatever it was. If only he could get home to his comfortable, narrow bed, and if only it weren't so close and smoky in here.

AE, his pipe billowing, approached him solicitously. "Ah, Padraic, a little under the weather, are you?"

The little poet felt his stomach heave, and he staggered up and lurched for the door.

"Gussie," said Willie Fay quickly, "go with him."

Sally narrowed her eyes as she watched Gussie help the little poet out. "It's got to be something in the Gort cake," she murmured. "Just look at everybody."

Ambrose Power swayed back and forth in his chair, his eyes closed and his large hands clutching his stomach. Brigit O'Dempsey, quiet for once, sat palely on the couch. O'Rourke slumped against the wall, forgetting even to light the cigarette in his mouth. Sinclair sulked and groaned softly.

"No," said Molly, "not everybody. AE seems all right, and Willie Fay and Gussie and the slimy Limey."

"You don't look so well yourself."

"I'm a bit queasy," Molly admitted.

"I've always thought her Ladyship's cake too heavy," said Sally.

"I didn't have any of it," said Molly.

"Well, whatever it was," said Sally, "I want you to go over to the couch and sit down. I'll just wash up some of these dishes."

"Ah," said Purefoy, appearing at her side, "allow me to be of assistance, dear lady."

"No!" Molly cried and jabbed her sister in the ribs. "We'll wash up later!"

"No trouble at all," smiled Purefoy, picking up a cup and saucer.

"No, Sal!" Molly whispered urgently.

"Give me those," said Sally, trying to snatch the cup and saucer from him. "You'll only be in the way. Just like you were earlier."

He, however, was chivalrously reluctant to surrender the cup and saucer, and in the struggle they fell to the floor, spilling tea on the worn carpet.

"Ah, wouldja ever look at that," he mourned, "and shure and I only after tryin' to help."

Restraining an impulse to box his prominent ears, Sally produced a rag from her apron and thrust it at him. "Pass them dishes up to me, and then wipe up your mess."

"Faith and bedad," he said, abjectly going down on his knees, "and why wouldn't I, and a bonnie, fine woman the like of yerself telling me to. Arrah, whisht, ochone."

Sally snatched the cup and saucer from him and stalked irately to the sink. Molly followed and passed her two plates.

"Now what is all this?" Sally said, under her breath.

"There was something in Mr. Holloway's tea."

Sally paused. "Well so, I'll gather everything up and stack them. But you sit down. Go on, do what I tell you for once."

Molly nodded tiredly. "All right, but don't pour anything out. Anything."

Sally swept around the room, gathering up plates and cups and saucers, and stacking them on the drainboard by the sink. Most of the cups, she noted, were empty, but what was left in the others looked normal enough. As she collected them from the top of the piano, a slight rustling caught her ear. With difficulty, she pushed past AE who was taking up most of the piano bench, and peered into the space between the side of the piano and the wall.

A little figure was crouching there.

"Who," demanded Sally, "are you?"

"Oooh!"

"Come up out of there!" said Sally, reaching down and securing a thin arm.

A dishevelled little woman arose somewhat dustily in a maid's uniform, her starched cap wilting and askew.

"Well, I never!" wondered Sally. "Now just who might you be?"

"Ch-Ch-Ch—," the little woman stammered tearfully.

Sally looked around the room. "Mrs. Mulcaster?"

"Ah?" Mrs. Mulcaster rumbled sleepily from the couch where she had collapsed, shoes off. "Don't be persecutin' me. I'm off duty."

"Who is this?"

Apathetically a few heads turned to look.

"She's helping," said Mrs. Mulcaster, closing her eyes.

Sally glanced to the door where Willie Fay was assisting Gussie back into the room with an ashen-faced Padraic Colum.

"Very well," said Sally, turning to the little woman. "Help. Gather up all the plates and bring them over to the sink."

"Yes, yes, yes," said the little woman, stepping out with a clink and a crunch from her den beside the piano.

"What's that now?" said Sally.

"What's what?" said AE placidly puffing.

Sally held onto the little woman's arm and looked down into the space between piano and wall. "What in heaven's name are all those cups and saucers doing down there?"

"I, uh, eh, I was putting them out of the way," the little woman remarked.

"Just put them over by the sink, and if you break any more, it'll come out of your wages."

Manoeuvering over AE's outstretched, tweed-covered legs, Sally saw Purefoy at the sink. She crossed to him and jabbed him in the small of the back. "Clear off outa this!"

"Certainly, certainly," he said, beating a hasty retreat. "Just trying to be of assistance, dear lady. Musha, wisha."

Dear God, she thought, what a night.

Mrs. Mulcaster began to snore.

"And that's his story," said Oliver Gogarty.

Synge grunted, and thought inconsequentially that they needed to put a more powerful light bulb in the little upstairs hallway.

"Whether we're to believe him. . . ," Gogarty added with a shrug.

"It's no secret that Lawrence detests Yeats," Synge brooded.

"Yes, that," conceded Gogarty. "And there's also the fact that we can't believe Lawrence entirely."

"Oh?"

"He told me he was in the balcony trying to find his lost wallet. Well, he didn't sit in the balcony. He was one of the first speakers in the debate, and he spoke from the pit. . . . Nevertheless, he was quite definite that he saw Yeats."

"But we both know that Yeats is totally incapable of —," Synge broke off with a futile flap of the hand.

"Incapable of anything except writing magnificent poetry," Gogarty concluded.

They stood there indecisively in the dim light.

"What," said Gogarty finally, "did Yeats think of Holloway?"

"Inasmuch as he thought of him at all, he probably thought pretty much what we all did."

"Which was?"

"Well, Holloway was always around the theatre. Miss Horniman engaged him to renovate the place when she bought it in 1904. So he had a sort of quasi-official standing, and was in the habit of showing up backstage and even at rehearsals."

"Did you like him?"

Synge frowned. "He was too much of a busybody. A gossip. And something of a bore. I generally tried to avoid him. And Yeats hardly noticed him at all."

Gogarty absently ran his hand through his hair. "What now?"

"I think, as you said, consult with Yeats and Lady Gregory."

Gogarty nodded, and they went into the office.

Yeats was behind the desk, scowling at a column of figures on a sheet of paper. "Absurd," he muttered.

Lady Gregory was at the window and turned to them questioningly.

"We need to talk," said Synge.

She gestured at a bulky figure on the couch. A blanket was thrown over it, but at one end an open mouth was breathing stertorously, and from the other two immense besandelled feet protruded and occasionally twitched.

"In the hallway," said Gogarty.

"Outrageous!" said Lady Gregory. "De man is mad."

"Of course," Gogarty observed, "it would be only Lawrence's word against Yeats'."

"Umm," said W.B. Yeats, absently brushing a raven lock from his noble ivory brow. "In the dock. Well, perhaps it had to come to that sooner or later. Emmet, Tone, the Sheares brothers. Traditional really."

"Willie," Lady Gregory said with an uncharacteristic snappishness, "don't be silly!"

"The point is," said Synge, "that the very least harm we can expect is a lot of nasty publicity. And that, coming hard on the heels of what we've had the last week. . . ."

"Oh, it would be disaster for de theatre," said Lady Gregory. "It would be de end of us."

They stood pondering.

"The really interesting point," Yeats said finally, "is who did do it? If we knew that, it would solve the problem."

"It would lessen de problem."

"Well," said Gogarty, "there are really only three possibilities. The stuff was put in by accident, which seems — if you'd seen and smelled it — rather farfetched. Or it was put in by Holloway himself, in which case it seems odd that he would try it out on the cat."

"If he were trying to kill himself," said Yeats, "perhaps he just wanted to see if it really worked."

Lady Gregory shuddered. "Willie, don't be macabre."

"Jabber," he murmured.

220

"Perhaps W.B. is right," said Oliver Gogarty, "but the third possibility strikes me as most likely. That is, it was put in on purpose by somebody else."

"There is a fourth possibility," Yeats remarked.

Again they turned to him.

He gave a pause long enough to evoke Synge's admiration. "I," he said mischievously, "put it in."

"Och," Lady Gregory snorted in disgust.

"Just a thought."

Oliver Gogarty cleared his throat. "Interesting as this discussion is, it's time we called the police."

"I would suggest," Lady Gregory said, weighing each word, "dat we hold off."

Oliver Gogarty was surprised. "But they should have been notified already. As a physician, I could get into quite a lot of — ."

"Oh, of course dey must be notified, but I suggest we wait for an hour."

"Madam," said Oliver Gogarty, "you astonish me."

"What do we need an hour for?" asked Synge.

"I thought dat we might quietly question people."

"There are quite a lot of them," said Oliver Gogarty dubiously. "Sixteen. Or no, that's wrong. Not counting us, there are fourteen."

"Fifteen," said Yeats. "You're forgetting the — damsel in the office."

"I think we could eliminate Miss McFitz," said Lady Gregory.

"Nooo," said W.B. Yeats judiciously. "One murder is enough."

"I mean," said Lady Gregory, "she was never backstage. So, if the three of us divided the others up — ."

"The four of us. Shouldn't you have a hand in it also?"

"Willie, I intend to. I was suggesting that Mr. Synge, Dr. Gogarty and I can handle it alone."

"Nonsense, nonsense," said W.B. Yeats. "I am quite addicted to detective fiction. It is much more stimulating than wild westerns."

"What would we hope to find?" asked Synge.

"Clues," said W.B. Yeats darkly.

"De thing is," said Lady Gregory, "dat de alternative is surely de end of de Abbey. I would do a great deal to avoid dat. So if we could take just a few minutes, five or ten, to talk to each person, and den meet back here to compare notes."

"Brilliant!" said Yeats. "I'm all for it! I must have pen and paper."

"Fine, Willie," said Lady Gregory, "you just sit quietly in de office and work on your poem."

"Poem!" he snorted. "Notes! Detectives take notes!"

She turned questioningly to Synge.

"All right, let's question them," he shrugged fatalistically.

"Dr. Gogarty?"

"We could all wind up in awfully hot water. Obstructing justice. I could lose my licence to practise."

Lady Gregory slumped. "Yes," she said. "You're right. I'm afraid I'm turning into a very foolish old wo — ."

"However," grinned Gogarty, "it would be good fun,"

"I should hardly," she said, suppressing a smile, "call it dat. Now, let's see your notebook and divide dem up."

"The subject interests me greatly!" said Frank Fay. "Yes, I have been reading and thinking about rhythmical recitation for years!"

"Frank," said W.J. Lawrence, "didn't you hear me? I have just been telling you that Yeets has murdered poor Joe Holloway."

"Most books of what is called elocution tell one to treat verse as prose, i.e. ignore metre, slurrrr rhyme and run one line into another."

"Murdered him."

"And all of them warn their unfortunate rrrreaders against what they call 'sing-song.' But I have heard many poets declaim!"

"Yeets — !"

"Certainly Yeats. And I have come to the conclusion that the elocution books are all wrongggg. . . ."

"Murdered," murmured W.J. Lawrence, his eyes glazing.

"Ah, AE!" said W.B. Yeats, with a slightly false enthusiasm.

"It's Arthur Sinclair, Mr. Yeats!" Sinclair blinked his sleepy eyes in irritation. "Mr. Russell is over there."

"Just so," said Yeats, making his way to the couch. He gazed down marvelling at how cruelly the passing years had treated his old school-fellow. "AE," he said solemnly, "'tis I."

"Aaatch!" bellowed Mrs. Mulcaster, "wouldja ever get off me corns!"

"Ah, Willie!" called AE from the piano bench. "Join me over here."

"Clumsy ould fool!" moaned Mrs. Mulcaster, massaging her foot.

"You really should wear glasses," said AE, making room on the piano bench.

"It is not my wish," retorted W.B. Yeats, sitting beside him, "to see through a glass darkly. Berkeley. Read much Berkeley, Russell?"

"Ah! Of all our Irish philosophers, the only one with the legitimate glimmer of truth," remarked AE.

"Do you think so?" said Yeats with interest.

Lady Gregory drew Sally over to the sink. "Are dese all of de dirty dishes?"

"No," said Sally, "For some reason, quite a few of them are missing."

"Missing?"

"I've noticed things going missing before. Never so many, though."

"Dishes?"

"All sorts of things. Make-up, packets of cigarettes, the odd couple of bob from your purse."

"Why didn't you mention it?"

Sally looked off. "Well, it was never very much, so you couldn't always be sure."

"Is dere anyone you suspect?"

"Och!" Sally rolled her eyes expressively to the couch. "It's her all right. No doubt about it."

"Mrs. Mulcaster?"

Sally nodded.

"She helped you serve de tea?"

"She did. After I sent someone to fetch her from the front of the house."

"Was dere anything you noticed at all out of de way?"

Sally frowned. "What do you mean?"

"I don't quite know. Was dere anything unusual when you served de tea?"

"No. No, nothing."

"Did anyone else help you?"

Sally grimaced. "Him — if you could call it help."

Lady Gregory turned to see Purefoy taking a volume down from the bookcase by the door. "The Englishman?"

Sally nodded.

"Anybody else?"

"Well, I suppose that woman you hired."

Lady Gregory blinked. "What woman?"

Sally's eyes roamed around the room. "I don't see her now, but she was here a minute ago. Strange little creature, done up as a maid."

". . . Oh yes," said Lady Gregory. "Yes. Anybody else?"

"No. Well, when everybody crowded in, and the party got going, somebody may have made a fresh pot of tea. Eh, I think I saw Mac of all people making one. And perhaps Frank Fay."

Lady Gregory thought for a second. "Sally, will you bring Mrs. Mulcaster over here? As quietly as you can."

"Is anything wrong? I mean, is Mr. Holloway going to be all right?"

Lady Gregory shook off the question with a vague nod and laid her hand on Sally's arm. "And dat woman, de new serving maid, see if you can find her."

Sally frowned. "Right away," she said, and went to the couch and bent over Mrs. Mulcaster.

Lady Gregory turned to the sink and regarded the neatly stacked cups. In a few, there was a half-inch or so of cold tea left. It appeared to be perfectly all right, but best to make certain. She found an empty jug, washed it out, and poured what was left of the tea into it.

It had been easy enough to slip out of the Greenroom when Willie Fay and that young actor were looking after Padraic Colum. But where could she go now?

Christina peeped about helplessly. It was all so dark and strange backstage. Not at all bright and glamourous, but dingy and dusty, and there were alarming objects to bump into.

Thomasina would be waiting for her now in the vestibule, but it was impossible to go out through the auditorium. She would be seen. No, best to find some little out-of-the-way corner, and wait till they all had gone away. So with her hands spread protectively out before her, she fumbled through the gloom. What were these objects stacked against the back wall? Parts of scenery. Perhaps if she could just quietly squeeze in behind them. . . .

Oh, there was more space than she had suspected. It was like a cave actually. And what a jumble of objects was stacked all around. Odd bits of furniture, a rickety table, and something that looked like a throne.

She could just crouch down behind it, and no one would ever find her.

Poor Guillaume. He was probably dead by now. She hadn't waited to see him quaff the deadly brew. Let her remember him as he was in life — tall, noble, deeply brooding. A small, grey tear furrowed down her cheek.

It was very cold, and there was a fierce breeze coming from somewhere. Looking up, she saw a broken window through which she could see the faint reflection of the city lights in the sky outside.

She clasped her hands around her thin arms, and made herself as small as she could. She would think of Guillaume and warm her heart at his dear memory. Perhaps his corpse was already stiff and rigid. Christina did not find such contemplation morbid. Poetically, her aesthetic predilections ran to the Graveyard School of Poetry.

From far away, a clock struck the hour. "Ah yes," Christina marvelled, "just as dear Edward Young had so thrillingly put it in his immortal 'Night Thoughts on Life, Death and Immortality'," whose 459 melancholy lines she had long ago committed to memory.

"The Bell strikes *One*" hath wrote (writ? wrat?) Edward Young. How deeply right, how profoundly true.

But it would never again strike One for *him*, Guillaume. Oh, if she could but be vouchsafed one last look, one parting glimpse to treasure in the sad recesses of her faithful heart. Even a glimpse of just his dear hand, with its lovely, long tapering fingers. . . .

And lo! Christina's prayers were answered. The moon, just for an instant, broke through the black and ominous clouds; and its weak rays, just for an instant, fell upon. . . the hand.

With a sharp intake of breath, Christina stared upon it. "Guillaume, you've come back for me! You've crossed back over! Now we shall always be together!" Impulsively, she reached out to clasp the hand, hardly noticing that the fingers were not really slim, long and tapering. They were rather pudgy actually.

"When AE reads his poems," continued Frank Fay judiciously, "some lines are given in a monotone, while others are spoken to a little tune."

"Murdered," mumbled W.J. Lawrence numbly.

"Now, in some of those tunes the notes could almost be recorded, but, between these sung notes, are indefinite and minute shades of tone more characteristic of the speaking voice, and. . . ."

"Mur. . . ," said W.J. Lawrence, his eyes fluttering shut.

Willie Fay brought her out to him.

"Johnny, what's happening?" she asked.

He took her hands in his. "We're asking some questions. Silly waste of time probably, but Lady Gregory's afraid for Yeats."

"Why?"

"Lawrence was in the balcony and says he saw Yeats actually give the tea to Holloway."

"Oh!"

"Would you mind," Synge asked, "quizzing Brigit O'Dempsey for us? It might be easier if you did. Try and find out if she saw anything at all out of the way. Particularly about the serving of the tea."

She nodded, hesitated, then pecked him on the cheek.

"Are you feeling all right?" he said. "You look — ."

"It's nothing," she said, and went back in.

After a second, he stepped up to the door, and, keeping in the shadows, whispered, "Fay!"

Willie Fay, who was standing just inside, came out to him. "How long is it going to be?"

"Not long. Are they getting restless?"

"Just grumpy. I think a lot of them don't feel too well."

Oh dear God, thought Synge.

"What seems to be the matter with them?"

Willie Fay shrugged. "Don't know. Colum's been pretty sick. Thrown up twice. And O'Rourke's not in the best, and neither's Mac."

"Umm. Send O'Rourke out, will you?"

Padraic Colum was slumped in a chair in the corner, just as far as possible from AE's puffing pipe.

Oliver Gogarty sat down beside him. "You don't look at all tip-top," he said.

"Something I ate, I suppose. I feel a bit better now."

"What did you eat?"

"Nothing much. A slice of Lady Gregory's cake. It's never agreed with me, but I don't like to hurt her feelings."

"And for dinner?"

"I had an omelette on the way to the theatre."

"Wouldn't seem to be much harm in that. Did you have any tea to-night?"

Padraic Colum's gaze slid away. "Do you think we can go home soon?"

"Oh, I should think so, yes. Did you drink any tea to-night?"

There was a long silence before Padraic Colum put his hand in his pocket and brought out a little tin container.

They paused for breath.

It is AE's language, Yeats decided. He writes "dream" where other men write "dreams," a trick he and I once shared, picked up from William Sharp perhaps when the romantic movement was in its last contortions.

It is Yeats' brain, AE decided. Perhaps I should open communication with him through the medium of astral light.

J.A. O'Rourke took the unlit cigarette out of his mouth and stared at it sadly. "Begod, I never thought there'd come a time I think twice about lighting a fag."

"When did you start feeling bad?" asked Synge.

"Oh, maybe thirty-forty minutes ago. First a quick, sharp pain in the belly, and then I got all nauseous like, and then — blupp! — up it all came."

"Anyone else under the weather?"

"Well, Mac wasn't his usual charming self, and I think Frank Fay and Joe Kerrigan had a touch of whatever it was too."

Synge nodded. "Did you eat anything?"

"Oh," O'Rourke said with a grimace, "just me usual penance of Gort cake, but it never affected me like this before. Eh, got a light?"

Synge produced one. "Did you drink much tea?"

"Oh, two or three cups." He inhaled deeply and then blew out a cloud of blue smoke and smiled. "Ah, that's good. I must be gameball again."

"Notice anything about the tea?"

"No. No, why, was there something wrong with it?"

"Probably not. I was just looking for something in common that would make several people ill. Eh, did you notice anything about the preparing of the tea?"

"I didn't pay any attention. Sure, there's nothing to making tea. Even Sinclair can do it."

Synge looked up casually. "Did Sinclair make tea?"

"Yeh. Astonished us all, he did. Usually, he waits for some slave to bring it to him."

Synge studied the red tip of O'Rourke's cigarette.

"How long are we going to be here, do you think?" asked O'Rourke after a bit.

"Shouldn't be long."

"And how's old Holloway?"

"About as — well as can be expected."

O'Rourke nodded and yawned. "Not a bad ould skin. Means well anyhow." He started off, and then turned back. "Eh, one thing — ."

Synge looked up.

"If there was anything wrong — that is, if someone was jack-acting — ."

"Yes?"

O'Rourke shuffled his feet. "We don't always get along too well, all of us, the actors I mean, on a day-to-day basis. But I wouldn't say any of us would actually do anything to, eh, harm any of the others, if you know what I mean."

Synge nodded.

"But the fact is, there's been some strange goings-on around the theatre lately. I don't know whether you've heard."

"I've heard something."

O'Rourke carefully tipped the dead ash off his cigarette into his hand. "Tricks like. Practical jokes. And some of them not so funny. So if there was anything odd-like going on to-night, well, I know where I'd look."

"Where?"

O'Rourke hitched up his left shoulder in a half shrug. "Ah, maybe I've said too much." And he slouched back into the Greenroom.

Sally brought a truculent Mrs. Mulcaster over to Lady Gregory at the sink.

"Whatever time of night is it a-tall?" Mrs. Mulcaster complained. "I don't know how I'll get home to the Coombe. Me poor husband will be sick with worry and suspicion."

"We're calling a cab for you, Mrs. Mulcaster."

Mrs. Mulcaster blinked in mollified surprise. "A cab, is it?" A pity that the neighbours wouldn't be awake to see her galloping up in state.

"I believe," said Lady Gregory sternly, "you were helping Mr. Synge gather up the box-office receipts in the vestibule."

"Eh, was I? I disremember."

"You can give me the money now."

"Eh, didn't I give it to him?"

Lady Gregory held out her hand inexorably, and Mrs. Mulcaster finally explored first one pocket and then another.

"Ah!" she brightened. "You're right!" And she drew out three crumpled notes and a fistful of coins. "Me mind's bamboozled, bein' up so late and all."

"Just so," said Lady Gregory, quickly totting up the amount in her mind. At least five shillings were unaccounted for. She decided not to mention it for the moment.

"Now, Mrs. Mulcaster," she said, "were you here in de Greenroom earlier, helping set out de things for tea?"

"Eh, you mean before the debate? Indeed, I was."

"You were not," said Sally hotly. "I set everything out."

"Oh yis, it comes back to me now. So you did. I had me hands full preparin' everthing out in the vestibule, and so wasn't able to give you the proper supervision. Ya did well though, ya did."

"Hmmph!" Sally sniffed.

"So you weren't here in de Greenroom until de debate was over," Lady Gregory said. "Den you came back and helped with de tea."

"Oh, I did, just as soon as me chores and duties in the front of the house permitted. I knew Miss Allgood would be busy, flittin' around jawin' to people. Oh, I had me hands full, what with the cuttin' and the slicin' and the pourin' and of course directin' the new girl."

"Ah yes," said Lady Gregory, "de new girl. Did you find her, Sally?"

"No. Maybe she's gone home."

"Take another look around. Try de women's dressing-room."

"Yes, ma'am."

"Now, Mrs. Mulcaster, did you notice anything at all curious about either de cake or de tea?"

This time the puzzlement in Mrs. Mulcaster's face was real enough. "No, nothin' curious, yer Ladyship, except that beardy man over there had five or six cups. He must have an iron stummick."

Lady Gregory regarded AE who was sitting on the piano bench with a gesticulating Yeats and puffing away impassively. He certainly seemed well enough. Which meant that whatever was in Holloway's cup was not in everybody's.

"Do ya think we'll be able to lave soon, yer Ladyship?" Mrs. Mulcaster whinged. "Me poor feet are only killin' me."

Arthur Sinclair was sprawled out in the one easy chair, his overcoat draped over him like a blanket.

"Ah, Sinclair," said Oliver Gogarty, "I haven't congratulated you on your splendid performance last week."

Arthur Sinclair half-opened one eye and groaned.

"You're being too modest," Oliver Gogarty said. "Are you feeling quite well?"

Arthur Sinclair belched and patted his belly solicitously. "Me stomach's upset."

"Ah yes," said Oliver Gogarty judiciously. "You hearty eaters. Of course, it might merely be indigestion. Probably not gallstones or a bleeding ulcer."

"Eh?" said Arthur Sinclair, sitting up alarmed.

"Have you thought of going on a diet?"

"Diet!"

"Yes, lose some of that weight. Puts a heavy strain on the heart, you know."

"Ah!" said Arthur Sinclair, feeling for his heart.

"Experience a bit of a flutter there, do you? I'm not surprised."

"No, no, not anything like a flutter, ah no. More just a — a . . . little bit of a murmur now and then."

"Worse yet," said Oliver Gogarty. "You'd better get onto the salads."

"Salads!"

"And the fruit. A few nuts possibly. Here, let's take your pulse."

Ambrose Power leaned over uncomfortably from the next chair. "Eh, Doctor, were you sayin' Mac here ought to go on a diet?"

"Hmm," said Oliver Gogarty, relinquishing Sinclair's wrist. "Not the best. Perhaps I'd just better take your pulse too, Power."

"Ah no! It's fine, grand!" said Ambrose Power nervously.

"Better safe than sorry," Oliver Gogarty said firmly, and took his wrist. "Yes, diet and plenty of exercise is what I'd prescribe for the both of you. You beefy young fellows all think you're safe, but — ." He shook his head glumly. "There's the real danger of dysentery, strokes, colly-wobbles."

"Ahhh!" cried Arthur Sinclair.

"How's me pulse, doctor?" said Ambrose Power. "Bangin' away like a Lambeg drum, I'd say. Eh?"

Oliver Gogarty consulted his watch, then shook his head des-pondently and dropped Power's wrist. "Can't find it at all."

"Ohhh," groaned Ambrose Power. "And I throwed up a while ago too. Everything in me poor stomach."

"Is that so?" said Oliver Gogarty. "That's bad. How many slices of Gort cake did you two have to-night?"

"Och," said Arthur Sinclair, "only two or three."

"Only three or four," said Ambrose Power miserably.

"And tea? I suppose you had tea too. The worst thing for you. As bad as porter. You had tea, Sinclair?"

"I did," said Arthur Sinclair forlornly. "Two or three cups."

"Oh, dear! And you, Power?"

"Only three or four or so," said Ambrose Power, with a quiver of his fat lower lip. "And, sure, I only sipped at 'em."

"There couldn't be any harm in a wee cuppa tea," said Arthur Sinclair. "With a good dollop of health-giving milk in it."

"Milk!" said Oliver Gogarty. "Milk as well, my God." He bent down and arranged Arthur Sinclair's overcoat around him. "Hmm," he sud-denly said, and extracted a dark bottle from the pocket. "What's this?"

"That's nothin'!" said Arthur Sinclair, his eyes growing alarmed. "Only a bottle of Kandee Sauce for me steaks and chops."

"Great stuff," said Ambrose Power. "Full of herbs and essences and all."

Oliver Gogarty raised the dark bottle to eye-level. "It's half gone," he murmured.

"Half gone!" said Ambrose Power. "And you only buyin' it on the way to the theatre to-night, Mac. You could probably get a replace-ment."

"Eh, never mind that," said Arthur Sinclair gruffly.

Oliver Gogarty screwed the cap off and lifted the bottle to his nose. His eyes glinted in recognition.

"Somebody nicked me other bottle from me coat," Arthur Sinclair explained plaintively. "Probably that villain Kerrigan."

W.G. Fay held his arm across the door. "Nobody leaves." he said sternly.

"But Miss Allgood just went out," protested Leslie Chenevix Purefoy.

"She was on a legitimate errand."

"But my dear fellow, I shall be locked out of my lodgings."

Synge appeared outside the door. "We'll take care of it, Mr. Purefoy. Now if you'll just sit quietly for another few minutes."

With bad grace, Purefoy stalked away.

"He puts my back up," muttered Willie Fay. "He's a jinx."

"Jinx?" queried Synge.

Willie Fay scowled. "There's a lot of quare old things been going on around here."

"Did you drink any tea to-night, Fay?"

"Tea? A couple of sips, that's all. Then I lost my cup, and I could never get that girl to bring me another."

"That girl?"

"Somebody who was helping out."

"Who were you talking to?"

Willie Fay reflected. "Nearly everybody, at one time or another."

"Who especially?"

"Well, the brother for a bit, but only for a bit. We're a little at odds lately."

"You and Frank?"

Willie Fay grimaced. "Ah, we had a bit of a set-to in Tommy Lennon's the other day. Nothing important. He'll come round. You know Frank."

"Was he drinking tea?"

"Can't remember."

"Who else?"

"Well, I was talking to Yeats. I wanted to have it out with him about Payne and the new arrangements."

232

Synge smiled noncommitally. "And was he drinking tea?"

"Bill Butler? Eh, he misplaced his cup too. You know how he is. But Colum gave him another."

Synge looked mildly surprised. "And did Yeats drink it?"

Willie Fay puzzled for a second. "I don't remember. He didn't seem to have it when we broke off."

"Think. Did he put it down?"

Willie Fay pondered. "I remember him gesturing with it and sloshing some into the saucer. Maybe he put it down then. I can't say as I actually remember him drinking it. He gets carried away when he's talking, you know."

Lady Gregory came up to them. "I've spoken to all of my people. Shall I see if Dr. Gogarty's done?"

"Yes," said Synge. "We mustn't take much longer."

Sally appeared at Synge's back and spoke over his shoulder to Lady Gregory. "I can't find her, whoever she is. She doesn't appear to be anywhere backstage."

"All right," said Lady Gregory. "I'll fetch Dr. Gogarty."

"Ah, Sally. . . ." said Synge.

She looked up at him with unconcealed hostility.

"Miss Allgood," he amended. "Would you ask your sister, Miss O'Neill, to come out for a minute?"

"My sister, Miss O'Neill," she said coldly, "is named Molly."

"Would you ask Molly to come out to me?"

She nodded briefly and stepped past him into the Greenroom.

"Most," said Frank Fay sagely, "of what Miss Farr did is similar to what one hears in the churches. She speaks on def-i-nite notes, and she speaks to a rhy-thm. But, I ask you, is it *the* rhy-thm?"

W.J. Lawrence rhythmically snored.

They gathered in the vestibule.

"I think," said Oliver Gogarty, "we've checked on everybody except Frank Fay who's in the men's dressing-room looking after Lawrence."

"We can probably leave out Fay," said Synge. "He's one of the ones who got sick."

"Has anyone talked to Kerrigan?" queried Lady Gregory.

"He was ill too," said Gogarty. "At least somewhat."

"There's no need to discuss it further," said W.B. Yeats impatiently. "The solution to this murder most foul is blindingly obvious."

With one accord, they turned to him.

"You mean, W.B.," said Oliver Gogarty, "you know how it was done?"

Yeats brushed the question aside. "Not how it was done, which is hardly a question of the first importance. I know *who* did it."

"Who, Willie?" asked Lady Gregory.

"In detective fiction," Yeats pronounced, waggling a tutorial finger, "the least likely suspect is inevitably the culprit."

"Oh really, Willie," Lady Gregory protested.

He frowned her down. "There is a psychological justness to that which the artist can appreciate, having by his intense perceptivity and heightened awareness — ."

"W.B.," said Oliver Gogarty, "it's late."

"The tragic artist," Yeats announced quellingly, "and I include even the phlegmatic Ibsen, realizes that."

Synge patiently began to roll a cigarette.

"I refer to the remorseless stripping away of appearance from reality. That is what we have in *Oedipus Rex*, in Ben Jonson and in, as Lady Gregory will tell you, Molière."

"I will not tell dem now, Willie," she observed.

He paced back and forth across the vestibule. "The fundamental problem for the artist-detective is to penetrate the veil of the 'seeming' in order to reveal the essence of the 'is.' Therefore, while you three have been framing your prosaic factual queries about teacups, I have been boldly striking at the dark heart of the mystery — the who?"

"What who?" queried Oliver Gogarty with a grin. "You, W.B.?"

"No!" thundered Yeats. "My personal transgressions are blunt, my sins are plain, and my villainies publicly flamboyant. No, I refer to a more dark, a more sinister intent, an intelligence one can only describe as malignantly daemonic."

"I give up," said Oliver Gogarty. "Who?"

Yeats magnificently folded his arms. "AE!"

Lady Gregory slumped on the bench below the stairs and absently tucked back a strand of iron-grey hair.

John Synge stubbed out his cigarette and rubbed his throbbing head.

Oliver Gogarty appeared to have trouble breathing.

234

However, he controlled himself, tore two sheets out of his notebook and presented them to Yeats. "Fascinating, W.B. I think you should write all that down at once."

"Yes," Yeats conceded. "Posterity."

"And the press," Gogarty added.

"Hmm, just so," said the poet, crossing to the tea counter and beginning to scribble.

"I can't understand," Synge said softly, "why everybody didn't get ill."

"Some didn't take tea," said Lady Gregory, "and some took only a little."

"True, but AE drank quite a lot, and he wasn't upset a bit."

Oliver Gogarty shrugged. "Well, I'm no expert in forensic toxicology, but the degrees of toxicity vary from one subject to another. Some individuals can build up an immunity to a particular substance."

"Dat," said Lady Gregory, "would explain AE's immunity. Once at Coole he drank ten cups for breakfast."

"Possibly," said Gogarty. "It's important to remember that poisoning doesn't have a necesssarily all-or-nothing effect. And, of course, many substances are toxic. Not merely potassium cyanide. Tobacco. Even common table salt, if you take enough. Even that staple of our Irish diet, the spud. It can be poisonous if the tuber grows at the surface and becomes green through exposure to the sun."

"Is there anything poisonous one could easily make tea out of?" Synge asked.

Oliver Gogarty thought for a second. "Lots."

"Dis is getting us nowhere," said Lady Gregory.

"Perhaps somewhere," said Oliver Gogarty. "We know that two people put alien substances into the tea. Sinclair poured half a bottle of Kandee Sauce into a pot, and some of it got into Holloway's cup."

"Dere wouldn't be anything in dat to hurt you."

Oliver Gogarty produced the bottle of Kandee Sauce and scanned the label. "Soy," he read, "acetic acid, salt, spices, caramel, garlic, onions, flavouring. I wouldn't think so."

"Acetic acid?" said Lady Gregory. "What's dat?"

"Only the essential compound," said Gogarty, "of ordinary vinegar."

"Colum," said Synge, "put some pills into Yeats' cup."

Gogarty produced a small tin box from his pocket and held it out for them to see. "A commercial brand of ordinary aspirin."

"But aspirin can kill," Lady Gregory said slowly. "Dere was a case a few years ago in Galway, a young girl who was pregnant and actually died from taking aspirin."

"Ah," said Oliver Gogarty, "but she would have had to have taken a lot. The normal person could probably take quite a few without ill effects, and this box contained only twelve."

"Wouldn't dat be enough?"

"I don't think so," said Oliver Gogarty. "If you drank the whole cup, it would probably make you ill. Or if you were a very small child, it could be lethal, but for a normal-sized adult — ."

"All right," said Lady Gregory, "but dere was something else in Mr. Holloway's cup. De colour was a dark, milky green."

"And," added Oliver Gogarty brightly, "the cup that Colum passed to Yeats — the tea in it was greenish, which would lead one to think that they were the same cup."

"So then," said Synge, "we have substance X, which was in the Yeats-Holloway cup along with the Kandee Sauce and the aspirin."

"Yes, yes," said Lady Gregory, "but substance Y may have been in that cup too."

"Substance Y?" Synge frowned.

"Whatever was in everybody else's cup and made some of dem ill."

They all paused, lost in their own thoughts.

"Well," said Oliver Gogarty, glancing at his notes, "that's about as far as we can go. We've established that there are at least three would-be poisoners, as well as three or even four would-be poisons. So I think it's time we called in the gendarmes."

"Let me see those notes of yours for a second, Gogarty," said Synge. He took the two scraps of paper and quickly scanned them. "The real poison," he said, "has to be this green substance, and we do know who put it in — the vanishing serving-maid."

"If dere was any such person."

"There had to be. Sally talked to her. Mrs. Mulcaster talked to her. Fay mentioned her to me. And Colum told you, Gogarty, that she gave him the tea cup. That seems pretty conclusive."

Gogarty grimaced dourly. "A conclusion that doesn't conclude. In fact, that leads to a dead end — pardon the expression. I simply mean that our mysterious lady has vanished. Miss Allgood thoroughly searched around backstage."

Lady Gregory nodded. "Yes, and Sally's very trustworthy. So perhaps our servant-maid came out through the auditorium."

"No," said Gogarty. "When I passed through, I called up to Kerrigan to ask if anyone else had gone out. Nobody, he said — except, of course, you two and Yeats."

"And I had Fay lock the side door to the laneway," said Synge. "I know he did because I saw Purefoy trying to get out that way."

Gogarty folded up his notes. "The police then?"

"Nobody has really questioned Kerrigan," Synge observed mildly.

"True," Gogarty admitted, "and doubtless we should have. On the other hand, Willie Fay trusted him enough to stand watch over Holloway."

"Oh, I'm not really suspecting him," said Synge. "I don't think he'd hurt a fly."

"Eh," said Lady Gregory, "just let me look at dose notes for a second, Dr. Gogarty."

Gogarty sighed softly, thought of his comfortable bed in Ely Place, and passed the papers over. She took them and stood peering at them closely.

"What we keep coming up against," said Gogarty softly to Synge, "is the problem of him." He gestured over his shoulder to the absorbed and scribbling Yeats. "We have eye-witness testimony that Yeats gave the cup to Holloway. That we can't get around."

"Dere is one other person we haven't really questioned," said Lady Gregory. "De English actor."

Oliver Gogarty wistfully fingered the watch in his pocket. "It must be very late. Has he been with the company long enough to loathe anybody?"

"We are not," Lady Gregory observed, "an entirely lovable lot."

"Purefoy's name does keep coming up," said Synge.

"All right," said Oliver Gogarty wearily. "Let's have him out, but let's, for God's sake, be quick about it."

"Yeats," observed Frank Fay, "laid ggggreat stress on what he called a 'wise mon-o-tony'."

W.J. Lawrence, sleeping, did not disagree.

Leslie Chenevix Purefoy had effected an exit from the Greenroom. It had entailed pleading an urgent call of nature to the unsympathetic Willie Fay, and being escorted by the faithful Gussie Gaffney who was now banging lustily on the door.

"Come on now, Mr. Purefoy darling, before you float the theatre away and drown us all."

"Momently, Augustus, momently."

A flurry of bangs from Gussie's thudding fists shook the toilet door.

"Come on now, Mr. Purefoy, or I'll have to be after bustin' it down!"

Smiling sweetly, Leslie Chenevix Purefoy unlatched the door and threw it open, managing, he was gratified to note, to bash the unwary Gussie sharply on the nose.

"Augustus!" he cried solicitously. "What have you done to yourself?"

"I dink me nobe if bleebin'!"

"Bedad and begorrah, but it is," cried Purefoy. "Allow me to be of assistance." He proferred the second-best handkerchief he had at some time during the course of the confused evening abstracted from the pocket of Mr. Joseph Holloway, deceased.

Purefoy had a magpie proclivity for acquiring whatever small pieces of property might be left lying about by their nominal owners. One never knew when handkerchiefs, small coins, pocket combs, holograph manuscripts or bottles of tangy meat sauce might come in handy.

As Gussie applied the cloth to his gory nostrils, the alert eyes of Leslie Chenevix Purefoy were arrested by something white on the floor, just outside the spill of light from the toilet door. Unobtrusively he bent down and picked it up. It proved to be a wilted maid's cap he had last observed perched upon the sparse hair of the little serving-maid, a.k.a. Miss Christina McFitz. As a matter of habit, he tucked it safely into his jacket pocket, mildly wondering once again just how Miss Christina McFitz, a semi-prominent poet, had sunk to that subservient position.

Something alarming, not absolutely unprecedented but of rare enough occurrence, was happening to George Moore. Scratchy, sand-papery — could they possibly be described as kisses? — rasped his pale cheeks.

"Stop! Have you no decency?" he cried weakly.

"None, Guillaume, I am in a tumult of passion!" came the intense reply.

A twisting, wiry weight squirmed and writhed upon him.

"This was destined before the beginning of time!"

"Edward!" he cried. "Edward!"

Leslie Chenevix Purefoy had been alternately concerned, helpful, respectful, puzzled and abjectly contrite in his inability to offer even one jot of illuminating information. A magnificent performance. One of his finest.

Synge had sunk down on the bench beneath the stairs. Lady Gregory was gazing unseeingly at J. B. Yeats' portrait of Sara Allgood. Oliver Gogarty was impatiently balancing back and forth on the balls of his feet. And Yeats was at the tea counter, lips silently moving and his left hand waving as if conducting some mute melody.

"Well," said Oliver Gogarty finally, "I think we had better — ."

"Eh, yer Ladyship," called Gussie Gaffney coming through the auditorium door. "Willie Fay wants me to ask how long will it be before we can send everybody home."

"Why Gussie," she said, surprised, "whatever have you done to yourself?"

"Ah," he said, daubing at his still flowing nose, "I just banged meself against a door in the dark."

"Your, er, bandage there," observed Oliver Gogarty, "seems a trifle unsanitary."

"Where," said Synge, a curious edge to his voice, "did you get that handkerchief, Gaffney?"

"Oh, Mr. Purefoy there kindly lent it to me."

Gingerly Synge took the handkerchief and held it up between thumb and forefinger. "This yours, Purefoy?"

"Yes, yes," said Leslie Chenevix Purefoy with a beautifully embarrassed little laugh. "Please excuse its lamentable condition. My laundry is a little late this — ."

"Purefoy," said Synge, "just why does your handkerchief have the initials 'J.H.' embroidered in the corner?"

"Ah, of course," explained Purefoy. "I believe Mr. Holloway dropped it yesterday, and I was returning it to him."

Synge gave him a long look. "Let's see what else is in your pockets."

"Now I say," exclaimed Leslie Chenevix Purefoy, "this is unheard of! This is unconscionable! I really must protest!"

Synge tightened his grip on Purefoy's thin arm. "Gussie," he said, "hold onto him and make sure he protests silently."

"Oh, very well," said Purefoy, starting to empty his pockets on the tea counter, "but you're making a colossal mistake."

"One bottle, empty," said Synge, "of Kandee Sauce."

"It's nice on lobsters," explained Purefoy.

"Item," said Oliver Gogarty, "one key ring with eight keys."

"Dat key dere!" exclaimed Lady Gregory. "Dat's de key to de office!"

"How do you explain that, Mr. Purefoy?" asked Gogarty.

Leslie Chenevix Purefoy smiled wanly.

"One wallet," said Synge, "containing a pound note and some identifying papers."

"Ah yes, poor O'Rourke has this weakness for betting on the horses, you see, and he wanted me to keep temptation from him."

"No," said Synge, "these papers belong to Padraic Colum."

"But," said Oliver Gogarty, peering into a second wallet, "the papers in here belong to O'Rourke."

"Well, eh, yes," said Leslie Chenevix Purefoy, "but it really amounts to the same thing."

"I shouldn't be at all surprised," Oliver Gogarty remarked.

"What I mean is, young Mr. Colum is secretly — I hope I am not breaking a confidence — secretly given to drink, a not unusual failing for artists, and I merely offered to protect him from the vice by holding his — ."

"One receipt," said Synge, "from James J. Fox, tobacconist, dated to-day."

"And five tins of Player's Rough Cut," said Oliver Gogarty, neatly stacking the five tins on top of each other. "You must be quite an addict, Purefoy."

"Ah yes, it's a bad habit," said Purefoy sadly.

"Sure, Mr. Purefoy, you don't smoke a pipe," said Gussie.

"Eh, I'm thinking of taking it up."

Oliver Gogarty opened a tin and looked inside. "Empty."

Synge opened another. Then they opened the rest. They were all empty.

"Eh," said Purefoy, "there are many tensions in the artistic life."

"Whatever is dat?" wondered Lady Gregory, probing a small furry object with her forefinger.

"Oh, that's Mr. Purefoy's moustache," explained Gussie. "One of 'em anyway. He's always puttin' one on and takin' somebody off. Fantastic."

"Yes," said Synge slowly, "I remember he does Mr. Holloway startlingly well."

"Oh, and lots more," said Gussie. "Frank Fay, Mac, Sally, Mr. Y — er, lots of others."

"Yes," said Lady Gregory, "Yeats is particularly fine."

"Thank you," said Yeats, poring over his manuscript.

"Hmm," said Gogarty. "And what have we here? Two interesting items of female apparel." He lifted a garter from the counter and twirled it around on his finger.

"That," said Leslie Chenevix Purefoy with a sad dignity. "has a sentimental value."

"Ah, but this next item?" Oliver Gogarty held up a wilted maid's cap.

"I wonder," said Synge, "if we haven't found our mysterious maid servant."

"No!" cried Purefoy. "I mean really *no!*"

Synge took the maid's cap from Gogarty and held it up to the head of Leslie Chenevix Purefoy, and then tied the strings behind his two large, prominent ears.

Thursday, February 5: II

Singly and in muted pairs, the actors trooped out into the laneway. From the door of the women's dressing-room, Sally watched them go. Then she turned back to snap off the light.

Her sister was still sitting limply at the make-up table.

"Come on, love," said Sally. "You look all in."

Molly shook her head. "I'm waiting for him."

"Oh, Moll," Sally said softly.

"He'll expect me to. I — think he'll expect me to. I've got to find out, haven't I, once and for all?"

Sally slowly nodded. "I suppose you do." She hesitated, then crossed to her sister and bent down to kiss her on the forehead. "I'll leave the door on the latch."

Molly smiled into the make-up mirror and listened to her sister's footsteps recede.

"Good night, Sally," she heard Brigit O'Dempsey say.

"Good night, Bridie. I hope you're feeling better, love."

"Ah, a good night's sleep, and I'll be right as rain. That is, if that man of mine thinks people should ever go home to their beds. Willie! Willie! Aren't you coming?"

"Ah, hold your horses!" called Willie Fay from somewhere in the empty, hollow-sounding theatre. "I'm coming!"

There were hurried steps outside. The door to the laneway slammed. And the theatre was quiet.

He'd taken her hand onstage. In front of them all. And that surely to God must mean. . . . Well! If he didn't mean it he didn't. And she could get along without him. Get along very well, as she always had. And she wouldn't give any of them the chance to pity her either.

But she felt the tears well up in her eyes, swell and drop, and — damn, spoil her make-up!

Angrily she rummaged in her make-up box for — and what was this?

She lifted up a little glass tube with a cork stopper in it. Now who had put that there, and whatever was it for? She was about to toss it away

242

when she saw that there was a bit of something in the bottom.

And then she caught her breath, for what was there was a murky, milky green.

"It's all gone quiet now, darling."

Darling, George Moore groaned.

"I believe it is safe to effect our escape."

He sat creakily up, every bone aching in his pear-shaped body. "How?"

"Shh," she said, touching him on the lips. "Oh! Guillaume, you've grown a hirsute moustache. How very quick! But I should have expected nothing less from one so physical. May I trim it for you in the morning?"

"No, you may not!" snarled George Moore. "All I want you to do is to discover how to escape from this hellhole. God, the folly of taking an interest in the drama! A low, crude, crass, vulgar and repellently disgusting form of art!"

"How profound!" said his companion, enthusiastically twining her bony arms around his neck. "You are always right, dearest Guillaume. We are both poets, and shall spend our marvellous days writing beautiful lyrics, and we shall spend our glorious nights — ."

"I don't want to hear about our glorious nights!" George Moore said vehemently. "I want to get out of here!"

"I have devised a way, dearest. Just above us is a broken window which we may leap through."

"Leap?" said George Moore.

"With love's light wings!"

"I assure you, madam, I am totally incapable of any such indecorous gymnastic feat."

"Not actually leap, beloved. I have discovered a sturdy box. You have but to stand on it, and — whoosh!"

"Whoosh?" said George Moore, feeling himself pulled roughly to his feet.

"Whoosh, the deed is done!"

"Do stop talking like Lady Macbeth."

"Now just place your handsome foot there."

"Ouch!"

"What is it, *mon ange?*"

"I have just got a splinter!"

"Don my sandals."

"I will not don your stinking sandals. Stop gouging me, you vicious harpy!"

"I am only helping you up. There!"

"Ugh!"

"Now rest your tum-tum on the window sill."

"Madam," said George Moore, "I do not have a tum-tum. I have an abdomen."

"Yes," she cooed, "soft as a pillow."

Briefly George Moore reconsidered that notion about writing his memoirs.

"Oww!" he cried, "there is glass in this window. Stop pushing! You are ripping my shirt! You are scraping my — !"

"Just a little more exertion, dear one. You pull, and I will push."

"I cannot move, you fiendish termagant! I am stuck in this damnable window!"

"But one last manly effort, sweetest, and the world will open before us with all its wild promise."

"Oh, shut up."

"This time we shall not fail. We are as two enchanted hearts that beat as one!" And putting both of her small hands upon his plump buttocks, Christina, with all the power her brave little spirit could muster, gave one mighty shove.

Like a cork exploding from a champagne bottle, George Moore flew through the window and lit with a sickening thud in the wet laneway outside.

"*Cherie?*" whispered Christina anxiously. "*Ne quittez pas!*" And she dropped feet first onto George Moore's soft, pillowlike tum-tum.

They had left Yeats and his muse in the vestibule and adjourned to the Greenroom.

Gussie grinned cheerfully at the wilting figure of Leslie Chenevix Purefoy on the couch. Sure, this was better than a Bronco Billy fillum.

"Let's sum the case up, Purefoy," said Oliver Gogarty. "You had possession of Holloway's handkerchief."

Leslie Chenevix Purefoy essayed a not entirely successful shrug.

"Also," continued Oliver Gogarty, "possession of an empty bottle of Kandee Sauce."

"But," complained Leslie Chenevix Purefoy, "I had most of that for lunch. Honest!"

"Such a bottle lately disappeared from the overcoat of Arthur Sinclair," Gogarty added. "And Kandee Sauce was poured into some of the tea. Also you had wrongful possession of a key to the office of the theatre, and wrongful possession of a wallet belonging to J.A. O'Rourke and another belonging to Padraic Colum."

Leslie Chenevix Purefoy squirmed in his seat and wiped a bead of perspiration from his upper lip. "Possibly I owe you some explanation."

Oliver Gogarty gave a quick nod to Synge. "Possibly!"

"It's very embarrassing," said Leslie Chenevix Purefoy, his face a study in chagrin. "In fact, it's a shabby story. I admit it is, and I would be grateful if it would go no further."

"That's to be seen," said Synge.

"Well. . . the fact is, I am the miserable victim of a lamentable psychological complaint. It has occasioned me untold distress and — yes, I candidly admit it — even certain professional difficulties. Why, you must wonder is an actor of my standing, with my experience in the major classic roles of the English stage, reduced to the degraded position of a lowly spear-carrier in an obscure provincial theatre? Pardon! I am overcome." And abruptly he turned away and dabbed his eyes.

"My heart is there in the coffin with Caesar," said Gussie Gaffney unexpectedly, "and I must pause till it come back to me."

"Get on with it, Purefoy," said Oliver Gogarty.

"Yes, yes," said Leslie Chenevix Purefoy bravely. "The fact is, gentlemen, madam, that I am the unhappy victim of what is known to the scientific world as kleptomania. It is an inherited trait. My poor father, the colonel, had his career blasted for the same reason. Reduced to the ranks, he the hero of Singh-Blatt, for purloining some trifling object — a collar-stud, I believe — from the company mess. The disgrace broke him utterly. He could never lift his head again."

"Stop blubbering, Purefoy."

"Yes, yes. Forgive my personal bereavement. Well, gentlemen, madam, I too am afflicted with this ghastly malady. I don't know what comes over me. It is an obsession. Oh, not that I ever take anything of real value — a pencil perhaps, a box of matches, an inexpensive bauble at most. And I have always in my moments of blessed sanity — my many, my frequent moments — replaced the purloined trifles. But I have occasionally in those rare moments of wild delirium been discovered as, alas, I have been to-night. Oh, it has been the bane of my existence, a wrenching personal tragedy that has kept me from assuming my rightful place upon the boards of Drury Lane. Irving himself once said to me, 'Leslie, my boy, you are more to be pitied than condemned.' Well, be that as it may, gentlemen, madam, I have never succumbed — no, never — as my poor father, the general. I have ever held my head high. I have . . . soldiered on."

"Begod, Mr. Purefoy," said Gussie, visibly affected, "forget about that half-crown."

"Thank you, Augustus," sniffled Leslie Chenevix Purefoy. "You are one of nature's noblemen. And thank you, gentlemen. Thank you, madam. It is not often a poor wretch encounters such compassionate hearts. I can only hope that, as I wend my weary, solitary steps from your hospitable green isle, you will sometimes, now and then, say a silent prayer for the lorn, the lonely and the sorely afflicted Leslie Chenevix Purefoy."

"Ah God!" said Gussie, a choke in his voice.

"Why, Purefoy," said Synge dryly, "did you put the Kandee Sauce in the tea?"

"A crotchet!" said Leslie Chenevix Purefoy deprecatingly, "a playful whim, a jape on the spur of the moment. Oh, childish, I grant you, and most ill-considered. But there is so little joy in my dreary days, that I sometimes cannot resist contributing to the genial social merriment. Well, gentlemen, madam, I trust this bagatelle is now completely cleared up. Nay, more than bagatelle — the fault, the fault I freely confess, that it is."

"Better than Italian opera," Gogarty murmured.

"There is still," Synge pointed out, "the curious matter of the five empty tobacco tins."

"I think," said Lady Gregory, "dat I can explain de empty tobacco tins." She brought a heavy teapot over to the table and set it down on a newspaper. Then she dipped a spoon into the teapot and brought something out and emptied it onto the paper.

"Dat does not," she said, "entirely look like tea leaves."

Oliver Gogarty probed the sodden brown mound and then lifted his forefinger to his mouth. "No," he agreed, "and it does not entirely taste like tea leaves."

The three turned to Purefoy.

"Well!" he said with a gay laugh. "You have found me out. Oh, that was too much, I frankly admit. I definitely shouldn't have done that. No, I shouldn't. And, indeed, it was far from my original intention. No, originally I meant to go to a certain chemist in Clare Street where I intended to purchase a tuppence worth of that harmless nostrum, Glauber's salts, and sprinkle a modicum of it into the teapots. Ha-ha! Oh, I am prey to excess of high spirits."

"Get on with it, Purefoy."

"Yes, well, my chemist was unfortunately closed, and so I was forced to improvise, and thus it was, in the guise of Mr. Russell, I visited the premises of James J. Fox, tobacconist, and there obtained the tobacco on his bill. Oh, my deplorable ebullience!"

"Nicotine," said Oliver Gogarty, "taken in sufficient quantities is a poison."

"Oh, well," said Leslie Chenevix Purefoy, "if taken in bushels, in tons — but who could ever sanely argue that a little tobacco is harmful to the health?"

"Dere is another matter," said Lady Gregory. "De entire company, Mr. Purefoy, has witnessed your remarkable ability to mimic people."

"Dat is so," he said Galwegianly, and with an engaging little laugh.

"And to-night, I saw you, standing on the stage, imitate Mr. Yeats."

"Yes, but I hope you don't think any disrespect was intended. Oh, dear, how distressing. Oh, madam! Oh, gentlemen, I yield to no man in my admiration for the poetic genius of Mr. Yeats!"

"In a darkened theatre," Lady Gregory interrupted impatiently, "I suggest dat you could come on to de stage and give Mr. Holloway a cup of tea. I suggest dat a person in de balcony, as I was later, could mistake you, as I did, for Mr. Yeats himself."

"And I suggest," said Oliver Gogarty, "that your youthful high spirits led you to place a very toxic substance indeed in Mr. Holloway's cup."

Leslie Chenevix Purefoy looked sadly from one to the other. "Well, you may, gentlemen; you may, madam, suggest." He crossed his legs easily and favoured them with his most charming smile. "But you cannot prove, can you?"

Synge rolled a cigarette. Behind him in the Greenroom, he could hear the plummy voice of Leslie Chenevix Purefoy discussing large damages for personal inconvenience and acute mental suffering.

"Johnny?"

"You waited."

"Yes."

"I'm glad."

"Is it about over?"

"Yes, we're letting him go, and then there's nothing for it but to call the police in, which is something we should have done two hours ago. Oh God, I don't want you here when they arrive. I'll have Gaffney get you a cab."

"I'd rather stay."

"I'd rather have you stay."

"I think I've found something. Come into the light and take a look."

He followed her into the women's dressing-room.

"It was in my make-up box." She opened her hand and showed him.

He took the phial from her and looked at the bit of green in the bottom. "Yes," he said. "You have found something. Stay here. I'll be back shortly."

In the Greenroom, Leslie Chenevix Purefoy was working himself up to a fine pitch of outrage. "I refuse to be kept a prisoner! I demand to be allowed to leave! To leave at once! Instantly!"

"Now, listen, Purefoy," said Oliver Gogarty with an irritated edge to his voice.

Synge pushed past Gussie Gaffney who was still at his post in the doorway. "I think," said Synge loudly, "Mr. Purefoy is quite right."

"Well!" said Purefoy, "That's more like it! But you haven't heard the last of this. Indeed, you have not. Oh, to be subjected to a vile barrage of humiliating questions! To suffer the personal indignity, the affront! To — !"

"It's very late," said Synge coldly. "Let me suggest we iron out these differences in the morning."

Purefoy favoured them with a withering glance. "I shall require my jacket," he said loftily.

"Expensive, is it?" queried Oliver Gogarty, "or does it have a certain sentimental value?"

"Gussie," said Synge, "would you fetch Mr. Purefoy's jacket from the vestibule?"

"I will, to be sure," said Gussie, turning away.

"Oh, and Gussie," called Synge, following him out the door. "When you're there, you might turn off the lights and check that the front door is locked. And also — ."

When Synge returned, the three others were exactly as they had been.

"Lady Gregory," he said, "there are certain matters about to-morrow — ." He drew her over to the sink, and they stood murmuring quietly for a moment.

"Yes," she said aloud. "I shall attend to dat." And then she went over to the easy chair and sank down into it.

"I fancy," said Leslie Chenevix Purefoy, "that I shall require a cab."

"Oh, go soak your head," said Oliver Gogarty.

Leslie Chenevix Purefoy arched his left eyebrow in a well practised disdain and held the pose until Gussie Gaffney's steps were heard approaching.

"Eh, here's his jacket," said Gussie, appearing in the door. "It don't look so expensive to me."

"I fear, young Gaffney," said Leslie Chenevix Purefoy loftily, "that your future success would seem to depend upon the acquisition of some other profession. Perhaps something having to do with dustbins might answer."

"Hah?" said Gussie.

"And now," said Purefoy, throwing his jacket insouciantly over his shoulders, "*Auf Wiedersehen*." He strode to the door, turned and smiled. "But not *Lebewohl*." He paused to savour the moment.

"Eh, Dr. Gogarty," said Lady Gregory quietly from her chair, "Did you turn out all of his pockets?"

"Eh?" said Oliver Gogarty, wearily passing his hand through his hair.

"Did we check de little breast pocket, de handkerchief pocket, of his jacket? Dat is easy to overlook."

"Do!" cried Purefoy. "Oh, by all means do! What matters one final ignominy?" He held his coat graciously out to Oliver Gogarty, who finally approached and took it.

There was a dead silence in the room.

"No," said Oliver Gogarty. "Nothing."

"Yes, one final expensive ignominy," mused Purefoy. "Could you recommend a good lawyer? Of course, I am not a vindictive man, despite the many hurtful and outrageous slurs cast upon my character. No, a rather kind man, forgiving and tolerant of error. Perhaps some under-standing might yet be reached. Yes, if one's salary, say, were increased. Also, if certain major roles were to be made available. . . ."

"Caliban?" suggested Oliver Gogarty.

"Eh, Dr. Gogarty," said Lady Gregory, "did you check de lining?"

Gogarty desultorily felt the coat. Then he looked up sharply. "There's something here."

He threw the coat on the table and ripped out the lining.

"That," pointed out Leslie Chenevix Purefoy, "will cost an addi-tional — ."

His voice suddenly died, as he and the others looked at what Dr. Gogarty produced and held aloft. A small glass phial, with a murky, milky green substance at the bottom.

"Help me," said Oliver Gogarty, "to lug the guts behind the arras." And he took the body of Joseph Holloway firmly under the armpits. "Come on, don't be so sensitive."

Reluctantly Synge took Joseph Holloway's feet, and he and Gogarty hauled the body behind the curtain.

"He's grown rigid," said Synge.

"Wasn't he always?" said Gogarty, "Now, the awkward part. You hold him while I slip off his jacket."

"This is insanity," said Synge.

"Not at all. Quite the drollest idea her Ladyship's had since *Hyacinth Halvey*. Come on now, yo-heave-ho! My word, Synge, you're as demure as a first-year medical student."

"Moreover," said Frank Fay, "when Miss Farr remained long on one note, certain words, such as 'birrrth' and 'mirrrth,' came to my ear as 'birr' and 'mirr'. And the sound became prominent at the expense of the sense, which is the very thing that. . . ."

"Cnonk," snored W. J. Lawrence. "Cnonk."

Lady Gregory frowned. "It is not quite right yet."

She made two small snips with her scissors. "Dere!" She turned to Synge and Gogarty. "What do you think now?"

"Yes, the moustache flops down over the mouth all right now," Synge admitted, "but I still don't know about those ears."

"Ears!" cried Leslie Chenevix Purefoy.

"And me without my scalpel," murmured Gogarty.

"De wig helps to cover dem."

"Try the hat on," said Synge.

Lady Gregory set the bowler hat squarely on the middle of Leslie Chenevix Purefoy's head. "Well?"

Synge shook his head. "He's too tall by a couple of inches."

"Dat," she said, "can be remedied by a slight stoop."

"Stoop!" protested Leslie Chenevix Purefoy. "I have an erect and manly bearing."

"A slumped and humble bearing will improve your character," remarked Gogarty. "However, you are much too skinny."

"An improved diet will remedy dat. De important thing is de general illusion dat is created. A great actor leads his audience to see exactly what he wants dem to see." She laid her hand lightly on the subject's shoulder. "Stand up," she said, "and let dem see you."

"Don't forget your slump," said Gogarty.

"Walk across de room. We can let dose trousers out tomorrow. Say something."

It was Leslie Chenevix Purefoy who glared at her, but it was Joseph Holloway who stood up, reflectively sucked the lefthand strands of his droopy moustache, plodded across the room, turned, directed an accusing finger at Synge and cried, "The evil genius of the Abbey Theatre! The dramatist of the dung heap!"

The three of them had to clap, but for the first time in his life Leslie Chenevix Purefoy did not relish applause.

"No," said Oliver Gogarty, returning from the laneway, "I won't need you. Gaffney and I have stuffed him in the boot, and he can help me lug him into the College of Surgeons. After that, it's just a matter of chopping and carving — ."

"Eh, yes!" said Synge hastily.

"And distributing the chunks unobtrusively here and there."

"Unobtrusively?"

"Well," shrugged Oliver Gogarty, "medical students regrettably tend to be a trifle casual, especially after a hard night, and so a stray femur or an extra arm can easily go unnoticed."

"Fine," said Synge faintly, "but what about —?" He gestured toward the Greenroom.

They both turned uneasily to the open door.

"Dere is no use protesting, Mr. Purefoy," Lady Gregory was saying. "We are letting you off quite lightly. And look on de bright side. It's a marvellous part!"

"I'll drop Purefoy off at Northumberland Road," said Gogarty. "Send him out to the car when her Ladyship has finished terrifying him. . . . Eh, confidentially, Synge, I've always found the theatre a little dull. Just goes to show that one should endeavour to keep an open mind. Ta-ra!" And he tripped out to his auto, airily reflecting that "endeavour" was not really a satisfactory rhyme for "cadaver."

Synge went into the women's dressing-room. "I can take you home now," he said. "Eh. . . what is it?"

"Nothing."

"Tell me."

"I was only wondering if we would ever have one."

"A home?"

"Sorry. Let's go. Sally's left the door on the latch."

He took her firmly by the shoulders. "We'll have one."

"Yes," she said wanly, "one of these days."

"No," he said. "To-night. We're going off in style to the Nassau Hotel."

It was half-three in the morning, and Lady Gregory was bone-weary and heartily disgusted with herself. How could she have suggested such an abominable idea? And how could Synge and Dr. Gogarty ever have accepted it? Yet it was to save the theatre. It — .

She pushed those thoughts from her. To-morrow would be time enough to cope with the guilt.

She turned out the Greenroom light and closed the door. What was needed? Pick up Willie from the vestibule.

A light from under the door to the men's dressing-room caught her eye, and she went to turn it off.

"No one," Frank Fay was announcing as she opened the door, "must take me as being a hos-tile critic of Mr. Yeats or Miss Farr. I merely state my impress-sions."

"Mr. Fay," said Lady Gregory.

"And indeed," said Frank Fay. "I am glad that Mr. Yeats has brought before the people the fact that speech — ."

"Mr. Fay!"

" — is of as much importance as songggg!"

She shook him. "Mr. Fay, it is half-three in the morning."

"Eh?" he said. "Rehearsal?"

"Cnonk," snored W. J. Lawrence. "Cnonk."

"You should wake up your friend," she said.

"Oh," said Frank Fay, punching Lawrence on the shoulder. "Lawrence, up, up. Is the man asleep? Extraordinary." And Frank Fay punched him again, this time vigorously.

"Murdered! " said W. J. Lawrence, abruptly sitting up.

"Who," inquired Lady Gregory, "is murdered, Mr. Lawrence?"

"Joe! Joe Holloway. I saw — ."

"Why," she purred, "Mr. Holloway went home hours ago."

He blinked. "Home? Hours ago? How can that be? I saw — ."

"Dey have all gone home. Everybody. You've been asleep."

"But," cried Lawrence, lurching to his feet, "I saw him foully poisoned! I saw Yeets himself — ."

She laughed and patted him on the shoulder. "You've read too many lurid Elizabethan plays, Mr. Lawrence. Go home, and drop in on Mr. Holloway to-morrow. I believe he was asking for you."

"He was ask — eh — eh — ."

"I'll walk with you till you find a cab," said Frank Fay. "We can discuss AE's views on poetic speech. Now, Lady Gregory here can tell you — ."

"Good night, gentlemen," she said, ushering them very firmly to the door.

As the roar of Dr. Gogarty's motor died away, Leslie Chenevix Purefoy paused before 21 Northumberland Road. A handsome and respectable house it appeared to be. Doubtless it was comfortably appointed inside, and possessed many of the niceties of life that Purefoy's wanderings among the seedier theatrical boarding houses of small English towns had thus far denied him.

Nevertheless, Leslie Chenevix Purefoy hastened away. What sort of fool did they take him for? They must be mad, the three of them. Oh, the sooner he put this insane island behind him, the better!

Somewhere a clock struck the hour, and he counted its hollow strokes. One-two-three-four. Three good hours before the maid would unlatch the front door and emerge to collect the morning's pint of milk, an amount deemed sufficient by the thrifty Mrs. Attracta O'Growney-Greenway for the austere needs of her guests.

Not that chez O'Growney-Greenway was any longer a sanctuary. No, it would be necessary most hastily to pack his few bits of soiled clothing and his scrapbook of clippings relative to past triumphs upon the boards of various provincial towns.

What was he thinking of? It would hardly be possible to pack those treasures into his battered valise. There was the slight matter of three weeks' rent outstanding, and even an old campaigner such as himself could scarcely hope to navigate the stairs without attracting the eagle-eye of Mrs. Attracta O'Growney-Greenway, not to mention her pack of sour-tempered small dogs.

Nor did he feel great relish for the inevitably ensuing scene with the mistress of the mansion and her redoubtable husband, the former Scourge of Kashmir.

He indecisively halted on the bridge over the canal.

In fact, even a brief return to the domicile of the hospitable O'Growney-Greenways was distinctly a dicey business.

At this point, a further matter for reflection broached itself; to wit, the climate of Dublin at four o'clock of a February morning might be appreciated by doughty Polar explorers, but by few others. He hunched himself more deeply into the comforting folds of Joseph Holloway's overcoat, but even that expensive garment was not impervious to the brutal, snarling wind. He plunged his hands into the pockets, and encountered a ring of keys. One of which must afford access to the warm and substantial home of the late Joseph Holloway.

No, it was impossible!

But it began to rain.

Gussie had never been in a motor car, and the wind which so dampened the spirits of Leslie Chenevix Purefoy seemed intensely invigorating. Begod, this was the way to live, he thought, as Dr. Gogarty roared through Merrion Square and hurtled into Clare Street. One of these days, maybe, when he came into his own and was playing Shawneen Keogh and Bronco Billy to admiring throngs, he too would have a grand, belching, exploding automobile, and — .

"Jaysus, Dr. Gogarty, somebody's standing in the middle of the street!"

Unperturbed, Oliver Gogarty swung the wheel sharply to the right and then as sharply again to the left, and thundered on down Nassau Street.

"Janey!" marvelled Gussie Gaffney, "that was a close one!" And he looked back, and saw two figures still standing, motionless and entwined, in the middle of the street.

"Sure, that's Mr. Synge and Molly," he cried. "I'd stake me life on it."

Oliver Gogarty took the corner into Grafton Street on two wheels, but Gussie did not appear to notice the feat.

"Well," he said, "I'd have to say they make a nice couple."

"They do," agreed Oliver Gogarty.

"Yeh," said Gussie a little sadly, "and you'd have to wish 'em well. A long life and a merry one."

Oliver Gogarty took his foot off the accelerator as they came out at the Green, coasted up to the College of Surgeons, and braked to a stop. He sat there for a minute without turning off the motor, and then said softly, "A long life and a merry one — I fear, for them, it will be neither."

Lady Gregory came out into the lighted vestibule. "Willie!"

He jabbed his pen at the paper. "Done it!"

"Willie, time to go."

"Read this!"

"It's after four."

"Read it!"

She took the paper and tried to focus her eyes. "I can't make it out. Not a word."

"Bah!" he exclaimed, "you're holding it upside down." He seized the paper, turned it around, and peered at it with delight.

"Hmm," he said, the delight dissipating a bit around the edges, "maybe you weren't."

She took him gently by the arm, walked him to the door and turned out the last lights.

"Probably," he pondered, "it will make more sense in the morning."

Probably, she thought as she opened the door into Marlborough Street, a lot will.

Leslie Chenevix Purefoy opened the door and entered the warm hallway. He pocketed the keys, closed the door softly, and looked warily around.

Not a sound.

Reflectively, he sucked some strands of crepe hair that dribbled down over his mouth, and then with both hands he lifted off the bowler hat that was set squarely on the middle of his head, and, without even looking, hung it on the hall stand that somehow, he sensed, must be just inside and to the right of the hall door. He would also, he was sure, find an easy chair, for an old sybarite like Holloway would surely have a comfortable one, and he could doze for a couple of hours.

Just for a couple of hours, out of the cold and the wet, and then he could slip out and escape from this dank, dismal island. And resume his triumphant. . . dank, dismal life.

There was a door on his right, and he turned into it. Through a window, the streetlight dimly lit the room. What a jumble. What an incredible jumble. Heaps of books. Stacks of papers. Pictures on every inch of the wall. Pictures even stacked on the floor against the wainscotting. And there over the mantel, that unmistakable print of Garrick, both hands raised in horrified alarm at — at, what was it? — the horror of Duncan's murder? The ghost of Hamlet's father? The future?

He was not thinking clearly. But he had not murdered anyone, not Duncan, not sleep. And certainly not Joseph Holloway.

And Joseph Holloway had not died from drinking that tainted tea, for he had not drunk any of it. He, Leslie Chenevix Purefoy, had watched Joseph Holloway savouring the effects of his conversation with the supposed Yeats. And Joseph Holloway had died a happy man, expiring with a happy sigh and a smile on his face.

Perhaps kindness had killed Joseph Holloway. Yes, kindness from one he thought to be Yeats, his heart overcome at. . . ? At communion with the great poet?

No one had ever particularly respected Joseph Holloway. A gossip. A busybody. A hanger-on. Even a rotten architect. He, Leslie Chenevix Purefoy, had the opportunity of changing all that.

No! No! Absolutely not!

256

What had killed the cat? That faintly familiar — yes, that one-eared alley cat! Was that not poison? Or was it age, hunger, homelessness? All those things could kill too.

Ah, there was the easy chair, just where it should be.

Gratefully he fell into it, and listened to the rain lashing the window pane.

Suddenly Leslie Chenevix Purefoy felt incredibly weary. What really was in front of him? What really had he to look forward to? A few dreary years dragging around cold and miserable theatres in Northumberland and Wales and Scotland. Playing Banquo, Casca, Kent, Horatio.

Never Lear, never Brutus, never even Polonius.

And then finally, and not all that far distant — his magnificent good looks could not last forever — playing Guildenstern. . . Second Soldier. . . a lineless spear-carrier.

And Purefoy wept. . . .

"A marvellous part," that horrid old woman had said. No, no. . . but what if he could really carry it off?

Beneath his droopy crepe hair moustache, Purefoy faintly smiled. His head nodded, his weary head. And then nodded again. And then slumped forward onto his chest.

Ellen hung up her bonnet and coat on their pegs, lit the range, and put a kettle on. Then she went upstairs to set the fire in the dining-room, but as she passed through the hallway a snore from the old fool's study arrested her.

She went in, blinked in the gloom, and made out the slumped form of her employer in his easy chair. The old fool had not even taken his overcoat off.

"Why, sir, have you not been to bed?"

"Eh? . . . Eh?"

"Mr. Holloway sir, have you not been to bed?"

He looked around vaguely, and then his old baggy eyes focused upon her. "Of course, I have been to bed," he snapped. "You know my schedule. Where is my breakfast?"

"But," she snapped, "it's not time for — ."

"It is my time and my breakfast! Two eggs, two rashers, two rounds of toast, butter, marmalade and tea!"

She bobbed her head obediently and returned to the kitchen. Silly old fool, he'd never change.

Time to go home. He came out of the cabman's shelter, sniffed through the rain at the lightening sky, and climbed onto his lowbacked car. He flicked the reins and gave a desultory "gee-yup." The horse roused itself stoically and moved. Two figures in the distance, both in black — one full, one lean — walked towards the railway bridge. The younger one sang boldly, but not loudly, "*Unde alle Schiffe brucken.*"

The cab driver turned off the quays and up Marlborough Street, nodding, half asleep, secure in the knowledge that the horse would find the way. As they passed the Abbey Theatre, an upstairs window banged open, and a muscular figure thrust its upper torso through, and bawled in a well-carrying baritone voice, "Rape! Abominable rape!"

Clop-clop clicked the horse's hooves up Marlborough Street.

"The crisis," yawned W. B. Yeats, sprawled in the most comfortable chair of their joint sitting-room, "seems averted, and I have an extremely interesting poem out of it. If it can be deciphered."

From the window embrasure, Augusta, Lady Gregory looked out. There was little to see in the grey dawn. The gaunt figure of a man in shabby working clothes shuffled sullenly along beside Trinity's wall, a tweed cap jammed down on his brow, a dead cigarette cupped inside his hand.

"Yes," she said, "but dere seem so many."

"Poems," he said happily. "Yes, there do!"

"Crises!" she said bitterly, and watched the shambling, surly figure mooching along the street beneath a faintly lightening sky.

"One would have to wonder," she murmured, "about de future of our Irish theatre."

Outside, in Nassau Street, the labourer looked dully down at the butt of his dead cigarette, his last one, and he flipped it into the gutter, and watched the rainwater carry it away. He blinked his red-rimmed eyes.

"Pain ever for ever," he muttered.

In an upstairs bedroom of Cooldrinagh house in fashionable Fox-rock, big, balding, bull-necked Bill Beckett stared glumly into the cradle.

On the other side of the cradle, tall, thin, hawknosed May Beckett also stared glumly into it.

"Maybe," said Bill, "you shouldn't have stopped breast-feeding him."

"He wouldn't suck."

"You'd think he'd get hungry."

"Food seems to disgust him."

"Just lies there, does he?"

May nodded. "All day long. Not a peep out of him. In fact, he hardly moves. He hardly even blinks."

Bill Beckett scratched his head. "Wonder what he's waiting for?"

The baby in the cradle stared bleakly into the middle distance and did not answer.

As the cabman came into Mountjoy Square, a stray dog barked. Once. Twice. And somewhere across the river another dog answered him. And then the clop-clop of the horse's hooves faded away too, and there was silence. Nothing but silence, for all Dublin was asleep.

John Synge and his Molly were asleep, their arms lovingly entwined around each other, in a warm bed in the Nassau Hotel, and he was dreaming of his Deirdre, and she was dreaming of her handsome, winsome Johnny. And on the floor below, W.B. Yeats was dreaming of the beautiful, imperious, forever elusive Miss Gonne. And in the next room Lady Gregory was dreaming of Coole and its seven lakes. And George Moore, home at last in Ely Place, was dreaming of himself so pleasantly that he did not even stir as Dr. Gogarty drew up with his usual roar across the street, and walked with a weary bounce up to his door.

And AE was snugly tucked in by his wife in Rathgar, his still warm pipe smouldering safely in the ashtray where he had deposited it, and he was dreaming of faeryland. And Padraic Colum was asleep in his narrow bed dreaming of an old woman wandering the roads, with no place whatsoever to lay her head.

And Kerrigan and O'Rourke and Sinclair and Willie Fay and his Brigit and Frank Fay and May Craig and Gussie Gaffney and Seaghan Barlow and all the others belonging to the little theatre, they were all in their beds too, and what they dreamed of we do not know.

So let us leave them there, to have such dreams as they can, for in a few minutes the first rays of the cold winter sun will bravely glint over the Irish Sea from Wales, and touch the towers and the turrets, the domes of the Custom House and the Four Courts, and Nelson on his Pillar, and the spire of Findlater's Church, and Wellington's monument in the Park — and a new day will begin in what once upon a time was Dublin.